THE VANISHING POINT

BOOKS BY MARY SHARRATT

Summit Avenue

The Real Minerva

The Vanishing Point

The Vanishing Point

MARY SHARRATT

A MARINER ORIGINAL
Houghton Mifflin Company
BOSTON NEW YORK 2006

For information about permission to reproduce selections from
this book, write to Permissions, Houghton Mifflin Company,
215 Park Avenue South, New York, New York 10003.

Visit our Web site: www.houghtonmifflinbooks.com.

Library of Congress Cataloging-in-Publication Data
Sharratt, Mary, date.
 The vanishing point / Mary Sharratt.
  p. cm.
 ISBN-13: 978-0-618-46233-9
 ISBN-10: 0-618-46233-3
 1. Maryland — History — Colonial period, ca. 1600–1775 — Fiction.
 2. Women immigrants — Fiction. 3. Sisters — Death — Fiction.
 4. Plantation owners — Fiction. 5. Plantation life — Fiction. I. Title.
 PS3569.H3449V36 2006
 813'.6 — dc22   2005019777

Book design by Anne Chalmers
Typefaces: Janson Text, Bickham Script

Printed in the United States of America

DOC 10 9 8 7 6 5 4

For *Joske*

Once upon a time the Americans were the British, lost. On the narrow lip of a distant continent, clutching their faith, songs, customs and memories, they were seventeenth-century space travelers, cut off from Planet Europe with its corruptions and tyrannies.

—Andrew Marr

Recorded history is wrong. It's wrong because the voiceless have no voice in it.

—Mary Lee Settle

Prologue

Gloucestershire, England

HANNAH POWERS'S FATHER taught her about the masters of painting and engraving, how Albrecht Dürer and Leonardo da Vinci had transformed vision into a new geometry. He lectured Hannah on scale and proportion. The place where a ship was lost over the horizon was known as the vanishing point.

Their servant, Joan, was a woman of fifty-three years with ropy blue veins bulging out of her red hands. She taught Hannah and her sister, May, about another kind of vanishing, about the lost people who had once populated the West Country, indeed the entire island of Britain. Their stone arrows, green mounds, and dolmens still marked the land that had swallowed them. The first people.

Once, according to Joan, the faery folk had possessed physical bodies as plain and ordinary as anyone else's. But over the centuries, they had become fey. Their bodies grew vaporous and insubstantial, visible only at twilight and in dreams. Fleeing church bells and the glint of iron, they shrank into their hollow hills.

"A mere optical illusion, Hannah," her father told her, referring to the vanishing point on the horizon. "In truth, the ship does not disappear. The vessel is still there, even if we on the shore cannot see it."

So it transpired that both people and ships could become ghosts without ever dying or sinking beneath the waves.

I

1
The Dream of Comets

May
1689

THE MORNING THE LETTER ARRIVED, May Powers awoke
with a premonition. Before she even opened her eyes, her heart
was pounding and her throat was so tight she thought she might
choke. The taste of iron filled her mouth. Throwing the bedclothes aside, she told herself not to be silly. She laced her bodice
over her shift and stepped into her skirt. After pinning her hair
into a coil, she descended the narrow staircase to the kitchen to
help Joan prepare breakfast. Father and Hannah were in the front
room murmuring over his pile of books. May listened to them
recite the Latin names of apothecary herbs.

The morning passed as uneventfully as any other, with wool
to spin and seams to stitch. Just past midmorning, Hannah left for
the market with Joan. In the garden, Father picked betony and
woodruff. It was the end of May, the lovely month after which
her departed mother had named her. The weather being fine,
she took her spinning wheel to the front of the house so that she
might look out on the village green, the sheep that grazed there,
and the hills beyond. That morning her eyes were too restless to
settle on the village; they kept wandering off toward the horizon.

When the rider trotted up to the garden gate on his mud-
spattered cob, she struggled to her feet as though waking from a
dream. "Is this the house of Daniel Powers?" he asked.

May nodded, and the milky-faced youth leaned from his

3

saddle and thrust a letter at her — a piece of folded paper, sealed with wax and marked by the many hands it had passed through until it had reached hers.

"The letter did come all the way from America," said the rider, too imperious to even flirt.

A peculiar tingling gripped her. She remembered the dream she'd had just before waking — a dream of her father showing her comets through his telescope. As she peered through that lens, the sky filled with shooting flames.

The letter was addressed to her father, Daniel Powers, Physician. She read the name of the one who had sent it — Nathan Washbrook, her father's distant cousin who had crossed the waters to Maryland.

"Father!" she cried, racing to the back of the house where he was gathering strawberry leaves. "Father, look!" A fever gripped her, the blood running in her veins like hot wine as she broke the seal herself, not waiting for her father's permission.

Under the hawthorn tree, beneath that canopy of foamy white flowers, she read the letter aloud. When she handed the letter to him, he nodded, as if he already knew its message. Father and daughter were silent, but the words May had read remained in the air, buzzing around them like flies.

"What think you of the letter, May?"

She plucked a handful of hawthorn flowers, crushing them in her left hand while holding the letter in her right.

Father wrapped his arm around her shoulders. "My dear, can you forgive me? A year ago, I took the liberty of writing to our cousin Nathan and telling him you were still unwed. In faith, it was I who planted the idea in his head."

Had Joan and Hannah been present, there would have been hysterics. The garden would have rung with shouting, curses, and tears. But between May and her father there was neither discussion nor debate. Her fingers went limp, hawthorn flowers and letter falling to the grass. Father took her hand.

"Could you consent?"

4

"You might have told me this was coming," she said. Then, looking into his eyes, she read his will. He had been praying for this offer, this miracle, to take the burden of her future off his hands.

Females are scarce in the Colonies, Cousin Nathan had written. *My Son needs a Wife. He is a healthy young Man of eighteen Years. I would rejoice to have your eldest Daughter May for his Bride. In Truth, I care not that your Daughter is without Dowry. I have Wealth enough and have already paid eight Hogs Head Barrels of Tobacco to the Ship Captain to assure her speedy Passage. Please be good as your Word and see that she sails out on the* Cornucopia *in August*.

He expected her to leave already in August, only two months away? And offering her a boy of eighteen as a bridegroom! She was twenty-two. May nearly laughed aloud. Aware of her father's somber gaze, she sobered and considered. On the one hand, what choice did she have if she wanted to save herself and her sister from penury? Though her father was a doctor of physick, making money had never been one of his talents. In recent years, his health had gone into decline. There was no son to carry on his business. When he died, she and her sister would have to sell his globe and telescope, his skeleton and surgical instruments, his books and diagrams of human organs. Even this house would be taken from them, for they merely rented it. She and Hannah would be dowerless spinsters, wards of the parish. After what she had done to disgrace herself, ruining her chances of honorable marriage, how dare she refuse? She was twenty-two, her sister only fifteen. The burden of securing their future fell upon her.

On the other hand, what an adventure! She half believed the letter had come to answer her own prayers of deliverance. When she was a young girl, long before she had discovered the lusts that plagued her body and spoiled her reputation, she had dreamt of setting sail for unknown worlds. Once she had declared to her sister, "If I were a boy, I would run away to sea." Only a roving young man could be as free as she longed to be. When she closed her eyes, she saw not a young bridegroom but herself at the bow of a ship.

5

Leaving Father alone in the garden, his query unanswered, she ran to his study, took the globe from its place on the shelf, and spun it until her eyes blurred. He found her there, twirling his prized globe. She laughed uncontrollably, her whole body shaking. Laughter was her weakness. May laughed the way other girls cried. Once she got started, there was no stopping her. Turning to her father, she laughed in his face. Without a shred of submission or obedience, she told him, "Yes, Father. Yes, I consent."

—◦—

"Fancy his name being Washbrook," May said, trying to make light of it in the face of Joan's glowering. "Is he descended from a line of launderers?"

"I have half a mind to throttle that father of yours," said Joan. "You know nothing of that boy."

May, Joan, and Hannah circled around a walnut chest carved with roses and thorns, which had belonged to the girls' mother, her maiden name having been Hannah Thorn. Once May had believed that the flowering white thorn bushes were named after her. May had lost her mother at the age of seven, so her memories of her were fleeting. Mostly she recalled her mother's cheer and wit, how she could draw Father out of his dreariness and make him smile. Father lived in a world of sickness, death, and bleeding that terrified May. She despised the skeleton in his study, the preserved calf heart in the glass jar. What good was her father's medicine if he had not been able to keep her mother alive?

As the eldest, May would inherit her mother's trunk and its contents. Joan dug out the clothes and linens, the tiny infant clothes and christening gown, and laid them out on the freshly swept floor. Every article would be washed and ironed before it crossed the ocean with May. At the bottom of the chest was a woman's shift and nightcap, but the shift was an odd one, being slit in front up to the waist. When Joan held it up to the light and shook out the dust, the sight was so lewd that May had to laugh, her fist covering her mouth.

"Our mother wore such a shift?"

Joan's reply was brusque. "It was her lying-in gown. The gown she bore you in."

The linen was so yellowed with age, it looked as if it had been handed down from their great-grandmother. Hannah went white in the face; her birth had caused their mother's death. As long as May lived, she would never forget the sight of Mother's drained face, mouth frozen open but silenced forever while the infant shrieked and shrieked. Hannah had been so frail, everyone feared she would follow her mother to the grave. When May looked back, she suspected the only thing that prevented Father from going insane from grief was his struggle to keep the baby alive. Ever after, he had harbored a special tenderness for Hannah that he had never shown for May.

It hadn't helped that May so resembled her mother. The likeness had only grown stronger when she became a woman. Joan said that even her laughter sounded like Mother's, her lightness and humor, her refusal to dwell on gloomy things. While Mother was yet alive, Father used to sit May on his lap. He taught her to read, do figures, and showed her shooting stars through his telescope. But after Mother's death, he had withdrawn from her, leaving her upbringing to Joan. Her resemblance to Mother had only caused him pain. If May allowed self-pity to creep into her head, she could easily convince herself that she was twice as orphaned as Hannah, but she brushed such thoughts aside. In August she would be leaving home forever; she refused to allow jealousy or resentment to cloud her final days with her family. Before anyone could notice her silence and ask what was on her mind, she folded the birthing gown and laid it on the floor with the other things.

Joan gripped her shoulder. "And on your wedding night, what will happen when he discovers you are no maid?"

At this, Hannah crept out of the room. May looked into Joan's eyes without flinching. "You know as well as I," she said, "that even the most hardened rake cannot tell a maiden from a whore if she holds herself tight enough." She swallowed and tried

7

to smile. "If he goes looking for blood, I shall prick my finger with a needle." Then she shook her head. "Oh, Joan, I don't think Father kept my history secret from them. I think they know already what kind of girl I am." Before Joan could berate her any more, May embraced the older woman, who wept noisily in her arms.

"Your own father is shunting you off for a pile of tobacco!"

"Hush," May whispered. "I go freely. I have chosen this."

2
Pot of Honey

May

At the age of fifteen, May had started with the boys. In the beginning, she had tried to be a decent girl, contenting herself with kisses, sweet words, and secret glances. But her hunger mounted, not leaving her in peace until she took her first love, the baker's youngest son, by the hand and led him to the copse of willows behind the churchyard wall. Opening her legs, she had drawn him deep inside her, let him pierce her through.

May and her first love took to meeting in the meadow near the gristmill. Those were the hours she felt most alive, sprawled in the grass, limbs flung open so that her body took the shape of a star. She felt as though she could rise and float up over the clouds, even as he covered her with his body, anchoring her to the earth. He brought her cider, which she drank until the stars began to spin and her throat burst with laughter. He called her his angel. She could sport all night, rolling in the grass with her sweet boy, threading her fingers through his hair, kissing the cider from his lips. She caressed him and rubbed her body against his until the stars fell from the sky and silvered their naked skin.

She took care not to get herself with child. Joan had grudgingly shown her the method she herself had used to prevent conception in her younger days. May took a tuft of clean sheep's wool, dipped it in honey, and thrust it into the mouth of her womb. There was no shortage of wool in her village. Every week May received a great heap of it to card, comb, and spin. Her fingers were so nimble that in a good week she earned nearly as much from her spinning as her father earned from his languishing practice of physick. As for the honey, Joan kept two hives at the bottom of their garden.

Her first love had called her his honey pot. That thrilled her. If only he knew how true it was. She was a walking pot of honey, the golden sweetness seeping between her legs. When he lapped it from her sticky thighs, he fancied it was her own unique sweetness he tasted. Honey was delicious and pleasing. It also killed a man's seed before it could reach her womb.

A few hours before daybreak, when May crawled back to bed with the honey still glazed on her thighs, she was too breathless to sleep. It was Hannah who eased her into slumber, Hannah with her sweet breath, her arm flung around May's waist, her red hair spread over the pillow like a silk shawl. Those in their village who dismissed Hannah as plain had no clue how winsome she looked in sleep, how innocent. May's trysts left her moist-eyed with love, not just for her lover, but for everything she saw. Those nights she thought she could embrace the whole world. She imagined that in her intimate encounters, she experienced the same ecstasies of universal love that holy men experienced in prayer. Her trysts gave her such an infusion of the life elixir that their household no longer seemed such a lonely and somber place.

In the morning, between spoonfuls of porridge swimming in thick cream, she smiled across the table at her father, who commented on the healthy glow in her face and inquired if she had slept well. Father, God bless him, slept so soundly she could creep from her chamber night after night without troubling him. Indeed, his thoughts were so immersed in his books and jars of physick herbs, it was as though he lived in a lofty tower far above ordinary affairs. The clucking of the village gossips never penetrated his ears. Hannah was too loyal to betray her. Joan only rolled her eyes.

Neither she nor her lover ever spoke of marriage. For a youngest son with few prospects, marrying her was a dream beyond his means. She knew that Father would never let her wed a baker's son. As for her own desires, trysting in the meadow was more beguiling than the prospect of setting up a household. She lived for that sweet excitement of brand-new love when she couldn't sleep for the pounding in her heart. When she saw the village wives with their pregnant bellies and gaggles of snivel-nosed brats, she pitied them. Yet before she could further contemplate her future with the boy, he left to visit his kin in Cornwall. Both he and May thought he would be gone only a few weeks. However, he never returned. Later May discovered that his parents, not approving of his infatuation for her, had arranged for him to be apprenticed to a cooper in Truro. Never having learned to read or write, the boy could send her no message of how he fared. In ballads, girls who lost their lovers drowned in a river of their tears. May did her share of weeping, but she reasoned that if her mother were alive, she would not want her to pine for him forever.

The young blacksmith, working half naked in the summer heat, had the most beautiful torso, golden and glistening. When he looked up from the anvil and met her stare, she winked and turned, inviting him to follow her into the alleyway, where he playfully pressed her up against the wall, his sweaty chest marking the front of her dress. She licked the sweat from his face like a mother cat.

Sometimes she felt as though she were questing after a dream lover, an irresistible phantom who enticed her from her bed night after night. His face kept changing. He could appear to her in any guise he chose — as the baker's son, the blacksmith, or even some young rag seller. Each time she took a new lover, swearing that he was the one she would love forever, another apparition appeared, stretching out his hand and smiling as if he had been her destined match all along. When she thought she had finally grasped him, the divine lover of her dreams, the enchantment vanished. She found herself embracing an ordinary village boy who taunted her for her loose ways and called her a trollop.

Before the illusion shattered, it was so sweet. The stars rained on her body as her lover plunged inside her. The next morning, she dredged out the honey-and-sperm-soaked wool and dropped it down the privy hole. Without uttering a word to Father, Joan brewed her decoctions of pennyroyal, tansy, and rue to ensure that her menses arrived promptly. May's belly remained flat as any virgin's. The village whispered it was witchcraft that she never got herself with child.

This was when May felt the first hint of dread. A few years before her birth, a woman had been accused of bewitching a married man and cursing him so that his wife remained barren. The woman had been tried, found guilty, then strung from the gallows. The story went that her body had been so slender and light-boned, the hangman had to grab her around the waist and yank hard until her neck snapped. Father said that no educated man believed in witches anymore, but Joan had warned May that in some villages, wanton girls like herself were publicly whipped, then locked in the stocks, and left there for everyone to jeer at and mock. Though the stocks in her village were rarely used, May felt a tremor whenever she walked past them.

Still, nobody troubled her. Father, after all, was a respected man. Half the village was in debt to him, for he treated the poor without asking payment. It helped that she looked so innocent with her large blue eyes. She never failed to appear in church, hands clasped and head bowed while the preacher railed on and on. When he addressed her sins—without naming her, thankfully—she put every ounce of will into appearing contrite. Only when the sermon was over did she raise her eyes to the Green Man carved in the church wall. His face emerged from a dense tangle of oak leaves. More leaves sprouted from his lips. The stone face smiled, as if to tell her that he understood her, even if no one else did. In the midst of all the talk of hell and damnation, the Green Man watched over her and gave her his blessing.

The year she turned nineteen, the innkeeper's son, smitten with her, declared that he would put an end to her wildness. When he asked for her hand in matrimony, Father agreed at once.

An eldest son, he had good prospects. Properly affianced, he and May could court in public with no subterfuge or shame. On Sunday afternoons, they went for endless walks, Hannah tagging after them as their self-appointed chaperone. Still, May could not quite fathom marriage. In her dreams, they simply went on courting forever. Eventually the banns were posted. Joan and Hannah summoned her to the market to pick out the satin and lawn for her bridal gown. The wedding date was set.

Three weeks before she was to be married, she and her fiancé went to the harvest fair in the next village. May wore green ribbons in her hair. She and her lover drank mead from the same cup. A piper and fiddler played, and all around them young people danced: shepherds and servant girls, milkmaids and farmhands. But May's fiancé did not want to join the dance. Instead he spoke with his brother about the cost of fixing the thatch on the inn roof, about how they couldn't afford to replace the thatch with slate. They spoke of their senile mother, how she needed a good nursemaid to look after her, and how none of May's father's remedies had done her any good. Then May's future brother-in-law, drunk on the mead, let his tongue slip, making a gibe about her lack of dowry. "What use is there bringing home a prized mare if she come not with a wagon of hay to feed her? And a used mare she is, besides."

May waited for her fiancé to speak up in her defense, but he just laughed and pinched her cheek. Not wanting to pout, she pretended to laugh along. She reached for the mead, only to discover that the cup was empty, and then it seemed that the empty cup was an omen, informing her that life as she knew it would soon be over. After the wedding feast, there would be no more dancing, no more slipping behind the hedges in the village green. She would be nursemaid to her mother-in-law, laundering the old woman's piss-stained sheets, enduring the old woman's insults and her brother-in-law's slights. She would hide her hair beneath a housewife's cap, keep her husband's house, bear his children. Her loins clenched at the memory of her mother's racked body on the blood-drenched bed. She almost fancied that her mother's ghost was warning her to save herself before it was too late. *Darling, you can see that this is no life for you.*

When she stepped away, she expected her fiancé to follow, take her hand, ask what vexed her. He still had the power to draw her back, charm away her doubts. But neither he nor his brother paid her any mind. With heavy feet, she marched into the thick of the dancers. They whirled around her, beat their feet into the earth, kicked up clouds of dust that shone like gold in the evening sun. A barefoot tinker stood on his own. His waving hair fell to his shoulders. His shirt, made of parti-colored rags stitched together, was open in the heat, baring his collarbone and smooth chest. His eyes were clouded hazel, full of mirth. Those eyes undid her. He winked, his face open and shining. When he held out his hand, she felt the overpowering tug, the intoxication sweeter than mead. Stepping forward, she squeezed his hand and let him pull her body against his as if they were already lovers. Then all was a blur of the dust they raised with their wild dance. When the music stopped she kissed him. His mouth tasted of wild blackberries.

Her fiancé and his brother left her there, in the tinker's arms. Rushing back to the village, her fiancé tore down the banns announcing their marriage. Meanwhile the tinker led May to his makeshift tent at the edge of the woods. When he pushed up her skirts and stroked the insides of her thighs, she felt so light, as though she had left her body and earthly existence behind. She kissed him fiercely and drew him inside her. Afterward they sat by the campfire and shared a supper of streaky bacon and bread. Then, despite his entreaties, May pulled herself away. She walked alone and unclaimed to her father's house.

Father could hardly look at her. Even Hannah appeared bruised and betrayed. Joan cornered May in the kitchen. "You have brought dishonor on us all. Your poor sister is ashamed to show her face in public. Did you ever stop to think about your father? Wherever he goes, people laugh behind his back."

May wept, but the shaming was nothing in the face of her desire, that pull on her that set her pulse racing. Within a fortnight she took up with a young weaver.

By the time she turned twenty-one, her pond had run dry. From the rich crop of boys she had once loved had grown a field of jaded men, most of them now married. They warned their wives what would happen to them if they ever started taking after May Powers. One morning she awoke with the taste of too much cider in her mouth, bruises on her arms and thighs. Boys followed her down alleys, singing not sweet songs but obscene ditties. *Cherry-red, cherry-red, like a slut's own bed.* At village dances, disgusting old men took liberties, pawing her bosom and rump, then laughing at her outraged protests. Joan told her she should have thought of the consequences earlier.

In the eyes of her village, she had become something much worse than an old maid. Joan said she was a fool for not marrying the innkeeper's son when she had the chance. He was a fine man these days, with money in his purse and a baby boy. His wife was a mild-faced, yellow-haired woman who never raised her voice. She had come with a dowry of two milk cows and eight pounds in sterling.

⁂

When Nathan Washbrook's summons arrived, May reminded herself that she had loved many men. Odds were that she could find something to love in young Gabriel. But in those final days, her bridegroom was far from her mind. At every opportunity she stole into Father's study to examine his celestial globe and maps of the heavens. In her dreams, she was not earthbound but flew unfettered through the endless vault of stars. Nothing could stop her, nothing could contain her. She imagined the unexplored new world that would soon be hers.

The night before she was to sail, at the hour when she should have gone to her bed, she smuggled Father's telescope to her room. She opened the window wide and gazed through the lens. For all their distance, the stars shone warmly, beckoning to her like long-lost friends. If she could find her way back to them, she would be complete. What path might her life have taken if Father had given her the same education as Hannah, if he had encouraged her to be studious, if she had spent those countless afternoons poring over books instead of sneaking out to meet boys? A whole other future could have been hers. Yet when she asked herself if she regretted anything, she had to concede that she did not. If she had been a good girl, Father would never have thought to send her on this voyage.

Peering through the lens, she entreated the night sky to reveal her destiny. A moment later she was rewarded with the sight of a meteor stitching its way across the sky in a brilliant streak. Soon there was not one but many. The heavens filled with shooting stars.

"Hannah, come look!" She handed her the telescope. "Surely this is a good omen."

Her sister glanced only briefly through the telescope before passing it back. Her face was pinched and her eyes were red.

May touched Hannah's cheek. "Will you not be happy for me?"

"They are sending you into a wilderness!"

May folded her sister in her arms while the girl wept like a lost child. Her tears soon soaked through May's nightgown. Stroking her hair, May remembered the first time she had held Hannah, a newborn with an angry red face, screaming for her mother, who was no longer there. *And now I am leaving her, too.* May struggled not to cry. There was no telling what might happen if she let this overwhelm her.

"Aye, a wilderness they say it is." May hugged her sister tighter. "But have you never wondered, Hannah, what a wilderness is like?" She thought of the tinker she had never seen again. If she could be born again, she would be that young man wandering from village to village with his satchel and tent, masterless and free. That night as she slept with Hannah in her arms, she dreamt she was a comet blazing her trail across the night sky.

3 Fog

Hannah

"IT'S NOT TOO LATE." Hannah tightened her grip on her sister's hand. "You can still say no." Lips to May's ear, she pleaded. "Say you'll stay here with us."

On the Bristol pier, Hannah struggled to hold on to her sister, whose body kept shifting under her green cloak. May was as slippery as a mermaid and as difficult to hold on to. Sometimes it was hard to believe this beautiful, capricious person was truly her sister. Since she and May were as different as day and night, Father's friends liked to joke that one of them must be a changeling. May was everything Hannah thought she could never be—tall and dazzling with her chestnut hair, her full bosom, her sky-blue eyes. Her wide hips promised ease in childbirth. Hannah was six inches shorter, skinny and hard. If she were to cut off her frizzy red hair and put on a pair of breeches, she could pass for a boy. The only womanly thing about her was how easily she wept.

"How can you leave us for a stranger?" she whispered. Even while she and May had embroidered the wedding dress, Hannah had prayed that her sister would have an outburst of her usual temper and declare that she was not really making the journey halfway around the world to marry some distant cousin. May had never obeyed Father or anyone else but done what she pleased. How had she consented to this? Hannah could not forgive May her eagerness, the way she gazed at the tall-masted ships and the sailors climbing the riggings. Some of the men were brown as bread, others black as molasses, gold glinting from their ears. When they came to port, Bristol smelled of spices and citrus fruit from faraway countries. Also moored in the harbor were the slave ships, human cargo chained in the hold. Hannah could not bring herself to look at those vessels. Father had told her that slavery was an abomination, and yet he was sending May to the Chesapeake, where rich planters built their fortunes on the backs of such slaves.

"You act as if it were some game," she told May. Then she closed her eyes as a queasiness passed through her, the skin around her mouth growing tight and cold.

"Oh, Hannah, you will not have one of your fits. You will *not*. Besides," May whispered, fingering a stray lock of her sister's red hair, "it *is* an adventure." The wind sweeping off the harbor brought out the bloom in May's face as she smiled. She kissed Hannah's forehead.

"The next one you kiss shall be him!"

May laughed.

Hannah wrapped her fingers around her sister's wrists. "What if he is a monster, a beast?"

"You think too much of tragedy and pain." May wiped Hannah's tears. "We shall only be parted a very short while. Soon enough you shall join me on the other side."

Hannah glanced at Father, who stood guard over May's trunk. He was growing frailer with each passing winter. Just as May considered it her duty to cross the ocean and marry, it was Hannah's lot to look after their father until his death.

"Two or three years, not more," May whispered. Sadness crept into her voice. "Then you shall sail over to me. By that time, you shall be all grown up. I shall have planted my garden with the seeds you gave me. I will plant more rosemary than anyone has seen. They say it grows well in that climate." She smiled, inviting Hannah to smile with her. *When rosemary grows in the garden*, the saying went, *the mistress rules the house*.

Hannah watched May embrace Father.

"Give my love to Joan," May called, about to board the ship with the two sailors who carried her trunk.

Hannah threw herself in her path. "I gave you quill, ink, and paper! I hope you shall put them to use."

"I shall write as soon as I am safe on the other shore."

"In your trunk there are stoppered bottles of water. Ration them well. And there are three loaves of bread besides, and a cake." Hannah had heard terrible stories of the food aboard those ships: nothing but brackish water in leaking casks, oversalted meat, and hard biscuit crawling with weevils.

"Dear Hannah." May held her as the crowd pressed around them. She gave her sister one last kiss before climbing aboard the ship. For a while she stood at the rail and shouted her farewells. Then, as more people pushed around her, she lost her place and was swallowed by the throng. The sailors untied the ropes, and the ship slowly pulled away from the dock.

"She will be one of those people waving," Father said. "She is there. We simply cannot see her amongst all the others."

"Look at the fog, will you? Why did they not wait until fair weather to sail?"

"Trust that the captain and his crew know the sea better than you and I. Pray, do not be overanxious. Your sister is ruled by passion, while you have a propensity toward melancholia. The humors must be in balance. My dear, my bones ache. Let us sit down."

"Go rest in the tavern, Father. I will find you soon."

As the ship vanished from her sight, Hannah stood on the pier, staring into the fog that rose from the steely water. She would always remember gray as the color of ghosts, the color of loss. *Please, dear God, do not let this overpower me.* She told herself she would not let the world grow dark around her, not fall writhing into a seizure, her body racked by spasms, blood and spittle flowing from her mouth.

The falling sickness had not visited her for more than two

years. Father said there was reason to hope it would never return. To ward it off, he had her drink a daily infusion of the berries and leaves of mistletoe mixed with peony root. He had also mixed for her a special salve with the anticonvulsive oils of nutmeg, lavender, marjoram, rue, cloves, and citron. May had always teased her when she anointed herself with it. *Oh, Hannah. You smell like the Garden of Eden.*

The first seizure had taken her when she was two. Joan had thought on the onset that it was a mere tantrum, then feared it might be madness. Father said that less learned folk might attribute her symptoms to demonic possession. His medical books told him that the falling sickness was a disorder of the humors in the brain. Apart from these episodes, she was healthy and strong.

She feared the seizures would follow her all her days like some dark twin, creeping out of the shadows at the least expected moment to undo her. For now, though, the pier remained solid beneath her feet. Holding her sister's image before her, she tried to trace the path of the ship she could no longer see.

—⁂—

Wig askew, Father huddled beside the tavern fire. His unsteady hands cupped a mug of ale.

"It is time to meet the wagoner," Hannah said. Finding Father's cane, she helped him to his feet and led the way out the door and into the street crowded with sailors, errand boys, and tradesmen.

"If I could call that ship back to port, I would," she told her father savagely. "We know nothing of her bridegroom."

"He is our kinsman."

"He is a distant cousin we have never met. You yourself conceded that you have not laid eyes on his father in nearly five-and-twenty years."

"Hannah, we have spoken of this before. Your sister will be a planter's wife." He uttered his words with weary authority, as if explaining a self-evident case in a court of law. "May will live like a gentlewoman with servants at her beck and call. Nathan and Gabriel Washbrook have seven indentured manservants and a kitchen girl besides. When I am dead, you will join her there. I can rest easy knowing that you both are provided for. In truth, it is not May I worry about but you."

4 The Earth Demands Blood

Hannah

WHEN THEY ARRIVED HOME in the August twilight, Hannah paid the driver and helped her father out of the wagon. It had been a bone-jolting two-hour journey, the splintered wagon bed cushioned only in straw. Hannah waited for her father to finish brushing off his breeches before he handed her the heavy brass key to their front door.

It struck Hannah, not for the first time, how dolorous their house appeared, untrimmed ivy smothering the pocked walls. Turning the key in the lock, she opened the door that led directly into Father's study and visitation room. With its big window, this room was the only one with enough light in which to prepare physick potions and study scholarly texts. She took her father's arm and helped him across the threshold into the clean-swept chamber. Then she went into the kitchen. Stirring the embers in the hearth, she stoked the fire and lit a lamp.

"Father?" Lamp in hand, she found him in his oak chair with his arms wrapped around the leather case that contained his surgical instruments. His face was turned away from her, signaling that he did not wish to speak. Hannah watched him open the case and gaze at the tools that provided their livelihood. The scalpel had seen innumerable operations. Hannah had sharpened and re-sharpened it countless times. Flexing her right hand, she recalled its smooth grip in her palm. Theirs was a family of concealments.

Father had always treated her more like a longed-for son than the daughter she was. He had held on to her tightly, even as he let May go her own way and slip through their fingers. His belief in her talents was vast. To his friends he had claimed that Hannah was so uncommonly clever that she had learned to read nearly before she could walk—surely an exaggeration, and proof of his blinding regard for her. Above all, she had feared disappointing him. To vindicate his pride, she had thrown herself into her studies. When she was a tiny girl, she had believed that Father was a wizard out of Joan's stories and that the Latin words he taught her were magical incantations. If she was a motherless girl, she was also the receptacle of her father's teachings.

But what if her mother had lived and given Father a real son? Then Hannah would have had to content herself with womanly tasks, as her sister had done. Sometimes she thought it would have been worth the sacrifice to have a mother as well as a father. A mother could have assured her that she was truly a girl, as much as her beautiful sister was, and not some lonely creature whom no one outside her family could ever hold dear.

Her consolation was this: Father had made her his right hand. The two of them had sworn a pact of secrecy. Though the law refused to recognize a female physician or surgeon, Father had taught her his arts. If May could spin and sew and bind any man to her will, then Hannah knew about the body and its disorders. Anatomical engravings covered the whitewashed walls. Bones, blood vessels, and vital organs were labeled in Latin. With Father's blessing, she had learned them by heart.

Her strange apprenticeship had begun at the age of seven, when she first held the dish to catch the hot red gush while Father bled his patients. She had lost her squeamishness long ago. Afterward she gave the blood to Joan, who hoed it deep into the soil of their garden. "The earth demands blood now and then," Joan was fond of saying. Their roses grew redder than any of the neighbors'. A few times a year, Joan went to the butcher's to get freshly chopped bones to bury among the rows of turnips and cabbages.

When Father went to his patients' homes to perform surgery, he had taken Hannah along as his handmaiden. After bolting the chamber door to make sure the proceedings would not be disturbed, he tied the patient to the bed, blindfolded him, and administered laudanum. Silent as a shadow, she stood by Father's side and handed him the instruments.

In recent years, Father's hands had grown unsteady with age. He no longer trusted himself to make the cuts, yet giving up his practice would mean poverty. Thus Hannah had become her father's hands. By the time she was thirteen, she had started making the incisions for him. Before an operation, Father explained the procedure, showing her diagrams from his anatomy books, pointing to the organs and major blood vessels. They did not speak during surgery but communicated in silent gestures, lest the patient discover that it was the handmaiden—not the physician—making the cuts. Afterward she cauterized the wound and sewed the flesh back together with a needle and silk thread.

Seven months ago, Hannah had removed a kidney stone, an especially perilous procedure. "Should you not cut clean and true," Father warned, "you will rob Mr. Byrd of his manhood."

Cupping the patient's cods in one hand, Father drew them out of the way, then nodded. Drawing her breath, Hannah had made the deep incision in the man's perineum. Sweat dripped from her forehead, yet her hands never trembled. When she had cut to the stone, she extracted it with a pair of tweezers and dropped it into a dish. The operation proved to be one of their great successes. Within six weeks, Mr. Byrd had healed. He thanked Father profusely and declared he was still in full possession of his virility.

Yet Father found his practice dwindling. He had lost much of his business to the young barber surgeon, whose shop occupied the best stretch of market square in the neighboring town. People came from miles away to visit the barber, drawn by his elegant storefront with its red-and-white-striped pole, signifying blood and bandages. Hannah raged over the injustice that common barbers were permitted to cut open bodies. She wagered that the barber surgeon had never put his nose in a book of science. She wondered if he could even read.

Hannah could read and write in English and Latin. Father had schooled her in algebra, geometry, botany, and astronomy, as well as the medical arts. Had she been a boy, Father would have gone begging to scrape together the money to send her to Oxford, where she would have worn the black robes of a scholar. The sign outside their gate would have read *Powers and Son, Physicians*. With her youth and energy to complement his experience, they would have drawn in more patients and made a handsome income. Her sister would not have been obliged to marry a stranger.

As a girl, however, her learning was a liability, something monstrous that clouded her chances of marriage as surely as her sister's loose ways had damaged hers. Unlike May, Hannah knew she was neither a beauty nor sufficiently versed in the arts of housewifery. She could not spin half as well as her sister could and had more experience stitching wounds than ordinary seams. Joan joked that her cooking was so bad that her future husband would wind up as thin and sorry-looking as the skeleton in Father's study.

When she walked through the village, men and boys shifted away from her, as if they half feared her for her witch-red locks and her eccentric education. Though she was thought to be merely her father's handmaiden, everyone knew she had seen things a girl should never see. Passing her in the street, Mr. Byrd would lower his head and cross to the other side, even though he greeted her father with his best manners. The gossip of her seizures had not helped matters. Hannah decided Father was right to fear for her future. It was time she faced the truth that Father would not live for many more years. One day she would be on her own, and what would become of her then? Who would ever love or want someone like her?

As if reading her thoughts, Father closed the case of surgical instruments and held it out to her until she took it from him. "When you leave to join your sister, you must take these with you. Perhaps over the water, where such tools are rare, you can sell them at a good price." He tugged off his wig, holding it like a small dog. "Bring me a candle, dear, and I shall retire."

—+—

Hannah climbed the stairs to the room that she had shared with May. Moonlight poured through the tiny, curtainless window. Washed silvery in its light, her nightdress and apron hanging from their pegs resembled ghosts.

She had always clothed herself in what May had outgrown. Joan took in the seams and shortened the hems. When she was a child, she believed that she would one day grow into her sister's voluptuousness and stature, that she would be able to fill one of those abundantly cut dresses without a single stitch being altered. But at fifteen she was still small and thin, and May was sailing away from her. *She could not wait to be gone.* The wave of anger subsided when she remembered how her sister had sometimes derided this house, Father's obsession with death and disease, his talk of purgatives and emetics, the stench of his herbal brews filling every room. Once, in a fit of temper, she had called it a house of pain.

When May stepped off that ship, she would first exchange vows, then lie beside that unknown man. What would she do if he was hideous, his face covered in pustules? Hannah thought of Joan's folktales of strange bridegrooms who turned out to be criminals or even the devil himself. When she tried to envision her sister's future husband, she saw neither a monster nor a handsome young planter but a void—a space filled with fog. The only sound in that gray mist was the keening of gulls.

As she nestled under the bedclothes, Hannah sensed that somewhere out at sea her sister walked the ship's deck in darkness, feeling her way along the rail and trying to spot constellations through the patchy clouds. Though May had not cared for physick or surgery, she was well versed in other arts, the ones Joan had taught her and that Father dismissed as outlandish superstition. She would look for the stars that spelled out her fortune.

The thought was comforting. May's essence filled the room like candlelight.

Hannah remembered the times her sister had crept into bed in the early hours, returning from her trysts. She tried to imagine what May and her lovers had done together. Her sister had never told her anything. When Hannah had begged her for details that would give life to the diagrams in Father's anatomy books and the drugged, blindfolded men strapped to the operating table, May only laughed. *Poppet, you will find out for yourself soon enough.* Sometimes May had neglected to wash herself before coming to bed and carried with her the salty smell of a man, which resembled the odor of flowering hawthorn.

The scent of hawthorn haunted Hannah when she and her father went to church the next morning. She stared at the carved stone face of the Green Man, whose questing eyes never blinked but burned into her until she almost looked away. She tried to picture her future brother-in-law.

After the service, Hannah lingered alone in the churchyard, winding her way among the graves. Ninety-nine yew trees grew in that churchyard. People said that if a hundredth tree were planted, it would die. Ninety-nine was the magic number that guarded the flat tabletop graves, peculiar to their village. Paths among the yew trees twisted and threaded around the limestone slabs raised altar-like to the sky.

Hannah knelt on the grass beside her mother's grave, rested her brow against the stone. Silently she entreated her mother's bones. *Keep watch over us. Don't let anything ill befall our May.* She pricked her finger on the thorny stem of the rose that she and May had left on the grave the previous week. Licking the wound, she tasted iron in her blood.

5 The Cards

Hannah

WEEKS LATER, as summer waned and the days grew shorter, Hannah cut onions for soup. It used to be May who helped Joan with the kitchen chores. When she was in a good mood, Joan teased Hannah, saying she would make a cook of her yet. But the onions made her eyes water, and the old knife couldn't cut properly.

"This blade wants sharpening," Hannah said, unable to keep herself from sounding strident.

Joan was in no mood to entertain complaints. "Cut it with your father's scalpel, then. Your sister never fussed like that."

Hannah wished she had held her tongue. Setting down the knife, she wiped her eyes on her sleeve.

"What is it?" Joan asked.

"I miss her," Hannah said. "Sometimes I can't sleep for thinking about her." It was September. May should have arrived in Maryland by now, but they couldn't expect to receive a letter from her until the following summer when the ships returned from the Chesapeake.

Joan patted her shoulder. "May has a good sister, she does." She put her face close to Hannah's. "What do you say I read the cards?" Without waiting for a reply, Joan lumbered to the far end of the kitchen where her pallet lay. "Come here, dearie. Your knees give you less pain than mine. If you tell your father, I'll skin you."

Hannah rooted under Joan's mattress. She didn't care if fortunetelling was superstitious nonsense or deviltry. She wanted some sign of May's fate, some message of comfort.

"Here they are." She presented Joan with the pack of cards, concealed in a knotted rag.

Joan sat at the table and began to shuffle. Pulling up a stool, Hannah watched in silence as Joan's red fingers plucked two cards from the deck and laid them down. The three of spades and the queen of diamonds. Joan's jaw sagged.

"What is it?" Hannah clutched Joan's wrist.

"Spades are no good. Especially the three of spades. Now, the six of spades would be a different story altogether."

"What does it mean?"

"The heart pierced by three blades."

"But this one." Hannah pointed to the other card. "The queen of diamonds. Surely this is a good card."

Joan grunted. "It tells us nothing of her husband."

"Then it must signify May . . . her good fortune."

Joan muttered something, then swept the cards off the table and wrapped them in the rag. "Enough for one day."

"Joan, *tell* me! What did you see—"

Her interrogation was cut short by a rap on the door that opened onto the study.

"Hannah!" Father called. "Will you come?"

Joan hid the cards in her lap while Hannah darted into the study.

"I heard raised voices in the kitchen." Father frowned. "What were you and Joan speaking of?"

"Nothing, Father. Nothing of importance."

"Were you quarreling?"

"No, Father." Hannah bowed her head. On a normal day, Father would have pestered her until she confessed the truth, but presently he appeared too weary to pursue the matter.

"This morning I examined Mr. Thompson. He suffers from a weak and troubled heart and has told me of palpitations."

The heart pierced by three blades. She tried to put Joan's cards out of her mind. Father was right—nothing good could come of fortunetelling.

"Upon hearing this diagnosis," Father continued, "what remedy would you prescribe?"

Hannah breathed deeply. In the past weeks, he had been teaching her ceaselessly, as if attempting to cram as much of his knowledge into her head while he was still well enough to do so. "*Digitalis purpurea* to regulate the heart, Father. Common foxglove. But it must be well diluted in a tincture with a gin base that the patient should swallow three times a day, but only a teaspoon. This tincture should include a tiny amount of *Helleborus niger* to warm and stimulate the heart. And also, very well diluted, *Convallaria majalis.*"

"The common names of the last herbs, if you please."

"Black hellebore and lily of the valley."

"Tell me the lesson of Paracelsus."

"All depends on the dosage. Any medicine may heal or poison according to its dose."

"What will happen if *Digitalis purpurea, Helleborus niger,* and *Convallaria majalis* are dosed immoderately?"

"The patient may die, Father. The herbs could induce heart attack."

"What oath did I make you swear before I began to teach you about the physick herbs?"

"The Hippocratic Oath, Father. That I will use this knowledge only for good, to heal and never to harm." Hannah wondered why he had bothered making her take the oath, seeing as she would never be permitted to practice these arts on her own. If she remained a spinster, midwifery would be the loftiest profession to which she could aspire. But there were plenty of midwives in the district already, each of them jealous of newcomers stealing their trade. Maybe she would be lucky enough to marry a physician or an apothecarist and be his helpmeet, measuring out the herbs as she did now for Father.

He unlocked the cupboard where he kept the gin. Working beside him, with the late-afternoon light pouring through the big front window, Hannah weighed herbs on the brass scale. Then she added them to the measure of gin. Next she needed to dilute the alcohol solution with an equal measure of fresh well water. Passing through the kitchen on her way to the well, she found Joan at the table. A new card was laid out before her, the eight of clubs.

"What does this signify?"

"Arrows." Joan caught her hand. "Arrows traveling at great speed through the air. She is thinking of us."

6 The Seeds

Hannah

MAY'S FIRST LETTER arrived on June 16, 1690, just as the hawthorn in the garden had ceased its blooming, fragile white flowers turning brittle and brown. Rain drummed softly against the kitchen door as Hannah, Father, and Joan gathered at the hearth. Hannah broke the wax seal and unfolded the letter. Mindful to conserve precious paper, May's handwriting was tiny, lines crammed together so that hardly a dot of white space remained. Father put on his spectacles and squinted, but only Hannah's eyes were strong enough to make out the crushed and distorted words. So Father sat down with Joan while Hannah read the letter to them slowly, with long pauses between the sentences as she struggled to decipher the words. When she came to a passage she deemed unfit for Father's and Joan's ears, she silently omitted it.

OCTOBER 25, 1689

Dear Father, dearest Hannah, to-morrow when we bring our Tobacco to Banham's Landing, I shall press this Missive in the Shipman's Hands. May it travell safely Home to you. Hannah, though you and Joan would not have it so, now I am a Wife. Ere I first set Foot off the Ship in Anne Arundel Town, Cousin Nathan did spirit me to Church where I wed Gabriel. "What of the Banns, Sir?" I ask'd. Cousin Nathan replied that he posted them three Months before I had e'en arrived!

Hannah stopped short. That meant Cousin Nathan had posted the banns before he had known if her sister would consent to the match.

"Why are you so quiet?" Father asked fretfully. "Read on. Let us hear the rest."

Bowing her head, Hannah obeyed.

Sister, the Dress we sew'd together with Joan looked right Comely, with the Lace and Ribbands and the embroider'd Stomacher, but I fear so great was the Haste with which Cousin Nathan rush'd me to Church, I had no Opportunity to procure a Wedding Bouquet.

Joan shook her head and muttered something indistinct. Father threw her a cross look and cleared his throat. "Read on, Hannah."

Lest any Person envy my new Station as a Planter's Wife, may I say that our Plantation consists of Tobacco Plants struggling to grow amongst the Stumps of fell'd Trees. It is a veritable Wilderness we live in. Let me tell you that I enjoy no Excess of Leisure. With the two Mr. Washbrooks, the seven Indentured Servants, myself, and the Maidservant to feed and clothe, I bide my Days spinning, mending, and cooking. In Truth, Joan would roar in Laughter to hear of my many labours, remembering how oft I shirk'd my Duties at Home. I share my Chores with the Serving Girl call'd Adele. She is just your Age, Hannah, and from the West Indies, born a Slave on a Sugar Plantation. She speaks often of the Cruelty she endured.

Hannah's voice trailed off as she read the rest of the passage to herself, a chill moving through her.

Adele believes in Spirits and Ghosts. It is rumour'd amongst the other Servants that she can work Hoodoo Witchcraft. But worry not. She seems a sweet and loyall Girl and greeted me upon my Arrival with Wild Flow'rs.

"Is there no more?" Joan demanded, swollen fingers tangled in her knitting.

"Read the letter to the end," Father said.

Hannah continued.

Cousin Nathan carries himself as if he were some Biblickal King. It is not enough that I address him as "Sir." He would have himself be call'd "Worthy Sir." He oversees Gabriel and the Boundsmen as they fell Trees to clear Land for Planting next Spring. Being from Ireland, the Boundsmen are a musickal Lot. Whilst they work, I hear them singing mournfull Songs in their own Tongue. Sister, come Spring I shall plant the Seeds you gave me. God willing, the Rosemary, Camomile, and Thyme will flourish here. Most of all, I long to plant the Foxglove, for it reminds me of Home. Please give my love to Joan. I miss her terribly. I pray that you and Father are in good Health. Ever yr devoted May

Hannah folded the letter and held it in her lap.

Joan rubbed her wet eyes. "Poor wench. So far away. She's lost to us." She glared at Father. "Planter's wife, indeed. More like a drudge, she is."

Biting her lip, Hannah waited for Father to rebuke Joan for her outburst. Instead he remained quiet for a long while.

"She writes nothing tender of Gabriel," he said at last. "Not a word." Then he crumpled in his chair.

—✦—

The next morning Hannah sat in her father's study with a freshly cut goose quill in her hand, a blank sheet of paper before her.

Dearest May,

How we all miss you. Joan will never forgive Father for letting you go. The House is quiet as a Tomb with you gone. I am a Year older but apart from missing you, my Life has hardly changed. The Days pass in Dreary Monotony.

Sister, I beg you to tell me of Gabriel. Has he brought you Happiness? How I wish we had at least met him before you sail'd.

34

I am as healthy as ever, no Fitts or anything to cause Trouble. Given their Age and Constitution, Father and Joan are as well as can be hoped. They send you their Love.

Though an Ocean lies between us, we are ever with you in Spirit. Keep it a Secret, Sister, but every so often Joan reads the Cards to know of your Fortune.

With this Letter, I send more Seeds. Father expects the Feverfew and Artemisia to be of Use in your Household Physick. Joan told me not to forget Heartsease, seeing as you have always loved that Flower. May you and your Husband remain healthy and sound.

Ever yr loving Sister Hannah

━╋━

The unseasonably cool summer dragged on, bringing too much rain, which blighted the wheat and barley crops. The price of flour was higher than it had been in years.

"We must be more frugal," Father told Joan, instructing her to bake only once a week. He economized by eating very little. By the time winter set in, his paunch had melted away and his cheekbones sprang from his face.

"You mustn't grow too thin," Hannah scolded. "We aren't such paupers that you must starve." It shocked her to see him looking so old and feeble.

He dismissed her remarks with a flick of his bony hand. "The ancients taught us that corpulence breeds all manner of disease." He cast a pointed look at Joan, who remained resolutely stout.

━╋━

June 1691 passed with no letter from May. Father hardly spoke, hiding himself in his herb garden. His ascetic diet left him constipated, obliging Hannah to administer purgatives once a week. To cure his ill humors, he applied leeches to his skin.

"The unhealthy blood must be drawn out," he told his daughter. "The teachings of Galen would have it so." Still, his melancholy clung to him like a heavy cloak he could not throw off.

Whenever she could slip away, Hannah spirited herself to the marketplace in the next town, ears pricked to any gossip from

Bristol Harbor. Had the ship carrying May's letter sunk to the bottom of the ocean? One of Father's patients said he had heard rumors of Atlantic squalls.

In the late hours when Father's snores rattled the beams, Joan laid out the cards. "We must not give up hope," she whispered to Hannah. "I keep turning up the eight of clubs. A message is on its way."

However, she kept drawing the eight of spades as well, which made her curse. She refused to tell Hannah what it signified.

⚓

In August the letter arrived. Hannah read it aloud, too anxious to remember to censor it for Father and Joan.

> *I write with Mournfull News. The End of Summer here is the Season of Fevers and Sickness. This Climate breeds Contagion. Just after Harvest, Cousin Nathan was taken with Ague, shaking and shivering all Night. He complained of High Fever and Fearsome Pain in the Head. The Disease is called the Flux and the only Remedy comes from the dry Bark of the Cinchona Tree. We begged this Medicine from our nearest Neighbours. Father, you must believe I tried my best. I gave him Decoctions of Cinchona thrice a day, as well as Willow Bark and Mint. I lay cool wet Cloths on his Brow and Chest. I went down on my knees and prayed to God, but all in vain . . .*

"What blasphemy does she write?" Father interrupted, his voice querulous. "Does she dispute the mercy of God?"

Hannah sighed. "Surely she wrote in a moment of sadness. I doubt that she intended to be heretical." Clearing her throat, she read the next line, then stopped abruptly.

Cousin Nathan did die.

Hannah waited for the grief to grip her, yet it left her untouched. She had never met the man. As far as she was concerned, he was the faceless stranger who had arranged for May's marriage and exile.

36

But Father's head sagged. Something glinted in his eyes. "Let us pray for his soul." Hands folded, his lips moved, but no words were audible. At last he gave her permission to read on.

Adele and I dressed the Body. The Men dug the Grave. As we must wait a long while for a Clergyman to come our Way and perform the Funeral Rites, we did for ourselves. Gabriel read from The Book of Common Prayer. In Faith, Nathan Washbrook was quarrelsome and over-proud, yet I miss him. I have been troubled by Nightmares of late and think ever on Adele's Stories of Ghosts, even tho' I know Father would think it Wicked of me to succumb to Superstition.

Hannah flushed and looked at Father. His eyes were shadowed.

At least I can send the two Hogs Heads of Tobacco to pay for your Passage. Pray, come when you are able. Tho' I miss you sorely, it would be a Great Sin to wish you to sail soon only to ease my Loneliness. May God grant Father a long and robust Life. Hannah, at long Last, I do have some Good News to impart. Soon I shall be a Mother. The Babe shall be born in a matter of Weeks, and my Belly has grown thick as a Vicar's. In Truth, I am a little frightened of the whole Matter. If it weren't for my good Adele, I would stow away on the next Ship Home to you. If I bear a Son, I shall name him after Father, and if I bear a Girlchild, I shall name her Hannah. Ever yr loving May

The letter ended at the bottom of the paper, the words squeezed as close together as could be. When Hannah looked up from the page, she saw Joan hobble out the back door, hands clasped to her face. Hannah was about to follow her when Father took her arm.

"Daughter, you tremble. You are white around the lips. Tell me you are not succumbing to one of your fits."

"I am fine, Father." Swallowing, she tried to ignore the tight knot in her belly. She thought of the infant clothes that May had taken with her. The letter was dated October 10. By now the child must be half a year old. *If* all had gone well with the birth. Hannah wouldn't allow herself to think otherwise. May had wide hips. May was strong and fearless.

"Father," she said softly. "You are a grandfather. I am an aunt." She was disappointed that May still hadn't answered her questions about Gabriel. However, she had written the letter in the depths of mourning. Perhaps she feared it would be disrespectful to write of conjugal happiness in the same letter that announced her father-in-law's death. And the letter paper was so small. She wouldn't have been able to squeeze in another word.

"She is troubled in spirit," Father muttered. "And lonely. She said so herself. She needs you. I am keeping you from her."

"Father, don't say such things." Her voice was sharp, then it broke like glass as she started to cry.

"If I were gone," he insisted, "you would be free to join her." He spoke without bitterness or self-pity. As Hannah wept, he drew her into his arms and hushed her. "Tomorrow you will write a letter to her. Give her as much comfort as you can."

Dearest May,
We send you our Love and our Sorrow for your Loss. In this Parcel you will also find a Pound of Cinchona Bark from the Apothecary.

Hannah did not write that Father had sold his telescope to pay for the expensive medicine, which came from far Peru.

God willing, your next Letter will be full of Happy News of the Child. Is it a Boy or a Girl? Perhaps by now, you are expecting your Second Born.
Please give our Love and Regards to your Husband. Though we have never met him, it does seem Strange not to greet him in our Letters.
We are well and think of you every Day.
Ever yr loving Sister Hannah

38

"I must purify my spirit," Father said. "There is no denying the fact that men of my years die in their sleep." The time, he informed her, was at hand to begin preparing his way for the world beyond.

"Father!" He was so exasperating, she thought. "While you are yet alive, please don't speak of the grave."

Although Hannah upbraided him for eating so little, he held to his course. He prayed and fasted, continued with leeches and weekly purgatives. She watched him grow even thinner, his hands feeble and papery. He was vanishing before her eyes, slowly reverting back to incorporeal soul and spirit. An expression of peace and resolve illuminated his face, as though his eyes saw things of heavenly magnitude that Hannah could not begin to grasp.

—✝—

A damp winter followed, which brought one of the worst epidemics of the grippe in Father's long memory. Weakened from his fasting, Father had little fuel to fight the sickness. Joan's lungs clogged with catarrh. She took a fever and one day could not rise from her pallet. Hovering at the hearth, Hannah made sick food and physick decoctions. Sometimes she thought it was only through dogged force of will that she did not succumb to the grippe herself. Someone had to be well enough to empty chamber pots and administer medicine. Someone had to light the fires each morning, draw water from the well. With Joan too ill to work, Hannah finally learned to cook a decent chicken broth.

The fever would not let Father go. Hannah wrapped his legs in cold wet cloths. His forehead burned and his eyes were glassy.

"May," he said. "May, you are the very image of your mother."

"Father, this is Hannah."

"You will forgive me, won't you, dear May? I don't want to leave this world without your forgiveness."

"Father, I am *Hannah*." She blinked back tears. "Now open your mouth." She managed to insert a spoonful of broth. Obe-

diently he swallowed. As his eyes focused on her face, she felt a
flicker of hope.

"Do you remember well the physick I taught you? What
planet rules the sloe bush?"

"Saturn, Father." *Cold distant Saturn.*

When he opened his mouth to say something else, she slipped
another spoonful of broth inside. She succeeded in getting him to
consume half the contents of the bowl before his eyes clouded
once more. His thin face erupted in a blinding smile.

"Hannah, is it truly you? Are we reunited? It has been so
long."

"Father, I have never left your house."

But her words did not seem to reach him. The smile still on
his face, he closed his eyes, head sinking back into the pillows. She
drew the covers to his chin. Hannah had been her mother's name,
too. Poor Father thought he was already in heaven. Setting the
bowl aside, she stroked his cool hand, trying to warm it. He slept
on soundly.

⁂

If Joan was weak, feverish, and coughing up green phlegm, at least
she had full command of her senses. "The door is shut for your
sister," she said hoarsely between mouthfuls of broth. "Don't let
it close on you."

"What door?" Hannah lowered her voice. "Have you been
reading the cards?"

"Her match was made for her," Joan wheezed. She paused to
cough into a sodden rag. Hannah took it from her and gave her a
clean one.

"Hush, now. Take your broth."

Joan struggled to swallow with her infected throat. "They
say love matches are unlucky," she rasped. "But that's just the talk
of men who can't think of anything but dowries and . . ." Her
speech subsided in a fit of coughing.

"Let me bring you the coltsfoot syrup."

Before Hannah could leave her side, Joan seized her wrist.

"Listen, dear. You make your own match. For love and affection. Find someone to cherish you."

"I will, Joan." Hannah tried to smile.

At last the older woman's fingers relaxed, relinquishing their hold.

⚓

Early the next morning Hannah carried wood and kindling up the stairs to light the fire in her father's room. He lay utterly still, a smile glowing on his face. Hands shaking, she turned her back to him and knelt to stir the ashes, uncovering a few embers, then built the fire, fanning the flames until they nearly licked her face. Cheeks smarting, she went to her father. When she touched his hand, it was as cold as the floorboards beneath her thin slippers. The cold crept up her legs, making her shudder.

"Father."

She opened his eyelids and saw the irises rolled back. Sinking to the frigid floor, she began to wail.

⚓

Father's coffin was so light, two boys could carry it easily. Hannah stood in the wet churchyard and watched them lower him into the freshly dug pit. He would finally rest beside her mother.

Though well-wishers crowded around her, Hannah had never felt more alone. Joan was too ill to attend. People offered kind words and genuine compassion, for there was hardly a family who hadn't lost at least one relative to the grippe. But no confidante stood beside her, no special friend or sweetheart, no sister.

How could he be *dead*, the man who had fed her with all his learning? As they shoveled dirt over her father's coffin, a few clods of damp earth stained the hem of her good dress. Fist to her mouth, she poured her entire concentration into keeping her spine erect so she wouldn't double over.

⚓

Hannah paid the rent and funeral costs by selling her father's globe, his clothes, and the furniture she could spare. The barber surgeon offered to buy Father's skeleton and anatomical dia-

41

grams. Hannah would never forget the way he stood there with his shoulders thrown back, his hat at a rakish tilt to show off his brand-new wig. She wanted to slap him for the way he strode through Father's study as if he were the new landlord. If he made a show of expressing his condolences, she knew he was also glad that his only competitor was gone.

Bargaining hard to raise the price, she sold him everything except what he coveted most — Father's books of physick and the leather case that housed the surgical instruments.

—+—

When spring came, Joan recovered. "I knew my time wasn't up," she told Hannah. "I read it in the cards."

Thin from her long illness, she used one of Father's old belts to hold up her skirts. "Ooh, look at me." Winking at Hannah, she paraded through the kitchen. "Slender as a girl again."

Joan's belongings were tucked neatly into three wicker baskets lined up beside the back door. She was going to join her niece's family who lived in a village south of Bristol. "My lungs and knees are still weak, but I will do for Nancy and look after her children. Poor wench has seven already, with one more on the way. She'll need her aunt Joan, she will."

While they waited for the niece's husband to come fetch her, Joan and Hannah drank cider in the kitchen.

"Remember this," said Joan. "Your father wouldn't want you to squander your youth mourning him. Go to your sister and look after her. Give her a kiss from old Joan."

—+—

Alone in the empty house, Hannah packed for the journey. She found a wry comfort that it was not a maiden's hope chest that contained her future but her father's heavy old trunk carved with rectangles and stars. Among her father's papers she found the letter from Cousin Nathan asking for her sister's hand for his son. Yet another letter described the beauties of Maryland. She enclosed both letters in the velvet-lined case with her father's surgical instruments. If she had lost her father, she would at least regain her sister. Hannah sat on the bare floor and hugged herself. May had always chosen a life of adventure. Her own adventure would now begin.

In August 1692, she boarded the *Cornucopia* and sailed out of Bristol.

II

7 The Bower of Eden

Hannah
1692

*In Faith, I assure you Maryland is so beautifull and abundant
that many have called it the Bower of Eden. Our Bay is full of
Oysters and Striped Bass. The Land about the Bay is rich in
Soil. Here do grow many towering White Oaks as grand as any
in England. Indeed, when the Land is cleared and cultivated, it
does resemble our native Gloucestershire. The Season for Growing and Planting is long and Winters but a mild Interlude — a
mere Dream, if you will. In our Forests grow Wild Cherrys,
Plums, Persimmons, and Strawberrys. Hickory and Walnut
grow in plenty, and we do have Tulip Trees with flame-like
gold and red Flowers. I need not tell you that many a Gentleman Planter has made his Fortune growing Tobacco in our
Tidewater Districts. A full-sized Ship can sail up the Chesapeake and there reach the most far flung Plantations. The
Indians here are peaceable. There are many who say that
Maryland and Virginia shall be the wealthiest Region in the
Americas.*

Trying to keep her balance on the rocking deck, Hannah re-
read Cousin Nathan's letter to her father. "The Bower of Eden,"
she murmured as people shoved past to spew over the rail. A storm
had blown the ship off course. The journey ahead would be long.
After two weeks of staring into the waves, she had come to believe
that the ocean itself was her new world, possessing a topography

47

all its own, with precipitous mountains the ship barreled over only to slip into treacherously deep valleys.

The sailors had told her to banish seasickness by looking at the horizon. But how could she when the horizon was as ever-shifting and inconstant as everything else? There was much that confounded her. May's letters had not made Maryland sound like a Bower of Eden in the least. By this time her sister had been married for three years, with one baby born, perhaps a second on the way. Would she even recognize May? Had motherhood and the hard life in the wilderness made her robust and ruddy like Joan, or thin and haggard? And what of her husband? He would cease to be an enigma, Hannah thought. She would finally get to see him face to face.

—+—

She shared her sleeping box with a woman named Elizabeth Sharpe and her two sons, Will and Ned, aged eight and ten. Elizabeth would not allow her boys to sleep in the men's quarters. "God only knows what unsavory characters are lurking on a ship such as this. And you," she said, "must stay close by me. Let no one know you are an orphan. There are evil men what prey on girls such as you."

Elizabeth's husband had gone over eight years before as an indentured servant. "Last year he got his freedom," she told Hannah. "His master gave him seventy acres on the Eastern Shore. He's the first of our folk to ever have his own land."

Although Elizabeth's hair was thin and she was missing half her teeth, Hannah sensed that she had once been pretty. When she spoke of her husband, her eyes shone with pride. "My Michael can read and write, he can. When he was a lad, he had a kind master what taught him his grammary." Back in England, Elizabeth had begged the vicar to read her husband's letters to her. Now Hannah read them aloud as they huddled on the deck, trying to shelter from the wind.

Her husband's reports had made Elizabeth wise to the ways of the colony. When Hannah told her that her brother-in-law was a tobacco planter, Elizabeth just laughed. "A planter! Every cracker and freed slave calls himself a planter. Half of what folk call plantations are miserable smallholdings. After three years, the land goes barren, and they try to sell it back to the Indians. I hope your brother-in-law owns a few hundred acres." She pressed her hands together. "We only have seventy, but my Michael is a clever farmer. I hope we pull a decent crop the first year and buy more land. If we have enough acres, some might lie fallow until the soil is fertile again."

—+—

The ocean seethed. Hannah learned to walk in broad strides, shifting her weight from one foot to the other with the roll of the waves. She tried not to stare at the indentured servants, whose threadbare clothing and gaunt faces set them apart. They received the scantiest rations. In the hold, they slept six to a box. Most were men and boys, but there were a few women and girls. Elizabeth told her that many of them had been let out of debtors' prison, poverty being their only crime.

"When we get into port, the gentlemen planters will buy all the healthy young ones. But the sickly ones will be shipped straight back to Bristol Gaol."

"Do they not get their freedom back after seven years of indenture?" Hannah asked.

"If they survive the climate and fevers of the place," said Elizabeth. "Pity the servants what are wenches. In no time, their masters will be at them, seeking to roger them at every turn. If a master gets a wench with child, he can prolong her indenture. The only virgin in the colony is a girl what can outwit her master."

She clutched Hannah's arm and pointed at a pair of gentlemen planters striding across the deck. Their linen shirts, even after seven weeks at sea, looked almost clean. The feathers in their hats bobbed like living things.

"They do own many servants," Elizabeth whispered, "and many more slaves besides. Africans are the only ones what can bear the climate. Mark my words, Hannah. Late summer is the season of fevers. Many an English servant will sicken and die ere he sets foot off the ship. But the Africans will go on working."

—+—

After ten weeks on board, everyone on the vessel stank like a goat. The gentry tried to mask their stench with eau de cologne. The salt pork ran out, and the biscuit was infested with mold. The water tasted foul. One morning Hannah awoke with a burning forehead, her bowels in agony. Half the people on board were ill. Weak as she was, it was too awful to stay in the dank hold and breathe everyone else's offal and sickness. Swollen-headed, she leaned against the ship rail. In her fever, she fancied she saw tulip trees rising from the waves. Their crimson-gold flowers were like shooting flames.

She cleaved to her vision of those radiant trees, trying to see only them and not the corpses that the sailors launched overboard. Elizabeth's boys pointed and shouted as sharks devoured the bodies.

8 _Anne Arundel Town_

Hannah

HANNAH SQUEEZED ELIZABETH'S arm as they leaned over the ship rail to view the harbor front of Anne Arundel Town. The place appeared to be little more than a village of around forty roughly constructed houses. Cows and sheep grazed in pens between the buildings. Her eyes anchored on the church where her sister and Gabriel had married.

"Oh, Hannah. Somewhere down there will be my Michael. I wonder if I'll recognize him after all these years."

Most of the people on the pier wore buckskin and rough homespun, except for the gentlemen planters in their linen and brocade. Everyone seemed in good cheer to see the ship. Yet something about the crowd troubled Hannah—there were no old people. She remembered Elizabeth's talk of contagion, the toll the brutal climate exacted.

"Of course, you will know your own husband," she told Elizabeth, hoping to chase away dark thoughts. She asked herself if she would be able to pick May out of a crowd when the time came. Her sister didn't know she was coming—there had been no chance to send a letter that would arrive before the ship did. Hannah would disembark at Banham's Landing, fifteen miles up the Sequose River from the Washbrook Plantation. She had heard it would take another two weeks before the ship reached the mouth of that river. But the Washbrooks would be there to deliver their tobacco harvest. Wouldn't May be surprised to see her? Wouldn't it be a dream to see her sister again?

"How do I look?" Elizabeth asked. "Clean and decent?"

The night before, they had moored at Jamestown, Virginia, where the crew had brought barrels of fresh water aboard. The captain would fetch better prices for the indentured servants if they washed before the auction. Hannah and Elizabeth had soaped and scrubbed themselves from their toes to their hair, then Elizabeth had given her boys a good sponging. Hannah dug to the bottom of her trunk for a fresh shift, but she was saving her good bodice and petticoat for her arrival at Banham's Landing.

"Look," said Elizabeth. "They're lowering the gangplank." Ned and Will edged away from their mother as she began to weep. "Oh, what if he hasn't come for me, Hannah?" She looked terrified. "What if he's forsaken me? What will I do?"

"Stop talking nonsense." Hannah took her hand. "Of course he'll be there."

"Come down to the pier with me," Elizabeth begged her. "Hannah, please. I don't want to stand alone down there like a servant waiting to be sold off."

They waited until it was their turn to file down the gang-plank.

"Don't leave my sight!" Elizabeth shouted to her boys. "Stay close by me. We mustn't lose one another." She took each of her sons by the hand. Hannah watched her search the sea of faces for her husband.

There were few women in the crowd, but Hannah's heart surged when she saw a young mother with wide blue eyes who was struggling to quiet a squalling tot. Of course it couldn't be May. Yet the illusion was perfect. Hannah allowed herself to pretend that the moment of reunion was upon her. Then the strange woman turned her head, revealing a pockmarked cheek. No, it couldn't be her May. No pox had ever touched her May.

Elizabeth made a noise from deep in her throat as a man approached. Though he was scarred in the face and thin as a barber pole, his smile was enough to bring fresh tears to Elizabeth's eyes. "Is that my Betty?" he asked. "Is that my girl?"

Hannah looked away to give them their privacy. She heard

her friend crying in his arms, heard him gently hushing her. Ned and Will hung close by Hannah and traded nervous glances. Eight-year-old Will had been in his mother's womb when his father sailed to the colony. Hannah reckoned that even ten-year-old Ned couldn't have much memory of him.

Their father called their names. "Are these my little men?" He threw his arms around them, drawing their heads to his bony chest.

Elizabeth took Hannah's elbow. "This is Hannah Powers. She read your letters to me on the ship."

Michael Sharpe bowed to her. "We live near Cambridge on the Eastern Shore," he said. "You are always welcome."

Hannah smiled. "You are kind, sir." It was comforting to know she already had friends in the New World.

"Look!" Little Will grabbed her hand and pointed.

The auction had begun. A girl she recognized from the ship stood on a barrel while planters in plumed hats pointed their walking sticks at her and placed their bids.

"Two hogsheads for that wench."

"You say two for a healthy girl of seventeen?" The first mate, presiding over the auction, lifted his eyebrows incredulously. "Young and pretty, no pox on her. Sure she'll make some lonely man a good wife."

Laughter shook the crowd. The girl on the barrel stood without flinching, her strong chin pointed toward the distant hills. The rumor on the ship was that she had been a kitchen girl made pregnant by her master's son. Her baby had been stillborn.

A man in homespun clothes with a hickory walking stick stepped forward. "I bid four."

A while later, Hannah heard Michael Sharpe tell his wife that their ferry for the Eastern Shore was about to sail. Elizabeth threw her arms around Hannah's neck. "If you ever need anything, write to my husband."

"I am happy for you," she whispered, holding Elizabeth tightly before letting her go.

"Can Hannah come with us?" Will asked.

53

"No," Hannah told him firmly. "I am to meet my sister and her family."

"Does she have little boys?" Will sounded jealous.

"She has a child I have never met." Hannah stooped so that her head was level with his. "I don't know if it's a boy or girl."

Elizabeth embraced her again while the boys waved goodbye. Michael Sharpe doffed his hat. "Good luck to you, Hannah Powers."

Hannah waved until she lost sight of them in the crowd. Suddenly alone, she wondered what to do with herself. The smell of roasting meat caused her empty stomach to growl. Beyond the pier, she made out the cookstalls. After twelve weeks of dry biscuit and weak beer, she couldn't imagine anything more delectable than freshly cooked food. Her fingers weighed the cloth purse that hung from her belt and contained her small hoard of coins. On her way to the stalls, a man stepped in her path and smiled, revealing a row of rotten teeth.

"I see, mistress, you are yet unclaimed. Let me tell you, I have two hundred acres and am looking for a wife. Timothy Sower is my name, and I am a widower with four boys in need of a stepmother."

"I am not seeking a husband." Hannah spoke sternly. "I am bound for Banham's Landing to join my sister."

"Banham's Landing, you say?" He grinned lewdly. "Is your sister one of Banham's whores?"

Hannah could only gape as he melted back into the throng.

"You must forgive him for his words," a voice behind her said.

She swung around to see an immense woman with a body like a proud galleon. Her skin was indigo-black. "The men come to sell their tobacco and buy a few nice things from the ship. There are so few Englishwomen here. When they see a girl like you, they act like fools."

Hannah could not think what to say. She had never stood

face to face with an African before, but something in the woman's gaze reminded her so much of Joan that she ached.

"I am sure you are right," she said at last, dipping her head.

—+—

"What meat is this?" she asked the man at the cookstall while he ladled thick brown stew onto a wooden trencher.

"Venison," he said without ceremony, as though he were dishing out pigs' feet. Hannah shook her head in amazement. At home only the gentry were allowed to hunt deer and eat their meat.

After she had finished the stew and was wiping her trencher with a hunk of coarse bread made from Indian maize, she realized that every man within twenty feet was staring at her. This time she tried not to let it unnerve her. She reminded herself that she was brand-new to their world, still unmarked by this country. She was fresh from the land most of them would never see again. How could they help but stare?

—+—

As the sun crept toward the western hills, there seemed little point in remaining on shore. The auction had ended. The sailors had unloaded the goods for Anne Arundel Town and were ready to sail north up Chesapeake Bay at first light. How many days, she wondered, would it take them to reach Banham's Landing? Now that Elizabeth was gone, the ship was a lonely place. Crawling under the bedclothes, she couldn't wait for the voyage to be over.

She had just dozed off when a sailor carrying a lantern awakened her.

"Hannah Powers," he said, "two women have come to take Elizabeth Sharpe's place in your sleeping box." At that, he was gone, taking his light with him.

One of the women, however, held a guttering candle. Her face above the unsteady flame was black. Raising herself on one elbow, Hannah recognized the woman she had spoken to earlier that day.

"I am Lucy Mackett," said the candle bearer. "And this is Cassie." The face of a younger woman hovered over Lucy's broad shoulder. "We are free midwives bound for the Mearley Plantation."

"I am Hannah Powers," she replied, her voice hoarse with sleep. "Bound for Banham's Landing."

"You are the girl I saw before."

"Yes."

"Banham's Landing, you say? Your journey is longer than ours."

How long? Hannah wanted to ask when Lucy and Cassie turned their attention to moving their things into the narrow space and spreading their blankets on the shared pallet. Lucy set her candle in the tin sconce, then began to undress. Shadows flitted across the rough walls.

"You are midwives." It was too awkward to just lie there in silence as the two strange women prepared to bed down beside her. "Have you been to the Washbrook Plantation? It's upriver from the Banham Plantation. My sister bore a child . . . almost two years ago. Her name is May."

"I have never heard of the Washbrook Plantation," Lucy replied. "Cassie, you ever heard of it?"

"No." Cassie's shadow was girlishly slender.

"Good night to you," said Lucy, lowering her heavy body on the pallet. The sleeping box filled with the scent of dried herbs. Cassie blew out the candle, then squeezed into the space between Lucy and Hannah.

Rolling over to face the wall, Hannah tried to ease herself to sleep, but Lucy Mackett's words hung heavy in her mind. Her journey was far from being over. The waters of the Chesapeake swayed and surged beneath the ship as though she were still—and would always be—at sea.

9 The Dark Green Place

Hannah

ANNE ARUNDEL TOWN fell behind, lost and forgotten as a dream upon waking. With each hour they sailed, the land grew wilder and stranger. It reminded Hannah of the stories her father used to tell her. Once Britain had been covered in forest. Centuries ago, before the Civil War, before Henry VIII and the Reformation, before the tall trees had been cut down to make ships, there had been a lost wilderness full of bear and wild boar.

The ship sailed past harvested tobacco fields where the stripped earth stood out like a giant wound against the dense woods beyond. She sighted a group of black men burning harvest stubble. Although it was halfway into October, they worked shirt-less, their backs glistening in the fire's heat. Their voices rose on the wind with the smoke as they sang in an unfamiliar language, their music so haunting that it made her shiver.

Those men, she gathered, were not free like Lucy and Cassie. She turned as the two women walked toward her.

"Soon we anchor at the Mearley Plantation," Lucy said when they joined her at the rail. "The ship only comes once a year, and when it comes, it is like Christmas."

"Christmas?"

"You will see for yourself," said Lucy.

Cassie said nothing, only cracked a smile.

The ship swung around a bend, revealing a plantation that reminded Hannah of a prosperous yeoman's farmstead at home.

57

The two-story house had a steep-pitched roof and red shutters flanking gabled windows of real glass that glinted in the dazzling autumn light.

"Do they make glass here?" she asked.

Cassie snorted.

Lucy shook her head. "I heard that the Mearleys did order their glass from Holland."

Scattered around the house were outbuildings of more primitive construction. Lucy pointed out the livestock barns and tobacco sheds.

"That little cottage you see with the smoke coming out the chimney," said Lucy, "that is the kitchen. They cook in there so the big house doesn't get too hot in summer."

"Then it must be very cold in winter." Hannah could not imagine a house without a kitchen.

What Lucy did not point out were the hovels half hidden among the bushes and pines. Hannah reckoned those were the slaves' quarters.

"Look," said Lucy. "The children are blowing horns." She raised her hand to wave at the cluster of young ones jumping and whooping. One boy shouted to the sailors to throw him a mooring line so he could tie it to the dock. A woman in a russet-colored dress waved so wildly, Hannah thought her arm would loosen from its socket. Hannah waved back. She was beginning to understand why Lucy said the ship's arrival was like Christmas. The woman in the russet dress was obviously the planter's wife and the mother of those children, yet she was waving with the enthusiasm of a young girl. Did May also wave to the ship like that?

Everyone clapped and cheered. Black men began rolling huge hogsheads from the tobacco sheds down to the dock.

"That is their entire fortune," Cassie said.

"What happens if the harvest fails?" Hannah asked.

"They go into debt to the ship captain. They pay by credit—as long as he allows it. If the debt keeps rising, they lose their leasehold. Not a single planter here truly owns his lands. All is on lease from the Lord Baltimore."

"Further north I hear that storms have ruined the crops," Lucy ventured.

May lived north of here, Hannah thought. What if her harvest had been lost?

When the sailors lowered the gangplank, the first mate stepped ashore, saying he had letters for Mrs. Mearley. Hannah watched how eagerly she took them from his hands, how she hugged them to her breast as if they contained jewels. Hannah allowed herself to pretend she saw May clasp letters from home.

Meanwhile the men unloaded the goods that the Mearleys had ordered the previous year. She listened to the first mate read the inventory to Mr. Mearley. "An oaken table and eight chairs, two casks of Rhenish wine, a box of China tea, a bolt of India silk, six cones of sugar, one steel plow . . ."

"Do they not have ironmongers here?" Hannah asked Lucy.

"Who would be an ironmonger when he could be a planter?"

"Come." Cassie tugged Lucy's arm. "Let us go down and see if we are needed."

"Is Mrs. Mearley expecting a baby?" Hannah asked. The woman on shore did not appear to be pregnant, though the fabric of her dress was bulky enough to hide a growing belly.

"We tend to the others, too." Lucy nodded toward the shacks in the pines.

—+—

Hannah wandered down the gangplank, but soon lost sight of Cassie and Lucy. Mrs. Mearley beckoned people off the ship to a table of rough planks, where a cask of ale and a plate of crabcakes were laid out.

"Come and refresh yourselves!" she cried. "I'll let no one say that the Mearleys are not liberal and generous."

Mrs. Mearley looked about thirty-five, still handsome, but when she smiled, Hannah saw the gaps in her teeth. *For every child, a tooth*, the saying went. She wondered if May had lost a tooth with her first pregnancy. Hannah reckoned Mrs. Mearley was hiding something behind her smile—she could make out the strain in her face as the lady pressed a pewter tankard of ale into the ship captain's hand.

"I cannot tell you how pleased we are," Mrs. Mearley said to the captain, "to finally have the good table and chairs. For years we made do with what the servants could cobble together. At last we shall be able to receive guests in style. There is nothing Mr. Mearley likes better than company."

Mr. Mearley, busy overseeing the loading of tobacco barrels, did not strike Hannah as a man who enjoyed guests, or much of anything. She observed him limping along as though every step caused him pain. His posture was one of forbearance, spine hunched and arms clutched to his belly as if to protect his inner organs.

"In his condition, he should rest indoors." The captain spoke delicately. "I heard the news of his malady in Anne Arundel Town."

A fretful look passed over Mrs. Mearley's face. "I tried to persuade him to book passage to Bristol so that he might have the care of a physician, but he refused." She lowered her voice. "He fears sea travel. Last time he boarded ship, he caught a fever that was nearly the end of him."

"Madam." Hannah spoke before she could stop herself. "What is the nature of your husband's illness?"

Mrs. Mearley and the captain turned to her with puzzled faces. Mrs. Mearley appeared affronted.

"This is young Mistress Powers from the ship," the captain said.

"If you please, madam, my father was a physician, and I know something of physick myself. Perhaps I could be of service." Hannah curtsied with what she hoped was appropriate deference.

"My dear girl, I think you overestimate your powers." Mrs. Mearley spoke in a high and brittle tone. "This is no matter for amateurs."

"Begging your pardon, madam." She swallowed. "I only wished to offer help."

"Your offer is kind, mistress," said a man who appeared at

60

Mrs. Mearley's elbow. Hannah hadn't seen him until now. His voice was conciliatory and smooth as cream. "But Mr. Mearley requires a surgeon, not a nursemaid, however solicitous."

About forty years old, the man was easily the most sophisticated person she had seen on this shore. He wore a doublet of wine-colored leather over his voluminous linen shirt, which was laundered to such whiteness that it hurt her eyes. His wig, if modest, appeared brand new and of the latest fashion. His breeches were linen and his boots were of claret leather to match his doublet. Unlike the strutting planters she had seen on the ship and in Anne Arundel Town, there was a look of true nobility about him. He didn't need jeweled rings and silk waistcoats, Hannah thought, to prove he was a person of distinction.

"A surgeon, you say?" Her hands itched for the box of surgical instruments hidden at the bottom of her locked trunk.

"Seeing as you have so kindly expressed your concern, I trust Mrs. Mearley will not object if I share this revelation with you." He inclined his head. "The good lady's husband has a stone in his kidney."

Hannah opened her mouth in an O. She saw Mr. Byrd splayed on the table, the scalpel in her hand as she cut to the stone. How cleanly she had made the incision. How proud Father had been. She raised her eyes to the gentleman, about to tell him she could indeed operate on Mr. Mearley, when she caught herself. What possibility was there that Mrs. Mearley would let a strange young woman with a scalpel anywhere near her husband?

The gentleman addressed Mrs. Mearley. "If I were you, madam, I would try once more to persuade your husband to sail back to England at the first opportunity and there make use of a surgeon. In the meanwhile," he nodded to Hannah, "I understand there are two herb women aboard the ship. If you could fetch them, Mistress Powers, perhaps they might at least provide enough physick to dull Mr. Mearley's pain."

"Lucy Mackett and Cassie, you mean." Hannah ducked her head. "I will see if I can find them, sir."

Hannah joined Cassie and Lucy in the cooking house, where they measured out herbs for Mr. Mearley's remedy.

"Lucky for him, I had the witchgrass in my pouch," Lucy said.

Their tincture required young birch leaves, speedwell, and chicory. The last two they procured from Mrs. Mearley's store of dried kitchen herbs, but no new birch leaves would be found until spring.

"We must make do," said Lucy. "An incomplete remedy is better than none."

Cassie squatted at the hearth and poked the fire with a stick while waiting for the kettle to boil.

"If his stone is small, such a tincture might help him pass it," Hannah said. "But if the stone is large, only a surgeon can save him. Why can they not find a surgeon for him on this shore? The voyage to England might well kill him."

"My girl," said Lucy, "there *are* no surgeons on this shore."

"How can that be?"

"Who would trade a life of comfort in the mother country for this?" Lucy waved her hand around the cluttered cooking shack. "The patients are so far-flung, he would spend all his time traveling."

Cassie lifted her head from the hearth. "I hear in Anne Arundel Town there is a trained blacksmith. They could summon him to cut for the stone."

"A common blacksmith?" Hannah felt sick.

"Aye," Lucy said shortly. "Then he would die from the bleeding afterward."

"My father was a physician and surgeon." Hannah spoke rapidly so they wouldn't interrupt her. "Many times I assisted him. I saw him make the cuts. I have the instruments in my trunk. If the Mearleys would allow it, I could remove the stone."

Lucy laid her hand on Hannah's shoulder. She was struggling not to laugh. "You would offer to cut into a strange man's privy parts?"

Cassie guffawed.

Hannah's face burned. "But I—"

"No." Lucy spoke firmly. "A girl like you should not meddle in these things. Besides, the man is fifty. His sons are nearly grown. He has lived longer than most. God has not been unkind to him."

⚓

When the tincture was bottled and ready, Lucy and Cassie presented it to Mrs. Mearley.

"We are obliged," Mrs. Mearley said. She gave them a small cask of home-brewed ale as payment.

Back on deck, Hannah waved again at the children on the landing. She thought of Mrs. Mearley with her new oak table and chairs, of Mr. Mearley with his pinched gray face and his look of perpetual torment. What if she had been brave enough to present the scalpel and her book of anatomy? What if she had been courageous enough to tell them how she had successfully removed a kidney stone from Mr. Byrd back home? *They would never believe you.* She recalled the look Mrs. Mearley had given her. *They would call you a lying, deluded girl.*

"Still feeling pity for Mr. Mearley?" Cassie approached with a traveler's tin cup of Mrs. Mearley's ale. "The brew is weak," she complained.

Hannah looked out over the ship rail. The Mearley house had already vanished from view.

Cassie grinned. "Did you not say your sister lives upriver from the Banham Plantation?"

"I did."

"Well, there he is," she said coyly. "There is your Mr. Banham." She pointed to the man in the leather doublet who had told Hannah about Mr. Mearley's kidney stone. He sauntered past, a shining sun surrounded by a coterie of lesser planters who were like moons reflecting his brilliance. They competed for his attention and hung on his every word.

"Are you certain?"

Cassie nodded. "I heard the captain introduce him to some other men."

"So he is my sister's nearest neighbor." Hannah remembered what the man with the rotten teeth in Anne Arundel Town had said. *Is your sister one of Banham's whores?* Mr. Banham was certainly pleasing to look at. May would think so, too. Unwelcome thoughts crowded her head. No, surely May would have renounced her loose ways by now. She was a married woman, a mother. Surely she would not ply her charms on Mr. Banham.

Hannah clutched the ship rail. The man in Anne Arundel Town had said *one* of Banham's whores. Did he have a reputation as a libertine, then? He had not struck her that way. His gaze had been frank and open, befitting an upright man. *Enough.* She couldn't afford to tear herself apart over every scrap of gossip. Soon she would see May and be able to speak to her about everything. May would laugh at her worries.

"Why is he traveling at this time?" she asked Cassie. "Why is he not at his own plantation to oversee the loading of the harvest barrels?"

"A true gentleman never works," Cassie said slyly. "For that he has servants and slaves. I heard he has just returned from Virginia. He bought land there." She raised her eyebrows. "Two thousand acres."

Hannah could not fathom one man owning so much land.

"So you see," said Cassie, "he is far too busy to oversee his own harvest." At that she drained her cup of ale.

—◦│◦—

Hannah waited for a chance to ask Mr. Banham about her sister, but it was hard to approach him. He ate with the captain and slept in prime quarters with the ship's officers. She did not succeed in catching his eye. Before she could question Cassie further, the ship anchored at the Turlington Plantation, where Cassie and Lucy said their goodbyes to her.

"If you are ever in need of a midwife, send for us." Lucy

winked, then shouldered her small trunk and trundled down the gangplank.

—+—

The journey up the Bay continued. The ship emptied of passengers and goods from England, but filled with hogsheads, which weighed down the hold. Their passage was so sluggish, Hannah wondered whether she would ever reach her destination. When at last they arrived at the Gardiner Plantation at the mouth of the Sequose River, word came that storms had knocked down trees, blocking the waterway. Even the sandbars had shifted. The ship would not be able to navigate the river.

Hannah stood on the pier in the midst of the men struggling to load tobacco and unload cargo before darkness fell. Judging from the way Mr. Banham leaned against a crate and smoked his pipe, the ship's blocked passage appeared to cause him no anxiety. His men had loaded the harvest barrels onto smaller boats and sailed them down to Gardiner's Landing. She could only hope that the Washbrooks had done the same.

"Any news of the Washbrooks?" Hannah shouted at two men rolling a barrel.

One of them laughed. The other shook his head in annoyance. "The Washbrooks? How should we know their business?"

When she approached Banham, one of his servants was addressing him. "There is no damage to your house or any of your buildings, sir, although some fences were knocked down. Mrs. Banham took a fright, she did, sir, but she is better now."

Before Hannah could hope to get a word in, a man in an embroidered waistcoat swept up and embraced Banham. "Never fear that you must make the journey home by darkness, my friend. You are welcome, as always, to bide with us. Mrs. Gardiner would never forgive me if I didn't invite you to stay the night."

The ship captain approached. "Evening, Mr. Gardiner, Mr. Banham." He bowed. "There is another matter to discuss. A girl named Hannah Powers is also bound for Banham's Landing, sir."

Although she stood a few feet away, the captain referred to

her as if she were a child. Summoning her courage, she spoke up. "Mr. Banham." She dropped in a curtsy. "I am Hannah Powers, sir."

Banham smiled. "Ah, yes. The physician's daughter."

"Sir, I am bound for the Washbrook Plantation."

Something flickered across his face, but he said nothing. Inclining his head, he signaled her to go on.

"My sister is May Washbrook, wife of Gabriel Washbrook."

"Gabriel, you say?" He frowned. "I have only heard of Mr. Nathan Washbrook."

She flustered. "Gabriel is the young Mr. Washbrook, sir. Nathan's son."

"Ah, yes." He glanced around. "Have your people not come to meet the ship?"

"No, sir." Her voice shook. "I think not. The men I spoke to have heard no news of them."

"This is most unusual. Surely someone from their plantation must have made the journey down."

Hannah fought tears. "Maybe there was illness in their household, sir. Maybe their boats sank or their harvest was ruined . . ."

He held up his hand to silence her. "My dear girl, you are making yourself quite wretched, and probably for nothing. The tobacco was harvested in August, then hung up in barns to dry. Unless the storms brought down their barns, their harvest I'm sure is safe. Perhaps they are tardy because they could not yet clear the river for passage. Perhaps the storms damaged their boats. They might still bring their barrels down to Gardiner's Landing. I believe the ship will call here one more time before leaving the Bay.

"So you see, all will be well. Tomorrow I will take you upriver. When we reach my plantation, my men will take you on to the Washbrooks. Fret not, Mistress Powers. In the space of a day, you will be with your people."

Before she could thank him, he turned to Mr. Gardiner.

"The Gardiners, I am sure, will allow you to stay the night

here in safety. All you need do is fetch your things off the ship. Oh, and whatever the Washbrooks have ordered." He turned to the captain. "Any goods for the Washbrook Plantation, sir?"

"And how will they pay with no harvest?" the captain inquired.

Hannah covered her mouth.

"Courage, my child." Mr. Banham spoke gently. "I can extend credit to the Washbrooks, sir. Now have you any goods for them on board?"

Hannah smiled, almost faint to witness such goodness.

"I think not, Mr. Banham," said the captain, "but I will look at the inventory."

Banham winked at her. "That's sorted, then." He snapped his fingers at one of the sailors. "If you please, fetch Mistress Powers's box from the hold. She is leaving ship."

Moments later, Banham led Hannah up the path to the Gardiner house with its lit-up windows glowing in the twilight. He told Hannah that he had a daughter her age who played the spinet. A dancing master had come all the way from London to teach her the minuet. Among the young planters she had many suitors. His favorite among them was a young Virginian who bred racehorses. Mr. Banham also had twins named Eleanor and Alice. His oldest son was a scholar at Oxford, while his youngest boy was not yet old enough to cut his hair and wear breeches.

"My father went to Oxford," Hannah said, unable to hide her pride.

"I should have deduced when I first laid eyes on you that you were an Oxford man's daughter."

She flushed in delight. "Sir, I hear you are my sister's nearest neighbor."

"That is the most curious thing. Though they are also *my* nearest neighbors, I know little of them. The Washbrooks have never been neighborly. Nathan Washbrook's son—pray, what did you say his name was?"

"Gabriel, sir."

"Gabriel Washbrook." Mr. Banham spoke slowly, as though committing the name to memory. "Let me tell you of our Christmas parties at the plantation. They are famous. We invite every soul, rich and poor, in miles. There is music and dancing, food and drink in plenty. No one is turned away. People up and down the Bay come. Why, we have guests who hail from the Eastern Shore and as far as Virginia. But the Washbrooks never came once." He spoke with calm neutrality.

Hannah could not think what to say.

"Though on one occasion I did meet your sister," he said kindly.

"You did, sir?" She could barely restrain herself from kissing his hand in gratitude. "Do tell me of her."

"I only met her briefly." The expression on his face was difficult to read. "A proud and handsome woman. Maybe when you live there, we will see more of your people. Women are by nature more society-loving than men."

As they neared the house, Mr. Gardiner caught up with them, exchanging loud banter with Banham. Dropping behind, Hannah followed them over the threshold, down a wide central passageway, and into a chamber where a linen-draped table was set with china plates and silver goblets.

"Here is our hostess," Mr. Banham announced. "The incomparable Mrs. Gardiner."

A heavily pregnant woman extended her hand for Banham to kiss. She was lovely and golden-haired, and her belly thrust out grandly beneath her gown of watered silk. Mrs. Gardiner did not look a day over eighteen. Her bodice, cut fashionably low, exposed her breasts, which were even whiter than her face. She gave off the scent of tuberose. Behind her was an open doorway leading into a bedchamber. In the middle of that room, a black woman sat on a stool and nursed a white child who looked about a year old.

"Our son." Mr. Gardiner smiled indulgently. The boy had his mother's golden curls.

When everyone was seated, servants poured claret into the

silver goblets. They brought out platters of pheasant, oysters, roast pork and beef, and sweetmeats. The smell of the food alone nearly undid Hannah. This feast on the remote plantation seemed fabulous, like Joan's tale of the weary traveler who stumbled into the faery palace. If she blundered, the illusion would shatter. The fine victuals would turn into a pile of dry old leaves and empty acorn cups.

Gardiner and Banham spoke heartily of tobacco prices, the London market, and the West India Company. Hannah imagined she should make conversation with Mrs. Gardiner, but she didn't know what to say. For all her blinding beauty, the lady was vacant-eyed, smiling dimly without quite meeting anyone's gaze. She didn't utter a word, but merely went on chewing and swallowing the food that her servant placed in front of her. She sipped wine from her goblet until her face and breasts were rosy and flushed.

⁓✦⁓

Afterward Mr. Banham retired to a pallet set out for him in the room where they had dined. Hannah slept in a narrow chamber with the wet nurse and the little boy.

In the pitch-dark, she awoke to the sound of footsteps on creaking floorboards, strange noises, dove-like cooing. The wet nurse muttered in her sleep and rolled over while Hannah froze, rigid on her pallet. Her skin burned as she listened to muffled laughter. There was a voice she distinctly recognized as Mr. Banham's, then Mr. Gardiner's. A woman sighed like a pigeon. Hannah thought of Mrs. Gardiner's breasts, trussed up and on display for the men. Her pregnant belly. A whimpering voice murmured unintelligible words.

A strand of her own hair caught in Hannah's mouth like a bit. She thought of May and her lovers, then of her own maidenhood, her ignorance. Even if it disgusted her to admit it, the moans and cries moved her. Closing her eyes, she imagined an invisible hand stroking her belly and thighs. She recalled the times May had crept into their bed in the early morning, still glowing from her trysts, the scent of her lover rising from her skin. How peacefully her sister had slept afterward. *One of Banham's whores.* Had he also made her sister cry out like that? A sob caught in Hannah's throat.

While the nurse slept on, the little boy began to cry. Hannah crept to his crib and tried to soothe him. "Shh," she whispered. "Shh."

—+—

The following morning, Mrs. Gardiner did not appear at breakfast. Her husband explained that owing to her delicate condition, she needed her rest. With perfect equanimity, Mr. Banham inquired if Hannah had slept well.

The convoy of low-slung boats set off early for the Banham Plantation. The first two boats were loaded with the supplies Banham had bought off the ship. Six men rowed each of these craft upstream. Hannah sat with Banham in the third and smallest boat, which had four men rowing. Huddled at the rudder was a boy of about sixteen — a new hireling Banham had bought off the ship. Silent as stone and looking weak from his poor rations, the boy was obliged to take his turn at the oars to relieve the other men. Hannah nearly offered to row in his place — he hardly looked sturdy enough to hold his own against the swollen river's current. Mr. Banham dozed most of the morning while his oarsmen labored, their faces impassive.

Storm damage notwithstanding, the forest appeared impenetrable. Immense trees that had never known a white man's ax closed in around the waterway. Blood-red maple, golden ash, and birch stood ablaze against dusky pines. It would take a hundred strong men or more, Hannah thought, to clear the land for planting. Deer flitted through the foliage. Were there still Indians in these woods? she wondered. Cousin Nathan's letter had claimed that the Indians here were peaceable, but she'd heard from Elizabeth Sharpe that there had been massacres on the western shore a few years back. She wished Mr. Banham were awake so she could ask him.

The wilderness made her think of the ancient forests of Britain where the first people had lived. Once, when digging in the garden, she had found a stone arrowhead. Joan had told her it was elf shot—a faery's arrow. Now she pictured the silent ones moving through the woods, watching their boats as they struggled upriver. She could not escape the notion that they were being watched. Shielding her eyes from the sun, she scanned the forest for staring faces. The first people were observing her from the dark green shadows where they hid. She imagined a head emerging from the oak leaves. The Green Man.

Mr. Banham grunted in his sleep.

A while later, on a rocky outcropping, a huge black shape reared, maw open. Screaming, Hannah clutched the side of the boat. Mr. Banham lurched awake and reached for his musket while the oarsmen laughed. The bear dropped to all fours before melting back into the forest.

It took some time before her heartbeat returned to normal. She had seen a bear only once before, at a country carnival, and it had been a tame and toothless old beast dancing on its hind legs. But the animal she had seen on the outcropping could have ripped out her throat had she stood undefended on land. The true meaning of the word *wilderness* sank into her. Beasts, not men, ruled this forest. This was their world.

They rowed past abandoned fields, the soil exhausted from tobacco. Weeds claimed that forsaken earth. Soon the forest would return, she thought, even thicker and darker than before.

To pass the time, Mr. Banham chatted about various subjects, such as the cultivation of tobacco and which fish could be caught in the river. Hannah could hardly concentrate on his words. Her eyes kept slipping toward his hands, resting neatly on his thighs. She imagined those long fingers all over Mrs. Gardiner. All over her sister.

"Mistress Powers, are you quite well?" he asked. "In another hour or two, we will reach my plantation. My daughters, I am sure, will be very curious to meet you."

He slapped at a fly that lighted on his sleeve. "Be glad it is late in the year, otherwise the mosquitoes would devour us."

Hannah nodded and tried to appear grateful for his kindness. Every pull of the oars was bringing her closer to May.

—◆—

By noon they reached the Banham Plantation. Stiff from the journey, Hannah lurched out of the boat. Three pretty girls floated down the dock, rushing past her as though she were invisible. "Father!" they cried, fighting to see which one would embrace him first. Hannah noted that Mrs. Banham had not come down to greet her husband.

"Easy now!" Mr. Banham laughed. He was busy seeing that his men unloaded the cargo properly. "Careful with that parcel!" he called out. "There's a skein of Flemish lace in there!"

"Lace!" the girls all shouted at once. "Oh, Father!"

Finally Mr. Banham appeared to remember Hannah. "Ah yes, I must introduce you." He put his arm around the tallest and prettiest of the girls. "This is Anne. Those two are Alice and Nell."

How clean those girls were, their creamy faces protected from the sun by wide-brimmed hats and parasols. They were delicate as snowdrops while Hannah was gritty from the boat, her face scorched from the sun. Her once white neckcloth was mottled brown and gray. The Banham girls glanced at their father, as if to inquire how they should address her.

"This is Hannah Powers, sister to May Washbrook," he explained. "She just sailed from England."

The girls blushed. Hannah concluded that they probably assumed she was a new servant their father had bought off the ship. Her sunburnt forehead throbbed. After such a long voyage among strangers, how was anyone to know that she was a physician's daughter, a planter's sister-in-law? How was she herself to remember who she really was?

"I think you would like a meal," Mr. Banham said mildly, "and perhaps a bath before your journey onward."

Hannah saw how his daughters exchanged looks, wrinkling

their noses and curling their pink lips into mocking smiles.

"Sir, if you please, I wish to continue on." She willed herself to speak with the authority of an Oxford man's daughter. "My sister will be happy to see me in any case."

Mr. Banham found two fresh oarsmen and a smaller boat, then sent her on her way.

⚓

According to Banham, the trip would take another three hours upriver, but the afternoon dragged on. Fallen trees and beaver dams blocked the watercourse. At least a dozen times, the oarsmen had to unload her trunk, climb out of the boat, then heave the craft around a dam or a logjam.

"Why can't your kinsmen keep their part of the waterway clear?" one of the men asked, glaring at Hannah as though it were her doing. "We'll be damned lucky if we make it back before nightfall."

"Maybe they have not enough hands to clear away all these trees," she said, mostly to herself. In her letters, May had said there were only seven manservants. If Banham truly considered himself a considerate neighbor, he should send some of his many servants to help. She had heard him say he had sixteen indentured servants and more than forty slaves.

When they weren't cursing, the men lapsed into sullen silence, rowing hard against the current, muscles straining under their skin.

⚓

At last they reached a dock with missing slats and a boathouse with a caved-in roof, the sight of which sobered the oarsmen.

"Are you sure your people are still here?" one of them asked. His anger had vanished.

"Of course they are." Hannah's heart was beating too fast to entertain any other possibility. Before they could stop her, she leapt onto the dock. A weather-worn sign said *Washbrook*. "Give me the rope." She barked the command as though she were some highborn lady and not an unwashed orphan alone in the wilder-

73

ness with two strange men. When they threw the line to her, she tied it to a post. As the men hefted her trunk onto the dock, she heard a chorus of barking.

"Aye, they are here!" Her heart brimmed with happiness. "Can you not hear the dogs?"

Reaching into the cloth bag that hung from her belt, she extracted bright silver pennies, tuppences, even a glittering shilling. For once in her life she could be generous without a thought to economy, spending the entire contents of her purse as if she were a true gentlewoman. She had rejoined her sister and all would be well. The men stared in astonishment when she pressed the money into their blistered hands.

"Thank you for bringing me here." Picking her way over the broken dock, she shouted to the boatmen over her shoulder. "You may leave me now. You may return home. Go while there is still light." Their journey downriver, at least, would be swift.

Racing up the overgrown path, she failed to notice the weeds grown high in front of the tobacco barn door. Out of the tangled blood-red leaves, dogs jumped at her, barking excitedly, snapping at the air. "Leave me," she commanded, hoping to sound fearless as she darted past them. They chased her, nipping at her skirt. "May!" she cried.

Sprinting up the narrow path, she ducked her head under a low-hanging bough and lost her linen cap. Her hair flew out of its coil. From beyond a stand of dogwood, she saw a shingled roof, a stone chimney with a plume of smoke curling in the golden evening sky.

Smoke in the chimney! May and Adele must be preparing the evening meal. Lifting her skirts, she ran toward the house. An exposed tree root caught her foot and sent her sprawling. The dogs were on her, their paws on her back, their hot breath and tongues on her nape.

"Away!" Gasping, she struggled to her knees. She heard a shout, then the earth shuddered with pounding footsteps. A young man's startled face emerged from the autumn leaves. His eyes were dark pools. When he stepped forward into plain view, she saw that he was dressed entirely in buckskin. His long black hair hung loose and uncombed. A sparse beard grew on his face. With one shout, he called off the dogs. She rose to her feet while the dogs circled around him, whining and slavishly nuzzling him, licking his hands, which hung slack at his side.

"Who are you?" Hannah asked, temples pounding. Her eyes rested on the sheathed knife on his belt.

"Gabriel Washbrook." His voice was strained, barely audible over the dogs. "This is my land. Who are you?"

"Hannah Powers, your sister-in-law. Where is May?" He looked just like a tinker. Had Father only known, he would never have allowed May to marry him.

The young man shook his head.

She tried to collect herself. It was understandable that he would be surprised, seeing as there had been no chance of sending a letter announcing her arrival. But why did he look at her that way, as though she were a ghost?

"How came you here?" He spoke with antiquated speech. "Did you not get the letter?" His voice sounded rusty, as if he had lost the habit of conversation.

"May's letters are in my trunk," she replied. "Your neighbor Mr. Banham brought me upriver."

"Banham!" His jaw tightened. "Is he here?" He gripped the handle of his sheathed knife.

"No," she said warily. "He sent me on alone with two of his men."

Finally the young man looked her in the eye. His gaze was stern, even angry. "You will return with them anon. There is nothing for you here. *Nothing.* Get you back to the dock. Go!" Raising a trembling hand, he pointed toward the river.

"What of my sister?" She shouted with such venom that the dogs flew at her again.

He called them off. His pointing arm fell back to his side. Again he looked right through her as though she were vapor.

"Your sister is dead. The baby didn't live." He covered his eyes. "My father died of the flux. Then after . . . after your sister died, there was no rule, no rule . . . The servant girl ran off and then I gave the boundsmen their freedom. There was little else I could do. I am the only one left."

"My sister," Hannah kept repeating. "My sister." She had to dig her toes into the soles of her shoes to keep herself upright. Then it sank in. "You sent no word!"

"I did send word. I told you already of the letter. When I gave the boundsmen their freedom, one of them promised to post it in Anne Arundel Town, to the ship that was to sail out in spring. Mayhap you set sail before it arrived. Mayhap it was lost."

He said something more, but Hannah was beyond hearing it. She couldn't feel her own heartbeat anymore. May's green cloak floated before her. Her sister's hair was soft and heavy in her hands as she plaited it. She heard her sister laughing, teasing her. *Oh Hannah, you were always so somber!*

The dogs bayed and May's widower stared, but their attention was of no consequence. It was coming. It had been years since her last attack, but the fog rolled in, carried her away. This time the fog was not gray but green as her sister's cloak. Her legs caved beneath her as she fell down the well, plummeting into the dark green place where May called to her.

III

10 A Fish on Land

Gabriel
1692

THE GIRL'S SMALL pointed face reminded Gabriel of a cat. What struck him most was her hair, not chestnut like her sister's had been, but the shrill red of lichen and poisonous toadstools. There was nothing pretty about this girl who shook like an aspen leaf, whose witch-green eyes flooded with tears. While he looked on, not knowing what to say, the blood drained from her sunburnt face until it was as gray as a corpse. Her eyes widened, pupils dilating. From the blankness of her gaze, he knew she saw nothing. Before he could reach out to steady her, she collapsed, banging her head on the earth. Convulsions racked her body, spittle flowing from her mouth. He wondered whether she was ill. Or mad. If Adele had been present, she would say the girl had devils trapped inside her. His dogs pressed around her, whining as she thrashed like a fish on dry land. They tried to rouse her with their licking and barking until he ordered them away.

He fell to his knees and tried to hold her, tried to restrain her from hurting herself. Her head thrashed against his chest. A streak of blood running across her cheek stained his hand. His throat went dry. He could not believe that this was the sister after whom May had named their short-lived daughter, and to whom she had written those letters, crying over the page when she thought his back was turned. This girl was as different from her sister as a

79

sibling could be. Her wrist in his hand was so slender, it reminded him of a birch twig he could snap between forefinger and thumb. Though he himself was short and slight, she was so tiny that she made him feel gigantic. May had been half a head taller, always looking down on him.

Just as unexpectedly as her fit had started, it stopped. Her limbs ceased twitching. She lay utterly still, her head against his chest. He wiped the blood from her face with his fingers. Something about her helplessness left him helpless. After brushing the hair from her forehead, he gently laid her on the ground. He told himself not to touch her anymore.

When her eyes finally flickered open, she looked at him first dully, then fearfully, as though she did not recognize him or remember anything that had transpired before she had gone down. He looked up at the fading sky.

"Are you well now?" he asked. Then he ventured, "Are you hungry? There's a fish I caught today."

The girl raised herself on her elbows. When she opened her mouth, blood spilled out, staining the front of her dress. He reached to help her, but she warded off his hands. Unwinding the kerchief from her neck, she used it to wipe the blood.

"May," she murmured before gazing up at him with shame-filled eyes. Still holding the kerchief to her mouth, she scrambled to her feet.

"You did bite your tongue." How strange it was to be speaking to another human after two years of solitude.

"The boat," she said. "I fear it must be gone." She started off unsteadily toward the river. Sniffing the air, the dogs trailed at her feet.

"Wait," he called out. "You do not look well." It took him only three long paces to catch up with her. "Rest you here." He pointed to a tree stump where she could sit. "I will look for the boat."

Running hard down the path, he whistled for his dogs to join him. If only it were possible to outrun the heaviness that plagued him, the desolation crushing him. Just when he thought he had learned to master his grief, that girl had come out of nowhere, that broken girl falling into convulsions at his feet. When he reached the dock, he found her trunk but no sign of the boat. He shouted and raced down the bank, craning his neck to see as far downriver as he could. The waterway was empty.

His own boats were long gone. He had given the best boat to young Finn, who had promised to post his letter to May's family. The others had been stolen. He counted the things the fleeing servants had robbed from him. His dead father's silver, boots, and signet ring. Father's good clothes and the few pewter plates. He had been left with nothing but three graves, his dogs, and the empty house.

How could he take this girl back to the land of the living? Making an Indian dugout canoe entailed a week's labor at the very least. First he would have to cut down a suitable tree, hack the log to the right length, then burn out the inside. Building any other kind of boat would take twice as long. Besides, he lacked the nails.

The way overland would be slow and cumbersome. It was fifteen miles to the Banhams', and he had no horse. A patient scout could pick his way through the forest, it was true, but not with a frail girl and certainly not with her baggage. Her trunk was a huge piece of carpentry, massive walnut from the look of it. He wondered whether he would be able to lift it on his own. What would a girl like that have to transport? May's box had not been half as big. Defeated, he sat on the chest. The heaviness bore down on him. Once his father had told him of a collapsing tin mine, boulders crushing men's lungs, forcing the very breath from their shattered bodies.

His dogs barked and stood at attention. A few paces away, the girl watched him in silence, kneading her bloodstained kerchief.

"The boat is gone," she said.

He nodded.

"My trunk." Gingerly approaching him, she grabbed the iron

ring on one end and he took hold of the other. For a girl so small, she was strong. Between them, they heaved the chest up the overgrown path to the house. Gabriel didn't know whether to curse the devil or cry out to God. What would he do now that this girl had come? What would he do?

11 The Whole Cloth Unraveled

Gabriel

GABRIEL HAD NEVER CHOSEN to be a planter. His father had chosen for him, had made him work twelve-hour days, sweating in the fields beside the indentured servants. Nathan Washbrook had ruled his life with shouts, threats, and blows. He had whipped the boundsmen until welts laced their backs. "A man must show he is master," his father had told him. "If he doesn't, the servants will get the upper hand. There must always be a master."

When Gabriel was five, his mother died, bitten by a copperhead snake in her own garden. His father had never cared to remarry. They had lived in Anne Arundel Town until Nathan, consumed by his envy of the rich planters, decreed that they would be planters, too. He promised Gabriel what a fine life they would lead, waxed on about the wealth they would enjoy. Despite his temper, his father could be jovial—or more precisely, he could be like Jove, as pompous and grandiose as the Roman god whose image adorned his rum flask. Deceived by Paul Banham, who sold him the backcountry land, he paid too much for it. Surveyor that he was, he should have known better. The summer Gabriel turned fifteen, they had come to live in this wilderness. The first year, Gabriel and the seven Irish boundsmen had done nothing but chop down trees, to clear the land and build with their own untrained hands the rough hovel his father called the plantation house. Though Gabriel worked as hard as the servants, and though his hands were as callused and scarred as theirs, the Irishmen held themselves apart from him. They spoke their own incomprehensible language, sang their doleful songs, pretended to smile at Gabriel's father while cursing him as a tyrant under their breath.

His father had never joined in the labor but merely supervised, carped, cajoled. The plantation house consisted of a main room, a storage room, and a drafty attic, where the servants had slept until they built a shack of their own. They had transported the furniture upriver in a shallop boat. No one but Father was allowed to sit in the carved chair with the back and armrests. His father found a twelve-year-old mulatto wench named Adele Desvarieux to keep house for them, had bought her cheap after her previous master had cast her away on account of the savage bite she inflicted on him. For a mere girl, she was fearsome. Once, after a whipping, she left a pile of chicken bones on Nathan's bed, spilling the blood on his fine cambric shirts. She purportedly possessed voodoo magic and warned the men that if any of them tried to touch her, she would curse them and cause their pintles to shrivel to the size of gooseberries. She slept with a kitchen knife and a curious cloth doll in her arms. Gabriel thought she could have spared herself the trouble, for he wasn't the least bit taken by her, and his father, for all his other faults, did not lust after young girls.

The first year, with the tree-felling and building, they planted no tobacco but lived on corn mush and whatever fish they caught in the river. Each Sunday Adele slaughtered a capon. The summer Gabriel turned sixteen, their first tobacco crop failed. Banham came gloating, offering false sympathy and farming advice. Banham brought his three tittering daughters, paraded them before Gabriel, then declared he would marry them off only to established planters with sufficient means. Gabriel had not cared a whit for those spoiled girls.

"Not all who would be planters succeed," Banham had told them grandly, sipping from the claret he had brought upriver, ostensibly as a neighborly gift for the Washbrooks, though he drank most of it himself in front of them that day, he in his doublet of Spanish leather. It was common knowledge that half the freehold tobacco planters failed, had to give up their land to the debt collectors and work as tenant farmers for gentlemen like Banham. Gabriel's father was convinced that Banham was biding his time until they were ruined and had to sell back the land to him at a fraction of what they had paid for it.

After Banham and his entourage had sailed back downriver, his father had taken Gabriel aside. "It is time, my son, to get you a wife."

The year he turned seventeen, the tobacco crop had been a moderate success, allowing his father to send eight hogsheads of it across the ocean to buy a bride, the daughter of some distant cousin. He had not allowed Gabriel to read the letter from May's father privately but had insisted on reading it aloud in front of the servants while his son struggled not to squirm.

"By all rights, you should be well pleased," his father informed him. "Daniel Powers assures me his daughter is comely and healthy. No pockmarks on her face."

Looking back, Gabriel wondered what would have happened had he refused the match, if he had told his father he wanted no part of it. He had made his peace with being alone and friendless. If he were bolder in temper, he would have told his father to marry May Powers himself. But Father had cared little for women. He seemed prey to none of those common lusts at all, though he favored one of the Irishmen, treated him almost as a son, in his way. He would give him choice pieces of meat, praise his cleverness and strength, then beat him over some transgression, real or imagined.

Gabriel suspected that his father had thought that a daughter-in-law would be easy to dominate and that she would surely provide him with an heir. If Nathan Washbrook had failed with his own shy and faltering son, then he would succeed with the grandchild, whom he would mold like clay into the form of his choosing.

But May was not demure in the least. When she and Gabriel first met in Anne Arundel Town, the look she gave him was frank and challenging. She was four years older and five inches taller than he was—the shining Englishwoman in her embroidered gown. Her beauty was enough to melt away his misgivings and yet, as dazzled as he was, he sensed she was hiding something from them all. She wore green, the unluckiest color for brides. It was as if she carried a shadow with her. She made no secret of the fact that she was no maid. He was the untried virgin in their bed, too ashamed to take off his nightshirt lest she see the scars from his father's whip. Yet he had striven to befriend her, to make himself a worthy husband. His memories of her, both tender and bitter, seared. Once he had caught her lifting her skirts to show the servant men her shapely ankles and strong calves. She laughed and jested with them, begged them to sing ballads and airs in their language. Then she asked them to tell her what the words meant. When Gabriel could bear no more of it, he stole into the woods and carved his name on the trees to prove that he still existed.

Father ruled that plantation as if it were his kingdom. For as long as he lived there had been order, if not joy. There had been continuity. But when he died, the whole cloth unraveled. There was no patriarch, no master, no authority. Gabriel had never possessed an ounce of mastery, and then it had been too late to claim it. If he tried to give the servants orders, they laughed, knowing he wasn't man enough to reach for the whip. May had never listened to him anyway. Heavy with child, she blamed him for the humiliation of her body, the agony and tearing it would bring, though Gabriel wondered who the real father was. She ran off into the woods, crying for her sister back in England. Adele ran after her, pleading for her to watch out for snakes.

After his father had died, Gabriel threw his old bullwhip in the forest. He hated the sight of it. May went into labor, screaming that she hated him, that he had murdered her. Then she clutched the sickly child in her arms, weeping over it. That was where his memory stopped. Patches remained. How the cow had died from eating some poisonous weed. How, to spite him, the Irishmen had stolen his father's signet ring, his dead mother's last silver cup, and the secret cache of sovereigns.

They were all gone now—had died or run away. He was abandoned. In a way, it was a relief, a comfort, for in spirit and soul he had always been alone. Now at least it was a true life he lived, and not a lie. There was no more pretending to love the wife who betrayed him, and the father who had made his life a pit of obedience and toil. Yet he stayed in his father's house. Where else had he to go? A man alone with no hired men, no living kin, no wife—he could not be a planter. So Gabriel became a hunter. It was the simplest thing, the natural conclusion to what had happened. Wasn't hunting what he had always loved best? Roaming through the forest with his musket and dogs, no one to order him back to work. His skin grew dark, burned by the sun. He let his hair grow, forgot to shave. He hung a string of brilliant wild-turkey feathers over the mantelpiece. When storms knocked trees over the river, blocking the route to civilization, he exulted that no one would come here to disturb his hard-won peace. Solitude had finally made him master of this place. Only in this loneliness and grief had he come into his true powers.

He planted no tobacco but spent days in the forest where the tree trunks bore his name. The Gabriel woods. Then it seemed that he had always lived this way. His father, May, Adele, and the Irishmen shrank to tiny motes. They receded to the land of distant dreams. He never went to the graves he had dug for his father, his wife, and her baby. The property was vast enough that he had no need to go there.

And then she came. His dead wife's sister.

12 The Bed of Skins

Hannah

HANNAH COULD HARDLY look at the young man who carried the other end of her trunk, bearing most of its weight as they trundled up the path. She found it hard to think of him as Gabriel, simply by his Christian name, as if he were familiar to her. *Mr. Washbrook.* That was what she would call him. Her sister's widower was stranger to her than any soul she had ever met. Even Mr. Banham and his daughters had seemed less alien. She had half a mind to corner him, take him by the shoulders and shake him. *How did my sister die? Did she suffer long? How did the infant die?* The deaths in and of themselves were nothing out of the ordinary—new mothers and babies died in droves. But that May had died! It seemed impossible. May had been the strong one, the fearless one, the one who had always laughed. If she questioned him again, she would fall apart into nothingness. She would be lost.

A break in the trees afforded her a view of a harvested maize field. Rotting tree stumps rose like warts among the brittle wasted stalks. Beyond this lay a fallow tobacco field, thick with weeds. The forest closed around the land like a living thing with a will of its own. Left to its own devices, the wilderness would soon reclaim the cleared land. Deer would eat next summer's corn. Snakes would make their home in the old tobacco barn. The plantation house would collapse into a pile of rotting wood. How quickly a home could disappear.

They neared the house. A porch ran down the side, and under its roof, animal skins were pegged to the outside walls. Her eyes rested on one enormous pelt of thick black fur. With a shiver, she remembered the bear she had seen that morning. It was only eight hours ago or so, yet it seemed like days and weeks had passed since the morning boat ride, when she had been full of happy anticipation, thinking her sister still lived.

Gabriel hefted the trunk over the threshold. "Come in," he said.

Kneeling at the hearth, he added fuel to the dying fire until the flames leapt high, casting an unsteady glow. Hannah made out the sparse furnishings in the dim room. Two backless benches, one carved chair, a trestle table, a dresser, and a chest of drawers. Two curtained beds were pushed against the far wall. A ladder led to a trapdoor in the ceiling, and a door beside the hearth indicated there was another ground-floor room. Heaped in one corner lay a pile of animal skins. On the trestle table lay a gutted fish.

"I was cleaning the fish when you came." He gestured toward one of the benches. "Sit down."

She watched him rise, an iron skillet in his hand. A jar on the table contained some kind of fat with which he greased the pan. In went the fish. He rested the skillet on a grate in the hearth. The fat snapped and crackled, and soon the smell of frying fish filled the room. Outside, his dogs whined and scratched at the door, but he ignored them. Hannah turned to the only window, facing west and stained with sunset. If she closed her eyes, she could pretend she was back home with Joan.

He hung another pot on a hook over the fire. It began to simmer with the homey scent of cabbage and onions. Hannah coughed from the smoke, which brought tears to her eyes. She began to weep again, just couldn't seem to stop. How kind he was, treating her as though she were a dignified guest and not some bawling stranger who had fallen in a fit, thrashing around like a madwoman.

Once it had been May who knelt at the hearth and prepared

the food. Hannah pressed her kerchief to her mouth and stifled a sob. Father's death, at least, she had been able to prepare for, but this was so unjust. How could her beautiful sister be dead?

"Hannah." How curious her name sounded when he spoke it. "You grieve sorely, I know it. Grieving was nearly the end of me, too. First my father, then the baby, then her."

Hannah lifted her head. "Was it a boy or a girl?"

He was silent for a moment. "A girlchild. She only lived a few days. Your sister named her Hannah."

She covered her face.

"You mustn't," he said. "You'll drive yourself mad." His voice broke. "Come now. You must eat."

She shook her head. "I don't think I could."

"You are thin as a starveling."

She thought of May's rich and abundant body, her curves. What would May say if she saw her sniveling like this?

"Here, Hannah." He placed a wooden trencher in her lap and handed her a spoon carved of horn and a dull knife.

The fish was golden brown. Heaped around it was a thick stew of carrots, cabbage, and onions—the last vegetables from the autumn garden. He gave her a piece of dry cornbread and hovered near her until she cut a piece of the flaky white fish, speared it on her knife. The fish was tender in her mouth. This meal was better than the venison in Anne Arundel Town, better than the feast of pheasant, sweetmeats, and oysters served at the Gardiner Plantation. This was the finest food, made sweet by her hunger and her loss, made sweetest of all by the one who had cooked it for her. She stole glances at him when she thought he wouldn't notice. May's widower was the only family she had left. She sensed the cloud of sadness hanging over him. His grief locked into hers like a twin spoon.

At least I do not mourn alone, she thought, cleaning her plate with cornbread.

After the meal, Gabriel went out to feed the dogs. He returned with a bucket of water and one of sand. She watched him gather the trenchers, spoons and knives, skillet, and iron pot.

"Let me do that." Hannah went to the table, where Gabriel poured the water into a wooden bowl. It seemed ages since she had last washed crockery and pans. Taking the rag from him, she went to work. First the trenchers, then the spoons and knives, then the skillet, which she scoured with sand to remove the last traces of grease. She filled the cooking pot with water and hung it over the flames again until the water was lukewarm. Then she tossed in the sand and scrubbed away. At home, Joan used to scour the pots with rushes.

She worked by firelight. Gabriel didn't light any candles. They must be precious out here in the wilderness. Perhaps Gabriel hadn't mastered the art of candlemaking. That would have been May's job. Hannah bit her lip to keep herself from crying as she wrung out the rag one last time and wiped down the trestle table.

He took the bowl from her and dumped the water outside. Frosty night air flooded in through the open doorway. Her eyes dropped to the pile of pelts on the far side of the hearth. Bearskins, with deerskins on top. For a moment she thought of the living animals, then of a sharpened knife skinning the hide off the flesh.

Gabriel returned with a fresh bucket of water. "If you need to wash or drink," he said, "here is a dipper." He headed across the room to the wall opposite the hearth and pulled back the curtains on one of the two beds. "You can sleep here." He dragged her trunk across the floor to the bed.

Outside, it was quite dark. Stars shone in the window.

"Anon I go to bed," Gabriel told her. "I rise and retire with the sun."

In the firelight she caught his eye, then looked away in embarrassment. He wanted to undress, she thought.

"Where's the privy?" she asked.

He found a candle stub in a brass holder, then opened the door and pointed. "The dogs sleep. I hope they will leave you in peace. But fear them not. They are friendly."

—+—

When she returned to the house, candle in hand, she found the fire already banked. Scooping water from the bucket with the dipper, she drank. It was so cold, it hurt her teeth, but it tasted pure. After pouring water into the wooden bowl, she plunged her kerchief in and washed her face and hands. Gabriel had already turned in for the night—not to the other bed but to the pile of animal skins on the floor. The firelight caught his long black hair. He lay with his back to her, his face to the wall, his buckskin shirt still on him. Judging from the way his flank rose and fell with steady breathing, he was already asleep.

Taking the candle, she crossed the room to her bed, kicked off her shoes, drew back the bedclothes, hoisted herself on the high mattress, and drew the curtains shut. She stripped down to her shift, then whispered her sister's name and lay herself down.

—+—

Hours after darkness had fallen, Hannah lay rigid and awake. The night was too loud for sleep. Outside, the owls made as much racket as tavern revelers at home. She buried her head in the musty pillow and listened to her brother-in-law toss in his bed of fur, the floorboards groaning beneath him.

Why did he have to sleep in those skins? Hannah decided that the other bed must have been his marriage bed, where May had borne their child who had not lived, where May herself had drawn her last breath. That meant that the bed where she lay must have belonged to Gabriel's father. This was where Cousin Nathan had died of the flux. The thought made Hannah writhe in the bedclothes. Maybe that explained why she couldn't sleep. Gabriel was right for making his bed on the floor.

If Father only knew how this had turned out, he would die all over again. He would go down on his knees and beg her pardon for sending May across the water. But Father was in heaven with May and her baby. She pictured him with his arms around her sister while she held her infant. *No more pain or earthly toil for them. Only we on earth were meant to suffer and grieve.*

When she finally slept, she dreamt of her sister. May was as lovely as ever, but she no longer laughed. Her skin had a silvery cast. She had on her wedding gown of green lawn that she and Hannah had embroidered with rosebuds and soft-breasted doves. Sitting beneath the hawthorn tree in Father's garden, May cradled a bundle of bloodstained rags. The bundle became a limp baby with a withered blue face. May's mouth trembled. She threw back her head and wailed. Hannah reached out to embrace her, but her hands sliced through empty air. May rocked the lifeless infant and sang lullabies. *I gave my true love a golden ring, and this he loved above all things.* The rest of her song was lost as her words ran together into a madwoman's keening. A flurry of brown autumn leaves swept past, obscuring Hannah's view of her sister. When the wind died down, May was gone and the hawthorn was stripped of its leaves. Only blood-red berries remained where the foamy white flowers had been. On the grass beneath the tree were two wooden crosses and two mourning doves.

13
The Crack in the Cradle

Hannah

SHE AWOKE TO THE SMELL of frying eggs. Dressing behind the closed bed curtains, she made herself as decent as possible, combing her hair with her fingers. But she couldn't coil her hair and cover it, having lost her linen cap the day before. Her hair tumbled loose, spilling over her shoulders and down her back. She imagined she must look like a ghoul with her eyes swollen from too much crying. Opening the curtains, she stuck her feet into her shoes and made her way to the trestle table.

Gabriel's face was taut and drained, his eyes shadowed. He, too, must have had a hellish night. Without speaking, he passed her a trencher of fried eggs and cornbread, and a cup of milk. At least he still had hens and a cow, she thought, until she tasted the milk, which was so strong and musky it could only have come from a goat. She made an effort to empty her cup. Even goat's milk was too precious to waste.

This was her husband, Hannah thought as they ate in silence. *This was the table where they supped together.* She looked down at her own hands and saw May's hands. Finally she spoke.

"Will you take me to the graves?"

⬥

After feeding the dogs, he led Hannah down a narrow path through the trees. There was only room for them to walk single file. He spoke in a hollow voice with his back to her.

"My father thought he was clever, coming here to start his

own plantation. But the land was too wild for him. Killed him, it did. Just like it killed your sister and the child."

His pace accelerated to a march. Hannah struggled to keep up. Then he stopped so abruptly that she bumped into his back.

"There you see them." He pointed.

On a grassy knoll near the river were three weedy mounds, each with its own wooden cross. The first cross was the biggest, made of two sanded oak planks neatly nailed together.

HERE LYETH NATHAN WASHBROOK, ESQUIRE
PLANTER
1639–1690
R.I.P.

Each letter had been carved with precision. Hannah imagined Gabriel patiently working the wood with chisel and hammer. By contrast, the other two crosses were made of rough planks lashed together with rawhide. The epitaphs were scratched in the horizontal plank, as crudely executed as paupers' graves at home.

Here lyes Hannah Washbrook, aged 7 days
1690
R.I.P.

Plainest of all was May's grave.

Here lyes May Washbrook

Hannah dropped to her knees in the long grass. Tears stung her eyes. When she found her voice, it came out like acid. "This does not look like the grave of a cherished wife." She swung around and looked Gabriel in the eye, not caring if she offended him. She thought of her parents' tabletop grave at home, the marker as enduring as the stone from which it had been hewn. These two flimsy crosses looked as if they could barely last through one more winter.

Gabriel recoiled. The muscles in his throat twitched. "It is true I am a poor engraver, but I did my best."

She looked at him in confusion. "But your father's grave . . ."

"Not my handiwork." He turned away. "One of the servants did carve his marker. A lad called James. My father favored him." Something in his voice sounded devastated. Three deaths in the space of a year.

Hannah rose shakily to her feet. "I beg your pardon, Mr. Washbrook. I am so sorry."

"No matter," he said tonelessly. "I will leave you here. I have work to do."

Before she could say anything, he had gone. Hannah knelt again on the green mound that covered her sister's body. She clutched handfuls of weeds and pulled them up by the roots. She was tempted to dig into the earth with her bare hands, scratching like a mole until she came to her sister's coffin. *I shall never believe she is truly dead until I see her bones.* In one of Joan's tales, a conjurer gathered a dead girl's scattered remains and played his harp until he charmed the living flesh back on the skeleton and the girl returned to life.

"I will tend your grave," she whispered. She would plant flowers on the mound. Foxglove and heartsease. As long as she lived, she vowed, her sister would never be forgotten.

⚬━┃━

Walking back up the path, Hannah could find no sign of Gabriel. Even his dogs were gone. She cursed herself for her cruel words. The way she had spoken to him was like bludgeoning a wounded man. *May God forgive me for my sharp tongue.*

Had there been a funeral for May? she wondered. In her letter, May had written of Cousin Nathan's burial and the scarcity of clergymen. *We did for ourselves. Gabriel read from the Book of Common Prayer.* He must have done the same for May. She pictured him broken at her grave with the prayer book in his hand.

"Gabriel!" She called his name, but he had vanished. There was only the rustle of the wind in the trees, the rush of the river, the harsh music of crows. For some time she followed the paths that sliced through the underbrush. Eventually she discovered a garden enclosed by a fence. Unlatching the gate, she stepped inside. Cabbage, kale, and orange pumpkins held out bravely against the weeds. In her father's botany books, she had read of these large North American gourds and seen pictures of them. She crouched beside one and pressed her fingernail into the hard rind. It barely made a scratch. There were so many New World plants of which she was ignorant. If Father were here, he would send her out to study their properties. Lucy had spoken of powerful physick herbs that were native to this country.

Hannah spun in a circle. She felt a sense of lightness, her sister's presence. The garden was May's handiwork, to be sure, planted from the seeds Hannah had sent along with her. Here were the stalks of foxglove. Its season had passed, but in spring it would rise again. In a sunny sheltered corner, she found a few heartsease flowers still in bloom. Peppermint had completely overrun another corner of the garden, but it was brittle and dormant now.

How late in the year was it? She had lost track of the days. The cloudy sky was full of birds heading south, and the ground was hard. Winter would come soon. Bleakness settled over her again, making her wonder where she would spend the dark, cold months.

Not far from the garden she found two shacks, standing about thirty feet apart, with a clump of trees and bushes between them. They must have been servants' quarters. Both dwellings had dirt floors littered by dead leaves. One was roomy, the other small. On the doorframe of the larger one, someone had carved notches, probably to mark the days.

Hannah was about to return to the house when something drew her toward the smaller shack. Her pulse raced as she stood in the doorway. She couldn't explain why. The hut was empty and bare, not a spoon or rag left behind. The blood rushed inside her ears, rising in a red tide. She could almost hear her sister's voice warning her to be careful. *The rules here are different, love. Watch your step.* On the lintel someone had carved a heart pierced by three arrows.

A memory came back to her of Joan laying out cards on the kitchen table. The three of spades. She shook her head. What nonsense was this? She shivered, teeth rattling. It was really too cold to be out without a shawl. Lifting her skirts, she ran back to the house.

⁂

Hannah stood on the porch, one palm on the closed door. "Mr. Washbrook? Gabriel?" There was no answer. If he had work to do, he would be outdoors, not inside the house.

By daylight, the house appeared a different place altogether. Though the benches were battered and the table scored from knives, she was astonished how clean and well ordered it was, especially considering a man lived here on his own. Nonetheless, she found a broom in the corner and began to sweep. Joan, who had never believed in Father's medicine of the humors, had said that keeping busy was the only true cure for melancholy. *The devil gives idle hands work to do.*

Once the floor was swept, she decided to search the place for some artifact of May. Surely Gabriel would forgive her. This had been her sister's home, after all, and what a comfort it would be to uncover some possession of hers.

Hannah opened a door that led to a narrow pantry, lit by a high window. Bunches of dried herbs and strings of onions hung from the ceiling. Stoppered clay jars lined the shelves. She lifted the lid of one jar and sniffed a powerful-smelling fat that she recognized from the previous night. Gabriel had used this to grease the pan. The fried fish had tasted delectable, but the fat in its pure state made her slam the lid back down.

In the other jars she found dried beans and peas. There was a barrel of salt pork, another barrel of dry maize kernels, a basket of eggs, three boxes of apples wrapped in straw, two more of some unknown tuber. In the far corner was a butter churn that looked as though it hadn't been used in some time. On the floor, arranged in a row, were pumpkins and gourds. Though the pantry seemed well stocked, she wondered whether there would be enough to get two people through the winter. Gabriel had thought he would have to provide only for himself. If she remained here, she would be a burden to him. He had been hospitable enough, but he had not invited her to stay.

Leaving the pantry, Hannah closed the door behind her. It wouldn't be respectable for a man and a woman to live together, so far apart from society, without even a servant for company. People would surmise the worst. Her reputation would be as ruined as May's had been in their village, even if she remained as ignorant of the whole business as some papist nun. It would do nothing for Gabriel's good name, either. She would have to leave. Where could she go? Back to Anne Arundel Town? If only she hadn't lost track of Lucy and Cassie. They would be able to tell her what a spinster with her education might do.

As long as she was here, she should make herself useful. There was nothing worse than a lazy houseguest. She should wash the window, air out the bed linens and curtains. Hunting for cleaning rags, she went to the chest and opened each drawer in turn. She found a worn pair of men's breeches, two linen shirts with raveled cuffs, a brown woolen waistcoat, and a folded greatcoat. She found a drawer of men's stockings and underlinen. In the very top drawer there were rolled-up maps of the Bay and surrounding plantations, but nothing that could have belonged to her sister. Not even a handkerchief. What had become of her beautiful wedding dress? Her green cloak?

Maybe Adele had stolen May's clothes when she ran away. But when she thought back to her sister's letters, that made no sense. May had praised Adele, saying she was loyal and good, her only friend on this shore. Could that girl have been so treacherous to a mistress so fond of her? The hair on Hannah's nape prickled at the memory of standing before the hut with the pierced heart carved in the lintel. What a tangle. She couldn't begin to comprehend any of it without Gabriel's help. She would have to gather

her nerve, question him more closely, even if she risked offending him again. On her own, it was just one big riddle. The deductive reasoning Father had taught her was of no use. Joan could have made more sense of it with her cards.

She reached for the curtains of the bed she assumed had been May and Gabriel's. They were thick with dust and could use a good beating. When she unhooked them from the bed frame, she saw there was no mattress, just the mesh of ropes that had once supported it. Hannah stared at that blank space until her stomach clenched. She thought of May bearing down in childbirth. The mattress had been ruined. Perhaps after her death Gabriel had burned it for fear of spreading contagion.

But where could May's trunk be? It was too large an object to hide, too heavy a thing to be easily stolen. An impulse overtook her. Crouching down, she looked under the bed. Though the bed was high, there was not enough space to conceal a trunk. But some object was stored there. Her fingers grabbed the edge and slowly pulled it out into the daylight. When she saw what it was, she cried more than she had at May's grave. Grief was a terrible trickster, Joan always said. Just when you thought you could live with your pain, grief found a new way to twist its blade into your flesh.

The cradle was veiled in cobwebs, stuffed with stained rags. Though it was built of sturdy planks, one of the side walls was loose. A crack ran down the headboard. Hannah upended the cradle, dumping out the rags. Fetching a clean cloth and the bucket of water Gabriel had left on the table, she scrubbed at the dirt and grime until the grain of the wood was visible. The cradle was made of birch. Joan would be pleased, for she had always said that a birchwood cradle protected by a rowan cross would guard the baby from every evil. It would keep the faeries from stealing the child.

Hannah held the cradle as if it were an infant. Setting it down again, she rocked it gently. She ran her finger up and down the crack, which could be sanded smooth or varnished but never mended.

A fever moved through her. Before she took the curtains out to air, she had to find something else, another clue. The dresser contained only crockery, knives, and spoons. The oak box on top of the chest of drawers housed the family Bible and the Book of Common Prayer.

She climbed the ladder to the trapdoor. To open it, she had to push with both hands. After several attempts, she finally heaved it so that it fell on the attic floor with an explosion of dust that left her coughing. Climbing up the ladder, she poked her head in the opening. It was the darkest attic she had ever seen, no window to pierce the gloom. The light coming from below wasn't strong enough to illuminate more than what lay in the immediate vicinity of the trapdoor. The air was stale and smelled of mildew.

Backing down the ladder, she found the candle stub she had used the night before, lit it from the hearth embers, and picked her way back up the rungs. The ceiling slanted sharply on either side, but it was high enough in the middle to allow her to stand. She held out the candle in different directions. Indistinct shapes covered the floor. Sleeping pallets? The candle flame revealed cobwebs, thick as carded wool, that coated the eaves. Gritting her teeth, she took a few steps. A scuttling noise made her think of beetles rushing for cover. Her foot caught on some object. As she fought to keep her balance, her free arm flailed and brushed the cobwebs. Spider silk coated her hand.

She stopped short, trembling. What would Gabriel think if he knew she was groping around in his attic like a thief? She couldn't get down that ladder fast enough. Back in the main room, she snuffed out the candle and put it away.

⁕

Hannah washed her hands. She took down the curtains from the other bed and stripped off the linens. Carrying them outside, she shook out the dust until her arms ached, then hung them over bushes to air. She swept and scrubbed the floor, finding only a chamber pot beneath the bed where she had slept. She carried the furs Gabriel slept in to the porch and shook them out, too, then put them back, careful to make them appear as if they had not been disturbed. The skins still had an animal scent clinging to them. Or maybe it was Gabriel's smell, the piny odor of male sweat. She ran to the river to fetch fresh water, scrubbing down the table and dresser. Then she swept the pantry and wiped down the shelves. Last she washed the windows, hung the bed curtains back up, and made her bed.

When she had finished cleaning, she unpacked the bar of lye soap from her trunk, took the bucket, and headed for the river. In a sheltered place surrounded by bushes and pines, she filled the bucket, then stripped and soaped herself. The cold water ran in rivulets down her goose-pimpled skin. Joan would say she was courting sickness. Even Father would disapprove, but somehow, after seeing her sister's grave and the crack in the cradle, she felt dirty and had to be clean.

She dried herself on the cloth she had brought with her, then dressed again as quickly as she could. The blinding sun descended toward the treetops. It was much later than she had thought. There were so many narrow paths cutting through the woods, she was afraid of losing her way in the twilight. The forest echoed with noises she could not identify. Creatures slithered in the fallen leaves. Things crashed through the underbrush. A blurry shape came toward her. The bucket fell from her hand as she screamed. The thing grunted and squealed, dashing across the path. Hannah let out a long breath. It was just a pig, left to forage in the woods. But it could have been a bear.

If May were here, she would laugh at her for being so afraid. Hannah picked up the bucket. She should fill it up again. They would need water for cooking. Shoulders rigid, she forced herself back to the river.

The full bucket was heavy and slowed her progress. When the handle cut into her palm, she switched to the other hand. May was made of tougher material than she was. Her sister was bigger, stronger. She was brave. But had her fearlessness been her downfall? Hannah wondered as she trudged up the path. If May had been a more timid, careful soul, would she still be alive? Setting the bucket down, she rubbed her sore palms on her skirt. Nonsense. May had died after giving birth. That had nothing to do with being brave or cowardly. Then Hannah considered. Gabriel hadn't actually told her how her sister had died. She would have to ask him. As May's sister, she had a right to know.

—+—

A few yards from the house, she came to a halt, water sloshing from the bucket and wetting her skirt. Gabriel sat on the porch while his dogs watched him intently. When they tried to edge closer, he scolded them. Deep in concentration, he did not seem to know she was there. Even the dogs ignored her. Before she could announce her presence, she saw the knife in his hand.

He was skinning a rabbit, slowly working the hide off the body. He had already gutted and beheaded the animal. Where its legs had been were only stumps. Blood seeped from the open belly, falling in the weeds at Gabriel's feet. The dogs strained, as though longing to lick up the blood, but he spoke firmly, keeping them back.

A sick taste filled her mouth. Why did the sight disturb her? She had held the bowl to catch blood and pus when Father lanced his patients. She had cut into men's living flesh. This was just a rabbit.

Gabriel dumped the skinned beast into a bowl and set it on the porch behind him, out of reach of the dogs. Balancing the skin on a plank, he worked over the hide with the blunt edge of his knife, scraping away the bloody pieces of flesh and tissue that stuck to the soft inside of the pelt.

A dull pounding sounded inside her temples. She looked him over, from the worn soles of his buckskin boots, to his lean limbs and torso, to his young face with the shadowed eyes of someone much older. A wicked thing took hold of her as she pretended to look at him through her sister's eyes. In the golden evening light, she could not decide which shone more brightly, the blade in his hand or his long black hair. She imagined him holding her sister.

He looked up and caught her staring. Her skin burned. Remembering how harshly she had spoken to him that morning, she didn't know what to say.

"Did you go in the river?" he asked. "Your hair is wet."

Hannah fingered her damp red locks, now frizzing like wool. How immodest she had become, wandering around with her bare wet head. She would have to search her trunk for a new linen cap to cover her hair.

"You court the grippe." His eyes did not leave her face. "Bathing in the river so late in the year. You risk peril, too. A public waterway, it is, and you know not who travels there."

Hannah set the bucket down at her feet. "I fetched water."

"I only take water from the creek out back. Mayhap you have not yet seen the creek, but the water there is purer."

She nodded, feeling like a child.

His face softened. "Go in the house and sit by the fire until your hair is dry."

She carried the bucket inside. He had already built the hearth fire. Onions and white chunks of tuber simmered in the pot. The steam was fragrant with rosemary and thyme. Fetching her comb from her trunk, she sat on a bench and worked through her tangled hair.

A while later he came in and melted grease in the skillet. Then he chopped the rabbit into pieces and tossed them in. She had eaten nothing since breakfast, and her hunger left her faint. Gabriel stirred the pot of steaming vegetables with a wooden spoon.

Hannah looked at him shyly before turning to the fire again. "I quite forgot myself today. I had no right to speak to you the way I did this morning." She took a deep breath. "This has been so strange for me."

"You are in a strange land," he said. "Nothing is as you thought it would be."

She wondered if he noticed that she had cleaned the house. Or if he resented the liberty she had taken in doing so. This was his domain.

Moving away from the fire, Gabriel cleaned his knife blade, then sat down and began to sharpen it with a stone. Each movement was practiced. Hannah thought he must take great pride in his knife, the way he carried it with him everywhere. Such a sharp blade must be a treasure out here in the wilderness. It could make a difference, she thought, whether or not he had meat in his pot or skins to keep him warm in winter.

How far I have come, but to what end? The months of her passage seemed like years. England was a lifetime away. The girl she had been in her father's house didn't exist anymore. But she was still unsure who the new Hannah was. What shape would her life take now? Looking at Gabriel, she summoned her courage and will.

"Could you please forgive me one more intrusion? I must ask you how it happened." She clasped her hands in her lap. "How did my sister die?"

He put his knife away. "Two years ago she did go into childbirth. A midwife was sent for, but the child was sickly and died before it could be christened."

Despair closed her in its fist. She was a girl on the Bristol pier, holding on to her sister with all her strength, begging her not to go.

"This land does destroy people," he said. "It does demand blood like heathen sacrifice. I told you so this morning."

"The child lived only seven days." Hannah tried to picture the doomed baby. "But what of my sister? What became of her?" She leaned so close to the hearth that the heat blasted her like the flames of hell. If she got any nearer, a spark would catch her skirt and she would burn to cinders.

"She was sorely grieved to lose the child." He stood up and paced to the dresser. "Then she did perish, too."

Hannah fidgeted on the bench. "*How*, Gabriel?"

"What questions you ask."

"She was my only sister. I must know."

He stood frozen, his back to her. "The childbed fever."

"Were I only there." Hannah covered her face. "I know something of physick. I might have saved her. Did the midwife not give her medicine?"

Something came out of his throat. "By then the midwife was gone." He spoke as though each word had to be dredged from the bottom of his misery. "Midwives are scarce on this shore. They do not linger. Please," he begged her, his voice stretched painfully tight, "let's speak no more of it."

Hannah wept in silence. How had her May lost the will to live? "What will you do now?" she asked him.

"What can I do?" He turned at the noise of the hissing pot.

"It will boil over." Hannah covered her hand with a rag and moved the hook so that the pot got less fire. "How can you go on like this?" She stirred the pot of vegetables, then the chunks of rabbit meat frying in the skillet. "Alone?"

He said nothing.

"And what of your tobacco harvest?"

"There is no harvest." He laughed curtly. "Do you know how many hands it takes to raise tobacco? We barely pulled in a good crop when there were eight of us working in the fields from sunrise to dusk. After your sister died, they all fled."

"How will you keep your leasehold?"

"I will lose it." He spoke plainly. "There are many things that Paul Banham covets. And he does covet my land. When the news goes round that there is no more tobacco here, he will drive me away."

"It is true, he covets much." Hannah winced and thought about Mrs. Gardiner. "But to rob you of your land? When the ship anchored at Gardiner's Landing, he offered to deliver to you any goods you had ordered from the ship. He offered to give you credit in his own name."

"He would have me beholden to him. Credit would turn to debt, and then he would relieve me of my land and make me at best a tenant farmer."

He emptied the skillet of rabbit meat into the simmering pot of vegetable stew. The meat bobbed on the surface, the bloody red now brown.

"To survive here you must be either master or servant." Gabriel spoke bitterly. "My father was all for being master. He ruled his servants with a bullwhip. He didn't spare me, either." He broke off, nearly losing his grip on the spoon as he stirred.

"Then he did die, and that was the first breakdown of rule. Then your sister. She was so proud." He looked away. "Adele obeyed her, and the manservants, too, in the beginning. She knew how to work her will. But after she died, all was undone. I could be no master. The manservants had seen how my father had whipped me just as he had whipped them. They saw no difference between our stations. To be their master, I would have to show them. I would have to pick up the whip and do my will with them, as my father had done, but I could not."

The rising steam glazed his face. "My curse is that I can be no master," he said in a tired voice. "But neither will I have a master ruling me. I aim to be a free man, left in peace, with none but God above me."

"My father taught me the history of the Civil War," Hannah said. "Once there were many who thought as you do. The Diggers and the Levelers would have no masters over them and refused to pay rent to their lords. They thought the land itself was a commonwealth to be shared by all. The Quakers refuse to bow to any man, even the King." She stopped short, feeling foolish. He was so quiet, it was as though she were talking to herself.

She cleared her throat. "I will lay the table." Crossing to the dresser, she took out the wooden trenchers and the horn spoons.

"You are very different from your sister." The hearth flames caught his face and threw his shadow on the wall.

"In our village," she told him, "they used to jest that one of us must be a changeling."

He did not laugh but regarded her solemnly. "You have had an uncommon education, I think."

"Aye. It hardly mattered to Father that I was a girl. He taught me everything he knew, and he was a very wise man." Regret flared when the words had left her mouth. She hoped she hadn't caused Gabriel any more pain. If her father had been kind, Gabriel's had whipped him like a slave.

"You were fortunate indeed," he said. "My father taught me letters and sums and the art of surveying—that was his profession until we came here. But I fear he never knew what to do with me. My mother died when I was only small. He was left to rear me on his own. He thought he could make a man of me, but the harder he was on me, the more I resisted him."

"Can you remember your mother?" Hannah asked him softly. "I can't remember mine. She died when I was born." The family curse, she thought. To think May had come to the same end.

"She was a Welshwoman. Name of Olwen. Full of fire." A smile spread across his face, making him look for once like an unburdened young man. "Everyone who knew us in Anne Arundel Town said I was the spit of her. I inherited her stubbornness." He laughed. "She used to tell me stories about the faery ointment and the glamoury eye."

"The what?" Hannah leaned closer to him.

"Oh, it's just an old wives' tale, but it was my favorite." He gave the stew another stir. "Once there was a servant girl who could do the spinning of ten others. She worked so fast because the faeries were spinning for her."

Hannah bit her lip, remembering May at the spinning wheel, how swiftly she had pumped the treadle.

"Well, one night the servant girl wandered out to take the air and never came back. You see, she had struck a bargain with the faery folk. In exchange for their help with the spinning, she had agreed to marry one of their number. Her old mistress heard not a word from her until a year later, when the faery man came riding to her door. You see, the woman was a midwife and the girl about to deliver her firstborn."

Hannah wondered how, given everything that had happened, he could sit there and tell that tale. A look of pain crossed his face, but then it was gone and his eyes were far away, as though lost in memories of childhood.

"So the midwife went into the dank cave where the girl lived with the faery man. 'Ach, the wench has come down in the world,' the woman thought. The new mother had no bed but a pile of dead leaves, yet she seemed content enough, and the baby was bonny and strong. The faery man gave the midwife a jar of the faery ointment and told her to put it on the infant's eyelids. She did as she was told, but couldn't resist rubbing a little of the stuff on her own left eyelid. That's how she got gifted with the glamoury eye. With her right eye, she still saw the same cave with the new mother and baby lying on the dead leaves, but her left eye saw that the cave was a palace with golden ceilings. The mother and baby lay on a high, rich bed with silk draperies. The midwife had always thought the faery man a rough-looking fellow, but now he was as wondrous to look upon as the sun itself."

Hannah smiled. "I should like to see with the glamoury eye, too."

"When I was small," he said, "I dipped into my mother's jar of bear grease. I pretended it was the faery ointment and rubbed it on my eyelids."

"Bear grease?" Hannah thought of the mysterious fat he had used for cooking. "Did it give you the glamoury eye?"

"It might have done." He offered her a half-smile. "Sometimes when my father was at his wit's end with me, he used to say I wasn't real at all, but fey, like one of the creatures in my mother's tales." He leaned over the pot. "The stew is ready."

While they ate, she noted how lean he was, how he wolfed down his portion as though he had been famished for days. He ladled more stew on his trencher.

"What will you do," she asked, "if they take away your leasehold?"

He shrugged. "I always knew my father's house was only a way station. I am no planter, but I know enough of the forest. If this country is brutal, then it is also big. When they come to take the land, I will vanish into the forest."

Hannah shook her head. "You cannot live alone all your life. There must be some settlement, a village of Quakers mayhap . . ."

"I have spent too long with the dead," he said, "to go back into the world of the living."

Hannah shivered. "You cannot mean what you say. What of the Indians? I have heard of massacres."

"They only kill those who take their land. I told you I am no planter, just one lone hunter. I don't think they would trouble me. I am no harm to them or anyone." The fire leapt and the shadow of his hand lifting the spoon darted across the wall. "But I think I will be left in peace through the winter. Banham won't come upriver until his men clear the logs and beaver dams away." He glanced at her. "But you have more pressing troubles, I think. What will you do?"

"I will go downriver." There was no enthusiasm in her voice.

"It is better for you," he said, "to rejoin society. I will take you to Banham's as soon as I can build a canoe."

—⊹—

Asleep in the curtained bed, Hannah whimpered, dreaming of skinned rabbits hopping through the forest. They left behind a trail of blood, which seeped into the river, staining the water wine-red. The trees in the forest screeched and moaned, the clamor so great that she lurched awake, clutching the bedclothes to her chest. The wailing wound around her, a tightening cord. The noise came from the corner by the hearth, where Gabriel slept in his bed of skins.

Swinging her legs off the bed, she planted them on the cold floor. A few glowing embers in the hearth guided her path across the room. He cried and thrashed like a haunted man, so loudly that his pain took shape and substance. In the darkness, Hannah saw her sister's face, her sister's cold body in his arms as he carried her to the river to bury. *Grief has undone him. He's just as lost for her as I am.* Men were confounding creatures, as different from women as the sun was from the moon. She remembered how her father had shriveled up and withered away after May had left. Men didn't weep openly but held their sorrow inside, where it festered and poisoned them.

"Gabriel!" she cried hoarsely. "Wake up." She found his shoulder and gave it a shake before backing away.

He sat up with a gasp.

"You were dreaming, Gabriel." She hurried to her bed.

The next morning his face was gray. He couldn't seem to look her in the eye.

"You dream of her, too." Hannah looked down at her bowl of corn mush. "I have dreamt of her every night in this house." She put down her spoon. "I loved her more than anyone, even more than I loved my father." She had never made this confession before.

"Let's not speak of the dead, Hannah." He got up from the table. "I can't abide it. She's gone and I can't abide it." At that he walked out the door and whistled to his dogs.

Dispiritedly she washed the wooden bowls with the water he had fetched that morning. Gabriel had left her alone again. She had no idea what to do with herself. Rummaging through her trunk, she found her second linen cap. There was no mirror, but she tried to make herself as respectable as possible, even though it seemed rather pointless in this wilderness. May would have let her hair tumble free, but Hannah braided hers, pinned it to her head, and covered it with the cap.

She carried the dishwater to the porch and emptied it in the weeds. When she turned to go back inside, she saw the rabbit skin Gabriel had pegged up on the outer wall. Slowly she raised her hand to stroke the soft fur. Then she decided to hunt for the creek he had mentioned the day before.

Picking her way down the network of paths, she passed the garden and the servants' shacks. The path widened as it went by the chicken coop. Gabriel and his dogs were nowhere to be found, but she heard tinkling bells. Drawing to a halt, she held her breath as a goat ambled out of the bushes and gazed at her with its yellow devil's eyes. In the distance, beyond the house, smoke rose in a tall column. Had Gabriel lit a bonfire?

The earth sloped down a steep bank into a ravine where ribbons of white water gushed over rocks. She followed the footholds worn into the ground. Once May had gone down here to get water and probably to launder. She imagined her sister beating dirty clothes against the rocks, hands rough and swollen in the cold water. She remembered the way May had laughed and said, *Fancy his name being Washbrook*. Wandering downstream, she came to a still pool that reflected her forlorn face. Once Joan had told her she could look into the future by gazing into a pan of water. Hannah hovered over the pool until her neck hurt. After a time her reflection blurred. She fancied she could see her sister staring back. May had aged. Dark rings marked the skin beneath her eyes. Her hair hung loose and uncombed. Her lips were bitten and bleeding.

Hannah lifted her head at the sound of an ax striking a tree in the distance where smoke billowed in the sky. The ax blows were rhythmic as drumbeats. Gabriel must be cutting firewood for winter. He had so much work to do. Really, she should be helping him. She should weed the garden, gather eggs, prepare the evening meal. Filling the bucket, she trudged up the slope toward the house.

The sound of chopping continued. She heard an enormous creak as the tree gave way and crashed to the ground. The sound seemed to come from near the tobacco barn.

She stopped at the chicken coop and filled the water trough before marching back to the creek to fill the bucket again. The chopping resumed. Once he had felled the tree, he had to cut and split the logs. It might keep him busy till sunset. Carrying her bucket of water, she passed by the side of the house where a blood-red bird flitted through the trees. When she followed its flight, she noticed a shuttered window in the attic wall. If she wanted to search the attic for May's trunk, she only had to go to the window and open the shutters — then she would have all the light she needed.

⁓⊢

She mounted the ladder and heaved open the trapdoor. Gabriel wouldn't have to know. As long as she heard the chopping, she knew he would be away from the house.

It was a straightforward proposition. The attic window was on the wall opposite the hearth. Downstairs, she had already measured the distance by pacing from the ladder to the wall and counting her steps. Twelve measured paces would bring her to the shuttered window. Candle in hand, she put her feet down cautiously, aware that unseen objects might lie in her path.

At the count of twelve, she held the candle over the cobwebbed wood until she made out shutters and a latch, which gave way with a squeak. When she pushed the shutters open, light flooded through the glassless window. Blowing out the candle, she turned.

On the floor lay a pallet speckled with mildew. Near the trapdoor, she spotted the object that she had tripped over the day before — May's spinning wheel lying on its side. She remembered Gabriel's story of the girl who called upon the faeries to help with her spinning, only to be obliged to marry one of them. How could he have stored the spinning wheel so carelessly? May's had been her most treasured possession. After righting the spinning wheel, Hannah wiped the dust and cobwebs away with her skirt. She spun the wheel and examined the spindle and gears. By some miracle, it appeared to be in good order. Leaving the wheel in midspin, she moved to the other end of the attic. In a dark corner, away from the window, she found her sister's trunk and dragged it to the window. Outside, the red bird sang with unbearable sweetness. Holding her breath, Hannah threw open the lid and went through the chest, one item at a time. She recognized the infant clothes passed down from Mother and the quilted counterpane that she and Joan had helped stitch. But there was not a single item of May's clothing. What had become of her wedding gown?

At the bottom of the trunk was the first letter Hannah had written to her. With a sinking heart, she realized that May had been dead by the time the second letter arrived—if it had arrived at all. Also at the bottom of the trunk was the leather-bound book Hannah remembered Father giving May—their mother's receipt book of cookery and household physick. Father had kept it with his private mementos of their mother until the day before May had sailed.

Hannah Thorn Powers
This her own Book
1663

Underneath, May had penned her own name in a bolder hand.

May Powers Washbrook
1689

Though the ink had faded and the pages had yellowed, the script was clear to read. Looking at the pages, Hannah tried to catch some essence of the woman who had died giving birth to her.

To make a Soop
Take a Leg of Beef, and boil it down with some Salt, a Bundle of sweet Herbes, an Onion, a few Cloves, a bit of Nutmeg; boil three Gallons of Water to one; then take two or three pounds of lean Beef cut in thin Slices; then put in your Stew-pan a Piece of Butter, as big as an Egg, and flour it. And let the Pan be hot, and shake it till the Butter be brown; then lay your Beef in your Pan over a pretty quick Fire, cover it close, give it a turn now and then, and strain in your strong Broth, and a Handfull of Spinnage and Endive boil'd green, and drained, then have Pullets ready boil'd, and cut in Pieces, and Toastes fry'd.

The pages were well fingered and stained with broth. Hannah pictured the book lying open on the trestle table as May and Adele labored over the soup pot. She turned to the physick receipts.

A Stay to prevent a sore Throat in the Small-Pox
Take Rue, shred it very fine, and give it a bruise; mix it with Honey and Album Graecum, and work it together; put it over the Fire to heat, sew it up in a Linen Stay, and apply it to the Throat pretty warm: As it dries repeat it.

A Receipt for a Consumptive Cough
Take of the Siroop of white and red Poppies of each three Ounces, of Barley, Cinamon-water, and red Poppy-water, of each two Ounces, of Tincture of Saffron one Ounce, Liquid Laudanum forty Drops, and as much Spirit of Sulphur as will make it acid. Take three or four Spoonfulls of it every Night going to Bed; increase or diminish the Dose, according as you find it agrees with you.

Hugging the book to her chest, Hannah knelt on the dusty attic floor until she lost sensation in her legs. The red bird with its tufted head still warbled, but the chopping had ceased. She heard the noise of sawing. As pins and needles shot through her calves, she struggled to her feet and limped to the window. Already the sun was sinking. Soon Gabriel would return. She closed May's trunk and then the shutters, but took the receipt book with her and concealed it in her own trunk.

Heading in the direction of the sawing, she found Gabriel in the woods behind the tobacco barn. The felled trunk of a massive pine, stripped of branches and bark, rested on split logs. Gabriel worked the top of the log with a saw. His face was grimy, marked in wood dust. When he caught sight of her, he wiped his forehead on his sleeve. "This is for you."

She looked at him blankly. "What do you mean?"

"I am making a canoe to take you downriver."

Hannah lowered her head, not knowing how to thank him. "Where did you learn how to do such a thing?"

"When we lived in Anne Arundel Town, I apprenticed as a boat builder. A good skill to have in these parts." He held up his blistered palms. "Tonight I shall rub my hands with bear grease."

"Shall I fetch eggs and vegetables for our dinner?"

He nodded and began to saw again. "There is still a little more I can do before nightfall."

⸺✦⸺

Hannah noted she was a poor cook compared to him. Her stew consisted of cabbage, onions, and turnip simmered with salt and herbs. It wasn't nearly as rich as the rabbit stew he had made for her. She boiled eggs to serve on the side. When Gabriel dragged himself through the door, he ate three trenchers without complaint. After the meal, he took the jar of grease from the pantry and rubbed it into his raw hands.

"I have clean rags," Hannah offered, "if you want to bandage your hands for the night."

"No, I just want to sleep now."

Hannah washed up and retired early so that he could, too.

⸺✦⸺

May sat at her spinning wheel beside the bower of white roses in Father's garden. May was an unmarried girl again, the beautiful, loose sister for whom the boys yearned. She laughed as she spun, foot pumping the treadle until the wheel spokes blurred. Then she pricked her finger on the spindle, her blood spraying the roses red. *The earth demands blood.* And the deep red roses were so heavy, so huge, that they toppled from their stems, toppled on Hannah, pinning her to the mattress so she couldn't move. She could only choke on their musky-sweet odor. The roses took the form of a man, a red man whose flesh branded her. He kissed her violently, his breath on her face like heat from a brick oven. Wrenching herself awake, Hannah threw off the heavy blankets and fought for air. The darkness clung to her like a shroud as she listened to Gabriel toss in his sleep.

⸺✦⸺

Hannah rose with the first light, taking pains not to wake him. Putting on her cloak over her shift, she slipped into her shoes and crept out the door. She hurried to the creek, headed away from the worn path, beating her way through the brambles until she came to a still eddy enclosed in blazing red sumac. Shedding her clothes, she knelt in the cold water. Shivering and panting, she slapped the water against her belly and chest, then grabbed a fistful of ferns to scrub her skin until it chafed.

14 Rabbit Skin

Hannah and Gabriel

THE SMELL OF BUBBLING corn mush greeted Hannah when she returned to the cabin. The trestle table was set with a pitcher of fresh goat's milk, a single trencher, and a horn spoon.

"Gabriel?" she called, but he was gone.

She took the pot off the fire before it could scorch and ladled corn mush on the trencher. She was so hungry, her appetite frightened her. Surely all these animal hungers came from the devil and not from God. Her unholy dream raged inside her. What if she had called out something shameful in her sleep? Perhaps that explained why Gabriel had abandoned the cabin so early. But he had made breakfast for her.

Running a hand across her heated face, she thought of his blistered palms. He had gone back to work on the canoe. She could hear him chipping away. As a grateful guest and kinswoman, she should prepare his midday meal and carry it out to him. It was only right, considering everything he was doing for her. After her dream, she wondered if she could bear to look at him without burning up in humiliation. The only thing she could do was pray for release. As soon as Gabriel had finished the canoe, she would leave this place and be out of temptation's way. In the meantime, she would banish unclean thoughts with hard work.

Lest the leftover goat's milk sour, she churned it into butter. In the pantry, she took some apples and the remains of what had once been a big cone of sugar. In the wooden spice box she found a single nutmeg clove, a rare treasure. She had enough ingredients on hand to make apple tansey. Opening her mother's book to the receipt, she went to work with care and concentration, as though cookery, like surgery, were an art of dangerous precision, on which life itself depended.

To make an Apple Tansey
Take three Pippins, slice them round in thin Slices, and fry them with Butter, then beat four Eggs, with six Spoonfulls of Cream, a little Rosewater, Nutmeg, and Sugar, stir them together, and pour it over the Apples, let it fry a little, and turn it with a Pye-plate. Garnish with Lemon and Sugar strew'd over it.

Though lacking cream, rosewater, and lemon, the golden brown apples smelled like heaven. Covering the pie plate with a clean cloth, she set off down the path, hoping to deliver it to Gabriel while it was still warm. She no longer heard chipping or sawing but saw blue smoke rising from the trees. When she saw that the fire was burning inside the canoe itself, she nearly yelped, thinking that Gabriel had set to destroy his creation. Then she noticed that the front and back had been chiseled into points and the bottom carefully shaped.

Gabriel swung around, his face blackened by the smoke. "Now I burn out the wood in the center to hollow it. It is easier to burn the green wood away than to hack it out with the adze." He stopped short when he saw the covered pie plate.

"I made this for you." She bowed her head so she could avoid looking him in the eye. "I thought you might be hungry." She pressed it into his hands.

As he took the plate from her, Gabriel caught her scent. She smelled of apples and nutmeg, but underneath that was her young girl's smell that reminded him of wood anemones and freshly shucked corn. Like a Puritan, she had covered every lock of her fiery hair with her linen bonnet. In his mind's eye, he saw her hair as it had been the evening she had come back from the river, damp and tangled over her shoulders. Her face glossy and wet. She had looked like a mermaid tossed up by the sea. The startled look she had given him when he had warned that the river could be dangerous. The flush that had filled her face.

"It's apple tansey." She spoke as shyly as a child would. "I cooked it from my mother's receipt."

Before he could thank her, she scurried away. He couldn't find the words to call her back.

Sitting cross-legged on the bare earth, he uncovered the pie plate and saw the fried apples. She had tucked a spoon on the side. At first he could only stare at the tansey, inhaling its maddening aroma. Not since the days when his mother was alive had anyone taken such care to prepare a special dish for him. Everything May had cooked for him had simmered in resentment.

Eating the first spoonful, he remembered a line from an old song. *Apples are the fruits of paradise.* Hannah had cooked sweet apples for him. He wished she had stayed so he could talk to her.

His dogs pressed around him, begging for scraps, but he reprimanded them until they backed away. Each bite of apple tansey tasted the way Hannah smelled. He could toil on the canoe all the daylight hours, working with ax, saw, adze, chisel, and fire. He would work until his blistered hands bled, but he could not banish her from his mind. More than ever, he understood what it meant to be a haunted man.

His dead wife's sister. How dare he think of her that way? He was unworthy of her, for unlike May, Hannah was innocent, as wholesome and good as her plain Puritan name. Leaping to his feet, he tended the fire that licked at the inside of the canoe. How her hair had shone and crackled like flame the other night when she sat at the hearth with her head uncovered.

He was in thrall to her, and the only way he could free himself was by finishing the canoe and taking her downriver, out of his sight forever. After what had happened with May, he must remain alone, undisturbed. Everything hung in such precarious balance. If he didn't keep his solitude, it would all come crashing down.

Around sunset, he went to the creek to wash himself before returning to the house, where the smell of chicken soup greeted him. He had spotted the blood and feathers in the bushes. She had left the raw heart and giblets in the dogs' trough.

During the meal, Hannah shifted her face away from the hearth light so that he could barely see her.

"If I could trouble you for one thing," she said.

"What would that be?" he asked her.

"Before I leave here . . ." She paused. "I . . . I . . . would like to take with me some memento of my sister."

His gut tightened instinctively, the way flesh did around a wound. How long would this go on? he wondered. How long would it take for the bitterness to finally die away? He did not want to spend the rest of his life thinking hateful thoughts of the dead.

She turned, the light catching her face. Her eyes were wide and moist.

"Her trunk is in the attic," he said. "Tomorrow I will open the trapdoor for you. You may take what you like."

She looked down, as though collecting her thoughts. "I would like to see her clothing. I helped sew her wedding dress. Might I find that in the attic with her other things?"

Gabriel closed his eyes as the old pain surged. "Your sister was buried in her wedding dress."

Hannah shrank into the shadows. Above the crackle of flames, he could hear that her breathing had changed. She was crying, doing her best to hide it from him. It took his entire reserve of self-control to keep from going to her and wrapping his arms around her. What a pure soul she was, her wounded heart full of love and unsullied grief.

"What about her other clothes?" she finally asked.

He sighed, resting his forehead on his blistered palm. "The wench Adele stole them when she ran away. There is much the servants stole." He told her about the missing boats, and his father's sovereigns and signet ring.

Hannah said nothing. Her silence dragged on like agony. He

wished he could do something to bring lightness to her heart. It would be something to see her laugh and smile again, the way she had when he told the story of the glamoury eye.

When she rose to wash the pots and trenchers, he went outside with a candle and took the rabbit skin, now tanned and dry, down from the wall. By firelight, he cut it with his sharpened knife, then took his heavy needle and the thick thread May had spun while cursing him. Long after Hannah had retired behind the bed curtains, he stayed awake, stitching the pieces together.

⊶⊷

Despite the news that she would never see May's wedding dress—or any of her clothes—again, no disturbing dreams troubled Hannah. As if in answer to her prayers, she had her first peaceful sleep since coming to the Washbrook house. In the morning she awoke and felt like her old self again.

Whistling, she went to the orchard to gather windfall apples. Cutting away the bruises and worms, she simmered them with sugar and nutmeg to make compote. She made Gabriel cornbread-and-butter pudding with compote poured over it. When she brought it to him, he was chiseling out the charred center of the canoe.

⊶⊷

"I wonder what I will do in Anne Arundel Town," she said that night by the fire. "Do you know of a respectable place where I might go?"

"You must ask the Banhams." His voice rang spiteful when he mentioned their name, but then he continued in an even tone. "They are well connected. Mayhap they know of someone seeking an educated girl as a lady's maid or companion. Or mayhap you will find a place as a child's nursemaid. But you won't have to stay a servant long," he added quickly. "Healthy young women are scarce. If you wish to marry, you will find many suitors. No doubt you will find a worthy man."

Hannah struggled to maintain a polite demeanor, for she sensed that he meant to offer comfort. But the time had come for her to look at her future squarely. She placed each fact next to the other, lining them up like dominoes.

Father is dead, and I may no longer practice physick or make any practical use of my education. May is dead, and I am stranded in the New World. I cannot live with Gabriel, for that would ruin my reputation, even if we lived as chastely as brother and sister. I cannot stay here in any case; Gabriel has lost his tobacco harvest and will also lose his land. When I leave here, I will be either a servant or some unknown man's wife.

Maybe there was another possibility. Could she set herself up as a traveling midwife? True, she knew little of the birth process, but she could at least read about it in her father's books. Her knowledge of anatomy had to count for something. Unlike most midwives, she could read and write. But she would need to find a companion first, as Lucy Mackett had. No respectable woman traveled on her own for a living.

She looked up, aware that Gabriel was staring at her.

"Something troubles you," he said. "And I fear it is more than simple grief."

At first she wanted to demur, then it occurred to her that she had nothing to lose. "I have a secret."

"A secret? You?" It seemed that he spoke with relief, as though having a secret entailed some unspoken fellowship between them. For a moment Hannah could forget he was May's widower. She could forget she was a young woman alone with him in a remote house. The look of complicity he gave her reminded her of the way Father used to look at her when they went to perform surgery. It reminded her of the way Father had treated her — not as a mere girl but as an apprentice physician with an intellect to match his own.

"If I tell you," she said, "will you promise to keep my secret?"

"Aye, Hannah. I give you my word." He gave her a wry look. "Not that I have anyone out here to tell, at any rate." But he was not joking — his face was as serious as it had ever been.

"My father was a physician," she began. "He was getting old.

I was his handmaiden. He taught me things no other girl knows. He treated me like a son . . ." She broke off, thinking again of how Gabriel's father had treated him. "He was the best of fathers and the best of men. He taught me Latin and Greek. He had me read the works of Paracelsus and Aristotle. He had me study the writings of Dr. Harvey on the circulation of blood through the body. In my trunk I have books of anatomy. I know of physick herbs and their signatures."

He nodded. "You gave your sister the seeds to plant in the garden."

"He also taught me this." Hannah went to her trunk on the shadowy side of the room away from the fire. Even though she had no candle, her fingers easily located the leather box. She carried it back to the hearth and opened it in front of Gabriel, revealing the surgeon's knives of different sizes, the catheter, the razor-sharp scalpel.

Gabriel looked at the instruments and then at her. "These are things I would not think to find in a maiden's trunk."

"I have used them." Hannah spoke forcefully. "He taught me how." She told him how she had become her father's hands when his own hands had grown unsteady with age. She explained how they had kept their secret from the patients and the patients' families. Gabriel's face went bone-white when she told him of extracting Mr. Byrd's kidney stone. "I cut into him with this." She pointed to the scalpel. "And I pulled the stone with these." She took the tweezers from the case and held them so that they flashed in the firelight.

Gabriel regarded her speechlessly.

Hannah held his gaze without blinking. "Do you think me a monster?"

"No monster, but a thing of wonder. You have powers few possess."

Her skin prickled in pleasure. "You are the first I have ever told," she said in a warm rush. "Only Father knew, and he swore me to secrecy. Not even May knew."

"You honor me," he said. "I will keep your secret safe. In faith, I always suspected there was something uncommon about you . . . and now I know. I will miss you when you go." The last thing he said quietly. Grabbing the poker, he shifted the burning logs in the hearth.

"I wish I knew what to do." She leaned closer to the fire. "There are so few physicians here, and yet I have no opportunity to put my arts to use." She told him about her experience at the Mearley Plantation, how Mrs. Mearley had rebuked her for offering to help her husband. "Had they allowed it, I could have relieved the man of his agony."

"You expect overmuch from these people, I fear," Gabriel told her. "But do not fret about your future." He fed more wood to the fire. "A girl like you will always find her feet."

Each day when she carried out his midday meal, Hannah saw the progress Gabriel was making on the canoe. He used the adze to chip away the charred wood in the center. He kept burning and chipping until, three days later, the canoe was hollowed out. With the adze, he smoothed the bottom. Then he smoothed the sides to make sure they were symmetrical, so the canoe would be balanced on the water. Last, he cut down a slender birch and carved out the paddle.

The finished canoe was twelve feet long and so massive, Gabriel needed to heft it onto logs to roll it into the river.

"This will last many years," he told her. "Nothing is better than solid wood. If I run into a rock, it will not break." He slapped the canoe's golden flank. "The Indians used to make giant canoes. I did hear stories of war canoes that were fifty feet long. Each could hold forty men. But I made mine small enough so that I can row it on my own."

Hannah stood on the dock and watched Gabriel climb in. He sat cross-legged on the flat bottom and then paddled around in a circle, showing her how easily he could maneuver the boat in the strong current.

"I could never ride a horse very well," he called out, pitching his voice above the gushing water, "but I am a born boatman."

She had to smile to see his face so flushed with pride. When he paddled up to the dock, she tried to share his delight. He let her climb in and run her fingers over the satiny wood.

"I made it just the right size to take you and your trunk down to Banham's," he said. "There is even room for your sister's trunk."

⇥

Before sunset Gabriel climbed the ladder and opened the trapdoor to the attic while Hannah waited below. He went up with a guttering candle. She had taken care to close the shutters and to push the trunk back to its original position. She hoped he would never guess she had been up there making her own investigation. With the shutters closed, it would be too dim for him to see the footprints she had left in the dust. A sense of regret passed through her. Now that she had divulged her deepest secret to him, it seemed almost shameful to conceal anything.

First he handed down the spinning wheel. At home, an unmarried woman could make her living spinning, though she doubted such a thing was possible here. What would people have to pay her with — eggs and tobacco?

With some difficulty, he hefted May's trunk, bearing the weight in his arms and descending slowly, one ladder rung at a time. *Careful*, Hannah thought, afraid he would fall and the trunk would crush him. When his feet reached the floor, he set it down with a heavy bang.

"That is done."

"You are generous," she said, "giving me all her things."

Gabriel looked away. "We leave at dawn tomorrow."

"Tell me one thing." Hannah fought down her trepidation. After this evening, she might not have another chance to ask. "Was May happy here?" She could not bring herself to ask if her sister and Gabriel had been happy together.

He stared at her, stricken. How unlike May he was, so quiet and gentle. How had he fared with her? She thought of May's boldness, her vices. Had she been true to this man, or had she carried on the way she always had? In her letters, May had told them about Adele and Nathan Washbrook, but had hardly mentioned Gabriel. With a heavy heart, she remembered Father's words: *She writes nothing tender of her husband. Not a word.*

"Our life here was full of hardship." Gabriel bowed his head. "I think she missed society. Had she known how lonely it would be, I doubt she would have joined us here."

Hannah wanted to say something, but found she could not.

He raised his face to the ceiling then, as if about to make a confession to God. "I fear I was not all she hoped for, either. I could not make her happy as I should have." His voice was stark with pain.

"Gabriel, I loved her well, but I know that she could be a trying woman. You are a good man. I am sure you did everything in your power to be an honorable husband to her."

He blinked. "I know she missed you terribly, Hannah. Your letter brought her such joy."

She turned aside so he wouldn't see her eyes tear up.

—+—

Just as she was about to retire, Gabriel appeared with a cloth bundle.

"I know you are disappointed," he said, "not to have more keepsakes from your sister. This is a keepsake from me. Mayhap it will be of use to you this winter."

She smiled shyly as she undid the bundle. Inside was a pair of mittens, tanned hide on the outside and soft fur on the inside. "This is kind," she murmured. Putting them on, she held them up in the firelight and marveled. They fit her perfectly. How had he known the size of her hands?

"They're rabbit fur," he said.

—+—

She slept with the mittens under her pillow, clutching them for childish comfort. The prospect of throwing herself at the Banhams' mercy banished all hope of sleep. She pondered whether she could go to Michael and Elizabeth Sharpe's homestead on the Eastern

Shore and make herself useful in exchange for a pallet to sleep on and a place at their table. Over time she could establish herself as a midwife and herb woman. Possibly Elizabeth was already pregnant again after rejoining her husband. Staying with them seemed a happy prospect until she took their poverty into account. Before she became a working midwife, she would be a burden, another mouth to feed. It would be different if she were a strong man who could help in the tobacco fields. No, she could not impose herself on them.

Tossing in bed, she tried to envision her future, laid out before her like Joan's cards. She saw only a blank.

—+—

At first light, she dressed behind the closed curtains. Combing her hair, she coiled it and tucked it beneath her bonnet. She was nervous about meeting Banham again, but maybe he wouldn't be there. Perhaps he was off sporting, she thought, with some other man's wife.

Gabriel had set out a single plate of cornbread and a pitcher of milk. The trunks were gone. How had he been able to take them down to the dock without waking her? The cornbread stuck in her throat. Why was she so nervous? May wouldn't be filled with trepidation. If May were with her, she would whisper in her ear that it was an adventure. May would expect her to set off in high spirits.

Before going to the dock, she visited her sister's grave. The frost-whitened grass chilled her as she pressed her palms against the turf. It pained her enough to have left her parents' grave, and now she was abandoning May's last resting place as well. She was about to set off into a world where no one knew a thing about her or her family: how beautiful her sister or how sagacious her father had been.

—+—

She found Gabriel in his canoe, paddle across his lap. The trunks were stowed in the middle, and he sat at the rear. "You must sit in front," he said, "to keep the balance."

She warned him of the logjams and beaver dams blocking the waterway, but he insisted they would manage. "The way downstream is easier than coming back will be."

After she had settled into the boat, he untied the rope and pushed away from the dock. The downstream current was swift. Before Hannah could catch her breath, Washbrook Landing was lost. *Oh May, what will become of me?*

"You will tend her grave for me, won't you?" she asked. The churning river swallowed her words. She looked back at Gabriel. The wind blew his long hair off his brow as he worked the oar. To think that this was the last she would see of him. The thought of losing his friendship seemed unbearable. Although she had stayed in his house for barely more than a fortnight, he was the one person who knew her secrets. He had seen her in one of her fits. She had shown him her surgical instruments. This night she would sleep in the Banhams' house. How she dreaded meeting them again. How she dreaded those sneering girls.

They were heading for a patch of rough water lashing around big stones. "Hold fast," he yelled, guiding the canoe around the rocks with a dexterity that astonished her.

She had lost so much. May, Father, Joan and her childhood home, her country. Now this. Had she traveled this far to end up a servant or else married to some planter with rotten teeth, like the man who had accosted her in Anne Arundel Town and called her sister Banham's whore?

"Gabriel, stop!" Lurching in her seat, she shifted her weight so that the canoe rocked violently to one side.

"Hannah!" he shouted. "Have a care. You will tip the boat."

"Gabriel, please! Turn the canoe around. Let us go back."

"Have you lost your head?"

"Banham is a dishonorable man. He is a whoremonger. I won't go to him."

"Sit still, Hannah. Calm yourself," he pleaded, making for shore. Paddle on the river bottom, he pushed the prow onto a sandy bank. He slowly moved one foot over the side of the canoe, then the other, stepping into the shallow water. Grunting with effort, he shoved the canoe onto land. Then he tied the rope to a tree branch hanging over the water. He stretched out his hand, helping her ashore.

"Hannah, what is this? You wanted me to take you downriver. I made the canoe for you."

She couldn't see him anymore for her tears. "Will you let me stay with you, Gabriel?"

She covered her face, waiting for him to tell her no, it was impossible, there was nothing left for her there.

"You are overwrought," he said. "If you want to go back to society, we must do it now, before the first snow."

She wiped her eyes. "You are the only family I have left. I do not want to lose you."

He moved his lips, but no words came out. She had never seen a man's face go soft like that before. Then he stiffened. "Think well on your words. Is this what you truly want?"

"They are all fops and liars, those planters. You said so yourself. They do own slaves and treat them worse than cattle. When I traveled upriver with Banham, he and Mr. Gardiner both debauched Mr. Gardiner's wife, though she was huge with child."

Gabriel looked at her as though she were raving.

"But you," she said, "are a good and honest man."

He swallowed. "You have known me only a short time."

"But I do *know* you," she said. "There is a bond of kinship. Our fathers were cousins."

He took her hand and led her up the bank to a flat granite boulder.

"Sit here a while and think of what you have said." He let go of her. "You must know your mind. If we do not travel today, you might be stranded here for winter, and our winters can be long—"

"Gabriel." She cut him off. "My sister was fortunate in at least one thing." She looked into his eyes.

His face went dark red. "Do you even know what you are saying, Hannah Powers?"

"I think I am in love with you."

They stood on the boulder, three feet apart, the river rushing past. She stepped forward and touched his arm. Before he could stop her, she embraced him, pretending for an instant that he was May and that she could wrap her arms around him without shame. How easily her head nestled against his chest. His heart pounded against her cheekbone. Yes, she was carrying on like a wanton girl, but wasn't she May's own sister? Didn't May's mischief run in her blood?

"Hannah." He sounded helpless and overwhelmed.

"I'm sorry," she said at once, backing away. But then he wrapped his arms around her and pulled her tight against him. Closing her eyes, she soaked in his warmth, the muscle and bone beneath his buckskin shirt. She began to cry again.

"Sweet Hannah." He wiped away her tears with his fingers, then rested his palm on the side of her neck. She noticed for the first time that his eyes were not black but darkest blue, like indigo ink with a glint of fire behind them.

His lips brushed her forehead. "You smell of wood smoke. And lye soap."

She laughed.

He tugged at her bonnet. "Let me see your hair."

"It's ugly," she whispered.

"It's not."

So she undid the strings of her bonnet, and he pulled it off her head. Like a living thing, her hair sprang loose from the tight coil she had wound it in. He ran his hands through it, then buried his face in it. He cupped her face in his hands and kissed her with a hunger that made her gasp. How easy it was to melt in his embrace, to let him bend her backward. This pounding inside her, was this what May had felt with her lovers? Was this what had lured May from her bed night after night and left such a glow on her skin? People said it was wicked, but this was what her May had done, her beautiful May, and this was May's widower. Did she not haunt them both? Kissing Gabriel was the only way to break through the wall of loneliness and grief, the only way she could hold on. In the entire world, only one thing remained of her family and home, and that was Gabriel Washbrook.

"Sweet Hannah," he said again as he gently drew her down on the grass. He plucked a late-blooming dandelion and rubbed it against the inside of her wrist until the pollen stained her skin gold.

—+—

As Gabriel had predicted, the way back upstream was much slower. Rowing furiously, he battled the current. She wished she had a paddle, too. But finally they were back at Washbrook Landing. His dogs rushed out to greet them in a noisy chorus while she helped him hoist the trunks out of the canoe bottom and set them on the dock. She let the dogs jump on her and lick her hands. Together she and Gabriel carried first the one trunk and then the other back to the house.

"It grows cold." Gabriel kindled a fire in the hearth. "Soon the first snow will come."

He pulled the animal skins in front of the fire, sat down on them, and held out his arms to her. "Come, Hannah." His fingers stroking her hair were so tender. She closed her eyes and surrendered to the warmth of his hands, the heat of the fire. *Now you are home. Now you have come home at last.* Home wasn't a place anymore. It was the love that welled up inside her.

"I hope I am not a burden to you," she said. "Have you enough provisions to get us through the winter?"

"More than enough." He wrapped his arms around her. "There are pigs and goats I might slaughter. Chickens as well. The forest is full of game, the river full of fish. We won't starve, you and I." He lay back on the bearskin and gave her a playful tug, pulling her down beside him. "Even if Banham comes to push us off the land, we will survive. We will never be servants or tenant farmers." He rolled over, lying on top of her but resting most of his weight on his arms so he didn't crush her. Hannah closed her eyes and arched her neck. So this was what it was like to lie beneath a man. The animal fur smelled of his body. He stroked her face, and she kissed his hand.

"West of here are mountains," he said. "My father once worked as a surveyor, and he drew them on a map. We could settle there, build a cabin. The planters wouldn't want that land anyway. No one grows tobacco in the hills."

We will vanish from here, Hannah thought as he kissed her, *like smoke*. One day Banham and his men would come here and find only the shell of an abandoned house and a few dilapidated outbuildings and overgrown fields. They would wonder where she and Gabriel had gone but never find out. It would be like trying to track down a ghost.

"I will not miss the other world," she told him, "as long as I can be with you."

⸻

That night she slept in his arms in the bed of skins. He held her tight, molding his body to hers. He cupped her breasts and stroked her through her thin shift but didn't ask her to take it off. "We can go slowly." He ran his hands down her spine as though she were some delicate thing he feared he might break. "I don't want to frighten you," he said, his lips against her ear. "May God smite me if I ever hurt you."

⸻

When Gabriel went to check his traps, Hannah wandered in a warm haze despite the hard frost on the ground and the chilling north wind that tore the bright leaves from the trees. While she gathered eggs and fetched water, her feet hardly seemed to touch the earth. She had become another person, had been taken apart and put together again so that the pieces fit together in a different way than before. If she had a mirror, she knew she would see the difference in the glow of her skin and the sheen of her hair.

Bit by bit, she was becoming a part of this place, as he was already. She learned to sleep on the bed of fur instead of the dead man's mattress. One day, when gathering kindling, she broke the heel of her worn shoe. Gabriel threw her old shoes to the dogs and stitched her a pair of moccasins made of tough deerhide, lined with rabbit fur to keep her feet warm through the winter.

Though there was no receipt for it in her mother's book, she learned to make cornbread. First she mixed the cornmeal with butter, eggs, and milk, and then either baked it in a pan or fried it in the skillet.

She went into the woods and collected walnuts and hickory nuts. Gabriel taught her which wild mushrooms were edible and which were poisonous. He showed her an edible fungus that grew in brackets on tree trunks. When she fried it, it tasted just like chicken. He introduced her to native plants to be avoided, such as poison ivy, as well as beneficial herbs like jewelweed, which was good for treating poison ivy rash and insect bites. She began to list these plants and their properties in the blank pages at the back of her mother's receipt book.

At sunset she went down to meet him near the tobacco barn where he split logs for winter. They stood on the riverbank, his arms around her waist, and she begged him to tell her the story of the faery ointment again. Love allowed her to see the world anew, with the glamoury eye. See behind the masks and outer trappings. The Gardiners' residence, for all its imported finery, was hateful as a charnel house. A rough cabin could be as splendid as a palace if she dwelt there in happiness with her beloved.

That night he pushed her shift up to her throat. A thousand things rushed through her. It was strange to be stripped naked like this. She didn't know which way to move, but he held her fast, fixed in place. "I want to see you," he said. The fire warmed her bare skin as he pulled her shift over her head and threw it aside. He turned her over so that she lay on her stomach, then he rolled her on her back again.

"You're so small," he said.

His exploration of her body left her shy and half skittish. As

134

much as she longed to meet his embrace with equal passion, she was suddenly nervous. She thought of May's lush body, and then her own, so flat and thin. Was he comparing her to her sister? But he looked at her with longing, stroking her until the blood sang in her ears. The more he caressed her, the more pliant she became, lying back on the bearskin while he took each breast in his mouth. Under his touch, she bloomed, her skin coming alive. He stroked the inside of her thighs until she was in a frenzy, then he stroked her most secret parts. "You are soft as a little rabbit." He caressed her until she writhed, her hair in her mouth.

He tugged off his breeches and lay naked, letting her straddle him as she ran her hands over his body, which was hard where hers was soft. She had thought that all men were as hairy as those on whom she had operated, but Gabriel's skin was smooth. She wasn't ignorant of male anatomy. She had seen Mr. Byrd splayed like a plucked rooster. But Gabriel wasn't a drugged, blindfolded body tied down on a table. His flesh rose to meet hers. She squeezed him in her hand until he pressed her back down on the bearskin. Opening her legs, he entered her slowly, his eyes never leaving hers.

"You have an angel's name," she murmured, wondering why she had never thought of that before. "They named you after an angel."

Then she cried out so sharply that the dogs outside howled and scratched at the latched door. It hurt more than she had thought possible, but she clung to him, wrapping one leg around his back so he wouldn't pull out of her. As he kept moving inside her, she felt the blood trickle down her thigh. It would leave no stain on the bearskin. So this was what they sang the songs about, what the preachers railed against, what had ruined her sister's name. This was the moment in which she finally became a woman. She closed her eyes and saw the face of the Green Man in her old village church.

"I love you, Hannah." He shuddered and lay still, his body covering hers. She thought he would kiss her then, but instead he trembled, his face in her hair.

"What is it?" she asked.

When he lifted his face above hers, she saw that he was in tears. "I don't deserve you."

"Gabriel." She twined her arms around his neck, not letting him go. "Shh." As she embraced him, she felt the raised skin on his back—scars from his father's whip. He hid his wet face between her breasts. After what seemed like a long time, he sat up. He touched her bloody thigh, then raised his hand in the firelight and stared brokenly at his shining red fingers. When Hannah saw the blood, she, too, was overcome. She wanted to tell him it was only a little blood, it didn't hurt anymore. The bleeding was such a small thing compared to what stirred inside her. But when she saw the horror on his face, she couldn't speak. Why did he look so terrified to see her blood on his hand? She knew May had not come to her wedding night a maiden. Was he so shocked because he had never been with a virgin before? For an instant, Hannah saw her sister's ghostly face superimposed on his.

"Gabriel." She took him by the shoulders and kissed him until he kissed her back, marking her arms with her sticky blood as he held her. Barefoot and naked, she hobbled across the freezing floorboards to the table, took a clean rag, and returned to him. She wiped his hand, then wiped the blood off her own skin. Crumpling the stained rag, she threw it into the fire. "There," she told him. "It is done."

They slept with their hair tangled together, limbs intertwined. Each time she rolled over, he rolled with her, tightening his arm around her waist as though now that he had her, he would never let her go.

—✦—

In the morning she searched the creek bank for late-blooming flowers. She found a clump of autumn crocuses tucked in a pocket of mossy earth. With the spade she brought with her, she dug them up, then placed them in her basket. Shaking the dirt from her skirt, she made her way to May's grave.

For the first time, she felt a sense of apprehension as she knelt on the mound that covered her sister. Blinking back tears, she set to work. When the hole was dug, she planted the crocuses, patting down the earth around them. Afterward she took the sharpened kitchen knife from her basket and cut off a lock of hair. She plaited it in the shape of a heart and set it beside the flowers she had planted.

Lying down, she stretched her body on the grave, her head where May's would be. She pretended they were children again, back home in their own bed, whispering under the covers and telling secrets.

"Don't hate me, May." She stroked the brittle autumn grass. "It was only because we were both half mad for missing you."

IV

15 *Near Drowning*

May and Gabriel
OCTOBER 2, 1689

THE MORNING MAY STEPPED off the ship in Anne Arundel
Town, drizzle fell, dampening her hair, which she had combed
so carefully before leaving the hold. She had bitten her lips and
pinched her cheeks to make them red. Now she asked herself why
she had bothered. Clouds hung over the harbor town with its
crude jumble of houses. A cow lowed from a distant paddock as
the drizzle dimpled the pewter water. May observed the bewigged
planters and the sailors unloading cargo. She clutched her cloak
around herself, and her eyes searched the scene for something
exotic to ease her disappointment. To think she had sailed this
far, breaking her poor sister's heart, only to arrive at such a dismal
place. She had expected to see the flowering tulip trees Cousin
Nathan had described in his letter. She had expected red Indians
with feathers in their hair.

Surveying the crowd, she wondered which of these strutting
planters was her bridegroom. When her eyes met those of a curly-
haired young man, she winked at him before she could stop herself. Though the days of her freedom were well and truly over, old
habits were hard to kill. She needed some bit of cheer to lift her
spirits. This was the Chesapeake, after all, not some dour Puritan
settlement like the ones in New England of which she had heard.
In his letter, Cousin Nathan had written that people here were
merry, loving nothing better than horseraces, hunting parties, and

cotillions, where they got themselves up in handsome clothes.

Her thoughts turned to her wedding dress, folded away inside her trunk. She, Joan, and Hannah had spent six weeks sewing it. She could still feel the crisp lawn, the silk embroidery thread slipping along her fingers as her needle guided it through the fabric. Hannah had baptized the gown in her tears. Although it would have been unpardonable for her sister to abandon Father in his old age, she wished Hannah were standing beside her now. Hannah wouldn't be so easily discontented. Eyes big and wondering, her young sister would clutch her arm, both amazed and a little frightened by the strangeness, while May reassured her that all would be well. No, they were not abandoned at the pier; the Washbrooks would find them any minute.

A commotion drew her attention to the waterfront. The crowd pressed forward, cheering and then jeering at some spectacle. Standing on tiptoes, she tried to see what it was about. Though she didn't want to abandon her trunk, it was impossible to get any view where she stood, so she pushed her way to the front of the throng.

Beyond the harbor wall, a shallop boat skimmed the water in wide circles. One man worked the rudder, another controlled the sail, while a third man stood at the prow, arms outstretched, welcoming the applause. At first she didn't understand what the fuss was about, then she spotted the rope dragging something in the boat's wake. Straining her eyes, she finally recognized the body at the end of the rope, the long skirt trailing. May snorted and shook her head. What manner of sport did these bumpkins play at, pulling a dead woman behind a boat? But the woman, she realized, was still alive, though only barely. She clung to the rope, struggling to keep her head above water. The boatmen showed her no mercy. The scene reminded May of a line in one of Joan's dark old ballads. *Sometimes she sank, sometimes she swam.* The woman's drenched head crested above the white foam before the current slammed her beneath the surface. Fists clenched, May glared around at the clapping crowd. Were they just going to stand there like grinning half-wits while the woman drowned?

"Do something!" she shouted. "They will kill her!"

No one paid her any mind. It was like a nightmare where she was forced to witness a masked stranger slitting her sister's throat and she was powerless to do anything but watch. Just as she thought the woman would surely drown, the men in the boat tugged on the rope, dragging her out of the water. May watched her spit and vomit overboard. No one helped her, even to give her a handkerchief or to put a blanket around her quivering shoulders. The man who had stood at the prow sat down, his back to her.

"That'll teach the trollop," a voice behind her said.

May whirled around to confront the speaker, but there were so many faces, she had no idea who had spoken. Among the men and boys, there were also women who pointed and laughed. It dawned on her that this near drowning was punishment for some crime—much like public flogging or putting someone in the stocks on the village green. As the boat sailed out of view, May imagined the woman quaking in fear and cold. What would happen to her now? Shoving her way back through the crowd, May decided to return to her trunk before someone made off with it. Her thoughts were in such a muddle that she hardly looked where she was going. Before she knew it, she had trodden on a boy's foot.

"Begging your pardon," she muttered, though if he had gotten any pleasure from watching the proceedings, she was not sorry in the least. If she caused him pain, then so much the better. Half a head shorter than she was, the boy glanced up at her in confusion. Brushing past him, she strode toward her trunk, only to find a stout man peering over it. With his gloved hand, he traced the letters of her name carved on the lid.

"What business have you with my baggage, sir?"

Straightening his back, he looked her over carefully, as though a merchant inspecting a bolt of cloth to see if it met his satisfaction. She held his gaze without backing down. They were the same height. His wig, she noted, was woefully out of fashion.

It looked as if he had affixed a spaniel's pelt to his skull.

"Are you May Powers?" he asked, doffing his hat. When he bowed, the spaniel wig nearly slid off. Although he looked like a rustic, there was a hint of steel in his voice, no deference in his bow. May sensed that he was not a man she would wish to cross.

"That is my name, sir," she replied, matching his haughty air. Joan had always scolded her for her pride. She dropped in a reluctant curtsy. If Hannah were here, she would bob her head as a modest maiden should. May stood tall and lifted her chin.

He appraised her. "You do resemble your late mother."

May dropped her eyes. Though only seven when her mother died, she still remembered her singing at the spinning wheel. She remembered brushing Mother's hair.

"As you have surely gathered, I am Nathan Washbrook, your father's cousin." A note of cheer mingled with the pomposity in his voice. She decided he was being convivial.

"Pleased to meet you at last, sir." She inclined her head.

"Here comes your bridegroom."

She looked in the direction he pointed and saw nothing. So he had only meant to jest with her. If her future father-in-law had a sense of humor, she just might be happy here. Then she saw the boy whose foot she had stepped on earlier. This could only be a joke. That boy was a mere stripling with a girl's long hair. He hardly looked to be eighteen, as the letter had claimed. She turned helplessly to Cousin Nathan, who still pointed at the boy.

"This is my son, Gabriel."

—+—

How the disappointment bloomed on her face. The way she looked at him, Gabriel thought, as though he would never do for her at all.

"Good day to you," she said, so tall and stately, so voluptuous and womanly, that he felt like a minnow before a queen.

"Good day to you also, Mistress Powers." He bowed.

"I trust your voyage was not too harrowing," said Father. "You look rested and well nourished." He was busy examining her. Gabriel almost expected him to open her mouth and inspect her teeth.

"I am blessed with good health, sir." May's attention was focused on Father, as if this business were strictly between the two of them.

"Very well, then." Father caught Gabriel's eye and grinned. "I have rented a chamber in the Shipwright Inn. There you may prepare for the nuptials."

For an instant, May looked so helpless and lost that Gabriel saw only beauty, the color high in her salt-stung cheeks. He searched for words of kindness.

"The nuptials, sir? But this day I have only just arrived."

"Do you have any other plans in mind?" Father's tone made her flinch. Gabriel watched her take a step back. "Do you wish to undo the arrangement I have made with your father? Am I to write the good man with the news that I must send you back?"

Gabriel pushed himself forward. "Don't be so harsh, Father."

May ignored him. It was as though he hadn't spoken.

"Send me *back*, sir? I hardly think I am a piece of cargo you might return." For all her brave words, she trembled. Father was sizing her up, seeing how far he could push her before she stood her ground. If she displayed weakness, she was done for. Gabriel took his place beside her, ready to step in and defend her. When he considered what she was up against, he could forgive her for being so mighty and proud.

"I merely wish," May continued, "for a chance to accustom myself to your country, sir, before the wedding." Defiance blazed in her eyes.

Father seemed to find her willfulness charming. He smiled, as though to a daughter. "See you the clock on the church tower?"

"She's not blind, Father."

"Shut your mouth, son. I will have no impertinence. Mistress Powers, can you read the time?"

"Nearly noon, sir."

"The wedding shall commence at two o'clock," Father announced, so full of himself that Gabriel wanted to throw a clod of dung at him. "That gives you two hours to make ready."

When she gaped, Father chuckled. "You see, my dear, we colonials must be expedient. There are no churches in the backcountry. It must be done today, before we return home. We will not see Anne Arundel Town for another year."

Gabriel wished his father would allow him a few minutes to speak to her on his own before he vowed to spend the rest of his life with her. But neither of them gave him a chance to squeeze in a word.

"But how did you know I would arrive this day?" she demanded. "The ship might have been blown off course."

Father beamed. "I arranged for the wedding to take place the day of your arrival. The minister has grown accustomed to performing the ceremony when the ship sails into port. And ere the ship was sighted in Port Tobacco, messengers traveled up the Bay, spreading the news."

James, Father's favorite servant, approached. "Master Washbrook, all is ready at the inn." His eyes sparked at the sight of May. When he smiled at her, she brightened like the sun breaking out of the clouds. Her eyes went soft and she blushed. Gabriel wondered what it would take to have her look at him that way. If he grew a foot taller, perhaps. Golden and shining, James dwarfed him.

While James bowed to her, Father rocked on his feet. Indeed he, too, loved to look at James and seemed to find it only fitting to see May so dazzled. "James and Gabriel will carry your trunk to the inn. Let me lead the way." He offered May his arm. "Fret not, my dear. I will buy you a cup of wine for courage."

James hefted one end of May's trunk and Gabriel took the other. It was not heavy; he could have carried it without assistance. To think she was an ocean away from her people and that this box held her earthly possessions. He listened to her question Father about the banns.

"I did post them two months ago," Father told her. "All was well prepared."

Gabriel saw her dig in her heels, as if she would not allow Father to drag her one inch closer to the altar. She came to such an abrupt halt that Gabriel bumped into her. In his surprise, he dropped his end of the trunk, which hit the ground with a bang.

"But Master Washbrook," she said to Father, "you cannot force me to marry in such awful haste."

Indeed, Father could not, Gabriel thought. If he and May both refused, Father would be forced to surrender.

"She is right," Gabriel said, but Father stared him down.

"After the many pains I have taken on your account, you defy my will?"

"I would at least have flowers," May said.

Father raised his eyebrows comically. "Flowers, you say."

"Yes, sir." She threw back her head. "A bride must have a bouquet. Such is the custom amongst civilized people."

Gabriel saw James grinning to hear her address his master with such spirit. His own spirits sank when he caught May stealing another glance at James. Father regarded her, his eyes lively and amused. There was nothing lecherous in his gaze, merely the pride of acquisition. Gabriel sensed that Father admired her for putting up a challenge.

"You heard your bride, son. She would have flowers. A charming request, do you not think?"

Gabriel had no idea what to say.

"After you have brought the trunk to her room, you must procure her some flowers." Father laughed at him.

Gabriel had half a mind to tell him to send James on the mission, seeing as he was the one for whom May had the biggest eyes.

—+—

One look at Gabriel's downcast face filled May with regret. With such a father, it was no wonder he was so shy. If it weren't for fear of backing down in front of Nathan, she would have taken back her request. Where could the boy hope to find flowers, anyway? It was October.

Nathan held out his arm to her again. "Let us be on our way."

Still she refused to budge. "Sir, I would know why the men in the boat did drag that woman till she was nearly drowned. What was her crime?"

He studied her for a moment. "Adultery."

May ducked her head. She felt too weak to resist him anymore. Though she stood on dry land, she felt cold salt water closing over her head. She had to fight just to breathe. Glancing backward, she tried to catch Gabriel's eye, but he was already walking away from them. Shouldering her trunk on his own, he receded into the crowd.

16 The Pact

Hannah
1692

GABRIEL'S BODY FIT perfectly to hers as if the Creator had indeed made them each for the other. She pulled him on top of her, opening her legs and arching her hips to receive him. Alone with him on this outpost, Hannah didn't give a care how loudly she cried out. These games of the body were brand new and filled her like wine. They didn't hurt her anymore. Loving was pleasure, pure and simple. It had become as easy as breathing, as dizzying as hunger, as breathless as hard running, as sweet and comforting as apple tansey. Afterward, when he tried to rise from bed, she pulled him down and made him kiss her again. Beyond their bed, the cabin slowly filled with morning light.

"I must be at my work," he whispered, stroking her body. For the cold months, they had moved from the bed of furs to his father's old bedstead. When it was drafty, they could close the curtains.

Outside, Gabriel's dogs barked and howled, anxious for their master to feed them.

"The goats want milking," he told her.

"Stay just a while longer." She lay on top of him, pinning him to the bed. "It's so warm here."

He kissed her until she reluctantly released him. They dressed quickly, their teeth clenched against the cold.

Hannah crouched at the hearth and nursed a spark from the

previous night's embers. Piling kindling and logs, she built the fire while Gabriel went out to milk the goats and feed the dogs. When he returned with the milk, Hannah cooked corn mush porridge.

"I should check the traps today," he said. "To do the skinning and salting by daylight, I must set off early."

Before he left, he put his fingers under her chin and tilted her face to his. "While I am gone, be sure not to go crossing the creek."

She laughed. "What reason would I have to go there? Do you think I would meddle with your traps?"

He didn't smile. "There is danger in those woods. I know where the traps are, but you would not spot them until it was too late." He showed her the bear trap he had oiled the night before. He possessed two bear traps. One already lay hidden in the forest. "Now it is closed and no peril to you, but mark you how heavy it is." When he gave it to her, Hannah needed both hands to hold it. "Look how sharp the teeth are. Its jaws are powerful enough to bring down a bear, Hannah. Think how easily it could snap your leg in two." He looked as stern as Father when he used to tell her not to play in the field where the farmer kept the bull.

"Gabriel, I am no reckless child." She kissed him and handed him the trap. "I know well enough to keep myself from harm."

He put the trap in his leather satchel. "Mayhap tonight there will be bear meat." He had told her that the best time to trap bears was late autumn, when they were at their glossiest and fattest, just before they retreated into their caves for their winter-long sleep.

"More meat than we can eat, even after I make sausages," she said. "Have we enough salt to preserve it all?"

"The dogs will eat the excess. But finally we will have more bear grease." The jar in the pantry was nearly empty. He kissed her again before putting on his heavy wolfskin coat and walking out the door.

—+—

With him gone, thoughts of May crowded her head. *Do I betray her?* Putting on her cloak, Hannah took the empty water bucket and let herself out. Her new moccasins fit her feet like velvet slippers. *Do I betray her, or do I become her?* So comfortably shod, she had a new way of walking, hips swinging, head held high — the way May used to walk. She needed no mirror to tell her that she had grown beautiful these past weeks. She saw it in the way Gabriel looked at her, his eyes drinking her in, his hands moving over her body. At last she had plumbed the body's mysteries. "Love." She said the word aloud. These days she left her hair loose and uncovered, the way he liked her best. The red bird with the tufted head hopped from branch to branch. His song was of aching sweetness. To think that such a bird would linger so late in the year, instead of flying south like the rest.

When she reached the creek, she studied her reflection in the black water. *You are the plain sister no longer.* This was the face that Gabriel loved. *Do I betray her?* The most confounding thing was that it was only after she had usurped May's place that she thought she finally understood her and the secret delight that had moved her from man to man. Except Hannah couldn't imagine any man but Gabriel. Now that she had found such joy with him, how could she possibly forsake him for another?

She looked out across the creek into the wild forest. If she chose to, she could cross the water easily, leaping across the narrow stream to the opposite bank, disobeying Gabriel's warning. He had told her that the strip of land between the creek and the river was protected, his dogs keeping the wild beasts at bay. The Indians would not think to come there. But across the creek in the wild woods, everything was different. About a mile from the creek was the path the Indians traveled when they went from north to south. Closer to the creek, Gabriel's traps lay hidden.

At this time, he would be wending his way from trap to trap. His dogs ran ahead, barking if an animal was caught in the iron jaws. Gabriel would drag the dead wolves, foxes, rabbits, and bobcats home on his sledge. If he was lucky enough to find a bear, he would skin it in the forest, then cut the body into pieces. He would load as much as he could on the sledge. Some of the meat he would feed to the dogs. The rest he would string up and hang over a high tree branch, out of the way of wolves and foxes, until he could come back for it. The crisp weather would preserve the meat.

"This is our wealth," he told her each time he brought an animal home to skin. "This is our fortune." If there was no more tobacco, then they were blessed with an abundance of fur and meat. Gabriel could sell or trade the furs for salt, sugar, lye, and nails. Beaver fur was especially prized. He piled the skins in the attic, which Hannah had swept and dusted. Gabriel said the forest would always support them.

When she filled her bucket, she wondered what the date was. She didn't even know if Christmas had come. It seemed a little sad to let the holidays slip by without celebration. She could ask Gabriel to slaughter one of the hogs so she could make a Christmas ham with apples. She could decorate the house with pine boughs and find some gift to give him. They could sing carols. Every day with him had seemed like Christmas. To think she had lost her sister, only to gain such happiness. Had her heart ever been fuller? The bucket handle bit into her hand as she lugged it back to the house. At the very least, she could have mourned a year, as was fitting, before throwing herself at May's widower. But May had known desire more than anyone. *May would forgive.*

The red bird sang in the branches above her head. The male was crimson as blood in the snow, and his mate was muted green, like a walnut before it ripened. Gabriel had told her they were called cardinals. In England she had never seen them. *May would have wanted us joined together.* Like the two birds, male and female. A spinster's life was unnatural, against the will of God. Every creature in nature strove toward its mate. *She loved me and would not want me to be lonely.*

How she wished he would come back now, this instant, and take her in his arms. How she craved him when he was gone, and what an appetite she had for his body, so slender and muscled. Now that her desire had been awoken, she would never be able to extinguish it. *Yes, I am her sister. This hunger flows in our blood.* Next time she would ask to join Gabriel when he checked the traps. She could help him. She would shoulder the rabbits and foxes while he dragged home the bear. She pictured the animals in their traps, the frozen stare of their lifeless eyes.

My sister is dead and I have never felt more alive. If Joan were here, would she call her a strumpet and a traitor? Would she slap her face for what she had done? Would Father look at her sadly, then turn away? Her heart hardened. May had had her chance with so many men. Hannah remembered the innkeeper's son and how cruelly her sister had spurned him, humiliating him in front of his brother and the whole harvest fair, on account of some tinker she never saw again. Happiness with one man hadn't been good enough for May.

At the sound of barking, Hannah looked out the window to see Gabriel dragging the sledge, laden with fur and chunks of raw flesh. Yes, he had trapped a bear.

Hannah worked beside him, as dedicated and unflinching as she had been in the old days with Father. They hung the sides of meat from a pole in the chimney to smoke. She boiled water and cleaned out the bear's intestines to make sausage. She ran the meat through the grinder with spices from the spice cupboard, dried herbs, salt, and cornmeal. While roasting a big chunk of bear meat, she salted down the rest of the meat in a barrel. Gabriel collected the fat in a special pot to make his bear grease. They worked long after sunset.

Gabriel caught her eye and grinned. "What a rude plenty we enjoy, Hannah."

—+—

Later, when they lay in bed, bellies full and bodies tired, Hannah bit gently into his flesh as though she were still hungry. Beside the bed, the candle still burned, allowing her to look into his eyes. Laughing, he put his finger in her mouth, then smoothed her red hair over her breasts. Out of nowhere, she found herself fighting the urge to cry. She wriggled away and pulled the bedclothes to her chest.

"What is it?" He touched her face.

"It seems strange to live with you in this house where once you lived with May, and yet you never speak of her."

He collapsed, flat on the bed, and was silent.

"You do not grieve for her as I do."

"What would you have me say, Hannah? I am not happy that she died. I mourned her passing, as I did my father's passing and the child's, but I cannot pretend that I cared for her the way I care for you."

Resting her head on his chest, she listened to his heart pound against her ear. "Was she untrue to you?" she asked in a small voice. "Is that why you will not speak of her?"

His body went rigid. "Would you have me speak ill of the dead, Hannah?"

"Back in our village." Her throat was so dry and tight, it hurt to get the words out. "She flew from one boy to the next. She was never true to anyone." Her voice broke. "I loved her well, but always pitied those boys."

"Is it true what you say? When I married her, I knew she was no maid, but I never suspected she had been so faithless to so many."

"She treated every boy the same. She could never love just one man." Hannah rolled away. "I have betrayed her."

He pulled her gently so that she faced him again. His eyes were moist, as though a terrible weight had been lifted off him. "Speaking the truth is no betrayal. You have done no wrong, my love. Before you told me this, I thought it was something in me that made her so capricious. My father used to say I wasn't man enough for her."

Her heart beat so fast that she was giddy. It lay revealed. Gabriel had never loved May. But he loved her.

"If I had been a good sister, I would never have lost my heart to you." She broke down in tears.

He embraced her. "Hannah, your sister and I did not choose each other. Never were two people more badly suited. Now you understand why I did not wish to talk about her. I know how you cherished her, and I did not want to say anything that would bring you sadness." His eyes, shining with love, fathomed hers.

She kissed him in wanton hunger, could not stop herself from tasting his flesh. He rolled on top of her, holding her in place.

"There is a pact I would make with you, Hannah." His face was so close that she could see herself reflected in his eyes. "Let us speak no more of her. It only brings pain to sully the memory of the dead."

Hannah nodded, a prickle of guilty relief running through her. Dwelling on May's past sins would benefit no one.

"Sweet girl." Gabriel kissed her until she pulled him fiercely inside her. *Just this one thing I want, now and forever.* How could May have squandered this on so many? He was right to make her swear the pact. Let her sister's name remain unspoken. Let her dead sister rest in peace.

17 Shadow Catcher

Adele

BROOM IN HAND, Adele Desvarieux stepped out on the porch and looked toward the river. Though trees blocked her view, she could hear the current, the promise of what the water would bring. Today Master Washbrook and his son were due back with the new English bride.

What, she wondered, would the new mistress be like? It was hard to imagine having a mistress instead of just the two masters. In the three years she had lived in this outpost, the only females she had laid eyes on were the Banham girls, the one time they had visited with their father. She hoped her new mistress wouldn't be haughty like those girls, but gentle and kind. Pretty, too. If she was a proper lady, she would call on Adele to brush her hair and lace her gowns, as Maman had done for her former mistress in Martinique. The mistress in Martinique had a face like a china doll, blue-marble eyes, and soft brown hair that Maman had curled with iron tongs.

All Adele knew from the letters Master Washbrook had read aloud to his son was that the new mistress's name was May, like the English month, and that she was healthy and twenty-two years old. Adele counted on her fingers. That made her four years older than Master Gabriel, seven years older than herself. Having a mistress here might finally put an end to her nightmares. Her hand moved inside the front of her smock to the small cloth bag that contained the white cockerel feather she wore for protection.

After sweeping the porch, Adele went back inside the house to make sure everything was ready for the mistress's arrival. This morning she had washed the window, scrubbed the floor, dusted the table, mantelpiece, dresser, and chest of drawers. But her hardest labor could not transform this shack into a proper home. The master and mistress in Martinique had owned a house built of stone with jasmine growing up the walls, a long veranda around it, glassed windows in each room. They had carpets, looking glasses, mahogany furniture, a spinet, and a parrot in a cage. Each Christmas the mistress had served roasted peacock. She tried to remember that place as she had loved it when she was a very young child—before she had learned to hate.

Yesterday, with no help from the lazy Irishmen, who sported and swam naked in the river when the master was away, Adele had stuck a small pig and butchered it. The bacon now hung in the chimney to smoke along with the sausages she had made. The loin she roasted in a pan with cider, apples, onions, and garden chard. Master Washbrook laughed at her cooking—he called it Frenchified and peculiar. The English like their meat the honest way, he had told her, boiled with turnips, not basted in cider and covered in fruit. Once he had given her a receipt book of proper English cookery, only to discover she couldn't make any sense of the words on the page. So it was either eat her Frenchified food or go hungry.

She missed the cooking she knew from her childhood—goat meat stewed in coconut milk, yams and mangoes, nutmeg and fresh pepper. Only dull food grew here. No wonder she had grown so thin. If Maman were with her, she would feed her guava fritters and sweet cakes until her hollow cheeks filled out. Although there was no looking glass in the Washbrook household, she had an idea how shabby she must look in her mud-colored homespun smock, her hair covered in a headcloth that had once been blue and was now a dull gray. She went barefoot, saving her shoes and stockings for winter's cold. Her skin wasn't coffee-dark as her mother's had been, but a lighter brown. She knew she was a half-caste, but didn't know anything more about her father. By the time she had been old enough to ask such questions, Maman was gone.

Adele went to the hearth to check the progress of the pork loin. When the mistress was finally here, she would fry corn-cakes on the griddle. Sometimes she wondered why she bothered cooking decent food for these people. Master Washbrook always prayed and read from the Bible before each meal. By the time he allowed them to eat, the food was overcooked.

She regarded the brand-new bedstead Master Washbrook had purchased from a ruined planter down the Bay. Previously young Gabriel had slept on a pallet, but now that he was to have an English bride, he must have a proper bed. Shyly she fingered the bed curtains and the linens she had washed in the creek. Bolder now, she sat on the edge of the feather mattress and bounced up and down. How inviting the bed was, how soft. How tempting just to curl up and doze until they arrived. But she sprang to her feet and smoothed the counterpane so no one would know she had tested the mattress.

Flowers, she thought. A new bride must have flowers. Of course, nothing beautiful could bloom in these forsaken woods. Her former mistress in Martinique had a garden so exquisite, none of Master Washbrook's descriptions of the Garden of Eden in the Bible could match it. Orchids and frangipani had grown there, gardenia and hibiscus flowers as big as her fist. When she was a child, Maman used to scent her braids with vetiver. She could still recall the earthy sweetness of that scent, her mother's hands in her hair.

The only flowers she would be able to find in this place were the ones that grew wild—the tall spiky purple flowers that shot up in the forest, the gold flowers that grew among the rotting tree stumps. She didn't know the names of those flowers, and it was no good asking the Washbrooks—what did men know about such things? Although her mother had brought her up to speak proper French and not just slave patois, her English was patchy.

Adele stepped out the door. She tiptoed past Master Gabriel's dogs, sleeping in a heap near the porch steps. She couldn't get away from them fast enough. Dogs terrified her. When she was eight years old, they discovered Maman was a shadow catcher, an obeah woman. Not only that, she had cast a spell on Monsieur Desvarieux, their former master, who had given his slaves his surname. Maman had cast a spell to turn his eye, to stop him from hurting Madame Desvarieux, the mistress.

In Adele's mind, the pictures revolved—one of Maman brushing Madame's brown hair as they laughed together; another of Madame weeping, clad only in her chemise, a purple bruise blooming on her cheek, her bare white arms around Maman's neck.

Shivering, Adele touched the bag that held her cockerel feather and pressed it against her breastbone. No matter how hard she prayed, the pictures in her head never stopped tormenting her. Maman worked her magic to help Madame, then Monsieur Desvarieux caught her strewing rusty nails in his path. He lifted Maman's pallet and the loose floorboard underneath to discover more evidence of her sorcery—chicken feet, white feathers, broken eggshells, lizard bones, cat teeth, and a bottle of graveyard dust. Some of the other slaves betrayed her, saying they had seen her in the act of the old night worship. Clemence, the laundress, saw her pouring offerings of milk, chicken blood, and pilfered rum on the roots of the cotton silk tree.

Maman's punishment was a whipping with the cat-o'-nine-tails, then twelve months of hard labor in the cane fields on the other side of the volcano. Clemence said Maman was lucky—other obeah women and men were hanged or burned alive. After they had taken Maman, Adele tried to find her. She ran away, cutting through the orange and lemon groves, the coffee plantation, and into the jungle that clad the steep volcano slope. Razor grass sliced her legs open and then dogs came out of nowhere, great mastiffs barking and growling, their teeth at her throat, paws on her chest, grinding her into the mud with the red and black ants until the master's men came and snapped iron manacles around her wrists and ankles. It didn't matter that she was a child; they whipped her until blood drenched her torn skirt. The welts still laced her back.

The whipping left her too weak for fieldwork, so they let her stay on as a house servant. She scoured chamber pots and polished Monsieur Desvarieux's shoes. With Maman gone, Madame fell ill, never leaving her bed. Eventually she died of the ague. When they buried her, the gravediggers raised and lowered her coffin three times so her ghost would rest gentle and leave the living in peace. Some said that her duppy would come back and haunt the master, punish him for his cruelty. Soon after Madame's death, the news came that Maman had perished in the cane fields, bitten by a snake.

Heart beating fast, Adele sat on a tree stump and smoothed her face with her hands, trying to draw herself back to the present. No one had died on the Washbrook Plantation yet. The place was free of ghosts. Maman had taught her that each person had two souls. After death, one soul went to heaven for judgment while the other lingered on earth as a duppy, taking up residence in the roots of a tree. A duppy could be good or evil; a shadow catcher like Maman could harness one to help or harm.

After Madame died, Monsieur Desvarieux could find no new wife. No white lady would have him. Instead he badgered the pretty young slaves, but sickened of them when they grew big with child. One night Adele woke to his weight crushing her into her pallet, his hands tearing open her shift. Eleven years old, she sank her teeth into his hand until she tasted blood. At the same time she scratched him like a wild cat, even managed to gouge his leg with her toenail. When he finally wrenched his torn hand from her mouth, she screamed and cursed, threatening to send his dead wife's duppy after him. She shrieked loudly enough to spook the horses in the stable. In the morning, he had her whipped, but he never dared to touch her again. People said that after that night, she had the eyes of a zombie.

Soon after, he sold her to an English sea captain, who spoke to her in a tongue she couldn't understand. She had to launder his clothes and wash the lice out of his bed linen before his ship set sail for the American colonies. The sea captain said the same words over and over until she understood. When he cornered her in his cabin and tried to lift her skirts, she kneed him in the pillocks. The following day she left a seagull's foot in his mug of beer and the rest of the dead gull on his pillow. After that, he left her alone, and soon sold her off so cheaply that Nathan Washbrook could afford her.

Adele stopped to pick the tall gold-flowering weeds that grew beside the harvested tobacco field. As she made her way down the path, she ran into Patrick, still dripping from his swim. Naked, he clutched his bundle of clothes over his groin.

Without wanting to, she jumped and let out a cry, dropping the flowers. Patrick laughed. "What are you looking at, Adele? Fancy a tumble?" Though the other Irishmen left her in peace, Patrick was cruel, always poking fun at how easily she startled.

Arranging her face in a scowl, Adele stared with a ferocity that made the little bit of color vanish from his pasty skin. "I will put the chicken foot in your pottage this night," she muttered. "I will put bones in your bed." Though she only pretended, the men on the Washbrook Plantation, even Master Washbrook himself, feared deep down that she possessed dark powers. It had been Maman's gift, not hers, but she did nothing to correct their assumption. Let them be afraid of her.

Muttering *Jesus* under his breath, Patrick scuttled away, allowing her to catch a glimpse of his goose-pimpled white ass. She spat in his direction, then picked up the gold flowers and headed toward the creek. Despite her fierce face, her heart pounded and her hands shook. Would the fear and hate of men ever leave her? Maybe when the new mistress came and she wasn't the only female. But what if the mistress was cruel? She had heard that Mrs. Banham whipped her servants at will, even if they did nothing to provoke her. They said she was driven to madness, wed to such a libertine, that she took it out on her maids and garden boys.

A crow flying overhead touched her with its shadow. Shivering, she crossed herself. *The purple flowers*, she thought. She still had to pick the tall spiky blooms at the edge of the woods. When she reached the creek, she knelt on the bank and cupped her hands to drink. Then she lifted her face toward the towering trees that grew on the other side. If she weren't afraid of Master Gabriel's traps, she often thought she would run deep into the forest and never return. If she squinted and prayed, she could see her mother dancing beneath the oaks. Tall and graceful with her too proud eyes. If Maman were here, she would take Adele's hands, raise her to her feet, tell her to be strong. *Never forget you are a shadow catcher's daughter.* When Adele was six years old, Madame had given her a silver bangle with *Adele Desvarieux* engraved on the inside, so she would grow up knowing how to write her name. The bangle was too small for her now. She hid it in her pallet.

Leaping across the creek to the lush bank opposite, she picked the tall purple flowers until her arms were too full to hold any more. Then she headed back toward the house. On her way, she passed Finn. He was her age, a quiet boy. If she had no fear in her heart, she sometimes thought they might have become friends. He wasn't cruel like Patrick.

"Adele." He nodded to her in greeting. "Did you pick those flowers for the new mistress?"

Even with Finn, the old panic wouldn't let her go. Ducking her head, she just nodded and hurried up the path. He stepped aside to let her pass.

Once she had heard Master Washbrook telling the Irishmen to leave her alone, stay out of her way, for she was touched by God. *Touched by God.* She imagined a golden hand emanating from Master Washbrook's huge English Bible and resting on her, marking her as different. *Please, God, let the new mistress be kind.* Let there be one person here she could look at without the dread rising inside her. Perhaps the mistress would have the power to still her hate, take away her fear.

Before reaching the porch, she slowed her gait to avoid awakening the dogs. Stealing inside, she found a jug for the flowers. There was enough water in the bucket to spare her another trip to the creek. As she arranged the purple and gold blooms, she decided that even though they were weeds, they were pretty in their way, brightening the gloomy house. Maybe when the mistress saw them, she would smile, knowing someone had thought to pick her flowers. Plucking one of the purple spiky flowers from the bouquet, Adele laid it like an offering in the center of the brand-new bed.

She jumped and swallowed a scream when the dogs started barking. Edging to the window, she saw them leaping down the path to the river. Her heartbeat quickened. That meant Master Washbrook and his son had returned with the English lady. She took a deep breath, decided this was the moment to be bold. In truth, she couldn't stop herself from rushing out the door and creeping toward the river. She held back, peering from behind bushes. Through the autumn leaves, she caught glimpses of the Irishmen walking to the dock. Finn held his straw hat in his hands. Patrick was clothed again, but his wet hair gave him the look of a water rat.

She saw James helping the young woman out of the boat. When he stepped away, providing Adele with a clear view of her, she forgot to breathe. The lady wore a green gown embroidered with flowers. Though it was October, she came dressed like spring, as beautiful as her name. The sun shone on her hair, which was the same color as Madame Desvarieux's mahogany dressing table. She was so lovely, she seemed to give off light, like the fireflies Maman had called *les belles*. As the Irishmen gathered at the dock, the lady smiled at them, hands outstretched like the Madonna. Adele could find no arrogance in her face, only curiosity. Something caught in Adele's throat. Forgetting her fear, she walked forward to greet her new mistress.

18 A Woman's Fate

Hannah
1693

THE DAYS SLID PAST in a happy blur. The pile of skins in the attic grew so high, it touched the ceiling. Gabriel stitched her a cloak of fox fur that kept her warm even in bitter weather, when the wind blew straight in from the Atlantic and she had to break the ice on the creek with a hatchet to get water. With snowflakes nestled in her hair and fur cloak, she looked like the Snow Queen, or so Gabriel said when he teased her. Sometimes they danced across the bare wooden floor, even though they had no music except the wind howling down the chimney.

"How do you keep track of the days?" she asked him one morning when they walked hand in hand down the riverbank. "I don't know if it is already the New Year or still the old."

"The Indians mark the time by counting the full moons, the summers and winters," he said. "Time passes differently here."

"I feel it too." Their youth could stretch on forever, she decided, if they stopped counting the years. This was probably the closest a mere mortal could come to touching eternity. She squeezed his mittened hand. "Now I know why you don't want to go back there." She looked down the river. "Back to that world." The world of calendars, planters, tobacco, and money counters.

He kissed her. "What need have we to go back there? We want for nothing. Do we, Hannah?"

The only two things left to desire were a ring on her finger and a minister to sanctify their union. In the eyes of the world, they were living in sin. But she didn't tell him this—she couldn't. What power did the word *sin* have on this dazzling white morning when the snow glittered like a crop of diamonds?

"No," she told him softly. "We lack nothing." She could walk the forest in a fur cloak like some highborn lady. Meat on her table every night, the love of an adoring man. She wouldn't trade places with any woman alive. Banham's daughters would be married off to planters of their father's choosing. Mrs. Gardiner would continue bedding her husband's friends until her beauty was gone. *But you, Hannah Powers, are a free woman, your own mistress.*

The days grew longer and the snow melted, leaving the earth springy and damp. Tiny white and yellow flowers carpeted the forest floor. The land claimed her and left its mark on her, as it had done with Gabriel. Soon all vestiges of her old life would be worn away. One morning she opened her trunk to take out her old Sunday dress of mustard-colored wool with the forest-green stomacher. Gabriel had never seen her in her good dress. But it was laced with moth holes. In a fit of disgust, she threw it in the midden heap. Soon she would have to dress in buckskin, as the Indian women did. An Englishwoman no longer, she would clothe herself in deerhide and let the sun burn her skin. When the weather grew warmer, she would go barefoot. Her foot soles would toughen into leather.

Hannah spread goat manure in the garden and hoed it into the soil. She planted the seeds Gabriel had saved in autumn. In a ring around the garden, pear and apple trees bloomed. Cherry trees blossomed in a pink cloud. Soon they were eating salads of dandelion and violet leaves. Not long after, the strawberries ripened. Hannah picked the first lettuce and tender peapods. The river filled with trout, which she fried in fresh butter.

"This feast never ends," she told Gabriel, thinking sadly of the plantation folk, who spent these lovely days working from dawn to sunset just to keep the tobacco alive. Gabriel had told her what a labor it had been. Each day during the growing season they had to strip off the beetles that could destroy the entire plant.

Summer came in waves of shimmering heat, far more ferocious than winter's cold. Mosquitoes rose in clouds on the riverbank, their bites peppering her skin like a rash. Gabriel taught her to rub bear grease on her skin to keep them off. They put the furs away for the warm months. Mosquitoes whined through the night while they slept with the window wide open.

Cherries ripened, redder than any apple. She developed a bottomless craving for them, devouring fistfuls of the sweet fruit even though she knew she should be making preserves for the coming winter. She gorged on cherries until she was half sick.

—+—

Cherry-red, cherry-red, like a slut's own bed. May chanted the hateful words before slapping Hannah hard across her face. She grabbed her by the shoulders. "Will you *look* at me, you dolt?" May wore her wedding dress, but it was soiled and torn, hanging from her tall frame like a beggar's rags.

"Hannah!" Gabriel shook her awake. "Hannah, why do you weep? It was just a dream." He cradled her against him, stroking her hair, lulling her back to sleep.

In the morning, she awoke fuzzy-headed and faint. After getting dressed, she made the fire, cooked the corn mush. Gabriel brought in the goat's milk. When she took her first spoonful, the milk curdled on her tongue. Rushing out the door, she spewed over the porch railing.

"Hannah." Gabriel held her around the waist until she had stopped. "What is it?"

"Nothing." She wiped her mouth.

"Stay out of the sun today. Mayhap you will be better by nightfall."

When he left to go fishing, she sat on the porch with her head in her hands. She felt so weak, her stomach twisted in a knot. Was it the flux? she wondered. The flux that had killed Gabriel's father?

A while later, she felt well enough to brew a decoction of bruised mint leaves, which settled her stomach. As the day progressed, she found she could work again, as long as she stayed out of the sun during the hottest part of the day. The sickness visited her only in early morning. The taste of food, however, changed in her mouth. She grew ill at the sight and smell of raw meat. She could no longer stomach goat's milk.

With her one good dress eaten by moths, she wished she had wool to spin so that she could weave cloth for a new one. She had seen an old loom in the tobacco shed. One day, she sat at May's spinning wheel, gave it a turn. The whirling spokes sent her into a trance. May was the better spinster. She could spin as much in a day as Hannah could in three. May didn't cry as Hannah did now. She never had nightmares that left her weeping and wretched.

—+—

"You were troubled by your dreams again," Gabriel said in the morning, lying beside her. "Your body does change. You think I don't notice?" He pulled down the sheet, baring her flesh.

Hannah flushed. Her body had ripened like the harvest; her breasts were full and heavy. Gabriel traced her nipples, which had darkened from pale pink to brown. He stroked the faint line that ran from her navel to her quim. He kept touching her until she raised herself on her elbows and looked at her body, seeing it through his eyes. Though she had always been scrawny as a boy, she was turning into a woman at last, her body growing nearly as lush and abundant as her sister's had been. Rolling over on her belly, she cried.

"But why?" Gabriel stroked her back with a gentleness that undid her.

She wrapped her arms around his neck.

"You are not ill," he said. "You know that, Hannah." He looked into her eyes until she nodded. "You know what it is." Taking her hand, he unclenched her fingers one by one, then laid her flat palm on her belly.

Hannah shut her eyes. "I am afraid."

"Why? You are a physician's daughter, not some silly ignorant girl."

It killed my sister. She held her tongue.

"You are healthy and strong. You thrive in this place. Our child will thrive, too. I promise." Gabriel rocked her in his arms while the weeping racked her body.

⸺+⸺

The weather grew crisp and the leaves turned color. It was time, Gabriel told her, that he went to trade his furs for supplies. The sugar was gone, and they were nearly out of salt to preserve meat for winter.

"The big ship will be coming in," he said, tying the furs in bundles with rope made from their own hemp. "The pelts, I think, will fetch a good price. Enough to bring home sugar, salt, and nails. And maybe a surprise or two." He kissed her forehead.

"How long will you be gone?" The inside of her mouth tasted like sour goat's milk.

"Not long. A few nights, a week at most."

"A week?" she echoed. "But you are only going to Banham's Landing, are you not?"

"No, Hannah. Not Banham's Landing. I will have nothing to do with them. I am going to Anne Arundel Town."

"Let me come with you."

"Hannah, there is no room in the canoe for you and all the furs. And you know it is not safe for you to make such a journey in your condition."

"You think I am safe left here alone?" Her heart raced.

"Safer here than anywhere else. The dogs guard the place. I will leave you with my father's musket. And my knife." He unbuckled his belt with the sheathed knife and handed it to her. "You know how to use a blade, Hannah. Woe betide the fool who crosses your path."

How could he make light of this? "I wish I could go with you." She touched his face. "In Anne Arundel Town we could finally be married."

"You forget the banns." Pulling her against him, he stroked her hair as he always did when he wanted to soothe her.

"Once you are there," she pointed out, "you could ask them to post the banns, could you not? In two months, we might go together to be married."

"I said before that such a journey would put you in peril. I can ask the minister if he can spare a traveling parson to come our way and perform the ceremony. It might take many months, even years. This is how it is in the backwaters. Do you think we are the only couple to live together without blessing of the clergy? Some have three children or more before they get their minister. You know I love you, don't you, Hannah?"

"But it is a sin. You know it well. Our child shall be a bastard." Her own vehemence shocked her. Something inside her was changing—it was more than just the child growing in her womb.

"A sin, you say." His face darkened. "I have given you my entire love and devotion. God has blessed us with a child. How can you call that a sin?"

"It's wrong."

"You don't mean what you say." He spoke passionately. "When did you suddenly get to be so pious, Hannah?"

"We should have waited until we were married. I should have mourned her for a year. You *know* it's wrong. We don't even dare speak her name."

He stared in disbelief. "It was you who started it all. Do you forget?" Betrayal shot through his voice. "I was willing to leave you alone, but you said that you cared for me."

"Stop." Turning from him, she walked blindly toward the garden. She didn't need him to remind her that she had brought this on them both. She had betrayed her sister more deeply than Gabriel ever could. Hadn't she forced him into divulging May's infidelity? Because of her prying, he had made her swear the pact not to mention May. He and May hadn't chosen each other, but Hannah had chosen to covet her sister's widower and wheedle her way into his bed.

Foxglove grew at the garden gate, its poisonous flowers pink as a baby's face. Remembering May's first letter, she sank to her knees. *Most of all, I long to plant the Foxglove, for it reminds me of Home.* She had given May the seeds.

When she heard Gabriel's footsteps behind her, she expected him to take her arm, raise her to her feet. But he didn't. He was in a temper. She could tell from his unsteady breathing.

"God has been kind to us, Hannah. Is it not an even greater sin to be ungrateful for all our blessings?"

With some effort, she struggled to her feet. From the look on his face, she saw that her words had wounded him deeply.

"All our happiness," he said. "Would you call that a sin?"

His face blurred. Her stomach was tight and her head swam.

"Do you regret it?" he asked her. "Do you wish yourself back?"

"Gabriel, no." She wished she had something to hold on to, to keep herself on her feet. "No, I . . ."

"Hannah." He caught her before she could fall. "Are you not well?" He held her as if they had never quarreled. "Tell me it isn't one of your attacks."

"*No,*" she said in panic as her mouth filled with the taste of iron. Then it passed and her heartbeat returned to normal.

She must have frightened him, though. He was in tears.

"I shouldn't go," he said. "What if you have one of your fits while I am away?" He looked at her with such love.

She drew a deep breath. "Gabriel, you *must* go."

She hated to have him think of her as a weak and helpless woman. If she had a fit alone or with him standing by, it was all the same. When the fog came over her, she was beyond his reach and help. The trip was no frivolous mission, she reminded herself. Without sugar and salt, they might not survive the winter.

"Gabriel, I am sorry. Of course, I do not wish myself back. I just wish I could be your wife."

"I will do what I can to see if a minister can travel here."

❦

The day before he left, he taught her to load and shoot his hunting musket. "If you are armed, you are as strong as any man." He squeezed her shoulders. "You were never a coward, Hannah Powers. Surely you have no cause to be frightened now."

Early the next morning, she ignored her queasy stomach and cooked him a huge breakfast of fried eggs, bear sausages, and griddle cakes. She filled his satchel with cornbread and strips of dried venison. She walked with him to the dock.

"Don't stay away long. Not an hour longer than you must."

She stood on the riverbank waving until he disappeared from her sight.

—†—

Hand on the sheathed knife in her belt, she wandered to the creek. Her eyes were raw from the tears she hadn't let him see. She had let him paddle away, let him believe she was self-sufficient and brave. How she wished they could have gone to Anne Arundel Town to be married. The minister would have spoken the blessing over them, absolving them of their sin, putting everything right. But it was futile without the banns. And here she was, alone in the wilderness with a child in her belly.

In the eyes of the world, she was a fallen woman. In her old village, there had been ruined girls turned out of their homes, forsaken by their lovers, and left to bear their babies alone on the alms of the parish. How she had pitied those poor stupid creatures with their cowed faces and great lobbing bellies. Pariahs, they were, the butt of every joke, the mainstay of the vicar's harshest sermons. Some had even taken their lives rather than live with the shame. At least May had been clever enough to keep herself from getting pregnant until she was married. Hannah cursed herself for never asking her how she was able to keep her belly flat and her courses regular all those years.

The cold creek reflected a woeful face. How long she stood there gazing she never knew. But the face in the water changed. She saw May at the age of eleven, blue eyes full of mischief. "Come, Hannah, I've something to show you. A secret!"

Little Hannah raced after her. Cutting across the pasture where the big white bull ignored them, they reached the spring tumbling over mossy rocks. Steep green banks rose on either side, hiding them. This was their special place. First May had to make sure it was safe. Body tensed and stiff as a soldier's, she came to a rigid halt and looked around. "*Now!*" She pulled her dress and shift over her head and plunged into the moss-colored water. Hannah was right behind her. It took her longer to get her clothes off, for her hands were smaller and clumsier, but soon she tumbled into the stream like a puppy. Water-washed agates caressed her feet. Tendrils of waterweed wrapped around her ankles as if to bind her forever to this secret green place where she could never come to harm.

The shock of cold water sent her and May leaping, splashing each other until they were as slippery as seals. Arms uplifted, May danced in the water. She was already beautiful, her soft chest sprouting breasts. Each time they played this game, May had a different body, hair appearing where there had been smooth skin before. She let only Hannah see her like this, her sole witness to how her body was changing. Teeth chattering, May reclined in the streambed, submerged to her waist. Her new little breasts hardened, pink nubs stiff and puckered. Hannah looked down at her own flat body. Her sister had powers, that was certain.

"Look, I am a mermaid!" Keeping her legs and feet together, May wriggled them as if they formed a great finned tail. "Look, I am a water faery!" She rolled in the streambed, staining her skin with green moss. "I am a hungry witch that eats little girls!" Turning her fingers into claws, she chased Hannah over the slick stones, both of them shrieking and laughing, until May caught her around the waist and gently bit her nape like a mother cat. Later, after they had dressed, skin still tingling from the cold water, May let Hannah comb her hair.

"I am a princess," said May. Hannah believed her.

The vision in the water shifted. Her sister was pregnant, with a belly like a sack of cornmeal. Sitting down heavily beneath a naked birch tree, May began to sew. She was not making baby clothes but stitching her own shroud.

Enough. Hannah struck her fist into the water, sending out ripples. What kind of woman was she, staring into the water, her head filled with such darkness? If she kept this up, Gabriel would think she was mad.

✛

The following day, she pulled the cradle from under the bed. Something awful ran through her when her finger found the crack in the headboard. How could that crack even be there? Who or what could strike solid birchwood with enough force to make that crack? It would be unlucky to lay her baby in the dead child's broken cradle. The crack spelled out a curse. Shoving it back under the bed, she decided she would ask Gabriel to make a new one. He had all winter to work on it. A brand-new cradle lined with rabbit fur.

Hannah knit her hands over her belly. She wished she had paid greater attention to the lore of pregnancy and childbirth. In truth, it had never interested her as much as Father's herbal medicine and the art of surgery had. Looking back, she could only laugh at her ignorance, thinking such calamities befell other women and would never touch her. *Did you believe you could escape a woman's fate?*

Physician's daughter, indeed. She had been playing the fool, bedding Gabriel without once thinking of pregnancy. Perhaps because her body had always been so flat and compact, she secretly suspected she might be barren. Or was it because May had been able to get away with it for so many years? She had wanted so badly to be like her sister. Well, she had gotten her wish. May's lot was now hers.

What's done is done. It was time to stop acting like a child and face her condition. Opening May's trunk, she took out the infant clothes and their mother's old birthing gown, with its slit up the front to make it easier for the midwife. Just looking at it filled her with dread. May was the robust one, with the wide hips perfect for childbearing. Hannah considered her own narrow pelvis. How was she supposed to survive this if her sister had not? It appeared that May had not worn the birthing gown, for it was still ironed in Joan's precise pleats, a film of dust clinging to the age-yellowed linen. May had refused to put that thing on.

Hannah tried to estimate how far gone she was, but it was difficult without a calendar. She had suffered her first morning sickness when the cherries were ripe. Now the leaves had turned red and gold. It must be October. Was she five months along or six? She was already showing. Her dress had become so tight, she'd had to let out the seams. When she stood in the sunlight and looked at her shadow, her belly stood out like a hump. Because she was so thin, it looked unnatural, as though she were a child play-acting with a pillow tied around her waist. The belt with the knife Gabriel had given her merely accentuated the belly that protruded beneath it.

She hung up the infant clothes and birthing gown to air on a rope tied between two trees. They fluttered in the wind like a ghostly mother and her babies, trying to fly away from this lonely place.

19 Above Rubies

May and Gabriel

OCTOBER 5, 1689

"THIS IS ADELE." Cousin Nathan nodded to the barefoot girl.

"A pretty name," said May.

The girl couldn't seem to take her eyes off May's dress, even though it was crushed from the boat. May had not wanted to wear her wedding gown on the endless journey upriver, but Nathan had insisted. *When you step out of that boat, the servants must see that you are a lady. You must show them at once that you are their mistress.*

When May caught the girl's eye, Adele smiled before her shyness got the better of her and she stared at the ground.

"A mere slip of a girl, she is," Nathan whispered. "But superstitious like the rest of her kind. She would have us believe she is a voodoo sorceress. I tried my best to set her right, but she needs a mistress to instruct her properly and guide her with a firm hand." He paused to look over his shoulder at Gabriel, who fussed over his dogs.

"She is barefoot." May's eyes traveled from Adele's naked toes to the Irishmen's shod feet. "Did you provide no shoes for her? It is October, nigh on winter."

The girl glanced at her so timidly that May wanted to take her hand. She reminded her of Hannah. She looked to be the same age, and Adele's eyes betrayed a secret wisdom, as though she were privy to things forbidden to girls. May thought of how Hannah believed that she didn't know about her helping Father with his surgery. Well, this girl possessed some similar knowledge. Her gaze, though bashful, was not servile. Adele was not backward in the least.

"She has been given a pair of shoes, to be sure," Nathan replied. "But she refuses to wear them unless snow does cover the ground. No doubt she is accustomed to going barefoot on her native island."

"Pardon me, sir." James addressed his master. "Shall I carry Mistress Washbrook's trunk to the house?"

When May smiled at James, he grinned right back at her. Out of the corner of her eye, she saw Gabriel watching. Although he said little, the boy noticed everything, every look that passed between her and his father's servant.

"Yes, bring her things to the house," Nathan told him before returning his attention to May. "You must be hungry, my dear. Well, soon you shall taste Adele's island cookery." Again he lowered his voice. "Her former master was French." He wrinkled his nose. "She douses everything in cider, fruit, and broth."

May's eyes followed the girl darting up the path. She hoped the house would be a sight nicer than the Shipwright Inn in Anne Arundel Town, which had been little better than a barn, with straw and horse blankets instead of beds and linen. After the wedding dinner in the tavern below, Gabriel had joined her in the bedchamber, barely bigger than a cupboard. She had held him off, saying she was too weary from her ocean journey. He hadn't objected. The narrow space obliged them to cram together, his slender back pressed to hers. In the night she had awoken, thinking she was back home with Hannah. She rolled over, thinking to throw an arm around the body beside her, hug it for comfort, when the sour reek of the straw reminded her where she was. The day after the wedding, they had sailed in the shallop boat to the river mouth and camped on the banks. Luckily it had been a dry night. She had huddled in her blanket and stared at the stars. The fact that their wedding had not yet been consummated provided a small degree of comfort. The thing was not carved in stone and could still be annulled.

Nathan addressed his son. "Why do you trail behind, boy? Leave the dogs for a moment and tend to your bride."

May felt her face contort. Patrick, the servant with the wet hair, smirked. They were all watching her. Nothing she said or did would escape them. She wished she were bold enough to slap Patrick for his insolence.

"Gabriel," she called, holding out her hand. When she smiled, he blushed the way any other young man would. It wasn't his fault that their fathers had made the wrong match. Although she had known at first glance that she would never feel passion for him, she wanted to like him. There was no reason why they had to be enemies.

His hand in hers was hot and dry, which indicated a choleric humor, according to her father. She detected a sharp intelligence in his eyes. Although Gabriel was as quiet as Nathan was loud, she sensed that it would be too easy to underestimate him. How could she ever come to know him in a natural way with Nathan's merciless gaze bearing down on them both?

"What think you of our plantation, May?" the boy asked her. "I'll wager it is different from what you are used to."

"Indeed, this was not what I expected." She struggled not to appear too crestfallen at the sight of the harvested tobacco field, studded with tree stumps, where goats wandered loose, gnawing at weeds that grew amidst the harvest stubble. Planter's wife, indeed! Her dreams of a life of adventure seemed a mockery. Some adventure to wed a green boy and live at the back of nowhere under Cousin Nathan's thumb.

"What was your home like?" Gabriel sounded genuinely curious.

"Have you never been to England yourself?"

"I was born in Anne Arundel Town."

Poor child, she thought, remembering that dingy jumble of houses. He had never seen anything. "Ninety-nine yew trees grew in our churchyard."

He shook his head. "What sort of trees would they be?"

She laughed in disbelief. "You cannot tell me you have never seen a yew tree." When she looked off at the forest, the trees rose like giants, utterly foreign. Her heart thudded and her chest felt hollow. She was so far from everything she knew. She would never see a yew or a hawthorn bush again. She thought of the roses that grew in Father's garden, how she used to bury her face in their soft petals. What if she lived on this outpost so long that she never saw another rose, never smelled that fragrance again?

"I do hope you brought your spinning wheel." Nathan fell into pace with her. "Your father did write that you had quite a talent for spinning."

"Do you keep sheep, sir?" Sheep, at least, would remind her of home.

"I fear not, my dear," Nathan replied.

"They would not fare well in this place." Gabriel spoke with an authority that took her by surprise. "Easy prey for wolves."

"You have wolves?" May looked from Gabriel to his father.

"Aye." Gabriel laughed. For the first time since she had met him three days ago, he looked happy. "Bears and wild cats as well. I set traps for them in the forest."

The boy certainly showed enthusiasm for blood sport. May snatched her hand free from his grip and rubbed it. She turned to Nathan. "If you have no sheep, sir, then what am I to spin?" It did not look as though they grew flax.

"We barter wool from the neighbors. The Banhams do keep sheep. They have slaves enough to guard the flocks by night."

"Here is the house," Gabriel said.

With its rough unpainted walls, it looked like a cow byre. To relieve Father of his burden of providing for her, she should have run away, living as she pleased. Her own mistress. It began to overwhelm her. She could not imagine bedding this boy, calling him husband. She clenched her hands into fists so she wouldn't lose her nerve. The smell of roasting pork and apples wafted out. Adele appeared in the open doorway and flashed her a smile before disappearing back inside.

"Once you are settled here," Nathan said, "perhaps you might tutor Adele in the ways of English cookery. Have you a receipt book with you?"

"My mother's, sir."

They stopped in front of the porch. Nathan spoke to his son. "What is wrong with you? At least take her arm and lead her over the threshold."

May winced. His face dark red, Gabriel wrapped his fingers around her elbow and walked with her up the porch steps and into the house.

A trestle table was laid with wooden trenchers, spoons, and knives—no forks. *Hannah, these colonials are so primitive, they do not possess forks*, she imagined writing home. A carved chair loomed at the head of the table. On either side were two backless benches. Then she noticed the jug of wildflowers.

She looked at Adele. "Did you gather those flowers?"

The girl smiled and lowered her head. "For Madame." She lifted her face. "Madame is hungry?"

"Oh, yes." May's mouth watered at the smell of the cider-drenched pork.

"You will mark, I hope, the new furnishings." Nathan put one arm around May, the other around Gabriel, and turned them so that they faced the other end of the room. When May saw the two curtained beds, she swallowed. One was narrow, the other broad with a spray of fireweed draped on the counterpane. So she and Gabriel wouldn't have their own chamber, only the curtains to pull around them, Nathan three feet away.

Her father-in-law glanced at them both and laughed. "Do not look so perturbed, children. Adele has prepared a pallet for me in the attic for this night. You two shall have your privacy." He smiled at May. "The bed does have a real feather mattress. We bought it to celebrate your arrival."

He spoke with such sincerity that she felt herself warm to him. A proper bed must be an untold luxury here. It had probably cost them dearly.

"Sir, I thank you," she said. "You have gone to great lengths on my account." She caught a glimpse of Father in Nathan's eyes. If she could persevere in finding a way around his domineering side, she thought she could like him.

"Let us sit down," said Nathan. He guided her to the end of one bench and had Gabriel sit opposite. Then he took his place between them in the carved chair at the head of the table. The servants squeezed onto the remaining bench space. Studying their faces, May committed the Irishmen's names to memory. *James, Patrick, Finn, Jack, Michael, Peter, Tom.* Adele sat beside her. Nathan murmured something to Gabriel, who then fetched a massive Bible.

The smell of pork made May dizzy. She was so hungry, she thought she could eat the flowers in the jug. But it appeared Nathan wanted to give them a sermon before allowing them to eat. When he folded his hands, everyone else did the same. Following suit, May peeked at Gabriel, but his head was bowed so low, she couldn't see his face. Nathan spoke in a sonorous voice.

"Our Lord and Savior, we thank thee for bringing thy handmaid May safely to our household. Let the union of May and Gabriel be fortunate and blessed with many children."

She swallowed hard to keep herself from laughing, then shot a glance around the table. No one dared to smile. Squeezing her eyes shut, she clasped her hands tighter. Nathan opened the Bible and read.

> Who can find a virtuous woman? for the price is far above
> rubies.
> The heart of her husband doth safely trust in her, so that he
> shall have no need of spoil.
> She will do him good and not evil all the days of her life.
> She seeketh wool, and flax, and worketh willingly with her
> hands.
> She is like the merchants' ships; she bringeth her food from
> afar . . .

May ached with the effort to keep her hilarity inside. Had Father told Nathan nothing of her past? Did he really think she had come here as a virtuous bride for his son? Her hunger died as the Bible verses spelled out her new world. She had given herself to this boy, this household, bound for life. This wasn't like the sweet game she had played at home. She didn't get to play by her own rules anymore; the rules were handed down to her. She was the prize mare they had procured at great cost, and they expected her to perform. Prove that she was worth the tobacco they had paid for her. Outside it grew dark, but candle flames illuminated the page as Nathan went on reading.

Favour is deceitful, and beauty is vain: but a woman who
    feareth the Lord, she shall be praised.
Give her of the fruit of her hands; and let her own works
    praise her in the gates.

Only then did he allow them to eat.

She picked at her portion of pork, apples, and chard. She sipped cider from the same silver cup as her bridegroom.

"This cup did belong to my mother," Gabriel said as he passed it to her. It was engraved with roses. "She did bring it with her all the way from Wales." Yearning tinged his voice. He told her that his mother died long ago. On the ship May had heard that women did not survive easily on this shore. She wondered if Gabriel's mother had missed her home, missed the scent of roses. His Welsh mother certainly accounted for how dark and small he was. Joan used to tell stories about the Welsh, how during battle they could melt into their wooded mountains and disappear. They were furtive by nature. But, May wondered, might Gabriel have grown to be a different young man had his mother lived to stand between him and his hectoring father?

When the meal was finished, the servants bade them good night.

James bowed to Nathan. "I take my leave, sir." Then he bowed to May. "I wish you every happiness, mistress."

Flushing, she nodded.

"And to Master Gabriel," James said. But his eyes lingered on May before he followed the others out the door.

Adele, meanwhile, washed the trenchers and scoured the pots. Her rolled-up sleeves revealed satiny brown arms that flashed in the candlelight.

"Let me help you." May took a clout to dry.

"No, no, Madame." Adele snatched the clout away. "This is your wedding night."

May felt the sinking feeling again, her stomach filled with lead. What she had put off the two previous nights, she would finally have to address. She might as well get on with it—after all, it was nothing she hadn't done before. In fact, a good romp might give the poor boy something to smile about. Still, she felt ridiculous—a grown woman initiating a boy who seemed to care more for dogs and trapping wild beasts than for any civilized pursuit. Growing up out here, he had probably never had a sweetheart, never even kissed a girl before their wedding.

Nathan and Gabriel walked outside, presumably to perform their ablutions, leaving her and Adele alone. Finished with the trenchers and pots, Adele threw the dishwater over the porch railing and hung the wet clouts on the drying rail over the hearth. Then she stepped up to May.

"Can I bring Madame anything?"

"Adele," she said softly, "please call me May."

The girl smiled. "May." On her tongue, the name sounded so lilting. "Yes." The golden hearth light moved across the girl's face as she pointed to May's gown. "I help you unlace, May?"

"No." May indicated the ribbons that crisscrossed over her stomacher. "See, it does lace in front. I can do it myself." It was charming that the girl seemed to regard her as a fine lady who needed a maid to undress her. "But thank you, Adele. You are kind to think on it."

The girl still hung close, seemingly reluctant to leave the warmth and light of the house for the wind and darkness outside.

How desolate it must have been for her here—still a child and surrounded by all the men.

"It is good to have you here." May spoke as bashfully as the girl had when first addressing her. "Being the only other female."

Adele met her eye and nodded.

"I hope we might be friends. I know such a thing is not customary, but in truth I've never cared much about what people thought of me."

The girl's forehead wrinkled as she struggled to comprehend the rapid flow of words. May reminded herself that English was not Adele's native tongue.

"I need a friend here much more than I need a servant. Will you be my friend, Adele?"

Her solemn face burst into a smile.

"I have a sister your age."

The girl grinned and ducked her head.

Not knowing what else to say, May glanced around the room. "I imagine I must make ready for bed before the men return."

"I will go now," Adele said. "Good night to you, May."

"Good night to you," May replied, watching the girl slip out the door and into the darkness. Adele had not taken a candle or lantern. The moon shone in the window, a big fat globe to light her path.

Picking up the candle Adele had left on the table, May decided to explore the nooks and crannies while the men were still away. Something wound up in a great circle hung from a hook on the wall. Her fingers traced rawhide, then the stout leather grip. The thing was a bullwhip. But they kept no bull. *The Washbrooks are most eccentric*, she would write to her sister. *Indeed, you would call them savages.*

Adele had left her a pitcher of water for washing. Under the bed she found the chamber pot—a blessing, for she had no desire to brave the bushes by night. Afterward she laid out her nightdress on the bed, settled on the mattress, and drew the curtains shut. Undoing the laces, she removed her dress, stomacher, underskirts, corset, and shift, and changed into her nightgown. Joan and Hannah had embroidered roses around the neckline. They had trimmed the cuffs and hem with lace. The linen was so finely woven, it draped her body like silk. May discovered that she was trembling as though she *were* a frightened virgin. She folded her wedding dress and underthings inside her trunk, closed the lid, and then entered the bed again, drawing the curtains around her once more. What was taking the men so long?

She picked up the spray of fireweed. At least someone had thought of flowers. On their wedding day, Gabriel had been able to find only a few shriveled asters, purloined from a housewife's doorstep. Folding back the counterpane, she inserted herself between the linens, which smelled of fresh air and sunlight. Adele had been industrious. The feather mattress, she had to concede, was enticingly soft. She was so exhausted. Her muscles were cramped from the boat journey, the play-acting and strain. Drawing the bedclothes to her chin, she allowed herself to drift off to sleep.

She awoke to Nathan's heavy footsteps. "Remember what I told you," she heard him say to his son.

May rolled on her side and listened to Nathan climb the ladder to the attic. The bed frame shook when the trapdoor swung shut. She counted his footsteps on the floor above as he made his way to the pallet. *Please*, she prayed, *let him sleep as soundly as Father.*

Sitting up in bed, she pulled back the curtains. At first she couldn't see Gabriel. Had he turned to vapor like a ghost? Then, moving her eyes over the walls, she caught his shadow. His back to her, he hunched on one of the benches and tugged off his boots. He removed his doublet and breeches, but left on his long shirt. The hearth light shone through the thin fabric, revealing the slim outline of his torso and hips. Facing the dying fire, he stood as though rooted in the floor. When she least expected, tenderness welled up.

"Gabriel," she called, hoping that her voice was just loud

enough for him to hear but not his father upstairs. It wouldn't be so bad, she promised herself. She only had to let him remove her nightgown and stroke her naked flesh. The rest would happen naturally. Boys his age, even timid ones, were perpetually excitable and cock-led. His animal instincts would take command, causing him to thrust into her. She only had to open her legs to receive him. With an inexperienced boy, it would be over quickly enough. He might even swoon away from the pleasure of it.

His face was in shadow as he approached.

With the majesty of a queen, his bride perched on the bed. Her loose hair shone in the light of the single candle. The thin stuff of her nightgown revealed the shape of her breasts. She was the most beautiful creature he had ever seen, yet there was something intimidating about her that reminded him uncomfortably of his father.

"Can you not bring another candle?" she directed, like a mistress to a servant. Never mind that there was already a candle in the sconce near the bed. Did she think they were extravagant as the Banhams and had candles to waste? If they ran out halfway through winter, they would be forced to go to bed at sunset and sleep the long nights through.

Rather than giving her a lecture on economy, he headed for the opposite side of the bed and climbed in. His heart pounded so loudly, he wondered if she could hear. His father had instructed him in what to do. Father had left them alone together, and now they were to mate like cow and bull left in the same pen. He was obliged to mount his bride, service her. Except he wasn't a dumb animal. He wished Father had chosen a girl closer to his own age. He thought he would have done much better with a shy, quiet girl.

May found his hand in the darkness and began to stroke it, which sent shivers through him. No one had touched him so gently since before his mother had died. All thought of rutting cattle vanished as she caressed his fingers.

"Gabriel, I hope we can be friends," she said.

He clasped her hand in his. "I would be your friend, too." His voice came out childishly high. He cursed himself for sounding so young. Her father's letter had informed them that May was no maiden herself. Once she had been betrothed to an innkeeper's son, who had taken her virtue and then refused to marry her. His bride was full of the knowledge that he lacked.

She took his face in her hands and kissed him deeply. This was his first real kiss. At the wedding, he had pecked her cheek. He hadn't known what else to do. His insides ignited when her tongue parted his lips. She lit a fire inside him and he burned. This night he would become a man. In the morning, he knew he would walk and talk differently. Everyone would know just by looking at him. Even Father would be forced to respect him. Her breasts pressed against his chest, making him breathe hard into her mouth.

But when she ran her hands down his back, he stiffened. Would she feel the whip scars through the thin fabric of his nightshirt? At the thought of the whip, the fire deserted him. May seemed to sense this. She stopped kissing him and got up from the bed. So it was all over. He had disappointed her, and she was walking away. In the morning, Father would somehow find out he had failed.

What was she doing, crouched before the hearth? When she stood and turned, he saw she held a lit candle, one hand cupped around the flame. Stately and calm, she glided back to the bed.

"It is better that you should see me." She set the candle on the floor, then pulled her nightgown over her head and let it fall. The candle flames bathed her naked body in gold. Every inch of him ached for her. She was even lovelier when she smiled and curled up beside him.

He kissed her and gingerly embraced her. He didn't want to displease her by doing anything wrong. He stroked her warm back and her hair until she took his hands and pulled them to her breasts, heavy and full. Burying his head between them, he thought he would die right there.

"May, oh May." He no longer cared how green and untried he sounded. He was close to tears.

A laugh ripped out of her throat. He pulled back, looking at her in bewilderment. Was his eagerness so amusing? Had Father heard her laugh?

"Come," she said. "Let's have a look at you." She took hold of his nightshirt, about to whisk it over his head. She would see his lash scars, see how her laughter had made his member shrink. He flinched and pushed her hands away.

"What, so modest?"

For all her laughter, he saw no mirth in her eyes, only exasperation. With as much dignity as he could muster, he stood up.

"I think we can bide our time." He searched for words. "Until we come to care for each other."

"You do not care for me, then?" She laughed as though he were the biggest fool she had ever suffered. Taunting him for his lack of courage, she didn't cover herself but sprawled in her nakedness. "Do I not meet your satisfaction, Master Gabriel, or do you not care for women at all?" Her voice was loud and ugly. Father would hear every word. "Perhaps you prefer your dogs."

Any desire or liking he had for her deserted him that instant. When he looked at her bare flesh, he could think only of his dog Rufus humping one of the bitches—an image that left him nauseated. The tremulous candle flames threw her shape against the wall. Her shadow resembled a giantess with monstrous breasts that would smother him. If he could look at her with the glamoury eye, he would see right through her beauty to how cruel she was within. Little wonder her father had sent her across the ocean; it was no mystery why her former fiancé wouldn't have her. At any rate, May had never really wanted him. Hadn't she balked like a calf led to slaughter when Father had rushed them to the nuptials? She had consented to marry him only out of desperation. She was clutching at straws.

"In your heart, you do not desire me." His disgust emboldened him. "My father bullied us to the altar, but I won't let him bully me in our bed. If we consummate this, it must be done out of love." He spoke coldly, watching her face darken. "Not to serve my father's will."

What was she to do with this petulant, contrary boy? Did he expect her to beg him — as if she hadn't already humiliated herself on his account. Any other girl would have wept herself dry, but May could only laugh. The misgivings and resentment she had bottled inside her since Anne Arundel Town exploded. If there was one thing of which she had always been certain, it was her beauty, the power of her body to bring men to their knees. To think that her lawfully wedded husband was the first man who had ever denied her.

At breakfast the following day, she could hardly look at Gabriel. When Nathan wished her a good morning, she wanted to cover her face. What if he had been serious about his threat to send her back to her father? She imagined returning home in her shame, the unwanted bride. Of all the dishonor she had brought on her family, this would be the most unspeakable, the deepest insult. Hannah's future depended on hers. God willing, her sister would join her on this shore and make a more fortunate marriage than May had done. But if she were forced to return, it would spell disaster for her and Hannah both, sully Hannah's name along with her own. She could already hear the village folk saying that her husband had rejected her on account of her being such a whore. After Father's death, she and Hannah would be impoverished, friendless, and forsaken. The blame would hang on May's shoulders for the rest of her days.

After the servants left to do their chores, she heard Nathan upbraiding Gabriel within earshot of the house. "What is wrong with you? She is handsome. You could not ask for a comelier bride."

Gabriel's reply was so bitter that it cut her to the quick: "Handsome is as handsome does."

20
His Wild Things

Hannah
1693

WITH THE RIVER GUSHING and the wind sweeping through
the trees, Hannah didn't hear the approaching horse, only the
dogs' wild baying. Then she heard a man calling, "Is anyone
here?"

Her stomach turned to water. She had left the musket in the
house. The sheathed knife in her belt offered little solace. Keeping
herself hidden in the bushes, she crept forward in the direction of
the barking. She spotted the stranger near the clothesline, where
the infant clothes and the obscenely slit birthing gown flapped.
The sun caught the golden hair of a young gentleman astride a
glossy bay horse. In his polished riding boots and crisp holland
shirt, he looked clean and beautiful, like a creature out of a vision.
Behind him rode two other men—servants, judging from their
clothes. One carried a musket, the other a sword, and both had
shovels strapped to their backs. The fair-haired young man was
unarmed.

The dogs circled them in a snarling dance, spooking the
horses. The two older men reined in their mounts, lest they bolt,
but the young man stepped down from his mare and spoke softly
to the dogs until they quieted down and rushed to sniff his gloved
hands. Unlike Gabriel, his face was clean-shaven. A whole year
had passed since she had seen a shaven man—or indeed anyone
apart from her lover. In the fray of leaping dogs, he knelt to fuss

over Bessie, the pregnant red spaniel that was Hannah's favorite. He stroked her and scratched her neck until she fawned at his feet, exposing her belly with the twin rows of swollen teats. Something in his solicitude toward the pregnant bitch made Hannah drop her guard. Smoothing back her hair, she stepped out of her hiding place.

"Good day to you, sir. What is your business here?" The dogs gathered around her as she spoke.

The young man bowed. "I am Richard Banham, your neighbor."

Could it be true? Did Mr. Banham have a son? Then she remembered him telling her that his oldest boy was studying at Oxford.

"And would you be Mistress Powers? My father said his men took you here last year." He spoke with perfect courtesy, but heat spread over her face. How beggarly she must appear to him, with her threadbare dress stretched taut over her growing belly. She clasped her hands behind her back lest he notice she wore no ring.

"Yes, sir. I am Hannah Powers."

"Yesterday my men saw Gabriel Washbrook traveling downstream in his canoe. Forgive my intrusion, Mistress Powers, but out of neighborly concern, I thought it best to come by and inquire after your welfare."

"My welfare, sir?"

"You are alone, are you not?"

She wanted to hide from his scrutiny. "If I am, what concern is that of yours?"

"It seems most unfitting to leave a woman alone in the wilderness. Forgive me for speaking so bluntly, but especially a woman in your condition."

At once she lifted her head. She didn't want his pity. "He has only gone to Anne Arundel Town to trade furs for supplies. We are wanting sugar, salt, and nails."

The young Mr. Banham shook his head in disbelief. "To

leave an expectant mother on her own in the name of sugar, salt, and nails? What manner of man would do such a thing?"

She felt as though someone had struck her. "Again, sir, I would say our business is of no concern to you."

Richard Banham tilted his head to one side. "We could have given him sugar, salt, and even nails had he asked. He needn't have gone so far."

"He will not be beholden to your family, sir. He told me that your father plots to take our land." How easily the *our* had slipped from her throat. She reminded herself that only Gabriel had legal claim on the property.

"Is that what he told you?" The young man seemed to ponder this. "It is true he hasn't seen a harvest in three years. I do not think the Lord Baltimore will let him linger rent-free for a fourth year." He nodded in the direction of the river. "It appears he has allowed fallen logs and beaver dams to clog the waterway to make it difficult for rent collectors—or indeed neighbors—to travel here. That is why we have come on horseback."

Hannah could think of nothing to say.

"But I fear, Mistress Powers, I have come here for graver concerns than any outstanding accounts Mr. Washbrook might have." Richard Banham had the wide-open eyes of a man with nothing to hide. "I do not wish to alarm a woman in your condition, but I fear you may be in danger. The rumors have traveled slowly northward from Port Tobacco. They are allegations, as yet unproven in a court of law, but if there is even the slightest chance the rumors are based on truth, this is serious business."

Hannah folded her arms. "You speak in riddles, sir."

"I think perhaps it would be best if you sit down."

The only place to sit was either on the ground or on a rotting tree stump. She was certainly not going to invite these men inside the house. "I will remain standing, sir."

"Could you tell me what relation you are to Mr. Washbrook? My father said that his deceased wife, May, was your sister."

An icy dread gripped her. "How did your father hear of May's death? I came here last year believing her to be alive. Your father, though he had not seen her of late, seemed to be of the same opinion."

"That is why you should sit down." He untied his cloak from the back of his saddle and draped it over a tree stump. "If you please, Mistress Powers."

Feeling very odd, Hannah did as she was told.

"What explanation did Mr. Washbrook give you for your sister's death?"

"He said she died of the childbed fever. Her baby daughter lived only a week and is buried beside her."

Richard Banham nodded grimly. "Well, let me tell you of the rumors flying around about Mr. Washbrook. The rumors were started by Patrick Flynn, a former indentured servant at this plantation. He was arrested in Port Tobacco on charges of thievery, being in possession of a gold signet ring and a set of silver knives and spoons that rightfully belonged to Mr. Washbrook. Now, some masters are indulgent with their servants, it is true, but the circumstances were suspicious, especially as Mr. Flynn had no papers saying he was a free man who had fulfilled his indenture.

"He was arrested and charged with thievery and desertion. The Port Tobacco authorities had every intention of returning both him and the stolen goods to Mr. Washbrook. Flynn was put in the stocks and whipped. But when the magistrate questioned him, something very shocking emerged."

He paused. "Flynn freely admitted to stealing the ring and silver and to running away from his lawful master. But he swore on the Bible that he had fled for his life."

Young Banham hitched up his breeches and squatted on his heels so that his face was level with Hannah's. "He said that his master, Gabriel Washbrook, flew into a rage, accusing his wife, May, of committing adultery with at least two of the servants, and that Mr. Washbrook murdered her in a most cruel way while she was still weak from childbirth."

Hannah shook her head. "No. No, sir. That is a falsehood." Her voice broke.

The young man handed her his linen handkerchief. "I know this is disturbing, but I beg you to hear me out." He paced in front of her. "The magistrates wrote down Patrick Flynn's testimony. He claimed that Gabriel Washbrook stabbed his wife in the chest before dragging her into the forest and laying her face-down with her leg inside a bear trap to make it look like a natural death—that she had met a fatal accident while running away from her husband, if you will. But the story went that it happened less than a fortnight after her giving birth. What woman just out of childbed would flee her husband? Unless she had good reason."

Still shaking her head, Hannah pressed her fingers to her temples to quiet the roar in her brain. *Don't go crossing the creek, Hannah.* He had always warned her to stay away from the bear traps. May accused of committing adultery with the servants. Yes, she could have done just that, as she had done all her life, her beautiful faithless sister. Gabriel had admitted she was untrue. Had he, then, stabbed her in a rage? Hannah touched the sheathed knife in her belt.

"You are overwhelmed, I am sure," Mr. Banham said.

Banham, is he here? She remembered Gabriel saying that on the day she had arrived, his hand gripping the knife handle. And his nightmares during her first week in his house—were they proof of a guilty conscience?

"Never fear, Mistress Powers. I offer you refuge. My horse is strong enough to carry two. I will bring you to my parents' house."

What would Gabriel do if he returned to find her gone? She remembered his gentle hands tracing her body. His hands stitching mittens for her. Those weren't the hands of a murdering man. How could anyone malign him like this?

"What charges stand against Mr. Washbrook?" she asked. "You said the allegations of murder stem from the testimony of a thief." She took a breath, building up her courage. "Vile slander spread by a runaway servant caught with stolen goods. Could he not have told these lies out of malice?"

Richard Banham bowed his head. "The fact that the suspicions stem from the words of a thief is the weakest part of the argument. Indeed, after Mr. Flynn's testimony was recorded, he broke gaol and has not been seen since. Without a witness to stand trial, evidence against Mr. Washbrook is slim at best. However, as his neighbor, I am duly concerned, for if there is any chance that he is a murderer, he must be brought to justice, for he endangers us all." He looked straight into Hannah's eyes. "Especially you, Mistress Powers."

"Do you intend to arrest him yourself? You have no authority."

"Granted, that is true. However, I have come with two witnesses, and I am a lawyer, having recently completed my education at Oxford."

Hannah wished she had the strength of mind to tell him that her father had gone to Oxford, that once she had been an accomplished, uncommonly educated girl and not just Gabriel Washbrook's pregnant mistress.

"Forgive me for asking," he said, "but I do believe your sister is buried on this property."

"She is."

"Can you show us where?"

Grateful for an excuse to get off the tree stump, she led him to the three graves by the river.

"My sister's is the middle one." The autumn crocuses she had planted the previous year bloomed delicate purple.

Mr. Banham's two companions unstrapped the shovels from their backs.

"We would ask your permission to exhume the remains of May Washbrook," Richard Banham said, for once not meeting her eyes. "If there is any truth in the story, it will be revealed by the corpse. If the leg is shattered or fractured, then Patrick Flynn's story about the bear trap will be proven true."

She thought the blood would drain from her body. "Surely you cannot do this."

"Mistress Powers, in the name of truth and justice, we must." Something about his highhanded tone told her that he had been condescending to her all along, making a great show of spreading his cloak on the tree stump. But if she scraped away the veneer of good manners, surely he held nothing for her but pity and contempt. A man of his station would look at her uncovered hair, shabby dress, and pregnant belly and see her as Gabriel Washbrook's whore. And if he was such an upright man of the law, what charges might he press on her if she allowed him to take her to his plantation, where she would be wholly under his power? Having a child out of wedlock was a punishable offense—she was guilty of both fornication and bastardy. Once the baby was out of her body, he could have her put in the stocks and whipped until her dress was in ribbons, her shameful flesh exposed.

Hannah pushed herself between the men and her sister's grave. "I forbid it." Abandoning all dignity, she threw herself on the grassy mound. "I do not give you leave to defile my sister's resting place."

Richard Banham let out his breath. "Not even in the name of your own safety? What if it is true that you live alone on this outpost with a . . . a base murderer?"

"If you are so concerned, why did you not come here earlier? Why did your father not tell me this last year?"

"The rumors have only reached us of late."

"*Rumors*," she said pointedly. She had never spoken out like this to a man so far above her. It was Gabriel's doing, Gabriel telling her he would have no master but God. The man's fancy clothes were mere outer trappings. If she stripped them off, he would be no different from any other man.

She looked straight into Richard Banham's eyes. "If you are as honorable as you say you are, you will come back when Mr. Washbrook is here and tell him these things to his face."

For a moment it looked as though speech had deserted him.

"If you bid me to leave, Mistress Powers, I must obey, but I do so with great reluctance. Think well on my words. Do you not put yourself in peril?"

Her words came out in a fervent rush. "Gabriel Washbrook is the kindest, gentlest man I have ever known. He could harm no one."

"So kind and gentle that he leaves you alone in the wilderness?" Banham shook his head.

Hannah clutched the soft tufts of grass that covered May's grave. "I have given you my last word."

"I see I cannot change your mind." He looked away from her, toward the rushing water. "But should you need to flee this place, follow the river through the forest. On foot it might take you a day's steady walking. We are hospitable people and welcome visitors. We turn no one away." At that, he gestured to his men and led them back to their horses. She remained on the grave until the forest swallowed them.

—+—

The night after Richard Banham's visit, the skies clouded over and burst. Rain lashed the window. A chill penetrated the chinks in the walls. Furs drawn over her, Hannah huddled in bed and prayed that Gabriel had found shelter. *Let him come safely home to me.* But the more she prayed, the more confused she became. Curling her body tight as a fern frond, arms and knees drawn around her belly, she wondered if she had made a brave stand that day, or if she had just been a fool. Would Richard Banham ride fifteen miles through the forest merely to slander Gabriel? Joan used to say that the devil could take many forms and handsome guises. But would Bessie fawn at the devil's feet? Dogs were wiser than humans in sensing good or evil in a person.

Granted, Richard Banham was no devil, but surely his words against Gabriel were touched and tainted by his father's designs on Gabriel's land. Still, Banham's words kept churning in her head. And his desire to open May's grave and see whether her corpse bore evidence of murder. What if she had permitted him?

Hannah buried her face in the furs. Why had Gabriel made her swear a pact not to speak her sister's name? *Did your own husband kill you, May? Am I carrying your murderer's child?*

——+——

When she went to fetch water the next morning, the creek seemed to whisper in her sister's voice, urging her to be bold, hike up her skirts, charge through the water and into the forest beyond where Gabriel had forbidden her to go. The notion came to her that the truth would be revealed only if she could summon the courage to cross to the other side.

The creek was swollen with rain, which made her way difficult, but she waded through, then clambered up the steep muddy bank. Once she entered the forest, she was dumbstruck. Pine, birch, oak, and ash rose over one hundred feet in the sky, their trunks so massive that they would break Gabriel's ax. She recalled the story he had told her of how the Indians took months to fell a single tree, first starting a slow fire, which burned in a ring around the base of the trunk.

The woods around the house and garden were thinned out, with saplings and underbrush growing among the dead stumps, but here the trees were tall and straight, with no low-hanging branches. A man might ride through the forest on a tall horse without having to duck his head.

Heart beating fast, she moved over the mossy ground. Gabriel's traps could be anywhere. She remembered when he had let her hold the bear trap. How could she forget those iron teeth? If she stepped in one, it would snap her leg in half, and then she would die a slow death of bleeding.

Bounding footsteps rocked the ground. She cried out, only to see Bessie charging toward her. The dog barked and jumped on her, muddying her skirt. Hannah bent down to pet her. Then she gathered herself together and resolutely set off, not knowing what she hoped to find. Despite her fears, the forest filled her with peace. Walking in the shadows of those massive trees purified her, wiping away the stain Richard Banham had left. She arched her neck to view the fluttering canopy of gold and red leaves far above her head. Feeling like a child again, she danced in a circle, Bessie nipping at her heels. Gabriel had carved his name on several of the smooth beech trunks, as if to mark these woods as his domain, the vast chamber reserved for him and his wild things.

Why had he excluded her from this beautiful place? Well, she wouldn't allow him to forbid her anymore. Echoing birdcalls drew her in deeper. Bessie sprinted off ahead, then looked back and wagged her tail, inviting her to follow. Hannah sprinted after her, filling her lungs with the pure air.

Bessie led her a few hundred yards, then stopped and barked, her whole body quivering. Hannah stroked the dog's head. "What is it?"

Then she caught the reek of feces, old blood, and rotting flesh. Flies swarmed through the air, a few landing on her face. She slapped them away. She and Bessie stood on the lip of a shallow ravine. On the bottom lay the trap, which held a severed animal paw in its steel jaws. The animal had gnawed through its leg to free itself. A trail of congealed blood led to a dead lynx. She wondered how long it had lain there. Flies gorged themselves on the decay. A few crows picked at the bloody stump.

Hannah attempted to walk away when her knees buckled, pitching her face-first on the ground. She pulled herself up and vomited, thinking of the furs Gabriel had taken to trade, the furs that warmed her on cold nights. If Gabriel were here, he would not be retching. He would be in his element—this was what he *did*. He would calmly walk down the ravine, take out his skinning knife, and go to work. He would take the pelt and leave the rotting flesh behind for the crows and wolverines. After cleaning the blood off the fur and tanning the hide, he would present it to her. "Spotted lynx," he would say, inviting her to stroke it, and she would tell him how beautiful it was. She would close her eyes and rub her cheek against it.

Bessie shoved her muzzle in Hannah's face, whining softly. Hannah wiped her mouth on her fist, then hugged the dog.

"Come on, girl," she said. Bessie led her back.

198

21 Cold Clay

May and Gabriel
November 15, 1689

NOVEMBER WAS THE MONTH of slaughter. Adele lit a bonfire outdoors, over which a cauldron of water seethed. Warming her hands in the rising steam, May watched Peter and Jack hold a struggling pig while James cut its throat. Blood laced James's shirt, spattered his face and bright hair. The squealing was frightful, yet she would not allow herself to look away. She could no longer live in ignorance of such things. At home Joan had kept a swine in the garden, fattening it over the summer, then butchering it in autumn. Joan had done it herself, letting May spin and stitch like a lady, sparing her the bloody work. But now Adele was going to teach her how to cut a pig apart. If Nathan ever granted Adele her freedom, the task would fall on May as mistress of the house.

Releasing the animal into the dark red pool pouring from its gash, James stood up, red blade in hand. Blood ran down his face. May took the clout from her waistband.

"Here." She handed him the clout and stood beside him while he wiped himself clean.

"I thank you, mistress."

She had learned that his given name was Seamus. The Irishmen had names in their own language; Nathan had given English names to all except Finn, James's younger brother. Patrick was Padraig, Jack was Sean, Tom was Tomas, Peter was Peadar, Michael's name in his own tongue was pronounced *Mee-hal*. Nathan had wanted to change Finn's name to Fred, but no one would call him that. On the last warm day of that year, May had by chance seen young Finn swimming naked in the river. How he had blushed before diving deep beneath the water to hide his embarrassment. Later she had teased him, saying they called him Finn on account of his graceful swimming.

While she, Adele, and the Irishmen were busy with the pig slaughter, Gabriel was off with his dogs, checking his traps. May thought he was shirking his duties, but James said it was better to have him take his dogs far away so they wouldn't go into a frenzy over the fresh meat. Nathan lay in bed, weak from ague. Last night May had laid compresses on him and made him drink a decoction of willow bark.

Patrick and Finn tied the stuck pig's hind legs together and hung the animal upside down on a pole stretched between two trees. Finn placed a bucket beneath the pig to catch the remaining blood.

Adele pointed to another pig, which had been hanging upside down for over an hour. "This one, he is ready. Bring him to the fire."

Tom and Michael each took one end of the pole, carried the pig to the cauldron, and plunged it into the boiling water. After a few minutes, they pulled it out and hung it back up.

Adele touched her arm. "You watch, May. I will teach you." The girl worked over the hide with rosin to strip off the hair. Then she took the long knife from James. "Fetch me the bowl," she told May.

When May returned with the wooden bowl and set it beneath the pig, Adele slit the animal's belly. May's hands twitched as the intestines tumbled out in a slimy mass. The smell was enough to make her retch.

"Later we wash them," Adele said, "for to make the *saucisse*." Bent over the knot of guts, she stirred them with a long stick. Her face was intent, as though she saw something in that revolting mess that no one else could. May wondered if she could read auguries.

"Please bring me another bowl," Adele said at last.

May fetched it. Adele cut out the pig's heart, kidneys, liver, and lungs. "We will bake them in pie with *épices* and onions," Adele said, as calmly as if she were discussing the weather, even though she held the raw heart in her palm. Joan would dearly admire this girl. *And you must become more like Adele,* Joan would tell her, *if you are to survive in this place.*

Adele dangled the pig's bladder in her hand. "On my island, the children they play with this. They blow it up with air." She blew into her cheeks, making them balloon. Her expression was so comical, May had to laugh.

She watched Adele cut away the best joints of meat for roasting that night. May brought another bowl for the scrap meat and the pig's head, which Patrick had sawed off. May cut off the tail and front feet. Finally Adele skinned the animal. The sides of pork went into the barrel of brine the men brought. The skin was left for Gabriel to tan.

"No one goes hungry in winter," Adele said. "This night we cook a big feast. Later we will take some pork from the barrel and hang it in the chimney for to smoke. Then we will have bacon." Fifteen years old, she spoke with the pride of an efficient housewife. May doubted that she herself would ever be as competent. She added wood to the fire before they plunged the next pig into the boiling water. There were still five more pigs to dress.

When they raised the swine out of the cauldron and hung it up, Adele handed May the rosin to strip off the hairs. "This time you try. I will go now to the creek for to wash out these." She picked up the bowl of intestines.

"Wait," May said. "I have heard that you can work magic." She smoothed her hands over her apron to hide her trepidation.

Adele lowered her voice. "Master Washbrook says if I talk of such things, I will get the whip."

"Oh, Adele." May touched her shoulder. "I would never betray you, I swear. My father had a servant named Joan. She was like a mother to me. In faith, I think you are like her. She was wise, and you are wise, too. She could read the future from a pack of cards." May took her clout and wiped the pig's blood from Adele's face. "I do wish to know my future." She laughed. "To know if I *have* a future."

Adele looked closely at May. "You are not happy here." Eyes shining with sympathy, she took May's hand. If she were any other girl, May thought she would have burst into tears and allowed Adele to comfort her. But she didn't cry, just hung her head. A few yards away the Irishmen sang to drown out the death squeals of another pig. They would not hear her confession.

"He does not care for me, Adele." Gabriel had never forgiven her for the way she had laughed at him on their first conjugal night. Loneliness devoured her. She had come to this shore with a head full of dreams of her new life, and here she was, wed to a boy who hated her. "Mayhap you will think me mad or wicked or both, but pray, can you not charm Master Gabriel into loving me? To make us care for one another as we should?" There was a tremor in her voice, but she chased it away with a hollow laugh.

Adele flashed her a warning look, eyes darting off to the side. May turned to see Nathan leaning on his walking stick. His face was drawn, his skin yellow with ague.

"Sir." The rosin fell from May's hand. "You do not look well. Should you not be abed?" How much had he overheard?

"I go to the creek." Adele snatched the bowl of intestines and hurried away.

May kneaded her bloodstained clout.

"I thought the air would do me good," said Nathan. "But I return now to the house. I only ask that you walk with me, May." He looked troubled. "I fear you and I must speak in private."

The moment has come. He would inform her that he had no choice but to send her back—a parcel of rejected goods. Father's ashen face paraded before her. Hannah's uncomprehending tears. *You've let us down, May.* She struggled to think what she would tell them, how she could beg their forgiveness for her ultimate failure. The smell of fresh meat and offal made her queasy. Everything reeked of death. But when Nathan held out his arm, she took it. He looked so weak, as though his walking stick could barely keep him upright.

"Let us go slowly, sir," she told him. "Take small steps. We may rest as often as you wish."

"Young Adele spoke the truth," he said. "You do look dreadfully unhappy. I fear that our narrow world has disappointed you."

May kept her eyes on the path in front of them. "We must all bear the travails God gives us, sir."

"I fear my son gives you no affection."

She wanted to dart into the bushes so he wouldn't see her face. After her first night with Gabriel, Nathan had returned to his own bed, only a yard away from their marriage bed. Had he spent the past five weeks listening with pricked ears for amorous rustlings behind the closed curtains?

To Nathan, she said, "The boy is yet young. Mayhap in time he will grow used to me."

Nathan clutched her arm. "May I tell you something, dear, that I have told no other living soul?"

"I am honored, sir, that you think me worthy of such a confidence." Her heart thudded as the premonition fell over her like a net. Deep down, she wanted to beg him not to tell her.

"Last night in my fever," he said, "I did dream of cold clay. You know, I think, what that portends."

"Pray do not speak of such things, sir. May God grant you many more years."

"In faith, none of us know how many days we have upon this earth." He spoke without self-pity. "This plantation may not be much, a mere smallholding compared to the Banhams' vast estate, but my dearest wish is that it should not die with me. None of the Washbrooks in England ever owned an acre. You may think I am too proud, but how I wish my descendants might transform this wilderness into a bower of abundance. I cannot entrust Gabriel to carry on for me when I am gone. The boy is too dreamy. At least I may thank God that my son has a strong wife." He cast her a rueful smile.

"Sir, you flatter me. I fear I am not as strong as you think."

"You are," he insisted. "I saw it from our first meeting. When your temper rises, steel shines in your eyes. I think you were descended from some barbaric warrior queen."

In spite of herself, May laughed.

"Forgive me," he said, "for speaking so plainly, but you would make me the happiest man on earth if you gave me a grandchild before I died."

"We must be patient. Gabriel needs more time."

"*Forget* Gabriel." Nathan's voice chilled her.

May stumbled over a tree root. "What do you say, sir?"

"You are a handsome woman. Any young man would be overjoyed to receive your favor."

"Sir . . ."

"Your father did write to me in all honesty of your history ere you came to join us here."

She pulled her arm away from him. "Sir, do you seek to shame me?"

Clinging to his walking stick to keep his balance, he managed to smile. "On the contrary, that is why I chose you. Better your blood should run hot than cold like my son's."

He looked so feeble that May took his arm again. "I do not understand."

"Sometimes I believe that Gabriel is no son of mine, but a changeling."

"You treat him with no excess of kindness, sir."

"You think me harsh?" He looked unbearably sad. "I mean well for the boy, I do. He is so like his late mother. Clever as a fox, but willful and stubborn, and a loner at heart. Someone has to toughen him up, prepare him to be master when I am gone. Yet when I try to guide him, he defies me at every turn."

They had reached the porch steps. She helped Nathan clamber up, then opened the door for him. "Get you straight to bed."

Instead he sat in his carved chair at the head of the table. "Would you bring me my Bible, dear?"

She brought it to him. "Anon I must return and help Adele before the meat rots."

"And beg her to work witchcraft over the severed pig's head?" Before she could walk away, he clasped her hand. "Pray sit with me. Just for a while."

Letting out her breath, she sat.

"Speak the truth to me, dear, and I will speak the truth to you. I have seen looks pass between you and James."

"Sir." She broke into a sweat, scalp itching beneath her linen cap. Her bodice, laced too tightly, chafed against her breasts.

"He is so young and handsome." Nathan's voice dwindled to a whisper. "How could you not desire him?" Head bowed over the Bible, he looked plaintive and vulnerable, no longer the master of them all but a soul snared, in thrall to a desire that he could neither confess nor banish. May had not failed to notice the way he gazed at James, never quite able to mask his longing. She could not see his eyes, only his tears splashing down on the calfskin Bible cover. Raising her hand, she stroked the back of his neck.

"Bless you," he said. "You are a dear child."

They sat a while in silence. It was a curious comfort that she and her father-in-law were both impure, each in their own way. Their secrets united them.

At last Nathan looked up from the Bible. "James has not had a woman in three years. I know he desires you."

May covered her face. "How can you speak to me like that?"

"I speak the truth," he said gently. He took her hands and pulled them away from her face. "If this household is to endure beyond my lifetime, we need an heir. Even if my son one day learns to use his pintle, I doubt that he can father children. Your father is a physician. You must have learned that a woman cannot conceive unless the man brings her to the heights of pleasure."

"Sir." If Nathan hadn't been holding her hands, she would have bolted out the door.

"Have other men before him moved you to ecstasy?"

She looked away. "What of it?"

"What I am telling you is that I shall welcome as my true and legal heir any child born of your body. I have already written as much in my will. If you gave me a grandson and heir sired by James, I would die a happy man." He pressed her hands between his own.

Blood rushed inside her head. When she closed her eyes, she saw stars. "You give me leave to betray your son and commit adultery?" Her voice hardened. "You would have me ruined. I have seen what men do to adulteresses here."

"May, no." Nathan's eyes filled with tears. "Anyone who wished to dishonor you would have to kill me first. I swear it in God's name." He laid his palm flat on the Bible. "I do solemnly swear that any child born of your body shall be my legal heir, as already written in my will, and I shall see to it that none trouble you with accusations of uncleanness."

After a long pause, she asked him, "What is Gabriel to make of this?"

"I think, in truth, he would find it a relief to be troubled by this business no longer." She saw a glint of fatherly compassion in his eyes. "The boy is happiest when left alone to wander the woods with his dogs."

May nodded. She could already imagine Gabriel's secret happiness in this reprieve of duty. Still, one thing troubled her. "Sir, forgive me, but what should happen when you are no longer here to enforce your will?"

Nathan looked at her not as a father-in-law to his son's wife, but as an equal, as though she were a man in his eyes. With a rush of emotion, she remembered that it was the same look Father had always given Hannah. "When I am gone," he said, "you will be mistress here and mother of the heir."

—+—

The following day, in the shed behind the tobacco barn, Gabriel worked the two-handled knife over the pigskin pegged over the fleshing beam. The beam was fixed at an angle, allowing Gabriel to press his body weight against the skin to keep it taut as he scraped away fat and membrane.

In one corner was a barrel filled with a mixture of creek water and pounded pig brains, which he would use to tan the hides he wanted soft and supple. These skins needed to be soaked for just a few days. A barrel of mashed oak bark and water occupied another corner. That was for treating the hides he wanted tough and waterproof for shoemaking. He would soak the chosen hides in the bark water for half a year, eventually moving the barrel into the pantry and placing it at the rear of the chimney so it wouldn't freeze.

Pigskin, pig fat, pig brains. The smell was overpowering. Outside in the fresh air and sunlight, the Irishmen split logs. But they dropped their hatchets and stood to attention when May came with the basket of midday victuals. Gabriel watched the manservants gather around her, getting as close to her as they dared, while she passed out the cornbread. Even when he reminded himself that he didn't care for her, Gabriel tightened his grip on the fleshing knife at the sight of James gawking at her with undisguised lust shining on his face. Gabriel waited for May to encourage him, proving how rotten she was beneath her pretty mask. Instead she averted her eyes and veered away from James as though she had some superstitious dread of him. Clutching her basket, she made for the tanning shed, then stopped short when the stench hit her face.

"Aye, it stinks," Gabriel told her shortly. "You can leave the basket out there."

He expected her to pull a proud face, but she simply nodded and set the basket down.

"Cornbread and pig's trotters this day." She looked troubled and oppressed.

"Are you feeling poorly?" He put aside the fleshing knife.

She shook her head. Something seemed to be poised on her tongue, yet she said nothing. The wind blew her hair across her lips until she tucked the loose strand back into her housewife's cap. Although she had arrived on this shore with a lady's smooth white hands, her fingers were now as red and cracked as any servant's.

"There's a jar of bear grease in the pantry," he said. "It will soften your hands."

"Bear grease?" She looked at him inquisitively. "You know this from tanning hides?"

He couldn't decide whether she was mocking him or not. Before he could take up the knife and start scraping again, she stepped forward, eyes lowered.

"Gabriel, if ever I offended you, I beg your pardon." Her face was scarlet.

He didn't know what to say. He could hardly go to her, stinking as he was.

From the house, Adele called for her. When May hurried off, her flying skirts revealed her worn-down shoes.

⁘

In the cold dawn, Gabriel awoke to whimpering. Fingers caught in his hair. She breathed in ragged gulps as though something were chasing her. She moaned a name. Hannah.

He laid his hand on her arm and squeezed. "It is only a dream."

Her eyes opened. She looked like a wild thing, mouth gaping, fingers still wound in his hair. Before he could stop himself, he stroked her tousled head. May's hair was even more beautiful than the rest of her, the russet of strong India tea. He waited for her to laugh at him, but she caught his hand and kissed it.

Had the moment come? Had she started caring for him? He kissed her mouth and she kissed him back. She clung to him. Her fingers feathered over his belly, slowly working downward. It happened then, that November morning. She opened her body, took him inside her. He buried his head in her hair as his body exploded. His tears filled her hair and she didn't laugh.

⁘

At breakfast, Gabriel couldn't take his eyes off her, couldn't hide his happiness. Her skin glowed, pink and fresh. Her eyes shone brighter than he had ever seen them. Let everyone stare at them both. Let them see how their lovemaking had made her radiant.

Father took him aside, gave him a swig of rum and a rough hug. "A man now, aren't you, my son?"

22 Quiet as Bones

Hannah
1693

ECSTATIC BARKING DREW Hannah out of the house. Feet flying, she dashed down the path. When she reached the dock, she was winded. Gabriel climbed out of the canoe, only to be engulfed by the dogs. Lost among the furry bodies, he did not look up to see her. She tried to observe him with clear, dispassionate eyes. Did he look like a guilty man?

Breaking loose from the dogs, Gabriel lifted a bundle from the canoe. Then he caught sight of her. "Hannah!" His voice was full of happiness.

He rushed forward, the dogs rushing with him. Soon she was wrapped up in the tumult, the dogs tumbling around her, Bessie tugging at her skirt. Gabriel set down the bundle and embraced her as though he had been gone a year.

"I came back with as much speed as I could. Hannah, what is it? You look so sad." He broke off to scold the dogs for trying to paw open the bundle. "Did something happen while I was away?"

"I did not like being here alone."

He kissed her. "Well, now I'm back. And I've a surprise for you." His arm around her waist, he led her into the house, then laid the bundle on the table. She had never seen him so excited.

"Go on and open it, dear. Pretend it's Christmas."

She untied the string, then pulled away the sacking to reveal two hard cones of sugar wrapped in stiff paper. If she had anyone to write letters to, the paper itself would have been a prize. There was a tin box of salt, a wooden box of nails, and a bolt of sprigged Indian cotton of pale green with a darker green pattern.

She fingered the exotic cloth. "This is an extravagance. It must have cost you many furs."

He shrugged. "Someone ordered it off the ship but couldn't pay for it. Too behind on his debts, I'll wager. I bargained hard and got a good price." He touched her hair. "The colors do suit you. Those spoiled girls down the river would be jealous if they saw you in that."

At the mention of the Banham girls, her heart thudded sickly.

"There's something else." He clasped her hands and sat with her on the bench. "Close your eyes."

"What is this? Do you play games with me?" When she closed her eyes, he placed something in her palm.

"Open your eyes."

Cupped in her hand was a gold ring set with a ruby and a seed pearl.

"Gabriel." Tears filled her eyes. "*How* did you find this?"

He silenced her with a kiss, then placed it on the ring finger of her left hand. "Now we are betrothed, my love, right and proper." He knelt on the floor and kissed both her hands. "I treasure you more than anything."

Had anyone ever looked at her the way he did? She was speechless, face hot and flushed.

He touched her wet cheek. "You still cry. Did you miss me so much?"

She clung to him. He rocked her in his arms.

"I am sorry I left you alone. But you like the ring, don't you?"

"It is the most beautiful thing I have ever seen. The most beautiful thing." She kissed him feverishly. But something in her manner must have betrayed her, something too frantic in her movements.

"What happened while I was away?"

"Nothing," she breathed. "Nothing happened."

He cocked his head. "Do you speak the truth?"

She embraced him again. The only way she could hide her face from him was by kissing him with such passion that all he could do was kiss her back. "I *missed* you." She licked his clavicle, tasting his flesh. The old hunger filled her. Taking his hand, she led him to bed. If she let him inflame her, it would drive the doubts away. He was careful not to hurt her. He held her alongside him and entered her from behind so that there was no weight on her belly. He cupped her breasts, which had grown so abundant they spilled out of his hands. She cried out her love for him, her legs knifing the bedclothes. His breath was hot on her nape, his face buried in her hair.

"There are no two people more fortunate than we are," he said.

She began to cry uncontrollably. He pulled her around to face him.

"*Tell* me what is wrong." There was an edge of exasperation in his voice. "Why must you torment the both of us by keeping silent?"

"It is only my condition."

"Hannah, you make a poor liar. It grieves me to think you could ever lie to me."

"To tell the truth, I must break our pact."

Drawing his hands away from her, he took a breath, then sat up cross-legged on the bed, his nakedness completely uncovered, as though he were Adam in the Garden and knew no shame. "Break our pact? What do you mean?"

"I must speak my sister's name."

He raised his hands to his eyes. "Why?"

Pushing her body upright, she groped for her shift and threw it over her neck. She drew her shawl tightly around her shoulders. The things she had to tell him could not be said while she was naked. She moved away from the bed.

"While you were gone, Mr. Banham paid a visit. The young Mr. Richard Banham."

"Banham. I should have guessed." He turned his back to her and dressed. "I reckon they saw me when I went past their landing. Such cowards they are, coming to call on you while I was away. Do they intend to petition the Lord Baltimore to take over my leasehold?"

Hannah sank down on the bench, faint with relief. There was no guilt in his voice, only anger at the Banhams' scheming.

Fully clothed, he turned to her. "Hannah, he did not frighten you, did he? If he laid a finger on you, I swear I'll slit his throat."

Without wanting to, she imagined him with the knife in his hand. "*No.* No one laid a hand on me."

"Something troubles you sorely, I can tell. I have never seen you like this."

"It was diabolical. He said such terrible things. There are base rumors going up and down the Bay. Rumors of you." She shook her head to show him her disbelief. "Yet he would have me believe this hearsay is truth." Her voice trailed off when she saw him go gray in the face.

He backed away from her until he leaned against the door. His eyes had gone red. He kept blinking at her. "Well, out with it, then." He spoke bitterly. "You've led me this far. Tell me those rumors."

Since she couldn't bear to spit out the accusation without preamble, she went through Richard Banham's story, piece by piece.

"Did you once have an indentured servant by the name of Patrick Flynn?"

"Aye. The thieving bastard stole the silver and my father's ring."

"They did arrest him in Port Tobacco and were going to return him and the goods to you."

He lifted his eyebrows. "That's a tale. The magistrates from Port Tobacco would bring that lying cutpurse back here?"

"This is what Banham told me." Her voice mirrored Gabriel's skepticism. "But that is not all. This Flynn told the magistrates that he fled you because he feared for his life."

Gabriel shook with laughter. "That is the cause of the vile gossip that drove Banham to speak to you behind my back? That I frightened a thief?"

"Flynn told the magistrates that you . . . that you did murder May." Clasping her hands in her lap, she waited for him to say something.

The house had grown cold. One of them needed to put another log on the fire, but his eyes pinned her to the bench. He stared at her, his face like a skull.

"Murder? I would never do such a thing." His voice was chilly.

"I did not believe him, how could I? Do you know what he wanted to do? He came with two men bearing shovels. They wanted to dig poor May out of her grave and inspect her body for evidence."

"Enough!" he snapped. He was trembling.

"Gabriel, I did not let them. Do you know what I did? I sat on her grave and wouldn't move. They saw I went with child and they didn't dare touch me. I sent them away, I did. Told Richard Banham that if he was a true gentleman, he would have to come back when you were here and say these things to your face."

He looked at her without recognition, as though he had gone into a trance.

She began to weep in hoarse noisy gulps. "I told him it was a pack of lies, Gabriel."

At last he seemed to return to his senses. Sitting beside her on the bench, he grasped her arms. "I am an innocent man. Do you believe even a word of those rumors?" Though he still looked shaken, the anger had drained out of him.

"How could I?" She let him brush the tears from her eyes. "How could I take a stranger's word over yours?"

"If you have judged me innocent, let us put this behind us and speak no more of it."

"It will be as you say," she replied. Inside her, the child shifted, pressing against the wall of her womb.

He grasped her hand fondly and tried to smile when a look of exhaustion crossed his face. His eyes were hooded, brooding. It was the old haunted look she remembered from when she first arrived—the expression of a man nearly done in by grief.

"Hannah, I have not eaten since dawn."

Without another word, she heaped wood on the fire and cut onions and salt pork to fry in the skillet.

~+~

After supper, Gabriel retired. The house was warm again, filled with the comforting scent of the meal she had cooked.

"Are you coming to bed?" he called to her.

"After I bank the fire."

When she clambered in beside him, he drew her in his arms and kissed her. In the bed with the curtains drawn shut, she couldn't see his face, could only feel his hands, warm and tender; it was as if they had never discussed murder. Nestling against him, she returned his kisses, but could not settle down. The baby would not stop stirring. She guided Gabriel's hand to her belly. "Feel it kick."

"A lusty child," he said. "He shows us his character already."

"You think it will be a boy, not a girl?" Inside her was a coldness she couldn't get rid of, even as Gabriel drew her into his warmth. If she had a daughter, she might want to name her May. But Gabriel would never allow it. *What use is there naming the child after a dead woman?*

"A strong fine boy," he said. "I sense it from the way he moves."

Not a weak girl, she thought, *who would live only seven days and then drag her mother with her into the grave.*

~+~

Wide awake, she listened to his deep, even breathing. How could he sleep when she thought she could never sleep again? That look in his eyes when she told him that Banham had wanted to open the coffin.

She and May used to wait until Father's snores echoed through the walls before they began their secret talks under the bedclothes. Sometimes they crept to the window to peer out at the moon. May put her white apron over her head and pretended to be a ghost.

Disengaging herself from Gabriel's arms, she rose from bed. May would have been proud of how noiselessly she moved over the creaky wooden floor. Feeling her way to the peg where her shawl hung, she wrapped it around her shoulders, then stoked the fire. By its dim light, she unrolled the bolt of cotton on the trestle table and stroked the soft fabric, tracing squares, rectangles, and circles. It looked as though there would be enough fabric to make both a new dress for herself and a gown and cap for the baby. Even if she had a boy, he would wear gowns and have long locks until he was old enough to be breeched. In his first five years, he would look like a little maiden.

Her hands found her sewing basket and the scissors inside. A pity it was too dark to start cutting patterns. She imagined a stack of neatly folded infant clothes. When she pressed the scissors' sharp point to her lips, it was not a smiling baby she saw, but her sister's bloodless face, her body draped in a white shroud. *Will it kill me too, then, the child inside me?* How would she survive the birth with her narrow hips? If Gabriel was right and it was a big boy inside her, how would she ever squeeze him out? She imagined her sister watching over her with cold, unforgiving eyes. Outside, the owls sang and the river surged in darkness.

—◦—

It had to be November. Only a few shriveled leaves clung to the naked branches. Frost bleached the grass, but the first snow had not yet come. November was the blood month of hunting, culling, and slaughter. Gabriel butchered two pigs and a goat. He went into the forest with his musket and returned with deer and wild turkey. The meat Hannah could no longer stomach piled on their table. She helped Gabriel salt the pork, then made sausages and blood pudding.

One day Bessie disappeared. In a panic, Hannah searched for her everywhere. Hours later, Gabriel found her in the tobacco barn with a litter of red puppies. "One of them can be yours," he told Hannah as she stroked the squirming bodies.

"I like this one." She lifted one of the females. The puppy licked her nose and playfully nipped her hand with sharp milk teeth.

"What will you call her?"

"I have to know her before I can name her. Maybe Ruby, since she's so red."

While the first snow fell, Hannah cut the pattern for her new dress to her old measurements. This wasn't going to be a maternity robe but a gown for the slender girl she had once been and hoped to be again, if God spared her through the birth. She stitched each seam carefully, as if the dress were a talisman of luck, promising her a long life and happy future. It was as though she were viewing the time after her labor in a fortuneteller's crystal ball. How handsome the future Hannah looked in the patterned cotton Gabriel had procured at great expense. He had clothed her like a gentlewoman, given her a jeweled ring to wear on her finger. Hannah in the crystal ball was happy, laughing the way her sister used to, her face turned lovingly to Gabriel, who held their son in his arms, the proudest father alive. When the little boy was old enough, the three of them would dance together, their feet picking a merry pattern over the floorboards, the lovely gathered skirt flying out to reveal her ankles, shapely again, no longer swollen from pregnancy. She was a beautiful young mother, gentle but strong enough to protect her child from every evil.

Keeping the vision in her head, she tried to banish her doubts and fears with each completed seam. After the dress was finished, she sewed baby clothes, tiny sheets, and pillowcases with the leftover fabric. When Gabriel praised her clever sewing, she held her tongue and didn't tell him she was a clumsy seamstress compared to May. *Our May could stitch in her sleep.*

May's ghost was at her elbow, making her seams crooked. Night after night, she dreamt of her sister walking barefoot through a forest of dead trees. A piece of mildewed sacking covered her wasted body. May no longer wept or cried out to her. She was quiet as bones. Silence settled around her grave with the drifting snow. It was the silence that oppressed Hannah most, that sent her fears into a deafening cacophony. Her doubts grew and grew, just like her belly, swelling like a gourd until she thought she would burst and that the bursting would kill her. Something inside her was going to wrench her open, tear her flesh, force its way out. Something she couldn't conceal from Gabriel any longer.

⁙

"A lonely life we lead," she said one evening as she filled Gabriel's trencher with slices of turkey she had roasted on the spit.

"It will be less lonely when the child comes," he said contentedly.

Hannah bit her lip before she spoke. "But will it not be strange and unwholesome for the child to grow up without playmates?"

Gabriel laughed. "We'll have to give him a passel of brothers and sisters, then, won't we?" He winked at her.

How could he speak so carelessly, talking about many births when she could not see beyond this one birth? She let her knife fall against the table with a loud clang. "I don't want to drop a baby every year like one of your goats."

"Hannah, what is this? You are in a temper."

"I am lonely," she confessed. "I miss the company of other females."

"There isn't much to be done about it."

She picked up her knife. "I wish there were neighbors we could call on."

"The Gardiners?" he asked her pointedly. "Or do you prefer the Banhams?"

"I wish we had other neighbors."

He gave her a wistful look. "You used to be happy here."

Laying his hand on hers, he fingered her ruby and pearl ring. "I cannot give you everything, but I give you everything I have."

She nodded and tried to smile. "I know, Gabriel."

"You will feel better," he promised, "when the baby is here."

"What if I am not strong enough?"

"What are you saying?"

She gazed into his eyes, hoping to see what lay behind them. "It killed her. What makes you think it would not kill me?"

"You said we would speak no more of it."

"Gabriel, I do not." Her voice shook. "I do not speak of rumors but of my sister. You say she died of childbed fever."

He was already turning away from her, one hand covering his eyes. "Why must you—"

She cut him off. "It could be the death of me, too. Women die having babies. Ladies of wealth write their wills before they go into childbirth."

"You are young and strong. We love each other. I will not let you die."

"*She* was strong and yet she died."

The breath seemed to leave his body. "You are not convinced of my innocence."

"If you are innocent, then there's no harm in mentioning my own sister's name." Her voice was raw and cruel. She sounded like the worst sort of harpy, but now that she had started, she couldn't stop. "What do you know of midwifery? Will you let me have this child all alone like Bessie birthed her puppies?"

"Hannah!" He slammed his hand against the table, causing the trenchers to skid. "I told you before." He spoke thinly, between clenched teeth. "When the time comes, I will fetch a midwife."

"I am ignorant of the days. I know not when my time comes and neither do you." Her voice ripped out of her throat with a violence that astounded her. It was as though she were unleashing demons. "What in the devil's name happened to that cradle?"

"What cradle?"

"May's cradle. The one pushed under the bed." Not caring if she hurt him or not, she let the words fly. "There's a crack running down the headboard. How did it get there, Gabriel? Who would crack a cradle like that?"

He struck the table again, this time with his fist. "What are you saying to me?"

"You never told me how her baby died." She looked at him, waiting for what would come next. "Will you let me die just as she did?"

He muttered something under his breath and walked out of the house.

After a moment had passed, she found her shawl and stumbled out the door. Looking neither left nor right, she lurched down the path. There was more than one way to kill a woman. If he hadn't killed May with outright violence, then could he have done it with neglect? If he had loved and cherished May, she would have held on to life after losing the baby. Why hadn't he taken better care of her?

Looking into her future, Hannah saw the green cotton dress folded in the drawer, not her body inside the dress. She had no reason to believe she would live when so many other women died. *May the devil take you. May you fester in hell for what you have done.* She didn't know whether it was Gabriel she was cursing or herself.

When she reached her sister's grave, she knelt in the shallow snow and wailed as she had never wailed before. She shrieked and keened like a madwoman. The dogs rushed over and sniffed her. They whined softly and licked her before trotting away. The cold wind stung her wet face. Her voice grew hoarse as a crow's. Still, she didn't stop shrieking until a shadow marked the snow in front of her. Gabriel stepped between her and the cross with her sister's name on it. He held the fur cloak he had made for her last year in one hand and Ruby, the puppy, in the other. Kneeling in the snow, he pressed the puppy into her arms, then wrapped the cloak around her shoulders. He raised her to her feet. Hannah cradled the little dog, let it lick her.

"Tomorrow I will go to the Banhams and ask them to send one of their women to stay with you until the baby is born." He spoke quietly, brushing her hair out of her face. "But please don't go on accusing me and giving me those looks. You know I can't bear it. If you think me guilty and wish yourself back, I'll sell everything I own and pay your passage to England. You can pass as a widow there and find another man who will make you happy."

Hannah looked at him through her tears. Her vision of him was so blurred. She wondered if she would ever see him clearly.

"Don't blame this entire misfortune on me. What can one man do? The woman's gone, and I can't bring her back." His voice broke. When he turned his face away from her, she knew he was crying. At last the moment had come. He was standing with her on her sister's grave, crying for May as she had cried. Setting the puppy on the ground, Hannah clasped his hands.

"Come, love," she whispered. "It's so cold out here." The puppy tagging along behind, she led him back to the house. Once in the door, he dragged the old cradle from beneath the other bed and sat down to repair it. He nailed the loose side so that it was solid again. Working with his adze, he smoothed the crack in the headboard. Hannah held the puppy in her lap and ran her numb fingers over Ruby's fur while she watched him work. She longed to ask him, this time in a calm way, how such a sturdy birch cradle could have been broken. But one look at his wounded face silenced her.

23 Made to Shine

May and Gabriel
NOVEMBER 1689

ONE EVENING, MAY PULLED a bench close to the hearth and invited Adele to sit with her. The male servants had already retired to their shack. Gabriel had gone out for his ablutions. Nathan dozed in his chair. When he awoke, he would send everyone to his or her bed, then bolt the door for the night. But May was too excited for sleep. She felt like a dull neglected thing that had been polished and made to shine again. Not only had she regained the power and pleasure of her body, she thought she had also, in a way, regained her innocence. She could sit beside the fire with Adele, who smiled at her as Hannah once had. In Adele's eyes, May was every inch the virtuous young mistress. *Above rubies.*

"You look pretty this night," Adele said shyly. "*Belle.*" The girl sidled up and whispered in her ear, "You no longer need the love charm?"

"No, Adele." She touched her hand fondly, then took the poker and drew random shapes in the ashes. A rose. A circle. A heart.

"You are happy." Adele spoke with awe.

"Yes." The flames leaping in the hearth reminded May of the fire in his eyes, the fire in his flesh when he took her. An idea sparked inside her. Running her sole lightly over the ashes, she rubbed out the shapes she had made. "If you like, I will teach you to read and write." She touched Adele's knee. "We can start with the alphabet."

Adele pointed her thumb toward Nathan, whose snores shook the floorboards. "He would forbid it, no?"

"I will persuade him," May promised. "He is a good Christian and would have his servants be good Christians as well. How can you read the Bible, Adele, if you do not know your letters?" Poker in hand, she went through the alphabet, having Adele trace each letter in the ashes beside her own. They kept passing the poker back and forth. In the meantime, Gabriel returned.

"Are you coming to bed?" he asked her softly.

The girl stood up, prepared to leave, but May caught her hand.

"Soon," she said, smiling at him until he blushed and disappeared behind the bed curtains. She winked at Adele, who swallowed a giggle. Uncommonly clever, the girl mastered the letters in no time.

"Tomorrow night, I will teach you to write your name."

Adele reached down the front of her smock and pulled up a tarnished circle of silver that hung from a string around her neck. When she held it up in the firelight, May saw it was a slender bangle with Adele's name engraved on the inner rim. Taking the poker, the girl copied the letters, spelling *Adele Desvarieux* in the ashes.

May fingered the bangle. "Who gave this to you?" Flashing the girl a conspiratorial smile, she imagined a secret sweetheart.

Adele's eyes moistened. "My old mistress." She turned the bracelet round and round.

May rested her hand on Adele's shoulder. "Your mistress from the island?"

Adele nodded.

"Do you miss her?"

"She is dead."

The girl's sadness pierced May. "I am sorry. Were you fond of her?"

Nathan snorted in his sleep, but did not wake.

Adele nodded, then looked forlornly at the bracelet. It was meant for a child to wear, May noted. Too small even for Adele's slender wrists.

"It is spoiled," Adele mumbled. "The silver it does not shine."

"I have a trick I will show you. Give me the bracelet, just for a moment."

Adele passed it to her. Scooping up a handful of cold ash, May rubbed it against the silver.

"No, no!" Adele tried to snatch it back.

"Adele, just watch." May patiently rubbed ash against the bangle until the tarnish was gone. "Don't you see?" It shone in her hand, gleaming and pure. She pressed it into Adele's palm. "Just like new again."

—+—

On a bright afternoon, Gabriel leapt across the creek. May had told him that she and Adele were going into the forest to gather pine boughs and pinecones to make the house pretty for Christmas. It would take a woman to think of such things, he thought fondly. Before her arrival, they had never bothered about decoration. Christmas was when he and the servants received their new set of clothes for the coming year. Father read a longer passage from the Bible than was his custom. Afterward they emptied a barrel of cider while Jack played his whistle, the manservants capering like drunken fools. But this Christmas would be different. May would civilize them.

Her laughter drifted through the forest like a silver thread, drawing him toward her. He had a surprise for her—a pair of soft slippers made of doeskin instead of common pigskin. One night after she had gone to bed, he had secretly traced her shoe soles on the hide to take her measure. Proper shoe leather took six months to bark-tan, but these slippers would do until the shoes were ready. They were for indoors, being too light to wear in the mud and rain, but they would be perfect for dancing, supposing she wished to dance at Christmas. He was too eager to wait for Christmas, or even until they were alone together in bed, to give her the present. He wanted to see her face in the daylight when he showed them to her.

It sounded as though she were singing. Her voice led him uphill, into the dense trees. This worried him. Hadn't he told her to stay near the creek and avoid the hills where his traps lay hidden? As long as he could hear her, he knew she was safe. But before he had walked another hundred paces, a cry stabbed the air. A yelp. He took off running, following the noise of her distress. Behind a stand of blood-red poison ivy, he came to a dead halt.

James was hurting her, pinning her against a beech tree while he hammered away. Hand on his knife, Gabriel was about to charge forward when he saw how her fingers clutched James's flame-bright hair as she moved her body in unison with his. She cried out in pleasure. So that was why she had stopped looking at James. Not because she had ceased wanting him, but to conceal the fact that they had become lovers. And if she coupled with him, her lawful husband, nearly every night, it was to cover her tracks. If she went with child, she would pass it off as his.

Gabriel backed away, his body gone cold. May was false, false. The promise of her had been so sweet, but she was like honey turned to snake venom on his tongue. *Poison*, he thought, remembering when his mother had been bitten in the neck by a copperhead in their own garden. Father tried to suck out the poison, but in vain. Poison had flooded her, made her face swell up until Gabriel could no longer recognize her. May was venomous as a snake and just as sly. He was tempted to drop the doeskin slippers in the creek as he crossed over again, but he held on to them. It had taken hours to tan the hide, cut the pieces, and stitch them together. He would not allow his labor to go to waste.

24 Snake-Tongue

Hannah
1693–1694

GABRIEL HAD GONE to fetch the midwife and everything froze. To draw water from the creek, she had to break the ice with a hatchet. Frost etched patterns on the window while the red bird sang. Inside the house, she sweated and shook. When she sat down to sew, her water broke in a warm gush. Hands crossed over her belly, she prayed. Let it not begin, not now. The first pains gripped her.

It was so cold, she had taken Ruby inside with her. The puppy looked up at her with anxious eyes and drooping ears. Hannah clung to her. At first the contractions were far apart, giving her hope in between. She could pretend all was well, but then they returned with a force that sent her panting.

Did May see her now? Was May watching? *At least you had Adele. You did not have to do this alone.* Was this her punishment?

The room went dark. He had been gone a day. How could he find his way in the night, through the ice and snow? There was no moon. She dragged herself across the floor. Shivering, she struggled to kindle a fire. There were only a few more logs in the house. If he stayed away much longer, she would have to go outside, stagger through the snow to the woodshed. Strangely, she was hungry, and what she craved most was bloody fresh meat, the thing that had sickened her throughout her pregnancy. In the pantry, she scooped salt pork from the barrel. The salt burned her tongue like sea brine. She was drowning. One of these waves would pull her under and she would never rise again. Cold, heat, hunger, salt, pain, fear, darkness blurred together. Ruby licked her hands as Hannah knelt on the floor and screamed.

—†—

Sweat dripped from her hair. She was so hot, it must be summer again. A strange face loomed over her. Strange hands pressed a compress to her forehead. The damp cloth smelled of witch hazel. The face peering down was luminously black, like a pool of molasses bathed in torchlight. A yelp ripped through Hannah's parched throat as waves of pain ran together in one pulsing angry tide.

The stranger spoke. "Aye, it hurt you like the devil. Shout and curse as loud as you like, my child."

She whimpered Gabriel's name, but he wasn't there. He had forsaken her and she would die, just as May had died. *You see, May, I got my comeuppance.*

The stranger's face faded. May shimmered in the distance. Sitting beside a foaming hawthorn tree, she embroidered green cloth. Cool and serene, no sweat drenched her brow. *May, I am coming now, coming to join you, if I can just cross this big gray sea.* Hannah shrieked with her last strength. Finally her sister heard. Looking up from her embroidery frame, she called Hannah's name. Her eyes were wide with forgiveness. *Come to me, darling. Everything's all right.* The image split and shattered.

I won't join her on the other side. She went to heaven, but my sin will banish me to hell. I shall never be with her again, not in this world, nor in the next.

Hannah bore down and bellowed. The stranger's face hovered above hers. Please let this woman give her one word of kindness and hope. One scrap. May had never been this wretched. She'd had Adele.

"Push, or the pain never end. *Push.*" The woman seized her shoulders and pressed her up against the bed frame.

But she could never push hard enough. The torment just

went on and on. Something stretched her so wide that she tore. The woman's big hands disappeared between Hannah's thighs. She kept shouting at her to push, push, push. Hannah cried as the woman pulled the misshapen thing out of her. It was covered in blood, in white and yellow muck. She closed her eyes and thought of the broken cradle filled with stained rags. A cold blue baby buried in the dirt.

"Now you have a son. Jesus have mercy on you both."

She opened her eyes to see the midwife cutting the cord. Hannah moved her arms toward the bloody wriggling mass. The woman pulled him up by his feet and slapped him until he wailed.

Hannah's eyes moved around the dark room. "Where is Gabriel? Where is my husband?" She had no right to call him that, but the word slipped from her before she could stop herself.

The woman muttered under her breath before turning to Hannah. "Why, of all men, you choose him?"

Silenced, Hannah could only shake her head.

"Once I meet your sister, May. Everyone love her but him. He break her spirit. Now they say he kill her."

Hearing those words from the woman who had pulled the baby from between her thighs was more devastating than any rumor voiced by Richard Banham. The midwife regarded her with such pity, as though she had been beguiled by the devil himself.

At that, the woman took the baby to the other side of the room where Hannah couldn't see him. She heard the sound of water splashing in a bowl.

"What are you doing? Bring me my baby. I want to hold my baby." It was hard to get the words out of her raw throat.

"You should give the child away," the midwife said, "to decent folk who fear the Lord." She washed the baby and put him somewhere out of Hannah's sight. Then the midwife returned to the bed, closed her fist around the cut cord still lying on Hannah's thigh, and pulled. "Now you push." She drew a bloody sac from between her legs. Afterward she pressed a cup to Hannah's lips, a decoction of herbs that sent her falling into a muffled sleep.

⋯⊹⋯

She dreamt that someone was pushing a pillow over her face, holding it down until she couldn't breathe. Voices broke through the fog. The midwife, Gabriel, and another man were shouting, their words fuzzy and indistinct. Gabriel's rage left her in a cold terror.

She couldn't see anything beyond the curtains that enclosed the bed. Somewhere the baby cried feebly. She struggled to get up, but the fog clutched her, dragging her down. It must have been powerful physick the woman had given her. Soon she left her body behind and traveled through the air, weightless as a ghost. She tried to find her baby, but a powerful wind sucked her in its current, dragging her back across the ocean. She was in her father's house, except it had grown bigger in her absence, sprouting doors, rooms, corridors, staircases, entire wings that had never been there before. It was night. A draft blew out her candle as she wandered, wondering if she would ever find her way back to the daylight world.

⋯⊹⋯

"Hannah."

Sun shone on her face. Someone had drawn back the bed curtains. Someone stroked her unwashed hair. Her eyes focused on Gabriel's drawn face, his red-rimmed eyes. When he kissed her dry lips, a tremor went through her. She remembered the shouting—or had she only dreamt that?

She wanted to ask him where the baby was, but her lips were too numb to form words. Her throat was too dry. Gathering her strength, she lifted her head from the pillow, but Gabriel pushed her back down.

"You must rest."

She wet her lips with her swollen tongue. "The baby."

"The baby is fine," he said. "We have a fine son."

He raised a cup to her lips. She shook her head, but he wouldn't take it away.

"Hannah, you must drink."

He tipped it into her mouth. To her relief, it was pure water, no more of the herbal brew that had turned her into a wandering ghost. She drank it down.

"Bring him to me," she said hoarsely.

"You're too weak. Just rest. Don't you worry about the baby. You must sleep."

"*Bring* him to me." Then she stopped short. "Or did they take him away?"

Gabriel blanched. "No one can take him away, Hannah. He's ours."

Cold tears blurred her eyes. "She said they would take him away and give him to decent people."

"She *said* that to you? What kind of fiend would torment you like that when you were so helpless?" He tried to stroke her hair, but she shrank from his touch.

"The baby," she said. "I want my baby."

He got up and crossed the room. She noticed that she lay on rough sacking cloth. Someone had laid sacking beneath her to spare the feather mattress. Shuddering from the pain, she forced herself into a sitting position. Now she could see the cradle by the hearth. How could he leave the wooden cradle so close to the flames?

"Bring him to me," she snapped.

"Here he is." Gabriel showed her the blanket-wrapped bundle with the tiny pink face. Hannah tried to take him, but he pulled the baby out of her reach just as the midwife had done. "Lie back against the pillow," he said, "and I will give him to you."

At last she held him and could gaze into his unfocused eyes. His nose was so delicate, like a little shell. She reached into the swaddling and pulled out his hand, counting his fingers. She kissed his downy head. His skull wasn't misshapen at all, as she had first thought. He was clean and rosy, no blood on him. She cradled him so she could feel his warm snuffling breath on her neck.

"We are a family." Gabriel tried to kiss her, but she twisted her head so that his lips grazed her ear.

Why, of all men, you choose him? The midwife's voice would not leave her head. If he hadn't killed May, had he broken her? In how many different ways might he have broken her?

"A healthy son and a safe birth." He tried to take her hand, but she snatched it away. "Are you not happy, Hannah?"

She couldn't bear to look at him, only at the baby. She tried to drown herself in those blue eyes that knew nothing of harm or betrayal.

Gabriel sighed. "You are tired."

He returned a while later with a bowl of broth, which she drank down obediently. She needed her strength; if she did not survive, the baby would die, too. Gabriel's eyes never left her face, but she refused to look at him. The only way she could live with her terror and her betrayal of May was by pouring her entire attention on the baby.

"You're white as a ghost, Hannah. That snake-tongued harpy must have frightened you. What else did she say?" When she didn't answer, he let out his breath. "Mayhap you are angry that I left you alone. I brought them back with me with as much speed as I could, but the river was frozen. I went down on foot, and we came back on horseback. But all is well now. You and the baby are well."

When the broth was finished, she sank into the bedclothes with her son. Stroking his face, she decided to name him Daniel, after Father.

"They are gone now," said Gabriel. "I hope we never have to see them again."

The baby snuffled against her chest. Turning her back to Gabriel, she opened her shift and drew the baby to her breast.

"The harpy said three days would pass before the first milk came."

Hannah ignored him. What did he know of such things? He hadn't been able to keep May and her baby alive. It took some time. She had seen women nursing babies on the ship. They had made it look so easy. But what if he didn't latch on to her? Finally the baby began to suckle, drawing a clear fluid from her breast. His greedy sucking allowed her to hope. He would be strong. She wouldn't lose him after a week. If she was a ruined girl who had betrayed her sister, then at least she had done one good thing. At least she had given life to Daniel. Closing her eyes, she curled her body around his.

"Leave us," she told Gabriel.

He stepped away and closed the curtains. Then she was alone in a warm cocoon with her baby.

She was no longer the old Hannah but a mother animal whose torn body leaked milk and blood. In bed with the curtains drawn against the cold, she lived in twilight. Day and night were all the same to her. She dozed a few hours, only to awaken to Daniel's cry, his tug on her body. His flesh was her flesh. When she held him, she lost track of where her skin ended and his began. When she counted his fingers and toes, she marveled that he had once fitted inside her body and now lived as a separate being. He was a part of her and yet he was his own. She loved him with a ferocity that made her ache. Sleeping with him in her arms, she couldn't bear the thought of anyone taking him away from her again.

—+—

She awoke to discover her arms were empty. Gabriel sat on the edge of the bed and held little Daniel, looking down at him while the baby stared up with his blue eyes. Something moved over Gabriel's face. He was utterly absorbed in his examination of the child, concentrating on him as though Hannah were no longer there.

"What are you doing?" The words slipped from her throat in a panicked gush. What was that look he was giving her son?

"His hair will be red." Gabriel spoke in a slow, perplexed voice.

It was true—shrill red fuzz already covered Daniel's head.

Hannah edged closer. "He takes after me." Without another word, she wrested the baby from him.

Not budging from his perch on the bed, Gabriel watched her

sink into the covers with Daniel. The look in his eyes, the graves by the river. As though sensing her fear, the baby cried. Bracing herself, she met Gabriel's eyes, staring him down. He glanced away and ran his hand over his face.

—+—

The following morning, after Gabriel had left to check his traps, Hannah crawled out of bed. She poured the creek water he had fetched into the kettle and heated it over the fire. With her last precious sliver of soap, she lathered her body and hair. Father said bathing in winter was courting death, but she couldn't bear the smell of her body any longer. She stank like a sickbed. Shivering over the wash pan, she scrubbed herself with a cloth, then rinsed out her soapy hair. All the while, Daniel lay nestled in her bed. She wouldn't think of putting him in that unlucky cradle.

After drying herself, she put on a clean shift and combed out her hair in front of the fire. When Daniel cried, she nursed him in the chair with the carved backrest, which she had never sat in before. She had never seen Gabriel using the chair either. He had told her it had been his father's chair, the master's chair, where no one else was allowed to sit. The backrest made nursing more comfortable. Her milk flowed easily now, her son's appetite summoning nourishment from her body. Yes, he would live. Stroking the red fuzz on his head, she blinked away tears. She didn't have the luxury of fear anymore. She would have to be strong, stronger than she had ever been.

When he was fed and sated, she tucked him back into the bed, then went to the chest of drawers. The top drawer contained her green cotton dress. It was more of a summer dress, from the weight of the fabric, but her old skirt and bodice had worn down to rags. Although her belly had shrunk back since the birth, there was a slackness in her abdomen that hadn't been there before. She was half afraid she wouldn't fit inside her new dress. The fabric was tight around her ribcage and belly, tighter still around her swollen breasts, but the snugness held her up, pulled her loose flesh together to fortify her.

It seemed impossible that she had once imagined dancing with Gabriel in this dress. Sweeping Daniel in her arms, she turned and swirled with him, her strong healthy boy. She would give her life to ensure that he outlived her and Gabriel both.

Having used all the water in the house for washing, she melted clean snow in the kettle and let it cool. Taking out the Book of Common Prayer, she laid it open on the table.

"I baptize thee in the Name of the Father, and of the Son, and of the Holy Ghost. Amen." She dipped her finger in the tepid water and traced a cross on his forehead. She prayed that God would smile upon her child. His soul was innocent and unstained, even if his parents were wretched and lost.

25
Join the Dance

May and Gabriel
DECEMBER 25, 1689

AFTER THE ENDLESS Bible reading, prayers, and hymns, and after the feast of wild turkey stuffed with apples and walnuts, Peter and Finn pushed the benches against the walls. James and Michael folded the trestle table. Once the floor was cleared, Jack played a jig on his wooden whistle with Tom accompanying him on the spoons, slapping them against his thigh. Reclining in his chair, Nathan smiled expansively and raised his hand as though in benediction. "Ah, let there be music. Let there be joy."

In recent weeks, he had recovered his health and high spirits. It seemed that the prospect of future grandchildren had aided his recovery. May tried not to blush when he peered hopefully at her waistline.

"I never imagined such merriment, sir," she said, pouring him another mug of cider.

The Irishmen performed the dances of their country, showing off their fancy footwork. Nathan clapped in rhythm, as did May, seated beside Gabriel, who did not clap along. His gaze was heavy-lidded. It appeared he had been forced to watch this spectacle too often. She wished she knew what to make of his moods. For about three weeks he had been happy and affectionate, doting on her, but lately he had gone sullen. Still, he had given her a pair of doeskin slippers, soft as butter on her feet. She tried to catch his eye and make him smile, but his gloom was too much for her to bear on this of all days. So she sidled over to Adele.

The girl fingered May's sleeve, marveling over the delicate embroidery. For Christmas, May had decided to wear her wedding gown, the finest thing she possessed. Adele had threaded green ribbons in her hair and curled her locks with iron tongs. The girl wore a band of dark gold velvet around her throat. May had found the velvet ribbon in her trunk. No doubt Hannah had tucked it in as a surprise, but the color suited Adele better. Instead of her usual workaday smock, Adele wore May's russet Sunday gown from home. They had taken in the seams and shortened the hem. The dress transformed Adele from a child to a young woman, the fitted bodice showing off her slenderness. Adele kept looking down, smoothing the skirt with her hands. May imagined how the full skirt would swirl out if Adele allowed one of the men to give her a turn around the floor.

"Do you dance?" she asked.

Adele shook her head.

Nathan laughed. "In this house only the men have ever danced. Adele refused every invitation."

The girl did not smile.

May touched her hand protectively. "Leave her in peace, sir." She whispered in Adele's ear. "But the music is cheerful, do you not think?"

She clapped her hands to the thunder of dancing feet. It was intoxicating to watch the men leap so high that their heads nearly touched the ceiling. They, too, were decked out in their best—Nathan had given them their new clothes for the coming year. She and Adele had sat up late stitching the breeches and shirts. Of all the dancers, James was the most graceful and jumped the highest. His eyes kept meeting May's. She had to blink and look down to her lap lest she give herself away.

Glowing with exertion, he stepped forward and bowed. "Will you dance, Mistress Washbrook?"

Did he presume too much? She turned to her husband. "Mayhap Master Gabriel wishes to claim the first dance."

Before the boy could protest, she pulled him to his feet. They had a turn around the floor, her steps weightless in the new slippers, but Gabriel dragged his feet like an old gelding. Had no one ever taught him to dance a simple reel? "This way," she tried to instruct him, but it was hopeless. When the song ended, he threw himself back on the bench and looked as miserable as ever. Did he expect her to placate him by forgoing the dance altogether? They had little enough festivity in this godforsaken place. She certainly wasn't going to allow him to spoil her Christmas.

When in a pleasant temper, Gabriel could be so sweet, and as long as he remained sweet, she enjoyed giving him pleasure. It was a comfort, after all, to share a bed with another body, to stroke his smooth chest in the dark, feel his heart beneath her hand. But her husband did not move her the way James did. If she wanted to conceive a child, she needed a lover who could stir her passion to its depths. A man and not a boy. She would not allow herself the humiliation of a barren marriage.

Her duty to her husband put behind her, she let James take her hand. Tom played a fast tune. The room blurred as James swung her in his arms until she was weak with laughter. How she longed for him. In dark midwinter with snow on the ground, it was difficult to find a place for their trysts. Lately they met in the tobacco barn. Afraid that someone might burst in, they had taken their privacy by lying together in an empty hogshead. Dancing with him, she struggled not to kiss him with her cider-sweet mouth.

Beaming at them both, Nathan clapped to the tune, which went faster and faster until she was too dizzy to stand. James's arm around her was the only thing that kept her upright as she panted.

"Not fair to keep the lady to yourself." Patrick took her hands, his eyes traveling over her bosom. In the wild dance, she had lost her neckcloth. While they danced to a slower tune, he gripped her too tightly, but she was too happy to care. Then Peter cut in. Since she liked him better than Patrick, she smiled and watched the color spread over his cheeks.

237

"Happy Christmas, Mistress Washbrook," he stammered.

Laughing, she looked at Nathan. "Do you wish to put a stop to this, sir?"

"Christmas only comes once a year," he replied, raising his cider mug. "For one night, let us be merry."

After she had danced with Peter, James claimed her again. He turned her around and around. As they spun, the faces of those watching seemed curiously disembodied. Nathan grinned and drank his cider. Adele gazed at her with solemn eyes. Then Finn led her in a country jig. Clumsier than his brother James, he kept stepping on her feet. She danced with James, Peter, and Michael in turn until her hair came loose from its ribbons and combs. When Patrick tried to cut in, she pulled away and called for James.

She danced with all the men except the musicians and Nathan, who shook his head and sighed about his age. The time had come to give her attention to Gabriel again, see if she could coax him out of his sulk, but his spot on the bench was empty. He was nowhere to be seen.

—⁜—

Head ducked down to shield his stung face from the wind, Gabriel labored uphill, his dogs racing around him. The declining sun cast a bloody shimmer on the snow. With each step, he sank to his knees. No one had seen him slipping out of the house, least of all his wife. That was the measure of how insignificant he had become. He had not been able to stomach another second of watching her dance with the men, with her head thrown back in delight, face and bosom flushed. Dancing in the slippers he had made her himself. If he confronted May, she would merely fix him with her big blue eyes, smile her false smile, and tell him not to worry his head about a thing.

He wasn't man enough for her. His father had always told him he wasn't man enough. James, Father's favored one, had stepped in to take his place. He hated his father for the way he had sat there and cheered her on while she floated in James's arms. It wouldn't surprise him if they had Father's blessing.

He was nothing, nothing. Neither his father nor his wife would deign to treat him as anything more than the muck beneath their feet.

Stopping to catch his breath, he watched Rufus, the top dog, wrestle one of the younger dogs into submission. Each animal fought for its position in the pack, and so it was, too, with men and women. James had bested him. Rather than be at the bottom, he preferred to break away from them all, become the lone wolf. He pushed onward, determined to reach the top of the hill, the stand of poison ivy, glittering with frost. The little clearing with the beech tree at its edge where it had happened, where James had propped May against the tree and taken her standing up, as if rogering some harlot. Shaking with rage and cold, Gabriel unsheathed the knife from his belt. The last rays of sun glanced off the blade as he drove it home.

Cast out of his home on Christmas Day. They had robbed him of his bachelorhood, his innocence, his wife, but they wouldn't take these woods away from him. They would not dare to sully his last refuge. He carved the letters of his name into the bark to prove that he still existed. *Gabriel.* He would mark this place, claim it as his own, his lawful inheritance. The trees would remain long after Father passed on, his name engraved on them. The Gabriel woods. The forest would remember him even if everyone else dismissed him.

JANUARY 8, 1690

The New Year brought a blizzard and a snap of deep cold. Midwinter was the worst time for tempers, all eleven of them cramped together, the servants' quarters having no hearth. Some nights the Irishmen slept body to body in the attic, where they at least had the heat from the chimney. Adele slept on a pallet near the fire.

On Sunday morning, everyone crowded around the table for morning prayers. Though Adele and the Irishmen were Catholic, Nathan would tolerate no papist nonsense. Everyone must sit with clasped hands while he read from the Bible and the Book of Common Prayer.

The Christmas festivities already seemed like a distant memory. On this cold January morning, May could see her breath inside the house. She wore her dress of blue worsted wool, two underskirts, her scratchy wool stockings, a neckcloth with a woolen shawl over it, and a linen cap. Though she had chosen her clothes for reasons of warmth rather than modesty, she imagined she must look every inch the sober Puritan goodwife.

Adele squeezed onto the bench. Because she was from the Sugar Isles, winters were particularly hard on her. While the Irishmen complained of the heat in summer, Adele shivered through the cold months, teeth rattling, as though the chill would do her in. She wore the Sunday dress May had given her, with two shawls wrapped around her.

May struggled not to doze as Nathan read a long passage from Proverbs.

As snow in summer and rain in harvest, so honor is not fitting for a fool.
Like a flitting sparrow, like a flying swallow, so a curse without cause shall not alight.
A whip for the horse, a bridle for the donkey, and a rod for the fool's back.

Head bowed, May made herself stay awake by thinking about spring, when she could plant the seeds Hannah had given her. Her attention wandered down the table to James. Their eyes met for an instant before she lowered her gaze to her clasped hands, her work-worn fingers with the dull gold wedding ring.

Across from her, Gabriel had fallen asleep. May tried to nudge his foot under the table before his father noticed, but it was too late. Nathan stopped reading and struck his son's shoulder. May averted her eyes. She did not want to see the look that passed between father and son.

When the prayers and Bible reading were over at last, May

and Adele laid the table and served sausages and Sunday chicken with fried corncakes, onions and turnips, cider, and a steamed pudding made of cornmeal and cherry preserves. Adele held the trenchers and May dished out the victuals. The best and biggest portions went to Nathan, as master of the household. Eyes watering from the hearth smoke, she saw only too late that she had given James a portion equal to Nathan's—something the other servants did not fail to notice.

Looking at James's trencher, Patrick said something to him in their native tongue that made James's face go red. James said something back. Then he said in English, "Mayhap you wish to trade portions."

Patrick said something else in his language, to which James replied swiftly. Leaping off the bench, Patrick dragged James away from the table and struck his face, bloodying his nose. Before May could even think to scream, James struck back, hitting Patrick in the belly so hard that he writhed on the floor, clutching himself and howling.

In the silence that followed, Nathan was too stunned at first to react. James's face was a mask of fury, fists still clenched. Then Nathan got up from his chair. With a shaking hand, he seized the bullwhip off its hook. Adele covered her face and cried. Even Gabriel went pale. May trembled when Nathan roared. Could this be the same man who had wept in her presence that day in November, allowing her to glimpse into the secrets of his heart?

"How dare you desecrate the Sabbath! How dare you strike blows in my house!" He turned to May and Adele. "Take the trenchers. If there is no gratitude amongst this lot, let all seven of them go hungry this day."

"But sir," May said, "only two have come to blows. Why must all of them be punished?"

"Silence, woman!" Nathan held up the whip. "Don't you dare speak against me."

May's face burned, but her eyes stayed dry, even as Adele sobbed. The very sight of the whip seemed to send the girl into a panic. May took her arm and led her to the other side of the table.

"Hush," she whispered, touching her face.

Methodically they took each of the male servants' trenchers and scraped the food back into the pots. May wondered if it would spoil. Maybe there was still a way she could smuggle it to them without Nathan knowing.

Meanwhile Nathan had donned his cloak, then marched Patrick and James outside. Barking out orders, he made Gabriel and Jack accompany them.

"What will he do?" May asked Adele. The girl only cried. She turned to Finn. "What will he do?"

"Go to the window, Mrs. Washbrook, and see for yourself."

May looked out to see Nathan lead the men to what she had always assumed was a hitching post. Only now did she discern its true purpose. Nathan's raised voice penetrated the closed window and door. At his orders, Gabriel and Jack stripped off the two men's shirts so that their bare backs twitched in the cold. They bound their hands to the post. Nathan unfurled his bullwhip.

May wrenched the door open. "Master Washbrook, no!" Of course, it was a master's right to chastise his servants if necessary, but a bullwhip was too cruel. Surely a birken rod would suffice. A well-placed blow with a bullwhip could kill a man. She dashed out the door, set to throw herself between Nathan and the men, when Adele and Finn grabbed her and dragged her back inside.

Finn placed himself in front of the door. "If you try to meddle, he will whip you, too."

Adele seized May's hand and guided it down the back of her dress, over the raised skin that crisscrossed her shoulder blades. "Once he whipped me. I have the scars still. He whips his own son."

May swallowed a cry. Adele was so small, so tiny. How had she survived the bullwhip? And Gabriel—she had never suspected Nathan could treat his son that way. No wonder Gabriel always kept his nightshirt on—he was too ashamed to reveal his naked back.

242

Nathan whipped Patrick first. When the singing crack of the whip landed on his back, Patrick screamed like a woman. Adele quaked so hard that May put her arms around her. The whip kept cracking. May saw the muscles bulge in Nathan's neck. She had never dreamed he possessed such strength. Or cruelty. Gabriel doubled over, vomiting in the snow.

"Mistress Washbrook, if you please." Finn looked as though he were struggling not to cry. "After the flogging, they will need you to clean their wounds. You must wash them and wrap them in dressing."

"Have we any bandages?" she asked Adele.

The girl nodded and rummaged through the dresser.

Meanwhile Patrick's back ran red. Nathan moved to the other side to whip James.

"This is madness." May tried to edge past Finn out the door, but he took hold of her wrists.

"No," he said. "You must stay inside."

"Please tell me what words sparked this brawl? What did Patrick say to your brother?"

The boy's cheeks went blotchy. "I would rather not say, mistress. Such words are not for a woman's ears."

She grasped his arm, making him blush even more. "Please." She shuddered as they listened to James cry out in pain. "If it concerns your brother, I must know."

Finn pressed his lips together before he spoke. "Patrick said to James, 'Not only does the master favor you indecently, but now the mistress as well.'"

May raised her hand to her mouth. Adele appeared at her side with an armful of bandages. Though they had been laundered since their last use, old bloodstains still marked them.

❧—

Adele prepared a kettle of warm water. May packed her basket with bandages, a cake of soap, and a washing rag, then climbed to the attic, where the whipped men lay prone on their pallets. Patrick's back was far more ravaged than James's was. The pity welling up inside her nearly made her forget that she detested the man. Patrick flinched at her touch and spat on the floor.

"There are words for women such as you," he muttered. But in his chastened state, he didn't appear to have the courage to tell her what those words were.

⚬╂⚬

That night in bed, Gabriel whispered in her ear, "On your account, the men come to blows and suffer the whip. Are you pleased with yourself, May?"

"Stop it," she begged him.

"What sport you play, woman! You think I am too blind or stupid to know your tricks?" He gripped her shoulder so she couldn't pull away. "You've sported with James like a mare in season. Well, now that he's had his whipping, all because of you, I hope he goes off you. Mayhap he has come to hate you. Mayhap the very sight of you will gall him like spoiled meat." His words rang out like a curse that would come true to the word. They turned her bones to ice.

It took her last strength to push him away. Rolling to the edge of the bed, she drew the bedclothes over her ears, but she could not keep out the sound of Nathan's choked weeping.

⚬╂⚬

Each evening that week, May climbed to the attic to rub James's and Patrick's wounds with bear grease. James no longer smiled at her. When she looked at him, his face closed and his eyes went blank. Had he really come to hate her, then? How could his love simply vanish out of her life?

"My dear," she whispered, kissing him when no one could see. "Beloved." She would dash herself against the stones at the creek bottom before she let Gabriel's curse come true.

⚬╂⚬

Adele took to her pallet with a terrible cold, leaving Finn to help May carry creek water to the house so that she could wash the soiled bandages. Each of them bore two buckets as they trudged up the path side by side. Their breath floated out of their mouths in the bitter air.

"Sometimes," said Finn, "I do have nightmares of whippings. When I awake, I have secret thoughts of us rising up against the master. I know it is a sin," he added forlornly.

"It must be hard to forgive him," she said quietly, "for what he has done to your brother."

"He has whipped all of us at one time or other. There is always some transgression."

They had nearly reached the house when Finn set his buckets in the snow. He took her buckets and set them down as well.

"You will try to protect us, won't you, mistress?" He pressed her hand, loosening something inside her. She thought she would cry. "We were praying that you could make him softer."

"I will try," she said bleakly. "I promise you that."

In the following weeks, she did her best to soften up Nathan. In March, when the snow had melted and wild anemones pushed their way out of the mud, she gave him the most softening news of all. She was pregnant. In spite of James's whipping and Gabriel's curse, in spite of all the trials and misfortune, she had succeeded in bringing forth this miracle, which she prayed would redeem her. By October, she reckoned, Nathan would finally have his heir.

26
Foxglove for the Heart

Adele
SPRING 1690

THE FULL MOON CAST silver on the foxglove May had planted that spring from her sister's seeds. They grew as grandly as if they had always been here, as though they belonged here, deep pink flowers as pretty as the woman who had sown them.

Adele held her breath. All was silent. The Washbrooks had retired for the night. No light shone in their window. Except for Peter, the manservants had also turned in after working from dawn to sunset in the tobacco field. Peter had stolen away in Master Washbrook's smallest boat. Adele had spied him creeping off at moonrise, heading downstream. He had been doing this for weeks. Finn had whispered that Peter had a sweetheart at the Banham Plantation, a kitchen girl named Rosie. Every other night, he rowed downriver, then labored back upstream in the early hours before dawn. A few times Adele had woken, hearing him pass her hut as he hurried to his quarters. If Nathan Washbrook ever got wind of this, he would give Peter the flogging of his life. But at least Peter had the sense to fall in love with someone other than Mistress May. Later, when his indenture was completed, he could marry his girl and start planting his own fifty acres.

Enough of Peter, she told herself. After glancing around one last time to make sure that she was alone, she set to work. Wrapping a rag around her hand, she grabbed hold of the stalk. With her other hand, she plunged her spade into the earth and dug up the root. She prayed that May would not notice one missing fox-glove plant. May had warned her never to touch the plant with her bare hands—it could raise a powerful rash. Adele laid the plant on the ground, took the knife from her basket, and cut off the root. The charm called for orchid root. Since she could find no orchids here, she had decided to use foxglove. May herself had told her it was powerful physick that worked on the heart.

Reaching into her basket, Adele took out the materials she had gathered. A handkerchief belonging to May, a long strip of linen cut from one of Gabriel's raveling old shirts, strands of May's and Gabriel's hair that she had plucked from their pillows, and an old stoneware flask containing a measure of Nathan Washbrook's rum. She had pilfered the turkey quill and ink bottle from May's trunk—tomorrow she would return them before May noticed they were missing. She had procured a scrap of paper torn from the sugar cone wrapping. Pricking the ball of her thumb with a knife, she let her blood fall into the inkpot. The charm called for dove's blood, but her own would have to do.

She placed the foxglove root in the center of May's handker-chief, then arranged the hairs and a few foxglove flowers around it. She closed her eyes and called the powers. Her mother's old chants came back to her, those words that weren't French or Eng-lish but African. Their music and rhythm issued forth from her mouth, though she didn't know what she was saying or what spir-its she invoked. If only her mother were here to guide her. She called on her mother's ghost.

As she dipped the quill into the inkpot, her fears paraded be-fore her. She might work the charm the wrong way. What if she unleashed forces beyond her control? Obeah was powerful magic. Her mother had worked spells only in moments of extreme need. Adele also feared that she was casting the spell too late. Really, she should have done it in November when May had first asked for it. But no foxglove had grown then. She hoped and prayed it was not too late to turn things around.

May was in grave danger. The certainty of this gripped Adele tighter each morning when she awoke from nightmares of May's destruction. She hadn't been visited by such terrors since leaving her island. May had set off down a path that could only lead to ruin. Adele had sensed the first prickle of dread the night of the Christmas dance when May had let the men spin her round and round like a child's top, faster and faster, until Adele had feared she would hit the wall and break. May hadn't been able to stop her perilous game, even after James had come to his senses and begun to withdraw from her. May wouldn't let him go, but kept trying to rekindle the flame. When he ignored her, she flirted with the other men—including with his own brother, Finn—to spark his jealousy. How could she carry on like that when she was at least four months gone with child? Somehow Nathan Washbrook didn't condemn her for it. But Gabriel couldn't look at May without his lip curling in spite. Adele's worst nightmares concerned Gabriel and what would happen when he could contain his anger no longer.

Shaking her head clear, she lifted the quill from the inkpot. Setting the paper on a flat stone in the bright moonlight, she wrote the passage she had learned by heart from the English Bible:

This is now bone of my bones and flesh of my flesh.

May had allowed her to practice writing with the quill on a scrap of paper. Adele was grateful at how easily the quill moved in her hand. When the ink dried, she folded the paper three times and wrapped it in the handkerchief with the root, flowers, and hairs. She twisted the handkerchief in a bundle and tied it shut with the piece of linen cut from Gabriel's shirt. She knotted it nine times. Throwing back her head, Adele whispered her mother's name. *Please give me the powers to save her before it is too late.* She poured nine drops of Nathan Washbrook's rum on the handkerchief, then spilled the rest on the earth as an offering. Adele breathed on the bundle and held it against her pounding heart. The thing was done. She had created a conjuring bag. Tomorrow she would hide it under May and Gabriel's mattress.

⚬┼⚬

Adele counted the passing days while waiting for the magic to take hold. When she carried the basket of cornbread and bacon to the men in the tobacco field, she observed Gabriel closely to see if her charm had any effect. He labored shirtless, uprooting weeds with his hoe, evidently unaware of her presence. She could see the muscles in his arms and back. One thing was certain—he was a beanpole boy no longer. He had changed since his marriage, had grown into a man who was stronger and tougher than anyone would care to admit. She tried not to see the scars left by his father's bullwhip. As the sun glared on his skin, slick with sweat, she could sense something brewing inside him, simmering beneath the surface. She had heard that quiet men had the most deadly tempers.

He wiped his forehead with his hand and caught her gaping. A few months ago, she would have set down the basket of victuals and fled. Now she looked into his eyes, pretending that she had the power to trap his spirit with her gaze. *Please, let the charm do its work.*

"What is it?" he asked. "Why do you look at me that way?"

She forced herself to stand her ground. May had made her bold, given her courage. If only Gabriel could forgive his wife and open his heart, allow May's beauty to conquer him, as it had conquered everyone else. If only he could grant her one more chance.

Patrick burst out laughing. "Taken a shine to the master, have you, Adele?" When she ignored him, he plowed right on. "I suppose someone has to, if his own wife won't."

Gabriel clenched his hoe in both fists. His eyes went black. He reminded her of a copperhead about to strike. For one awful moment, she thought he would go after Patrick.

Tom stepped between them. "Master, don't listen to the fool." He laid a careful hand on Gabriel's shoulder. Then he turned to Patrick. "You insult the mistress again, I'll tell Mr. Nathan."

A wary silence descended. She imagined they were thinking of the whipping Patrick would get if he overstepped his bounds again.

During the evening meal, Adele couldn't keep her eyes off May as she smiled and laughed with the men. Pregnancy had only made her more beautiful. Her hair had a special sheen to it. Her eyes seemed bluer than before. Finn gazed at her in adoration, as though she shone brighter than the moon and sun combined.

Gabriel bent his head over his food. When his trencher was clean, he left the table.

"Where do you go?" May called out.

"To feed the dogs." The door shuddered behind him.

Nathan merely sighed. May went on chatting with the others, taking no more notice of her husband than she would of a sulky child. Adele's eyes smarted.

She would have to talk to May, woman to woman. She struggled to gather her thoughts, translate them into English. Meanwhile the manservants filed out the door. Gabriel did not return. Nathan retired to the porch with his pipe while she and May scrubbed the trenchers and pots.

There is something I must tell you. She held the words ripe on her tongue.

May looked up from the dishpan and peered into her eyes. "You are so quiet this day. You have been sad of late, I think. Are you lonely here, Adele?"

"I was lonely before you came."

May took the clout and dried the last pot. "In faith, I don't know what I would do without you." She spoke with such kindness. Adele reminded herself that she had May to thank that she could read and write. May had given her two of her own dresses and made them over for her. She was beautiful and generous with both her body and her things. How was anyone supposed to resist her charms? *We were all so lonely and lost,* she wanted to tell her, *before you came.*

"Some creature has been into the garden," May remarked as she hung the clouts to dry. "It dug up one of my foxgloves."

Before Adele could think what to say, May took the Bible from its box and set it on the table.

"Are you ready for your lesson?"

She and May read from the Bible every night. Adele had nearly finished the book of Genesis and had memorized passages to trace in the hearth ashes. Taking the poker, she wrote:

Bone of my bones and flesh of my flesh.

"Ah, yes." May's laughter rang out like music. "Adam and Eve."

Once that story had been Adele's favorite in the Bible. She loved the description of the Garden of Paradise and of how God had given Adam a companion so he wouldn't be alone. Why had it ended so sadly, then? Why had Eve gone astray and destroyed it?

"Adele, you are crying." May searched for her handkerchief. Not finding it, she yanked her neckcloth from her bodice and used it to wipe Adele's tears. "What is it? Tell me."

Her breasts moved up and down with each breath, bathed gold in the firelight. Eve herself couldn't have been lovelier.

I am afraid. You lead yourself into danger. But Adele couldn't speak those words aloud. She could not bear the thought of causing May such distress. *Blood of my blood.* At that moment, it became clear. What her spell had accomplished was not the joining of May and Gabriel in conjugal love, but the binding of her own destiny to May's. Her blood in the ink with which she had written the charm. *Flesh of my flesh.* Their fate and fortune were intertwined, just as their fingers were as May held both her hands. It didn't matter that they were black and white, or mistress and servant. They were blood sisters.

27 Poison

Gabriel
1694

THOSE LIARS HAVE POISONED YOU. The words stuck in his throat. Hannah rocked their son in her arms, her loose hair falling around the infant's body like a ring of fire no one dare cross. She would not let him anywhere near the baby. If he picked up little Daniel when he cried, she snatched him away, as if from a thief.

Gabriel tried to look away from her, but he couldn't. She had never been more beautiful. The green of her new cotton dress set off her eyes and made her hair even more fiery. Her breasts poured over the top of the bodice. He had never loved her or wanted her more than he did now, but she froze up if he so much as touched her shoulder. Her eyes brimmed with tenderness, but not for him. She had fallen in love with Daniel, had named the boy without asking his opinion. He listened to her croon while rocking him. "Danny, my sweet Daniel." Her body and breasts, her love and attention belonged to the baby, only to the baby.

If Gabriel was fortunate enough to catch her eye, the look she gave him stabbed him like a blade in the chest. It wasn't the hurt, questioning look she used to give him. What was new in her gaze was the bald-faced dread. She feared him. It wasn't a question of doubts anymore—she had condemned him. He felt like a man at the gallows with the rope around his neck. He didn't dare argue or raise his voice lest he lose her completely. She was still frail from the birth. She needed to build back her strength.

He couldn't risk causing her any more anguish. Above all, he was afraid of her affliction—if something pushed her any closer to the edge, she might fall into one of her fits.

—┼—

Since Daniel's birth, the moon had waxed full, then dwindled again. A new crescent hung in the sky. In that time, the child had ballooned. Gabriel could hardly believe their son had once been a tiny wrinkled thing.

When he came in for the evening meal, Hannah set his trencher of stew on the table before retreating to the carved chair, where she nursed the baby.

"Will you not eat with me, love?" All he could see were her flaming locks snaking down the back of his father's chair.

"Daniel is hungry."

"You need to eat more yourself, or you will grow too thin." As much as it shamed him to admit it, he had come to think of the fat, ruddy-faced infant as a parasite sucking the life out of her.

"I eat when I can." Her voice was distant.

"Come sit beside me." He spoke so urgently that she turned her head, eyes wide and fretful.

"He is still nursing."

"Then I will sit with you." He took his place on the floor at her feet like a supplicant while she sat enthroned in his father's chair. During the old man's lifetime, no one but Nathan Washbrook had dared sit there. After they all deserted him, Gabriel had been tempted to ax the hated thing and burn it as firewood.

Hannah drew her shawl over her breast so he wouldn't see her nursing. Was this the same girl who had let him strip her naked on the bed of furs?

"I can take no more of this," he told her. "He's my child, too, yet you never let me near him. You treat me like an intruder in my own home."

The whites of her eyes flashed in the hearth light. She cowered.

"There," he said quietly. "You give me that look again."

253

His father's chair dwarfed her. She seemed so helpless, so young and lost. How he longed to take her in his arms — if she would only allow it.

"Banham has turned you against me," he said. "The midwife, too. I don't know what she said to you, but it has caused you to fear me. He fed her those words, Hannah. This is his game, and he has made you his pawn. Can you not see it?"

Daniel had stopped nursing. With trembling hands, she fumbled over the lacing of her bodice. Holding the baby over her shoulder, she patted his back until he burped.

"You would have me believe it is mere slander." Her hand cupped the back of Daniel's head. Her arm shielded the baby's body. "But why?" Her voice was tight and small. "Why would any man hate you so much to say such things if they are not true?"

Her fear was palpable, a presence that filled the room. He had sensed the same terror when cornering a deer with his musket. She seemed to be too scared even to cry.

"The Banhams have plotted against my family for years. Paul Banham sold my father this leasehold for far too much. When the harvest was poor, he came to gloat. We knew he was biding his time until we were ruined, so he could play the Good Samaritan and come to our rescue, only to buy back the land at a pittance."

None of this seemed to have any impact on her. She sat rigid in his father's chair, her breathing shallow.

"Mayhap you do not believe me," he said. "Mayhap you take young Master Richard's word over mine."

As if infected by his mother's unease, Daniel started crying. "Let me rise," she pleaded. "I must walk with him."

Gabriel leaned back as she got up and paced the room with the squalling baby. He listened to her sing a broken lullaby. When the baby was quiet again, she tucked him in the bed.

"You never use the cradle," he said.

She did not reply.

He crossed the room and took her arm. White-faced, she

shuddered and let out a gasp, which made him release her in shame. Her fear tore at him.

"The Banhams did their work well. Will you let them win their game? Will you let them take away everything we have?"

This time she refused to meet his eyes. A sick taste filled his throat, and then he could contain himself no longer.

"If you fear and despise me so much, there is little point in your biding here. When the snow melts, I will take you downriver. Do you not have a friend on the Eastern Shore? You can live with her and her people."

"You would turn me out?" Her face went ghostly. All the life inside her seemed to evaporate. She sank to the floor and pressed her hands to her forehead.

"I have done my best to make you happy." He knelt at her side. "I cannot bear to go on living with you if you hate me. You and the baby are all I have in the world. Before you came, I was alone. I had nearly mastered my loneliness. Now I cannot imagine my life without you. But I fear I have already lost you. I don't care if Banham takes the house and land, but if his venom has made you turn away from me, I will not be able to bear it."

She looked down at the floorboards. "When I lay in childbed, I heard you and another man shouting. I had never heard you so angry. I was afraid of you then. I have feared you ever since." The force of her confession made her quiver. So she had been torturing herself over this for the past month.

He couldn't endure the sight of her shattered face. Rubbing his eyes, he wet his fingers. "I was afraid for you and I lost my temper," he said. "Young Richard Banham came out with the midwife. I told him off for how he troubled you while I was away. Then he said that if you did not survive the birth, the blame would be mine." He fought to keep his voice steady. "He said that no one but a criminal would have a woman living with him in such a lonely place. He said you were a good woman and I did not deserve you."

There was nothing else he could say. This was the end, he

thought. He had already lost her, would never win her back. The log in the fire cracked and was consumed. The baby slept on. Buffeted by the wind outside, the house creaked like a ship on the high seas.

Then Gabriel started at the touch of her hand on his neck. His pulse rattled against her palm—the first time since Daniel's birth that she had touched him. Breathing her name, he wrapped his arms around her and held her close.

"May was not faithful," she said after a moment. "She must have caused you sorrow and pain. Perhaps you had reason for wanting her dead. Speak the truth. Did you . . ."

"Never." He held her at arm's length so she could read the truth in his eyes. "I could never raise my hand against a woman."

"And what of the baby?"

"You think I would harm a helpless infant? She was born sickly. She was not long for this world, but her death had nothing to do with me." He let go of her then. His head was splitting.

"What of the broken cradle?"

He held his head. "Out of grief . . ." His heart was pounding, his throat as dry as dust. "Out of grief and despair I did break it. Hannah, you must believe me." Her face blurred through his tears. "Though I did not love your sister, I never wanted her dead. I mourned her and the baby. I nearly lost my mind from grief."

"Let us settle this once and for all." Grave as a preacher, she fetched his father's Bible from the box and set it on the trestle table. "Swear an oath. Let's be done with it."

Gabriel laid his right hand on the dusty Bible. "I am innocent of murder. I never harmed your sister May or her baby."

28
Heart Pierced by Three Arrows

May
AUGUST 1690

ONE EVENING, oppressively warm and full of mosquitoes, May sat spinning on the porch while Nathan dozed in his chair. Gabriel was busy honing the metal jaws of his traps, preparing them for the coming season. He seemed to sense how the sound grated on her, sending an awful shiver through her bones, but he went on running his whetstone over the metal, over and over, as if to make her suffer. Had she truly sworn to obey this man and cleave to him forever? If Adele were here, she would not feel so desolate. She would put her spinning aside and give Adele her lesson. By now the girl could write the Lord's Prayer and Psalm 23 by heart. She could read aloud from the Bible. But Adele had been acting strange and troubled. That evening she had vanished after scouring the pots.

May held her breath as the baby kicked her beneath the heart. Lately the premonition had gripped her that this infant would be the death of her. Though she had two more months to endure, she could scarcely stomach another week. If she sat for one more second on this hard stool, she thought her belly would burst. Letting the spinning wheel whirl to a halt, she rose laboriously, hands in the small of her back. Without a word to her husband, she lumbered down the porch steps. Nathan slept on.

"Where do you go?" Gabriel called, his voice full of the usual mistrust.

"I am burning to piss," she replied tartly.

Before he could say anything more, she escaped down the path. But she did not go to the privy. In her condition, she could not bear the stench. Instead she squatted behind a bush and lifted her skirts. In this heat, she wore no underlinen. The sinking sun suffused the undergrowth in an unearthly orange light. *Used as a whore's cunny*, she thought as she pissed. Once she had heard Joan say that to her friends. They had been laughing about something May could no longer remember. What wouldn't she give to be with Joan now.

Wetness gathered under her armpits, sour as vinegar. At least the smell kept the mosquitoes off her. She longed to dunk her head in the river, let the coolness wash over her. Strip off everything and jump into the current, never mind that she couldn't swim. On Sunday last, she had seen James and Patrick swimming, naked bodies gleaming in the water. Since James had gone off her, the two of them had become tight friends.

She went instead to the creek, which was more private than the river, less deep and dangerous. When she reached the clay bank, she knelt down, not caring if she stained her skirt. She unlaced her bodice and chemise, wet her kerchief, then rubbed it against her skin. She wrung out the water over her hair, but it hardly offered relief. Finally she plunged her head underwater. Everything went dark. When she raised herself up again, her dripping hair spread coolness over her breasts, grotesquely swollen and sore.

Tugging off her shoes, she lifted her skirt and squatted in the creekbed, let the flow rock her gently. The water gushed between her legs and thighs, relieving her of her belly's weight. She could forget her puffy ankles and pretend she was a child again, playing in the creekbed with little Hannah, back when splashing naked in the water had been an innocent pastime.

She was well aware that she was courting danger. The sun had gone down. One by one, the night creatures would emerge. She might meet a prowling bear. Snakes hunted in the dark. Still, she was not eager to go back to the house. What would Gabriel say when she returned with a wet head? She flinched at the thought of him appraising her. Lurching to her feet, she wound her dripping hair in a knot, then closed her chemise and laced her bodice. Her legs were deliciously cool and wet, but her skirt was bedraggled and marked with clay. *Cold clay means death.* Her body was a dead weight. When she looked into the future, she saw a great wall of pain. She could not imagine herself as a mother with a rosy babe in her arms. Mothers were good. She was not.

Heading up the path, she passed near the Irishmen's shack, where she heard James's unmistakable laughter. Once she would have been bold enough to enter their circle and join the merriment. Hidden from sight, she hung back behind the sycamores and tiptoed toward the fork in the path that led to the house. She had to return before Nathan awoke in his chair to find her missing. Before he sent Gabriel out to look for her. *Lost your wife again, eh?* Gabriel would think she had been with a man, as if any of them would care to look at her now that she had grown so huge.

She followed the left fork to Adele's shack. She thought she could go on enduring her lot only if Adele would give her a few kind words. The full moon allowed her to pick her way along. She hoped that Adele had not already gone to sleep.

A few yards from the shack, May froze at the sound of a blade scraping wood. A tall shadowy form loomed in front of Adele's door. Trapped in her terror like a fly in a web, her palms dripped sweat. Beyond the curtain of trees, the Irishmen laughed as though this were a night like any other.

Taking a breath, May charged forward. She told herself that she had little to lose. One act of courage for Adele's sake. One act of courage was all she had to give. At the sound of her footsteps, the thing in front of the door cried out, then fell to the ground. Just as quickly, it scrambled to its feet. Moonlight glinted on the knife blade pointing at May. Adele's once familiar face was a horrible mask.

The girl stifled a cry, then lowered the knife. "You should

not creep in the dark like that." Before May had the chance to exhale, Adele's voice hardened. "Why are you about so late? Did you come now from the men's quarters?"

"You begin to sound like my husband. Pray, Adele, put away that knife. You gave me such a fright." She looked at the doorway, where she could just make out the stool on which Adele had been standing. The moonlight revealed Adele's handiwork—a carving of a heart with three lines passing through it.

"What is this? Do you work witchcraft?" The thrice-pierced heart disturbed her even more than the knife had. "Is this a curse, Adele?"

The girl grabbed her hand and pulled her away from the lintel. "Do not touch it." Her voice was tight with alarm. "Why do you come here in the dark? Your husband he will be looking for you. Let me walk you back."

May refused to budge. "Tell me the meaning of this carving, Adele."

"I did it for you. For to protect you."

"Protect me?" The sense of unease did not lift. "Protect me from *what*, Adele?" May's throat was so constricted, she found it hard to breathe. "From peril in childbirth?" When Adele remained silent, May fought the urge to shake her. "Have mercy on me, would you? Just spit it out."

The girl lifted her face to the moonlight. "I have terrible dreams." She paused. "In your condition, I do not want to say things that will make you sad."

May tried to keep from snapping at her. "Adele, I am as lost as a soul can be. Hearing of your dreams and portents cannot make things worse. If you are my friend, please speak."

"You are in danger." She spoke very softly, her voice nearly swallowed by the noise of the cicadas. "You must take better care. You ruin yourself going out in the night. You push the young master too far. In time, you might ruin us all."

"So if there is ruin, I am to blame. Do you condemn me, Adele? Have you grown to hate me, just like the rest of them?"

"You did make them hate you. It was your doing. You never loved no one. It was only a game to you, no? You made them burn for you. But you are cold. They say you have no heart."

Cold? Sweat dripped off May's face like tears. Was her need to be cherished so hateful? After James and Gabriel had begun to hate her, she had sought comfort from those who still cared. Did she not deserve a scrap of joy? But now she was a huge cow, her beauty vanished. She stank, nothing but a piece of rank flesh. She felt herself cracking, breaking, a raw egg smashed on a stone. How hot this night was. She recalled the cool English air, her sister begging her not to board the ship. *What if he is a beast?* For all she knew, Father and Joan might be dead. Her sister was probably the only soul alive who truly loved her. She wondered if she would ever see her again.

May no longer had the strength to stand. When her legs gave way, she found herself on her hands and knees in the dirt. She had to laugh at what a ridiculous creature she had become—a pregnant woman on all fours. Adele reached to help her, but May grabbed the doorframe and hauled herself up. Everything went dark as the blood rushed out of her head. Was it like this when Hannah had her fits? she wondered. Gulping for air, she prayed for the dizziness to pass. In the distance, James kept laughing. Maybe he was telling the others about her. She thought of the song that boys at home used to sing, following close behind her as she walked through the village on some errand. *Cherry-red like a slut's own bed.*

Still clinging to the doorframe, she looked again at the carving on the lintel. "The heart. Was that the purpose of your magic? To give me a new heart?" A noise came out of May's throat. She never cried, never let herself cry. Yet she was sobbing.

"You asked me to speak the truth." Adele held her the way Hannah used to, and May felt herself treasured once more. She was made human again, no longer a soulless, used-up whore. *Sweetness,* she thought, remembering a passage from the Bible. *The balm of Gilead.* If Adele still cared for her, then redemption might be within reach, even for someone as wretched as she was. But that hope vanished when the foreboding descended again.

"So you have the premonition, too." May spoke in a strangled voice, her mouth to Adele's ear. "I have seen it coming. Master Gabriel does not seem very frightful, and yet I fear him. I know I am to leave this world soon, if not in childbed, then in some other fashion."

"*No.*" Adele clasped her hands. "I will not allow it." Her voice rose loud and ardent. "I will curse him. I will strike him dead."

Her words hung in the air as the lantern shone on their faces. He had crept up so quietly. Blinded, May covered her eyes. Why did he need a lantern when he saw too much already? The shy innocent boy she had married had grown into such a bitter man.

"What do you speak of, Adele?" When he shone the light in her face, the girl bent her head and squeezed her eyes shut. Then he held the lantern to May's skirt, filthy with dirt and clay. To him it must look as though she had been rolling in the muck with a lover. His lantern picked out the knife lying on the ground and the carving on the lintel. "This is witchcraft." His voice was stark with accusation. "You both have been working witchcraft."

May thought fast. If Nathan found out, he would whip the girl.

"What nonsense, Gabriel!" Still faint, she needed his arm to make it back to the house, but she was afraid to touch him. She closed her eyes as he held the lantern in her face.

"Were you weeping, May?" he asked, a bit surprised, but without pity.

Adele took May's arm. "She misses her sister. She misses her home."

Ignoring her, Gabriel took hold of May's other arm. "Have you lost your tongue? Why do you not speak for yourself? Why are you out so late, if not to work mischief?"

"Madame came to me for medicine," Adele said. "A spider did bite her." She spoke so earnestly, striving to make Gabriel believe her, that May burst into tears again.

"Is that so?" Gabriel asked. "Show me where the spider bit you, May."

She could only hang her head and cry.

"It must be a painful bite."

"Let me be." She shrieked the words in his face. Abruptly the laughter from the men's shack died. They were listening to her bawl at her husband like a madwoman. "In my condition, I may weep if it pleases me. I know not if I will even have a midwife when my time comes."

Her outburst left her so weak that she would have collapsed had Adele and Gabriel not been holding her arms.

"I will sleep in the house from this night on," said Adele, "in case her time does come early."

Gabriel was about to say something when his father appeared. "By whose leave?" The light of his lantern illuminated his stern, tired face. "What makes you think you can simply decree—"

"By my leave, sir," said May. "When my time comes, I will need her there."

"Your time," said Nathan, "won't come until October."

"Mayhap I counted wrong, sir. Would you look at me, Mr. Washbrook? Can you not see how big I am?" Having never wept in his presence before, she had his full attention. "This night I felt pains in my belly, which is why I sought out Adele, sir." If Nathan believed her story, then it didn't matter what Gabriel believed. "You want your heir, do you not? You want me and the baby to live."

"May, you do pity yourself," said Gabriel.

"Please, Nathan." May dared to address him by his Christian name. She looked into his eyes.

"Very well," he said at last. "But anon I will have everyone abed so I might bolt the door. This ruckus has carried on far too late."

Before Nathan could turn to leave, Gabriel spoke up. "Father, there is something you must know."

When May saw the intent on his face, she thought she would

fall to her knees. What she dreaded most would come crashing down. Adele pressed her face against her shoulder. Gabriel only had to shine his light on the carving and tell Nathan that Adele had threatened to curse him.

"Well?" his father asked. "What is it?"

Gabriel clenched his jaw. Releasing May's arm, he held up the lantern, then lowered it again. The light bounced off May's skirt, his father's boots.

"Out with it, boy!"

Gabriel shook his head. "It is nothing, Father. Nothing." Turning his back on them all, he headed for the house.

29

If I Could Be Faithful

Hannah
1694

THE TIME HAD COME to put May's demise behind her. Living in peace with Gabriel was more important than mourning the past. Indeed she had little leisure for fretting. Daniel claimed all her attention, all her time. His crying shattered her sleep. She dragged herself from bed at dawn, which came earlier as winter lost its grip. She nursed the baby and boiled corn mush for breakfast. When Gabriel left to do his chores, she did hers, the same as before, except it took her at least twice as long, for Daniel had colic and she kept interrupting her sweeping and cooking to tend to his cramps. She lay chamomile compresses on his belly and gave him peppermint gripe water.

Gabriel shared her bed again. They kissed and held each other, but she had persuaded him to wait until Daniel was a year old before she risked another pregnancy.

After the snow had melted and the river and creek began to flow again, free of ice, Hannah hoed the garden for the first time that spring. She pictured the procession of the year: first the crocuses, then the violets and wood anemones, the first tender shoots of lettuce, the apple and cherry blossoms. This season she could watch her son develop alongside the ripening corn and baby goats.

The fuzz on Daniel's head grew into ringlets, and the harsh

red mellowed into a pleasing chestnut. His eyes remained dark blue. Even with his colic, he kept growing. It made no sense to clothe him in anything but swaddling, otherwise she would be forever sewing new gowns for him. When the boy could sit up by himself, Gabriel lost his awkwardness around him. He loved to carry him on his shoulders and swing him in the air.

"Which one of us does he take after?" he asked one night, lying on the furs and holding Daniel aloft. "He has your hair and my eyes."

Hannah held her tongue. It was so plain to the eye—how could Gabriel not see it? Daniel was the image of his aunt May, robust and bonny, with her blue eyes and chestnut hair, her glowing skin, her appetite and willfulness. He would grow to be a handful, she thought wistfully. He would be tall and strong, as handsome as her lost sister. If he had been a girlchild, the illusion would be complete. However, she was grateful that he was a boy, grateful that he would never suffer what her sister had suffered.

⚬┼⚬

One day when planting seeds in the garden, she sang a ballad that her sister used to sing. *If I could be faithful, then I would be true.* May's singing voice had been as lovely as the rest of her, but Hannah could hardly keep the tune. Still, she sang while Daniel watched from the willow-withy enclosure she had built him on the grass outside the garden. In his pudgy hand, he clutched a wooden rabbit Gabriel had carved. Ruby lay at his side, gnawing on a deer bone. If Daniel cried, she dropped her bone and licked him.

If I could be faithful. Joan used to say that if an unquiet spirit troubled a person, then singing a song could put the spirit to rest. It was like soothing a fractious child. *Then I would be true.* Moist dirt stuck under her fingernails and embedded itself in the grooves of her palms. To spare her good cotton dress, she wore her oldest clothes while planting pumpkin and Indian squash, potatoes and maize, beans, lettuce, cabbage, and turnips, sweet basil and thyme, heartsease and foxglove, with the seeds she had saved from the previous year. The smell of rain in the air made her cheerful, for the garden wanted watering. Pressing the last pumpkin seed into the soil, she sang a new song.

> Three maidens a-milking did go,
> Three maidens a-milking did go,
> The wind it did blow high, and the wind it did blow low.
> It tossed their petticoats to and fro.

It was a bawdy song, one of Joan's favorites. May would have laughed to hear Hannah sing it.

> They met with some young men they know'd
> They met with some young men they know'd
> They were only asking them if they had any skill
> To catch them a small bird or two.

> Here's a health to the bird in the bush,
> Here's a health to the bird in the bush,
> We'll drink down the sun, we'll drink down the moon,
> Let the people say little or much.

Ruby's barking interrupted her song. Hannah sprang to her feet to see the rider leap off his glossy bay mare. He bent over the withy wall of the enclosure and held out his hand to Daniel. "What a bonny boy you are."

"Keep your hands off my son." Before Richard Banham could doff his hat, she swept up Daniel in her arms. Ruby raced a circle around her and barked.

"Good day to you, Mistress Powers. I beg your pardon if I have caused you alarm."

Hannah's eyes raked past him to see if he had brought any men with shovels, but this time he had come alone. "What brings you here?"

He held his hat in front of his doublet. "I wanted to see if you were well. I would have come earlier had there not been so much snow." His clear brown eyes rested on her face. The wind stirred his blond hair. His voice was like silver. "You look to be in good health. The child has grown into a robust young fellow. And you, I think, were in good cheer before your dog announced my arrival. I did hear you singing."

Hannah flushed. "I did not think my voice could be heard above the wind."

"I came this day to ask your pardon," he said. "Master Washbrook told me that I caused you much dismay on the occasion of my visit last autumn."

Hannah dipped her face, remembering how she had thrown her body on her sister's grave.

"Indeed," he continued, "I remember the instance with shame. I should have shown more respect for your condition."

She told herself that she believed Gabriel, she trusted him; he had sworn his innocence. But this young man seemed so good-willed, it was hard to take Gabriel's word against him. Even his father, Paul Banham, had shown her kindness. His father was a rake, it was true, but Mrs. Gardiner, it seemed, had been a willing party. He had never troubled Hannah with unwanted attentions.

Her son stretched out his hand to Richard Banham, showing him his wooden rabbit.

"What is the child's name?"

"Daniel."

When Banham smiled, Daniel smiled back, jiggling his legs excitedly against her hips. First he had charmed her dog, now he charmed her son.

"I do believe," he said, sobering again, "that Tabitha, our midwife, might have spoken to you indelicately. She is skilled at her work, but sharp-tongued. I wanted to inquire about your welfare before I left last time, but it seemed immodest to visit a woman in childbed."

"You are kind to think of me." Hannah hugged Daniel tighter and smoothed his curls.

"If Mr. Washbrook is here, I will pay my respects to him, too."

Hannah shook her head. "He has gone into the forest to gather his traps."

"A pity," he said after a moment's silence. "My family sent a gift to you." He went to his horse, opened the saddlebag, and returned with a stoppered clay jar. "This is a pot of honey from our bees. My stepmother tells me it is the best thing for soothing a child's raw throat."

"I thank you." After setting Daniel on the grass, she took the pot from his hands. "I haven't tasted honey since I left my father's house." She thought of the two hives Joan had kept at the bottom of the garden.

Daniel looked up at Richard Banham with wondering eyes. She supposed this must be a fabulous event to him, considering that the only two people he was used to seeing were his parents.

"He is a beautiful infant," Banham said. "Indeed, there is something of your sister in him. Forgive me," he added hastily as Hannah turned away and set the honey pot on the grass. "I did not wish to make you fret."

So he saw it, too. He saw the resemblance that Gabriel refused to recognize. "You must have met my sister." Hannah spoke cautiously.

"Five years ago, I believe it was," he said. "The Washbrooks had brought their tobacco to our landing. Your sister was a new bride then, I think. Everyone said how handsome she was. Her bearing was very proud, yet her face was soft and kind. I remember she delivered a letter to the ship. It must have been addressed to you, Mistress Powers. She told me she had a younger sister back in England whom she loved and dearly missed."

Hannah pressed her fist to her mouth. She couldn't keep it in anymore. She began to sob helplessly.

"Mistress Powers," he said in alarm, "I had no wish to make you weep."

She took a few paces, filling her lungs with air, trying to regain self-control. "Did you come to torment me about Mr. Washbrook again? Is that your game?"

"Do you think it a game I play with you?" He sounded hurt.

"He said he was innocent. He swore he never harmed her. He swore an oath on the Bible."

"Mistress Powers, please. I did not come here to make trouble. I honor your loyalty to the man. Mr. Washbrook is most fortunate to have won your affection."

When she turned to face him, he held out a handkerchief. She took it from him and wiped her eyes. When the fine cambric touched her cheek, she remembered Gabriel's words. *He said you were a good woman and I did not deserve you.*

"I thank you." She tried to give him back the handkerchief, but he waved his hand.

"Keep it."

She regarded the crumpled cambric. He probably had more handkerchiefs at home, possibly a whole box of them.

"I've no wish to vex you as I did last time," he said. "But my conscience moves me to repeat my offer. Would you let me take you and your son back to my father's house? Your little one will have a playmate. My stepmother has a boy only a few months older than your Daniel. In truth, my sisters are silly, empty-headed creatures, but I think you would like my stepmother. She is lonely and longing for companionship. You would make her very happy if you accepted our hospitality. She wanted to come with the midwife this winter, but she was feeling poorly."

Hannah looked to the woods where Gabriel was collecting his traps.

"Do you ask me to abandon Mr. Washbrook?" Daniel started fussing. Soon she would have to nurse him.

"*Abandon* is a very strong word. Let me speak plainly. You believe Mr. Washbrook to be innocent. I grant you that we have no solid proof against him. Let me say for argument's sake that I share your conviction in his innocence. I would still make you this offer. Would it not be best for you and your son to live in society again? The almanac forecasts much rain this summer. In our climate, that means contagion."

He stopped abruptly. "Have you heard of the diseases we have here? The flux and the fevers?"

Hannah nodded.

"Last year we were lucky. I did not hear of many outbreaks, but I fear this summer will not be so kind. If you and Mr. Washbrook should both fall ill, what would happen to your child?"

Hannah remembered May's description of Cousin Nathan's high fever and shakes that had culminated in his death. "We have the bark of cinchona."

"And if you are both too weak to make the remedy? Of course, you must know that small children are at the greatest peril to disease."

She hugged Daniel tighter and kissed the top of his head.

"I do not think Mr. Washbrook would begrudge you for wanting to live amongst others again, especially for the health and safety of the child. He could visit you whenever he wished."

All she had to do was say yes. She could go into the house to nurse Daniel, then pack a small satchel. For an instant, it seemed within her grasp—she in her good cotton dress, seated with Mrs. Banham at the tea table. If the lady had a new baby, she couldn't be as old as her husband. She might be close to her own age. It would be such a joy to have companionship, to confide her thoughts and worries about Daniel to another mother. To lead a regular, civilized life, no longer isolated in the wilderness like some outcast.

Gabriel would come back from the woods to an empty house. She could find a piece of paper somewhere and write him a letter, leave it beside the pot of honey. *My dear Gabriel, I have gone to live with the Banhams.* It would be like stabbing him in the heart. How could he bear such a betrayal?

Richard Banham seemed to sense her discomfort. "Perhaps you wish to discuss the matter with Mr. Washbrook first. If you wish, I could return tomorrow."

She shook her head. "No, sir. I know he would be against it. He would not want me and the baby to live in your house." There seemed no point in varnishing the facts.

Banham let out his breath. "The man does cling to his grudges."

Hannah dropped her head. She wondered what would happen when Gabriel lost his leasehold. It would happen eventually, even if the Banhams bore nothing but goodwill toward them. The rents on the land had not been paid since 1690, the autumn her sister had died. Regardless of all the furs Gabriel had collected, they could not afford to keep the plantation. They were squatters.

"Is there nothing I can say to convince you?" He was certainly patient, almost as if he were paying court. Immediately she blushed and pushed the ridiculous notion away. Richard Banham would never court a woman like her. No doubt his father would find him some highborn virgin whose portion included several hundred acres.

"No," she said. "I am wed to him in my heart even if not in a church. My place is beside him." Her ringless hand moved up and down Daniel's back. She had left her pearl and ruby ring in the Bible box lest she muck it up with garden dirt.

Young Banham bowed. "I shall leave you in peace. But if you will pardon the liberty, I shall pay you another visit in the summer to see how you and the child fare." Clapping his hat back on his head, he mounted his horse.

Hannah raised her face to the bruised sky. "Travel home in good speed, sir, before the rain comes."

He waved to her before trotting back into the woods.

The clouds seemed low enough to touch the treetops. Hannah imagined them opening to drown her. Heavy rain would make the bay mare's hoof prints vanish; Gabriel would never have to know Richard Banham had come to call. She would hide the honey at the bottom of her trunk and dole it out only if Daniel had a cough.

<hr/>

Rain lashed the roof. Stirring the soup of beans, onions, and salt pork, Hannah prayed that the downpour wouldn't wash out the seeds she had planted. Their winter provisions were nearly gone.

This summer, I fear, will not be as kind as the last. Richard Banham's words lingered in her mind. She imagined the rain pelting his golden head as he spurred his mare through the forest. God willing, he would make it home safely without catching the grippe.

She had washed his handkerchief and hung it over the fire to dry. His initials stood out, embroidered in bold crimson. Had his stepmother or one of his sisters sewn him the handkerchief, or had he ordered it from a shop in Oxford? He must have cut quite a figure dressed in the black robes of a scholar. What would it have been like to be courted by a learned man, a man of the law? She dropped her spoon into the soup, then scalded her fingers when she fished it out. The heat and smoke from the fire were making her dizzy. She imagined herself legally wed to a man who owned an entire shelf of books. If she betrayed Gabriel, it was only in her thoughts. It was the loneliness that was making her half mad, the doubts and rumors hanging over them like a cloud. Surely people had been driven to lunacy by enduring less than what she had been forced to bear. Her sister buried in unhallowed ground as though she were a criminal or a suicide.

Outside, Ruby barked, and was answered by a chorus of baying dogs. Gabriel was back. Snatching the damp handkerchief, she stuffed it through the opening in her skirt and into the pocket bag that hung from her waist. She turned stiffly as the door banged open and he stumbled in, water streaming off his deerskin hat and coat. Mud dripped off his sodden boots. His breeches, too, were soaked.

"Crossing the creek, I stumbled," he muttered. "The traps do weigh me down." He could hardly speak for his shivering. When he shrugged off the traps, they hit the floor with a clatter that made Daniel wail.

"Hush, don't cry." Hannah scooped him off the floor. "That is your father."

Gabriel pulled off his hat, spraying water across Hannah's face. With his damp hair plastered to his skull, he looked like a stranger come out of the woods.

"Get those wet things off." She kept her voice brisk and practical. "Hang them near the fire."

Soon he was stripped naked, shaking and chilled. Setting Daniel down, she took a cloth and rubbed Gabriel dry, working as dispassionately as she used to with her father's patients. She took one of the deerskins from the bed and wrapped it around his shoulders, then sat him down and gave him a pan of warm water in which to soak his feet.

"You are good to me, Hannah." He lifted his hand to touch her face.

"When the beans are soft, we can eat the soup." She made her voice sound gentle. She loved him, she believed him. She had told Banham she was wedded to Gabriel in her heart. The ring was back on her finger. "I will fry you some griddle cakes."

Daniel was still crying.

"Give him to me," Gabriel said.

"You are too chilled to hold him." Hannah picked up the baby, bounced him on her hip, and set him down again. Then she went into the pantry. They had nearly reached the bottom of the salt pork barrel, and she reckoned only a week's supply of cornmeal remained. How could this be? The previous year, the cornmeal had lasted until the first runner beans were ripe and the river was leaping with fish. But this winter had been long, the spring late, and nursing the baby gave her such an appetite. She was eating more than she ever had, and yet she kept getting thinner.

She heard Gabriel's footsteps across the floorboards, the clank of metal hitting metal. The baby cried again. Rushing out of the pantry, she saw Gabriel, still naked, picking the traps off the floor. "I cannot leave these here," he said. "The child might get at them." His face was white with cold and his teeth were chattering.

"Gabriel, you do not look well." She took his arm and led him to bed. "Rest here a while." She tucked him under the blankets and skins. "I will hang up the traps."

"On the pegs." He pointed.

The traps were heavy, massive, the metal slippery in her hands. Their jaws were shut now and couldn't snap her fingers. The rusted teeth had grown dull over the winter, but Gabriel would hone them again. He would oil and polish them, sharpen each metal point. A dull trap was far crueler than a primed one, though slow death from a broken bleeding limb was agonizing in any case. She couldn't help thinking of May's smooth white leg, her grave by the river.

⊰—⊱

That night, having recovered from his chill, Gabriel embraced her in bed. He kissed her the way he used to when they first fell in love. "We can still be tender, Hannah."

She kissed him back so he wouldn't think anything was amiss. When he pushed her thighs apart and stroked her, she wanted to tell him to stop. It was no use. Since having Daniel, her body below the waist had become a lifeless thing, her old hunger gone.

"Hannah, what is it? Don't you want me anymore?"

Numbly she kissed him. If she pretended to feel something, it would comfort him. While he kept stroking her insistently, she closed her eyes and imagined Richard Banham. His face and his fair hair. The way he had looked at her when he said, *I did hear you singing*. The hurt in his eyes when he said, *Do you think it a game?* She sat behind him on the mare, wrapped her arms around his chest as the mare moved beneath her, taking them through the forest. If such thoughts were traitorous, at least no harm could come of them. Richard Banham was so far beyond her reach, she might as well be dreaming about the King.

The old hunger awakened, her body unfolding, opening up. Waves moved through her, mounting until they crashed. Eyes still closed, she blindly kissed Gabriel, reached out to stroke him, and whispered his name.

⊰—⊱

The next morning as the rain drummed down, Gabriel sat by the fire and sharpened his traps with the same whetstone he used for his hunting knife. He worked with patience, humming under his breath. He did not seem the least bit concerned about dwindling cornmeal.

Meanwhile Hannah washed the dirty clothes in rainwater. "What will happen when the rent collectors come?"

Gabriel nodded toward the rain-blurred window and laughed. "Let them try coming upriver in this weather."

Hannah thought of the path young Richard had taken through the forest. Soon the way would become treacherous. His mare would sink up to her knees in the mud.

"We cannot stay here forever," she said, scrubbing mud out of Gabriel's breeches. "One day they will come and drive us off the land."

Gabriel did not miss a single stroke of stone against metal. "The land stretches on forever. They might drive us from this house, but I could build another one. We will just wander out of their reach. Remember, Hannah, we are not like other people. We are not beholden to anyone."

⁜

The cornmeal ran out, but Gabriel told her they would never be hungry. He went into the forest and returned with a plump rabbit. When he slit its belly, there were six little rabbits inside.

Rain kept falling. Each evening at twilight, Hannah crushed snails in the garden before they could destroy the seedlings. While waiting for the garden to grow, they supped on eggs, goat's milk, and new dandelion leaves. Gabriel slaughtered a kid goat. Hannah thought of the jar of honey hidden inside her trunk.

She hoed eggshells and chicken manure into the garden, hacked up the bloody kid bones with Gabriel's ax and mixed them into the soil, too. The earth demanded blood. When the apple and cherry trees blossomed and the first strawberries ripened, she told herself they were over the worst. But the rain also brought a terrible crop of mosquitoes, far worse than anything she remembered from the previous year. Even in the house, with the door and windows closed, there was no escape. They came down the chimney and through the chinks in the walls. Their bites covered poor Daniel's skin and left him howling. She had to coat him in bear grease. At night Daniel screamed with teething pains. She fed him goat's milk, chicken broth, and mashed strawberries. It was time he was weaned; the erratic diet had dried up her milk. As long as he ate and kept growing, she could hope. She prayed over him as he learned to crawl. By the time the cherries were ripe, he seemed more like a little boy than a baby. Summer dragged on, bringing more mosquitoes. They whined in Hannah's ears each night, even plagued Gabriel, who had seemed impervious to them before.

When she looked back to the previous summer, Hannah began to believe that it was only the buoyancy of their new love that had raised them above the hardship. As the garden grew, she picked caterpillars off the young cabbages. She and Gabriel fought the insects over every ear of maize, praying they would have enough to see them through the winter.

⊶┼⊷

One sweltering afternoon, when she was pulling tassels off the maize, the dogs began barking wildly. She swung around to see Richard Banham and his horse at the garden gate. The sun shone on his golden hair and dazzling white shirt as he stroked Ruby. In his withy enclosure, Daniel squealed at their visitor.

"Good day to you, Mistress Powers. I see your son has flourished since I saw him last." He extended his hand to Daniel, who seized his thumb and grinned.

Tingling with gratitude, Hannah came to the gate. His voice was sincere; if he said her boy looked healthy, then it must be so.

He rested his hand on the gate, a few inches from hers. "I did come again, as promised."

"Sir, you are kind." Basking in her visitor's company, she smiled, then lowered her eyes. "Truly."

"How does your garden grow?"

She waved her hand toward the maize. "Every day I pluck off the caterpillars and weevils. A daily battle, it is. I do not know how people get on when they have acres of tobacco besides."

Banham was about to say something when the dogs started up again. Hannah took a step back from the gate when she saw Gabriel coming. He had been chopping wood and carried the ax in one hand.

"What brings you here?" Gabriel slapped the blunt end of the ax against his palm. "Did your father send you?"

Banham bowed. "Good day to you, Master Washbrook. I come with a gift for your household."

"We need no gifts from you."

"Gabriel." Hannah's throat was dry and tight.

Eyes locked on Banham, he ignored her.

Richard Banham's eyes moved warily over the ax. "This gift, I fear, might be indispensable in the next weeks." He cast a quick glance at Hannah before looking back at Gabriel. "I bring no trifles this time, but a pound of cinchona bark in case your supply runs low."

"What do you mean *this time*?" Gabriel's eyes were on Hannah now. "Do you mean to say you have come on previous errands bearing trifles?"

"Only the honey, Mr. Washbrook. I had assumed Mistress Powers told you."

"*Honey.*" His voice was incredulous. "What do you say to this, Hannah? Did he come with a gift of honey for you?"

"Mr. Washbrook, I rode out in early April, only to ask after her welfare." Banham spoke with quiet diplomacy, like his father. "It was meant in the spirit of being neighborly."

Even with her eyes closed, Hannah could feel Gabriel's stare. "You concealed both the gift and the visit from me?" he asked her.

Somewhere in the farthest reaches of her mind, she saw her sister spinning. May did not see her, did not look at her anymore. May had washed her hands of her.

"Mr. Washbrook, I hardly think this is cause for you to berate the woman."

Hannah cringed and stumbled away. So that was how Richard Banham thought of her—simply as Gabriel Washbrook's woman.

"*Mister* Banham." Gabriel mocked his civil tone. "I think it is time for you to leave."

Something inside her snapped. "Listen to yourself!" The anger surging through her gave her the courage to look Gabriel in the eye. "Why must you make everyone your enemy?"

The muscles in his face twitched.

"Will you make me your enemy as well?" she demanded. Marching out the garden gate, she climbed over the wall of Daniel's enclosure, picked him up, and went to Banham. "Sir, on my son's behalf, I accept your gift."

Richard Banham looked from her to Gabriel. His eyelashes, she noted, were sandy and thick. He went to his saddle bag and pulled out a cloth sack, which he handed to her.

"I thank you," she said. "God willing, we may one day be in a position to repay your kindness."

"*Hannah!*"

She had never imagined he could raise his voice to her like that, but she stood unflinching, her eyes not moving from Banham's face.

"Madam, do not speak of repayment. A gift is just that, a gift, freely given in the spirit of being a good neighbor."

"God willing, we will be better neighbors to you." She kept her voice strong. "Please give my regards to your family."

He bowed. "I will, Mistress Powers." Then he bobbed his head stiffly in Gabriel's direction. "Good day to you, Mr. Washbrook."

Her feet were rooted to the ground while she watched him mount his mare, one slender leg rising over her back. She watched him ride off. The mare's long tail fluttered gracefully.

"I scarcely think I know you anymore." Gabriel's breath touched the back of her neck.

She shivered but did not turn. "Nor I you." Holding Daniel on her hip with one arm, the cinchona bark in the other, she headed toward the house.

Gabriel came behind her and grabbed her arm. He took Daniel and set him down on the grass. She held on to the sack of cinchona bark with her free arm, clutching it like a shield.

"Why did you not tell me of his visit?"

"Because you hate him and all his family, but he was only being kind."

"Kind!" His mouth twisted. "He visits you in secret." Gabriel's fingers sank into her arm. "I saw the way you looked at him."

Hannah gritted her teeth. "Let go of me."

"I am losing you," he said in disbelief, "to that whoremonger's son."

She avoided his eyes.

"I never thought you could turn on me like that." Pain shot through his voice. "You are besotted with him. Deny it."

"My mind is my own. Don't you dare upbraid me like that. I am not your wife. I never vowed to obey you."

"You do begin to take after your sister."

She hugged the sack of cinchona bark to her chest. "What are you saying, Gabriel?"

"You heard me."

"You mean to say that if . . . if I cross you, I will meet the same end?"

He reeled backward.

"In a grave by the river?" She raised her voice to a shriek that made Daniel whimper. If she was being cruel, it was to punish him for the way he had chastised her in front of Banham, her one and only well-wisher.

"There it is!" His voice broke. "You would never believe, even when I swore an oath on the Bible. No words of mine will ever be good enough to convince you. Why do you not just call me a murderer to my face instead of meeting that yellow-haired fop behind my back?"

The dogs gathered around them and howled. Ruby nuzzled Daniel and licked his face.

"If you believe I killed her, you can go. *Now.*" He pointed to the woods into which Banham had vanished. "Take the child and run after him. Mayhap he will hear your cries and come back for you."

Wrenching her arm free, Hannah let the sack of cinchona fall and picked up the crying child. She buried her face in the crook of his neck. "Hush-a-bye."

"If you think they would treat you better than their servants . . ."

"Enough."

"They would call you a whore and our child a bastard, as surely as they call me a murderer. You know well what would happen if you put yourself in their hands."

She started walking away from him.

"Within the year, you would be big with Paul Banham's child, for they say that no female in his household sleeps in peace. Ah, but you prefer the son to the father. And I saw the way he looked at you."

Hannah swung around. "*In pity*," she said. "He looks at me in pity." She moved away from him as fast as she could with the screaming child in her arms. He could easily have caught up with her, but he let her go.

She dashed past the garden and the empty servants' shacks, leaving the cleared land behind. A trail of hoof prints and broken branches led into the forest. Could she still catch up with Banham? She whooped and shouted. Let him hear and turn back. She would allow him to take her and Daniel with him. She cried out as loudly as she could. Only the rushing river and the wind in the trees answered her.

She hugged Daniel, kissed away his tears. It wasn't an impossible distance to walk, but it was already late afternoon, judging from the sun's position in the sky. If she attempted the journey, she and the child would be caught out in the forest after dark. Flies buzzed around her head. She was too numb to swat them away. She didn't know how long she stood there, a damned woman, lost in that place between leaving and turning back. When she thought of facing Gabriel, her anger made her half blind. Daniel on her hip, she blundered down the paths, which eventually led her to the creek. Beside a shallow eddy, she stripped off his swaddling and soiled clouts, then bathed him, rubbing cool water over his hot sticky skin until he stopped crying. She sang to him until the fearful look left his face. If she could shift her shape, she would take the form of a bear that could provide for her cub on her own, defend him with teeth and claws. Why had God cursed human females by making them so vulnerable?

Soon Daniel was hungry. The only thing on hand to feed him were the raspberries that clustered at the creek bank, but she was reluctant to give him too many for fear of making his bowels run. When the sun dwindled behind the trees, the mosquitoes grew vicious. In the last light of day, she carried him back to the house.

—┼—

The door was propped open. The dogs, gathered near the porch, leapt to greet her, but she lurched through their midst, ignoring Ruby's quivering face. The smell of frying fish drifted over the threshold. Gabriel stooped in front of the fire. Sweat dripped off his face. Bruised dark circles rimmed his eyes. The look he gave her was haunted, as though he feared she had truly deserted him.

"You must be hungry," he said, voice choked.

After changing Daniel into a clean clout and swaddling, she sat at the table. Gabriel poured her a mug of goat's milk, which she spooned into Daniel's mouth.

When the catfish was golden brown, Gabriel cut it in two, giving her the bigger portion. He watched her eat, the way he had when she first came to his house. When Daniel cried, he took him before she could protest. How trustingly her son nestled in his father's arms, how tenderly Gabriel held him. For the first time in her life, she thought she had grasped the meaning of the word *mystery*. The longer she knew Gabriel, the more of a riddle he became. She would never unravel him. There was too much of him for her to comprehend.

"If you ever speak to me again as you did today, I will leave you," she said, "and never come back."

"I know, Hannah." He looked at her so sorrowfully that her eyes filled with tears.

Daniel nodded off to sleep against his father's shoulder. After tucking the boy into bed, Gabriel returned to the table and sat across from her.

"If it pleases you, we will be friendly with the Banhams. You have been lonely here long enough. I see how it pains you. If it would make you forgive me, I will take you downriver to pay a visit." It tore at her to see how much those words cost him. On her account, he was prepared to bury the grudge he had inherited from his father along with this land and the rents he couldn't pay. "I am sorry, Hannah. I beg your pardon." He folded his hands, as if in prayer, and rested his forehead on them.

⸺✦⸺

Hannah used Banham's honey to make cherry preserves. Then, a fortnight after his visit, Gabriel took her down the river, as promised. She carried the stone crock of cherry preserves in a basket packed with straw so it wouldn't crack on the boat journey. At Banham's Landing, she held the present before her, an offering in exchange for the gifts they had received, to prove that she and Gabriel could be gracious.

In his father's arms, Daniel babbled his excitement at the sight of all the new faces that came out to meet them. Hannah tried not to lose her composure under the observation of so many eyes, among them those of the midwife and the two manservants who had come bearing shovels, accompanying their master on his first visit. She prayed it would not be too awkward facing Richard Banham after he had witnessed her fight with Gabriel.

That morning she had bathed and used precious sugar for sugar water to tame her unruly curls. Despite the heat, she had ironed her good cotton gown. Gabriel had insisted on wearing his buckskins as though this were any other day, never mind the fact that he possessed good breeches and a decent waistcoat. Yet it was a miracle that he had agreed to come at all. Hannah had thought it unwise to protest his choice of attire.

As they neared the gabled wooden house with its shutters drawn against the July heat, a door opened. Richard and his kinswomen stepped out. The Banham girls were as jarringly pretty as she remembered, pink and white as apple blossoms, except this time there were only two of them.

Richard hailed his guests. "Master Washbrook, you do honor us with your visit." He made no attempt to hide his incredulity.

Gabriel nodded—the closest he would come to bowing. "It is Hannah Powers who honors you. She has come with a gift for your family."

While Gabriel remained bolt upright, Hannah curtsied, then held out the basket with both hands. "I have made cherry preserves with honey."

Bowing stiffly, Banham kept his attention on Gabriel. "You are both welcome here. I am sure my stepmother will be delighted to receive your gift."

Banham's overlooking her so completely left her punctured. Had he lost all regard for her after she had played the shrew by screaming at Gabriel in front of him? Or was this his way of showing deference to Gabriel, whose temper and jealousy he feared to incite?

"A present for your household," she said after Richard had introduced his stepmother and the twin sisters, Alice and Nell.

Mrs. Banham seemed a trifle nervous, the color high in her cheeks, but she also seemed genuinely happy to have visitors. "Most thoughtful of you, Mistress Powers, and how good to meet you at last. Our Richard has told me much about you."

Hannah took Daniel from Gabriel's arms. "This is our son. I hear you also have a boy only a few months older."

They stood eye to eye, young mother to young mother. For all her youth, Mrs. Banham was sallow-faced and hollow-cheeked. When she smiled at Daniel, Hannah observed that one of her eyeteeth was missing. But her neckcloth was filmy with Flemish lace and she wore pearls at her throat.

"Had we known you were coming, we would have waited until your arrival to serve dinner," she said.

Hannah's protest that they were not hungry was lost in the shuffle of feet as they were shown into the house. The white-washed hallway was refreshingly cool, the oak floorboards polished to a shine. Mrs. Banham opened a door to a bedchamber where a flaxen-haired boy fisted a rattle under the watchful eyes of his nursemaid. The boy's eyes widened when he saw Daniel.

"This is our Edward." Mrs. Banham reached down to stroke the child's downy head.

Hannah set Daniel on the floor beside the other tot, who reached out a shy hand to touch Daniel.

Mrs. Banham guided Hannah out of the room and shut the door. "Don't fret about leaving him. If he gets hungry, the wet nurse will tend to him."

Hannah was about to object to leaving her son with strangers when she reminded herself that this was the way of the gentry; infants and children were confined to the nursery until they were old enough to command adult manners. At any rate, she imagined it would be good for Daniel to share the company of another little boy.

In the parlor, servants arranged a circle of cherrywood chairs around a matching tea table. The shutter slats let in just enough light to reveal the room's elegance while still keeping out the heat. The massive looking glass over the mantelpiece reflected crystal candlesticks and walls stenciled to mimic patterned silk. A slender-legged spinet occupied one corner.

"The girls are accomplished musicians," Mrs. Banham said. "Perhaps later they will play for us."

Hannah gazed in awe at the wooden instrument, inlaid with ivory and different woods. She had never heard spinet music, though Father had described it for her, saying it sounded sweeter than the flute. Had May ever sat in this room and listened to the Banham girls play?

Servants produced a tray of buttered wheaten bread and red currant tart with clotted cream, which must have been left over from the main meal of the day. Mrs. Banham poured the tea herself with careful attention, as though this were what she had been born to do.

"Some prefer India tea, but I think China tea is the finest in the world. My father was a tea merchant, and that was what he always said."

She served the guests first. When she handed Gabriel a porcelain cup as fragile as an eggshell, he held it uneasily, as if afraid he might crush it.

Though it was comfortably cool in the room, Alice and Nell flapped their lace fans. Hannah wondered whether they did it out of habit or boredom. The soft hiss of moving air stirred the ash-blond curls around their white throats. Eyes darting over the top of their fans, they kept looking from her to Gabriel and back again. With his buckskins, sunburnt face, and long black hair, he looked like an Indian wandered out of the woods. His face was stoic, thoughts and mood well concealed.

Mrs. Banham made a great show of passing out the victuals, though she ate nothing herself. Her hands kept fluttering at her sides. She reminded Hannah of a high-strung horse. Any little noise or commotion might cause her to bolt.

"I believe you met the girls once before, Mrs. Powers?"

"Indeed I did," said Hannah. "And their sister. I believe her name is Anne."

"Anne is now married and in Virginia," Nell said. Then she lowered her eyes and fanned herself briskly.

"You must miss her." Hannah tried to soften toward the girls.

"She writes to us," said Alice. "But we've not seen her in over a year."

"I know what it is," Hannah said, "to miss a beloved sibling."

Silence fell on the room, heavy as a bear trap's jaws closing and cutting. The Banhams looked at Gabriel, who held his head without blinking. Hannah cursed herself.

To change the subject, she turned to Mrs. Banham. "I trust your husband is well."

A stricken look passed over the lady's face.

"You must pardon my father's absence," Richard said, addressing Gabriel. "He is in England on business of the West India Company."

Hannah caught her breath. To think the wealthy could sail back and forth across the Atlantic as if it were a mere river. The memory of the home she would never see again rived her.

The subject of her errant husband left Mrs. Banham out of sorts. The teacup trembled in her hand, splashing brown liquid into the saucer. Hannah searched for words that would brighten the conversation.

"Mrs. Banham, if ever you are in need of physick receipts, I would be most happy to assist. If colic ever troubles your son, I can mix for you an efficacious gripe water."

"The colic was nearly his death this spring." Mrs. Banham raised her handkerchief to her eyes. "I buried one little boy already. The seasonal ague took him."

"I am sorry, madam." Hannah's face went hot. "Forgive me. If ever I can help you in any way . . ."

The lady's eyes were downcast, lost in sadness.

"Drink your tea, Mother," Alice said, "before it gets cold."

"All is well on your property, Mr. Washbrook?" Richard asked.

Gabriel nodded.

Nell and Alice traded a covert look.

"Your gown, Mrs. Powers, is most handsome," Nell said, eyes flashing. "And so is your ring."

"Thank you," Hannah replied, flustered.

"India cotton," said Alice. "It looks to be of the finest quality." She regarded Gabriel's buckskins and then went back to fanning herself.

They had uttered nothing discourteous, but their sly smiles said it all. This unkempt man who dressed like a savage and who had neglected the rents for four years had somehow managed to clothe his woman like a lady of quality. The Banham girls seemed to find this hilarious.

Hannah struggled not to weep in humiliation. To think she had yearned for female companionship for so long. Their brother shifted uncomfortably in his chair but did not rebuke them for their disrespect.

"I prefer China tea to India tea," Mrs. Banham prattled on like an addled old woman. "Mr. Banham prefers India tea, but I say China tea is the best. My father was a tea merchant. He gave me a silver tea chest for my wedding."

"Have a piece of tart, Mother," said Alice in a too sweet voice.

"The colic was nearly Edward's death." Sloshing tea, Mrs. Banham rocked herself back and forth like a Bedlamite. "Two children born, one already buried. The flux eats me like a vulture. I was married off with a good portion, you know. It paid for two thousand acres in Virginia." Her eyes shone with a febrile glaze.

Nell snatched Mrs. Banham's teacup before it could be dashed to the floor. "Our stepmother has her fits and spells. It will pass. Won't it, Mother?"

"It's the excitement of having visitors," said Alice. "She says she can't bear another day of loneliness and then, when we do have visitors, she gets overwrought."

"Does she need physick?" Hannah asked. "There are herbs which can soothe a troubled humor."

"We have physick in plenty." Richard stared at the opposite wall. "Mercury and laudanum."

Mrs. Banham emerged from her mournful reverie with a jerk of her neck. She fixed Hannah with a stare. "I imagine one day the pair of you will finally fare to Anne Arundel Town to address the magistrates and atone for what you have done." Her face had gone hard and mean.

"Magistrates, madam?" Hannah thought of herself and Gabriel being interrogated. The graves by the river. The testimony of a thief. She burned, unable to hide her dread. Alice and Nell perched on their chairs like hunting falcons.

"To place the banns!" Mrs. Banham exclaimed. "Surely you intend to wed before another unhallowed child is born."

Hannah's spine slumped. Everything went out of her.

Gabriel spoke, startling everyone. "It grows late. If we would travel home by daylight, we must leave."

When he caught Hannah's eye, she thought he had been right about the Banhams all along, that in shunning them, he had been trying to shield her from their malice and condescension. Though the Banhams had nearly reduced her to tears, Gabriel remained in full self-possession. "I thank you for your kind hospitality." His irony cut through their pretense.

Following his example, Hannah did not curtsy or even incline her head before walking out of the room. Instead she sought to carry herself with Gabriel's proud indifference. Reaching the hallway, she burst without knocking into the bedchamber where she had left Daniel and found him playing with a painted wooden horse. The other boy slept while the nursemaid rocked his cradle. He looked pale and sickly. At any other time, Hannah would have offered physick, but now she just swept her own son into her arms and carried him away.

Richard spoke to Gabriel in the hall. "I apologize for my stepmother's affliction, which causes her to say improper things."

Hannah took her place at Gabriel's side. The Banhams no longer had the power to humble her, and Richard no longer had the power to slight her. Before God, all men and women were equal. This was what Father believed and what Gabriel had taught her better than anyone could. The glamoury eye saw beyond the finery in this household to the corruption that gnawed at its core. The Banhams were a sorry excuse for a family. The father was a libertine, and the stepmother was possessed of a troubled mind. Alice and Nell were biding their time before their father married them off to planters, who might well hold their dowries in higher esteem than their beauty and accomplishments. If Richard retained any spark of character or integrity, it was by virtue of his being a young man with all the liberties of his class. But only his money set him apart from Gabriel.

"Goodbye, Mr. Banham." She looked at him boldly until he went red in the face and bowed to her.

That night, when they had returned to their own home and after she had tucked Daniel into bed, she led Gabriel to the pile of furs by the hearth and let him unlace her gown. She pulled him down beside her, and it was as if they had never fought. When he kissed her, she laughed and twined herself around him, happier than she remembered she could be.

30 Down in the Hollow

Hannah
1694

HANNAH TOOK HER PAIL and went to pick raspberries, ripe and dark red in the thorny bushes that grew up and down the creek. Gabriel fashioned a buckskin packsack for Daniel so that she could carry him on her back. The little boy adored their forays into the woods. He squealed, bare feet kicking into her ribs as though spurring on a horse. Ruby trotted at her side.

Compared to the never-ending struggle with the garden, Hannah was amazed at how easily wild plants grew without sowing or tending. Native daisies and sweet cicely sprang from the earth, growing more luxuriantly than her heartsease. But the foxglove had gone wild through self-seeding, establishing itself in the undergrowth. Dark pink bells rose beside the rotted tree stumps.

She picked a pail or two of raspberries a day, and baked them in cobblers or served them with goat's milk and maize pudding. Gabriel found an old cask barrel and cleaned it out so she could make raspberry wine. Her mother's receipt called for six pounds of berries, a mighty endeavor, but raspberry wine was the best tonic for sore throats and it would cheer them in winter when snow lay thick on the ground.

The day she set off berrying, Gabriel lay abed with a low fever. "It is nothing to fret over," he told her. "Just a mild ague. If I rest a spell, I shall be better by nightfall." Hannah took the two big milking pails with her, reckoning that each held around three pounds of fruit.

Following the familiar path to the creek, she passed the garden and the abandoned servants' shacks. Something made her stop outside the smaller shack and look at the heart carved on the lintel. Gabriel kept the goats in the other shack, but he never went near this one. By now, the roof had nearly caved in. Hannah thought that he would at least want to salvage the wood for winter fuel. Foxglove sprang up all around the hovel.

The raspberry bushes on her side of the creek were almost stripped clean. The reddest, ripest-looking fruit was out of her reach on the other side. At first she hesitated. The creek was swollen with rain and she had Daniel on her back, but Ruby leapt into the water and was already paddling to the other bank. There was really no reason why she shouldn't go there, Hannah decided. Gabriel hadn't set up the traps yet. Lifting her skirts, she waded across, wonderfully cool water washing up to her thighs.

It was a fine day, not too hot. She was content to take her time and eat as many berries as she put in the pail. If Gabriel could rest a day, then she had earned a few hours' respite from the garden and household chores. She worked her way up the creek bank, plucking berries off thorny stems. She kept picking, allowing the lure of the berries to draw her farther up the bank and into the forest itself. When the first pail was full, she covered it in sacking to keep off birds and flies, then began to fill the second.

It was so delightfully shady and dreamy, with the birds calling and the wind moving through the leafy branches. To ease her aching shoulders, she shrugged off the packsack and nestled with Daniel against the trunk of a loblolly pine. Arms wrapped around her son, she let the drowsiness claim her. Just a little nap.

A low growl awoke her. A red buck with a full rack of antlers stared at her, his eyes dark and liquid, until Ruby leapt to her feet and barked. Lunging forward, Hannah grabbed her around the neck. The dog strained, eager for the hunt, but Hannah held on while Daniel looked off in the direction the stag had fled. "Dada," he said.

By the time she returned home, Gabriel was up, sitting on the porch and whittling a whistle for the boy.

—+—

In the weeks that followed, Hannah made the wine. First she washed the berries, put them in the biggest kettle, then poured boiling water over them. She stirred the mixture, covered the kettle with sacking, and left it for ten days.

She strained the ruby liquid through an old bit of cheesecloth she found in the dresser, added all the remaining sugar and honey they had in the house, stirred, and covered the kettle again. She stirred it daily for the next three days, then poured the liquid into the cask barrel and put the lid on loosely, allowing it to ferment. The wine would be ready to drink in six months.

Gabriel put maize through the grinder, filling up the cornmeal sacks in the pantry. He promised her they would want for nothing that winter. In autumn, when he went to sell his furs, he would buy another sack of cornmeal and a sack of wheaten flour besides. "You will be able to bake real bread again."

The year's struggle was nearly over. They had enough. Soon the apples would be ready for picking. Gabriel would cull the goats and pigs. Hunting and trapping season would begin. The heat would mellow into the pleasing crispness of autumn, but not before summer's last stand. One steamy afternoon, they swam naked in a shallow river eddy, passing Daniel back and forth between them. They danced in the water with the dogs barking from the shore.

Daniel was growing fast. Hanging on to the bedstead, he took his first steps. Gabriel made him a pair of deerhide slippers and nailed planks to the other bed to raise the sides so Daniel wouldn't roll out. Then he made him a mattress stuffed with fresh new straw.

—+—

When Hannah awoke one morning to a fuzzy head, her first thought was that she was pregnant again. They hadn't been taking care to prevent it. When she tried to get up and boil the break-fast corn mush, she nearly fainted. She was sweating, chilled, and trembling, her breathing shallow and labored. As hard as she panted, she couldn't get enough air.

Gabriel led her back to bed. "It is the flux. You must rest until it passes." He brewed her a heady decoction of cinchona bark and made her drink the bitter stuff until she was ready to spit up. He tucked the furs up to her chin and held her hand. "Never fear. It *will* pass. I have never seen the flux take a strong young person. I have had it myself since I was a boy."

She looked at him in confusion. A hazy halo formed around his face. "You never did tell me."

"The ague I had just weeks ago . . . that was it. It comes and goes in fever and shakes. I will have it all my life. It is a rare person in these parts who doesn't have the flux."

"It killed your father."

"He was old." Gabriel's face blurred. "But you are young." As he mopped her forehead with a cloth, his eyes came back into focus, inky blue-black. "You will endure this."

⸭

Hannah awoke to Daniel's crying. She lifted herself on her elbow to see Gabriel pick him up and tell him to hush, Mama wasn't well.

"Oh no, he isn't ill now, too." Panic rose in her throat.

Gabriel shook his head. "No, Hannah. He is healthy as ever, just bad-tempered today, I think."

⸭

As Gabriel had promised, her fever broke and the chills left her. She could breathe freely and soon felt well enough to get out of bed.

"You must rest easy," Gabriel told her, "until you are quite strong again."

Another week passed and she felt like her old self. She went with Gabriel to the orchard and helped him pick apples. Then, a few days on, Gabriel had the fever and shakes.

"It is nothing," he said. "Just the ague. It sticks with me like an old friend." He lay down to rest a few hours. But when Hannah brought him the decoction of cinchona, his forehead was blazing and his eyes were unfocused.

"Adele did this," he mumbled. "She poisoned me."

Hannah placed her hand on his chest. His heart was racing. She thought of the foxglove growing around the old shack. The carving of the heart pierced by three arrows.

"May asked her to work witchcraft on me. She wanted me dead."

"Hush." When she wiped his forehead, he flinched at her touch.

"That is why they do call them merry widows. She wanted me gone. But she couldn't kill me, for I was a ghost already."

"Gabriel." She took his face in her hands. "This is Hannah. No one is going to poison you."

"Foxglove flower in the stew, but it didn't kill me. I was dead already, living in a dead man's house."

"Gabriel, hush." She wrapped her arms around him and gently rocked him back and forth.

"Black widow," he mumbled. "Bitten by a black widow spider."

"Darling, hush." She sang a lullaby as she would to Daniel until he quieted down and allowed her to give him his medicine. She held his hand while he dozed off.

—+—

Hannah paced the floor with Daniel in her arms. Had Adele really tried to poison him? Because May had asked her to? Nonsense, he had been raving in his fever. Yet why did all that foxglove grow around Adele's old shack? She reminded herself that the plant could spread like a weed. Properly dosed, it was healing physick, not poison. Why would a servant girl try to kill him? She would be hanged for such a crime.

Surely May wasn't vicious enough to plant such an idea in the girl's head. May had been unfaithful, but not murderous, not capable of plotting her husband's death. May had not been evil. But neither was Gabriel evil, and yet his former manservant had accused him of murdering his wife. This knot was far too snarled for her to unravel. If only she had someone to talk to, not Banham or anyone who had ever quarreled with the Washbrooks, but someone impartial.

If Father were here, he would warn her about letting her passions and doubts sweep her away. She must keep her head. The key, he had always said, was the intellect. Rational thought and judgment. At home, when her thoughts were confused and overwrought, he used to tell her to collect herself and read the Bible for guidance. "Turn to the story of Hannah in the first book of Samuel," he would say, "for that is a story of the triumph of patience and humility." The biblical Hannah had been barren and thought herself forsaken by God, yet she had prayed and lived a virtuous life until God finally allowed her to conceive Samuel, the prophet.

While Gabriel tossed and groaned in his sleep, she opened the Bible box and carried the heavy book to the table. She added another log to the fire so she would have enough light to read. It shamed her to consider that she had lived in this house for nearly two years and had never read the Bible once. This wilderness had turned her into a heathen. No wonder her mind was so befuddled. She clasped her hands and whispered the Lord's Prayer before opening the cover. Turning the stiff pages to the first book of Samuel, she found a scrap of folded paper covered in her sister's cramped handwriting.

October ?, 1690

My Hannah,

  Should you ever find this, I must tell you that I have ruined Everything. My Husband hates me worse than the Devill. They all hate me now, save Adele. Only she can tolerate my Company. I am weak and sinfull and God has seen fitt to punish me. I could not even keep my own Child alive. Dearest, I think

you shall never see me again. I doubt I shall ever rise from this
Bed. It is with my last Strength that I hold this Quill. I did to
you a great Wrong in begging you to join me here. Now it is
too late to send a Letter warning you away. I have asked Adele
to hide this where you may one Day find it. Darling, you must
not linger in this House of Pain, for it will destroy you as it has
destroyed me. You must return with all Haste to Anne Arundel
Town. Make yourself known there. With your Learning and
Skill in Physick, you would do well as a Midwife. If you wish to
marry, you will have Suitors in plenty. Forgive me if you can
and then forget me, dear Hannah, for I was born under Cursed
Stars and only bring Pain and Misfortune. I love you and pray
for your Happiness.

Yr lost Sister May

Her sister's pain shimmered as the room around her dis-
solved. *My Husband hates me worse than the Devill.* May had pressed
the quill so hard when writing the word *hates* that she had pierced
the paper. *You must not linger in this House of Pain, for it will destroy*
you as it has destroyed me. What had she meant by that? What precisely had destroyed her? The hard life, the loss of her newborn,
and the childbed fever? Or was it Gabriel's hatred?

He had hated her, and she had died shortly after giving birth.
Childbed fever was the perfect explanation for such a death. He
had sworn that he never harmed her or raised a hand against
her, but might he not have been at least partly responsible for
her death? In her weakened state, May needed comfort, not hate.
Had he contrived to push her over the edge? No, not Gabriel. He
could never do such a thing.

The letter clutched to her chest, she wandered the room.
When she stood over Gabriel's bed on the shadowy side of the
room, she could barely make out his shape. She was tormented by
the fact that she had found May's message in the Bible on which
he had sworn his innocence.

Father had always told her that truth was a plain and
straightforward thing, as solid and unmoving as a church tower.

But it wasn't. The truth was a tangled web. In her letter, May had alluded to her sins. What had her sister done to Gabriel besides being unfaithful, and what had Gabriel done to May? The only hard fact she had was that Gabriel lived and her sister was dead.

With numb hands, she folded the letter, tucked it back in its hiding place, closed the Bible, and returned it to the box. She couldn't sleep beside him that night. Taking a blanket, she curled up with Daniel in the other bed.

—✢—

When she brought Gabriel his cinchona brew the following morning, he looked at her with clear eyes. "I think I am on the mend."

"Last night you did rave." She gave him the cup without touching his hands.

"The worst is past." He took his first sip, then made a comical face to demonstrate how bitter the brew was.

Hannah didn't smile. "Have you no memory of what you said?"

He wrinkled his brow. "What do you mean?"

"You spoke of May."

He blanched. She could see the bones beneath his skin. "What did I say?"

"Do you not remember?" Her sister's words still burned inside her. Hers was not the letter of a woman who had plotted to poison her husband, but of a woman who knew that she was going to die. Hannah didn't want to make it any easier by prompting him. Let the truth rise to the surface. If she waited long enough, he would spill it.

He went on gulping down the cinchona brew. His hands shook and he swallowed clumsily, letting some of the liquid run down his chin. His teeth rattled. "I am cold. Bring me another blanket."

"You said just now you were on the mend."

"Hannah, please."

"Speak first. Do you remember what you said about my sister last night?"

He shrank back into the pillow. "Why do you torment me?"

"Did you hate her, Gabriel? Worse than you hate the devil?"

"She hated *me*." He shivered even harder.

"Do you deny that you hated her?"

"Hannah, bring me the blanket."

"Answer me first."

"Aye," he said finally. "I hated her in the end."

"Hated her enough to let her die?"

His breathing was shallow and fast. "Why do you do this to me?"

"Answer the question, and I will bring you the blanket." She took him by the shoulders and turned his face to hers. Cold sweat covered his skin.

"You are cruel. You would never believe me."

"Why will you not answer?"

"I answered you before and it did not satisfy."

She made her face stony and impassive. "Why did you forbid me to go into the forest beyond the creek?"

He closed his eyes, his head rolling back and forth on the pillow. "The traps." He gasped for air, fighting for each breath. "You will kill me."

His words cut to the bone. She brought him the blanket, made him some chicken broth, and spooned it into his mouth. Questioning him further would be pointless. His eyes had gone blank.

Hannah washed Daniel's clouts while the morning slipped by. At midday she fed Gabriel more chicken broth. He was able to sit up, his eyes unclouded once more, but he had trouble meeting her gaze.

"Are you feeling well enough to be left alone while I go to the hen house for eggs?" she asked him.

He nodded stiffly, evidently still angry for the way she had treated him the previous night.

"I must fetch water, too, and cut herbs in the garden. I may be gone an hour." She put Daniel in his leather packsack, picked up her water pail and egg basket, and let herself out the door.

The winding path took her past the garden and the shack with the carving of the heart pierced by three arrows. It was some kind of charm, she decided. Possibly a symbol to ward off evil. Yet it disturbed her to look at it and then see the foxglove growing all around. Yes, foxglove was poison. She remembered the panic on Gabriel's face when he had said, *You will kill me*. Only Joan could make sense of his ravings and the symbol on the lintel. Joan and her pack of cards could unknot the things that Father and his logic could not touch.

Hurrying away, she left her empty basket and water bucket outside the hen house, then went to the creek. She didn't know what she hoped to find, but she whistled loudly, the way Gabriel did when calling the dogs. Three sharp piercing whistles and they came rushing. Rufus, the big red-and-white-spotted hound, was the leader of the pack. She pointed to the opposite bank and the dogs plunged across the creek. They were Gabriel's dogs and yet they followed her commands, charging up the bank. She nearly had to run to keep up. Bouncing in his packsack, Daniel giggled and pulled at her hair.

The dogs knew the forest as well as their master did. Gabriel had put out the traps some days ago. When he wasn't ill, he checked them every few days. Used to the routine, the dogs led her efficiently from trap to trap. Noses to the ground, they sniffed out the scent of blood. Hannah surveyed the dead rabbits and raccoons and the single dead bobcat. At each trap, the dogs looked at her and wagged their tails. They seemed disappointed that she didn't skin the animals and throw them the meat. She just pointed and urged them on. They obeyed, drunk on the excitement of sniffing out death, leading her past the scattered remains of earlier victims. Ruby picked up a bone and loped along with it in her mouth. Hannah counted the traps. They had visited eleven; Gabriel had twelve.

The dogs led her deeper into the forest than she had ever gone. Breathing hard, she followed them uphill. The dogs stopped abruptly, keeping their distance from the bear trap, still empty and unsprung. Rufus looked at her inquiringly, then set off in the direction from which they had come. Now he would lead her home.

Hannah whistled three times, calling them back. They wagged their tails and tilted their heads in confusion. She didn't know what order to give, just pointed blindly around. "Go!" Rufus started off again, the others at his heels.

It seemed a familiar path to Rufus, although some of the younger dogs whined and looked a little bewildered. Ruby kept glancing back at her.

Rufus led them down into a hollow where beech trees grew. A slender spring flowed from the hillside, then disappeared underground. Hannah's first thought was that it was a pretty, sheltered place. If they were driven off the land, she and Gabriel could build their new home here. It seemed so protected from the outside world. Picking her way down the steep incline, she saw the dogs sniffing and digging at a fallen log. A crow cawed harshly, then flew off a branch. When Hannah caught up, the dogs pawed at a piece of rotted fabric. Something turned in her stomach. Shrugging off the leather packsack, she set Daniel down so that he faced away from the log. He smiled at her, showing off his milk teeth.

Hannah kissed the top of his head before going to the log. "Rufus, away!" she ordered. He and the other dogs shrank back. The fallen log covered a shallow pit. Someone had buried something here, then a wolverine or raccoon had dug it up. Kneeling in the loose dirt, Hannah pulled up a piece of rotted cloth, slimy in her fingers. Bracing herself, she put it aside and dug to find more pieces of cloth underneath. They were too rotted and weather-worn to make out the original color, but their shape was still discernible. They were women's clothes. She shook them out and spread them flat on the mossy ground. Grabbing a stick, she dug deeper, finding another garment, heavier than the rest. The quality of the fabric had saved it from degrading too fast. It was filthy, beetles crawling in its folds, but Hannah recognized the lawn embroidered with roses and doves. Her sister's wedding dress. Beneath the dress was a glint of ivory. Bare bone with a bit of decayed flesh stretched taut over what had once been a face.

The bile rose to her mouth and burned her lips. On all fours, she spewed into the ferns. She roared, pummeling the fallen log until her fists were bloody. The dogs barked and whined and licked her face. Daniel howled. She wiped her hands clean on the damp moss and went to her son. "Just a while longer." She didn't dare touch him with the hands that had dug in her sister's grave. Instead she kissed him until he stopped crying. She made Ruby sit with him.

Soil tore at her fingernails as she dug with her bare hands. Only fragments of skin and rotted cloth clung to the bones. Worms lived inside May's skull. Wild animals had gnawed at her. To keep herself from screaming, Hannah thought of the ordered anatomical diagrams in her father's books, illustrated skeletons crisp and clean, clearly marked, not stinking of decay.

She could not pull the corpse out of the grave without tearing it apart, but could only dig slowly, revealing one bit of May at a time. When she unearthed her left hand, she found the wedding ring loose on the bone. She took it off and rubbed it clean on the moss. A plain gold wedding band with no ornamentation, not like the pearl and ruby ring Gabriel had given her. Her own ring was filthy from the digging. She tore it from her finger and stuffed both rings in her pocket.

At last she uncovered the legs. The tibia and fibula of the right leg were shattered. It might have come from the bear trap, matching the story Richard Banham had told her, or it might be that the bones had slowly disintegrated in their shallow grave. She didn't have the skill to know. But the bones of the left leg, though brittle, were unbroken.

Gazing bleakly around the hollow, her eyes came to rest on a beech trunk, which bore an awful scar where someone had hacked the bark away. The scar formed a rough rectangle. Shakily she stood up and walked toward it. It was as if someone had carved something on the tree and someone else had hacked the message away. She thought of the carving of the heart pierced by three arrows.

Daniel was crying again, no doubt from hunger. She had nothing to give him.

"Just a while longer!" she called. Stumbling to the spring, she washed her fingers until they were numb. "Hush-a-bye!" She kissed Daniel, strapped his packsack on her back, and squatted on her haunches to pick up May's wedding dress. When she tried to shake the beetles out, grave dust hit her face.

Whistling to the dogs, she started back toward the creek. Barking and sniffing, they led her up the steep hill. Daniel cried all the way back. "Hush-a-bye," she sang while the tears glazed her face. Reaching through the opening of her skirt and into her pocket, she fingered the two rings. One belonged to her, the other to her sister, both given by the same man.

Hitching up her skirt, she splashed through the creek, not caring that her feet were soaked. The dogs made for the house, but she went to the orchard, where she found one shriveled apple still clinging to its branch. She picked it, tore off the wrinkled skin with her teeth, and bit the soft flesh into small pieces, which she fed to Daniel, letting him take each piece from her lips so she wouldn't have to feed him with her hands.

Looking at the house, she saw the thin trail of smoke rising from the chimney. The dogs would wake him up. They would want to be fed. Hoisting Daniel back on her shoulders, she picked up May's wedding dress and made her way to the tobacco barn, where she took the biggest shovel from its peg. She carried it to the graves by the river. Setting Daniel and the wedding dress down, she dug, tearing up grass and the autumn crocuses she had planted.

Near the house, the dogs kept barking. Gabriel shouted her name. Ramming her shovel into the earth, she labored until she struck wood—the coffin lid of splintering pine. She continued until the entire coffin lid was uncovered, then forced the shovel under the lid and pried until the rotted wood and rusty nails gave way. Wrenching off the lid, she stared down into the empty coffin. To think she had planted those crocuses and pleaded so tearfully over a vacant box.

Daniel cried. The day had grown cold. He must be chilled and cramped in the confines of his packsack. His clouts wanted changing. Hannah rubbed her face with her filthy hands and stared at the river flowing past.

Unsteady footsteps moved up the path behind her. Gabriel called her again. He didn't sound like a man anymore but a ghost. Hannah watched him stagger forward, his face pale and tight with pain. He was too ill to be out walking. If he took another step, he would collapse. Part of her still wanted to run to him, take him in her arms, help him back to the house. The part of her that still loved him wept to see his body sway. He grabbed a tree trunk to hold himself upright. *They tried to kill me, but they could not. I was dead already, living in a dead man's house.*

She didn't have to say a word. His eyes moved from the opened grave to May's ruined wedding dress flung on the grass. He looked at her soiled hands, face, and clothes as though she herself were the dead sister who had clawed her way out of her own grave. He sank to his knees, the dogs circling around him. Rufus took position at his side.

Hannah regarded the bowed head of the man who had been her first and only love. The boy who had been so tender to her, opening up her heart and body.

"What did you do to my sister?" She pitched her voice above the baby's cries.

"Have mercy." He gulped for air as she strode toward him.

Rufus leapt to his feet and threw himself between her and his master. "I did not harm her."

"You think you can still tell the same lies?" Reaching into her pocket, she pulled out the plain wedding band. "Was this the ring you gave her?"

He jerked his face to one side as though she had struck him. "I did not kill her." He sweated and shivered with each word. "She ran away from me. She did step in the bear trap and perish. It was an accident, no murder."

How could he look at her like that, with those imploring eyes, as if he were the wronged one? He said her name over and over like a prayer.

"Then why did you lie to me of the childbed fever? Why the false grave?"

He collapsed against the tree trunk, eyes glassy with fever. She had left him alone for hours in this state. No doubt his throat was parched. He needed physick, but meanwhile Daniel was screaming and she could ignore the child no longer. Strapping on the packsack, she rushed away, leaving Gabriel beside the grave. Tears blurred her eyes as she broke into a headlong run. Father had told her that an opened, empty coffin was a symbol of resurrection. She could hear her sister's voice again, speaking the words of her last letter. *Forgive me if you can and then forget me, dear Hannah, for I was born under Cursed Stars.*

Remembering there was no water in the house, she went to the chicken coop where she had left her pail, then filled it at the creek. She washed the grave dust from her hands and face. Once back inside, she stripped the soiled clouts off Daniel, bathed him, and wrapped him in fresh ones. There was no time to wash the soiled rags; the goats wanted their second milking. Putting Daniel back in the packsack, she took him with her. The motion of her body seemed to soothe him. When the milking was finished, she cooked him cornmeal mush with hot milk—a proper meal to fill him at last. He devoured every spoonful, her robust boy. She still had him to live for, if nothing else. She had to endure long enough to raise him to manhood. She was thankful that he was so young: he would not remember this day. She wished she had the power to make herself forget. Sweet Daniel, the only innocence she had left. She kissed him and tucked him in his bed.

Outside, the dogs scratched at the door. Gabriel was out there somewhere, shivering and ill. Rain clouds were moving in. Following the dogs down the path, she thought of the biblical Hannah's song of praise in the first book of Samuel. The words of triumph and faith that Father had told her to commit to memory rang out like a curse. *The Lord killeth, and maketh alive: he bringeth down to the grave, and bringeth up . . . The adversaries of the Lord shall be broken to pieces; out of heaven shall be thunder upon them: the Lord shall judge the ends of the earth.*

She found him only a few paces from where she had left him. Evidently he had tried to drag himself back to the house and had fainted from the effort. She touched the side of his neck and felt his pulse. Though unconscious, he was breathing. She ran to the river and wet her neckcloth, then returned. Kneeling at his side, she wiped his hot face until his eyes opened.

Nearly two years before, she had been flat on the ground, coming out of her seizure to see the strange young man's face above hers, his dark eyes filled with such shy solicitude. How gentle he had been, cooking for her and comforting her while she wept for her sister.

Gabriel looked up at her without speaking. Maybe he was too ill to speak. God would take him, just as he had taken Father and May. An evil voice inside her said that if God punished him, she wouldn't have to. Hannah wept in shame. Long ago, her father had made her swear an oath to use her knowledge of physick to heal, to do everything in her power to help those who needed healing. If Gabriel died on account of her neglect, she would be as damned as he was.

"Water." His voice rasped like autumn leaves.

"Open your mouth." She squeezed out her neckcloth over

his parched tongue. It was only a trickle, but enough to moisten his throat.

"I thought you left me here to die."

Her tears fell on his face. "I must get you back to the house. Can you stand?"

She put her arms around his neck and pulled him so he sat upright. Slowly she helped him to his feet. Wrapping his arm around her shoulder, she bore as much of his weight as she could. He shuddered with each step. She had to urge him on.

"Look, you can see the porch. Just a little further."

When he faltered, she held on to him with all her strength to keep him from falling. At last they reached the house, where he collapsed into bed. Hannah piled blankets and furs on him. She brewed cinchona bark. He shivered so violently, she had to drip the brew into his mouth with a cloth.

"Just swallow." She made her voice gentle. These were her arts, and Father had insisted she use them to the best of her ability. *Love the sinner but hate the sin.* Gabriel sweated so much that she stripped the buckskin off him, sponged his body, and wrapped him in a man's nightshirt she found in the chest of drawers. It must have belonged to his father, for it dwarfed his thin body. She covered him up again, stoked up the fire, and made him onion broth. She brewed him a decoction of feverfew and sang to him as she would sing to Daniel. *Tirra lirra lirra.*

"It is only the ague," she said. "You are young and strong. You will endure this." She stayed up through the night, gave him more cinchona brew, and wrapped his legs in wet cloths to lower the fever before tucking him under the blankets again. But his fever didn't break until dawn.

⊷┼⊶

Rain fell softly, beading the hairy flank of the goat she milked. The rain wet her dress, stiff with yesterday's dirt. Her joints ached as she dragged the milk pails, then the water bucket and egg basket, back to the house. Her bones creaked like those of an old woman.

He lay in bed, still weak but out of danger. When she brought him corn mush, he ate in silence, not looking up from the trencher. She felt his eyes on her, though, as she fed Daniel his breakfast. She caught Gabriel watching them as if for the last time. After Daniel was fed and changed, she gave him his wooden rabbit and put him in his bed with its high sides to keep him from falling out. Then she took away Gabriel's empty trencher and spoon. She stood at the foot of his bed.

"You must tell me, once and for all. How did my sister die?"

"It is hard to remember. I tried so hard to forget."

Hannah crammed her fists in her pockets to keep herself from slamming them against the bedstead. "You buried her in the forest like an animal."

"Hannah, you have no inkling. She hated me, betrayed me, called me the vilest names."

"I found a letter that she hid away for me to find. She said that *you* hated *her*."

"She had no regard for me."

"Did you kill her for it?"

"I am no murderer."

"Patrick Flynn said you stabbed her in the breast, then put her leg in the bear trap and left her there to make it look like an accident. Flynn said he found her in the trap, then turned her over to see the wound in her breast."

"I never stabbed her. Mayhap Flynn stabbed her. Or one of her other lovers."

"Don't you dare insult my sister." It was all she could do not to scream.

"I never raised my hand against her. I swore that to you again and again, but you would never believe."

"What *am* I to believe?"

"She ran away and broke her leg in the trap."

"Patrick Flynn said she fled from you in fear for her life."

He writhed beneath the blanket as though some devil were riding him. "The words of a thief."

"Why did she flee you, Gabriel? Flynn said she was still weak from childbirth."

"The woman hated me." He tilted his face to the ceiling. "When the baby died, she blamed it on me."

"Did she have cause to blame you?" Sick inside, she took her hands out of her pockets and stepped around the side of the bed, placing herself between Gabriel and Daniel. "How did the cradle break?"

He had the shakes again, but she wouldn't allow herself to be moved. "She threw it at me," he said. "I ducked and it hit the wall." He raised an unsteady hand to point at a scar in the wood near the window.

Hannah shook her head. "You would have me believe she had the strength to hurl a cradle across the room when she was still weak from childbirth?"

"Have you ever seen that woman in a temper? She cursed me and called me a murderer."

"Why?"

He sagged against the headboard. "I did not send for a midwife."

Hannah's eyes stung. She remembered the pain that had nearly destroyed her during Daniel's birth.

"What in God's name were you thinking?"

"She had the girl Adele to tend her."

Hannah couldn't speak, couldn't even look at him. She rested a hand on the high side of Daniel's bed. Absorbed in his own world, the little boy patted his hands against the blanket, pushing down into the straw mattress so it crackled. That girl Adele had been barely more than a child, with no knowledge of birth. How could she have been expected to deliver May's baby and keep the infant alive?

"You wanted her to die." Trembling in rage, she turned to face him.

He lifted his hands as if to ward her off. "The child wasn't mine."

"How can you be so sure?"

"She told me as much herself."

"Why did she run away so soon after childbirth?"

"She threw the cradle at me and called me a murderer. I told her that if she hated me so much, she must quit this place."

Hannah went cold. She remembered their fight after Banham's last visit, when he had all but ordered her to leave. *If you believe I killed her, you can go. Now take the child and run after him.* "She was still weak from childbirth, and you turned her out?"

A moment passed. He stared straight ahead, his skin the color of ash. Then his head fell forward into his hands. She watched the back of his neck bob up and down. "I rue it. I do. I don't know what devil got hold of me then. I told her to get out of my sight or I would have her publicly chastised for adultery. Every day I beg God's forgiveness." He was sobbing very quietly.

"Why did you not beg May's forgiveness?" Hannah asked him coldly.

His breathing was ragged. "When at last I came to my senses, it was too late. She was dead." He spoke with a dead man's voice. "My dogs found her in the woods, her leg in the trap."

"Did she have a stab wound in her chest?"

"Aye." His voice was hollow. "All her clothes were scattered about. I think that thief Flynn robbed her of her valuables and fled."

"What of Adele?"

"Mayhap the girl betrayed her, too. Or mayhap the girl fled Flynn and disappeared."

Hannah sank to the floor. How could Adele have just vanished? A runaway servant like Flynn might get as far as Port Tobacco before the authorities arrested him, but a black girl? Perhaps she had lost her way in the forest and been mauled by a bear. And why had May run into the forest instead of seeking refuge at the Banhams'? Had Flynn dragged her down the hollow? Hannah wept and rocked herself. May was lost forever. She would never know what had really happened.

"You believe that Flynn stabbed her." Her tone matched Gabriel's. She had entered his world of shades and ghosts.

"Aye. He hated her sorely. Once, on her account, my father gave him a savage flogging." Gabriel looked so broken down, so cornered and wounded, that she knew he spoke the truth.

"Then why did you not tell anyone? If he is a murderer, he must hang."

"It was a shallow wound, not deep enough to kill. She died from stepping in my trap. I think she was running from him, not looking where she stepped."

Hannah could not speak.

"He vanished with my father's silver, my father's ring, my father's second-best boat. His sovereigns, too. The other servants fled. After I turned her out, they thought I had gone mad. Maybe I had. By the time I did find her, animals had ravaged her body."

Tears stung her raw face. "Why the false grave?" But she already knew the answer.

He told her in his dead man's voice that by the time he had discovered her there, she so was ruined that he couldn't stomach the thought of dragging her carcass to the river to bury. So he had made do with the empty coffin. "I did not kill her," he said, "and yet I know I am to blame for her death."

"You thought no one would ever know of it?" Her eyes anchored on the rain-smeared window.

"All I ever wanted was to be left in peace. Then you came." His voice wrenched her.

Her tears marked the dusty floorboards. "That is why you would not take me to Anne Arundel Town and marry me. You feared the gossip. You feared I would hear the rumors."

"Aye."

Daniel grew restless. She took him out of his bed. "You lied to me from the beginning."

"You grieved so deeply for her," he said. "You fell in a fit when I told you she was dead. I feared what would happen if I told you the whole truth."

She buried her face in her son's thick chestnut hair, so much like her sister's.

"Hannah," he said softly, "if I could have charmed her out of the grave for you, I would. You came here and you were so sad. I couldn't bear to make you any sadder."

She remembered how he had stitched her the pair of rabbit skin mittens, how she had slept with them under her pillow for comfort the night before she was to leave for the Banhams'. "How could you think I would never find out?"

Daniel wriggled out of Hannah's grip and tottered away. She watched him tug at the bed curtains.

"I could not tell you," he said. "You were my one chance for happiness. I loved you from the first day. If you knew the truth, you would have hated me. You were my one chance to know a woman's love. I thought love could restore me. Hannah, look at me, please."

He held out his hand to her. She took it, sat on the edge of the bed.

"I love you," he said. "I do not dare ask if you still love me."

She touched his face, his dry lips, but still she couldn't answer.

"At least say you do not hate me." He squeezed her hand.

"I do not hate you."

"If your father had only sent you instead of May." His voice was unbearably sad. "If you had been my wife from the beginning, I could have been a good man."

She lay beside him on the bed, hid her face in his chest.

"It is not too late," he told her. "We could marry still. As soon as I am on my feet again, I will take you and Daniel to Anne Arundel Town. We will post the banns."

Hannah pulled away. "Banham says that the rumors of you run up and down the Bay. If you show your face in Anne Arundel Town and post your name outside the church, people will question you, and not only of May. Think on it, Gabriel. You have not paid the rents in four years."

Once more, he looked like a ghost. She remembered something he had told her when she first came to stay with him. *I have spent too long with the dead to go back into the world of the living.*

"When you were raving in fever, you said Adele had tried to poison you. Is that true?"

"Poison me? No. But she did hex me. She said she had trapped my soul and imprisoned it in a tree. She said I would be wretched all my days."

31
Even in Death

Gabriel
1690

RUFUS DISCOVERED THE BODY before Gabriel did. The sight
and smell were enough to make him double over. The sound of
his panicked breathing drowned out everything else. Flies crawled
over her skirts, darkened with feces and old blood. The exposed
flesh of her severed leg had already blackened and gone putrid.
Maggots wriggled in the torn skin above the metal jaws.

She lay face-down, loose hair fanning out on the moss. The
cruelest thing was that her hair was still lovely, so shiny and soft-
looking that he almost wanted to stroke it. Stroke her hair and tell
her she could come home. Everything would be all right. Wasn't
forgiveness one of the Ten Commandments? He would take back
the hateful things he had said. *You know what they do to adulteresses*
here, don't you, May? With your own eyes you saw the slattern dragged
behind her husband's boat until she was nearly drowned. I could have you
put in the stocks, stripped to the waist, and whipped until your back is
bloody.

He hadn't meant any of it, had only wanted her gone, to end
the pain. In truth, he had expected her to disappear cleanly, vanish
like smoke. By all logic, she should have fled to the Banhams' — he
thought she would have been crafty enough to steal one of the
boats, let the current carry her downstream. The Banhams would
have taken her in. Paul Banham would have sat her on his knee
and clucked over her tears, and she would have allowed him to

undo her braid, as thick as a man's arm. Banham would have eventually sent her on her way and helped her in his own fashion, perhaps setting her up as his mistress in Anne Arundel Town or in Virginia. May would have gone on as she had always done, but far away from Gabriel, no longer his burden. How could she have met her end with her leg in his trap?

Before he could roll her over to look at her face, he saw the rusty knife in her gray fist. Had she tried to use the knife to free herself from the trap? he wondered. Then his eyes traveled from the knife's blade to the beech trunk only inches away from her head. In the smooth gray bark she had carved a message. *Murderer.*

Even in death she had to have the last word, had to stick her rusty blade into his flesh and twist. When at last he summoned the courage to turn her over, her face, though decayed beyond recognition, was frozen in a ghastly smile.

32 An Empty Chamber

Hannah
1694

SHE BECAME A HOLLOW THING. Something vital was ripped out of her. A phantom surgeon slit her open from breastbone to pubis, stole her organs, filled the bloody cavity with straw, and stitched her up again. Like Gabriel, she belonged to the dead. She still breathed, walked, and ate, but her life essence had fled. When she opened her mouth, she spoke in a dead woman's voice.

Poor lost May. First she had been obliged to leave her country and childhood home after Father had made her match for her. Then her husband had turned her out of this place. Yes, she had sinned, but her letter sounded so penitent. *I have ruined Everything. Forgive me if you can.* Hannah pictured her sister penning her final message in the hours before Gabriel had driven her out the door. *Dearest, I think you shall never see me again.*

May haunted her more keenly than ever. Her spirit inhabited every object in the house—each trencher and horn spoon, every board that quivered beneath Hannah's feet. She couldn't look at Gabriel without seeing the wasted carcass, the gold ring on bare bone.

"Can you forgive me?" he asked her.

"Only God can forgive you," Hannah told him. "Only God can forgive us both." She had stripped the linen sheet off their bed and was stitching it into a shroud. The least they could do was finally give May a decent burial.

Gabriel was back on his feet again, his ague gone, but the wasted look never left his face. When Hannah asked him to build May a new coffin, he took the lumber from Adele's shack, using the old nails he had pried loose to hammer the planks together. He took two smaller planks, smoothed the splinters away with his adze, then nailed them together in the shape of a cross. Working with pick and chisel, he carved out the epitaph.

Here lyes May Powers Washbrook
1667–1690
R.I.P.

Hannah tucked the shroud and cross into the coffin along with the shovel Gabriel had wrapped in sacking. Together they started off for the hollow, where the corpse awaited them. While Gabriel bore the coffin across the creek and into the woods beyond, Hannah followed with Daniel strapped to her back, the Book of Common Prayer in her hands. The day would linger in her memory, following her like a shadow for the rest of her days. The deep blue autumn sky with its innocent white clouds, red and gold leaves fluttering in the wind. Autumn crocuses carpeted the forest floor. Ruby darted around her, nipping at her skirt and running off to chase squirrels. The other dogs trotted after Gabriel.

Weak from his illness, Gabriel had to set the coffin down and rest. Bending forward, hands on his knees, he panted while sweat dripped from his hair. He looked so worn down, as though it were his own coffin he had to shoulder. Hannah took the shovel out of the coffin and carried it, to lighten his load. When they reached the lip of the hollow, his face was so pale that Hannah put down the shovel, prayer book, and Daniel, grabbed one end of the coffin, and helped him bear its weight.

They set the coffin on the moss beside the shallow pit. At the sight of the rotted cloth and dirty bone, Gabriel made for the stream. Hannah watched him splash water on his face. His dogs gathered around him. Rufus nuzzled him, wagging his tail attentively. When Hannah's eyes wandered back to the corpse, she felt the sick rising up her throat. Before it could overcome her, she fled up the hill for Daniel, the shovel, and the prayer book.

Gabriel was waiting for her, his back as stiff as the shovel handle. "Are you ready?"

She nodded. While he shoveled, she retreated to the spring and took Daniel out of the packsack. The fallen log blocked their view of the corpse. She cupped her hands and let him drink the cold clear water. In the beech tree above them, a cardinal sang. Hannah whistled to cover the noise of Gabriel's shovel. She rubbed Daniel's hands on the moss to show him how soft it was, but he kept looking in the direction of the digging.

"Da-da?"

"Hush." Hannah took his wooden rabbit out of her pocket. "Your father must work."

The cardinal sang as clouds traced their slow dance across the sky. Hannah lifted Daniel in her arms and pointed. "That is heaven."

Daniel looked up with May's blue eyes. She swung him around in a circle, then set him on the ground and held his hand while he took tottering steps along the stream. Out of the corner of her eye, she saw Gabriel resting, leaning on the shovel. Then he began to dig again. She hugged Daniel and smoothed back his chestnut hair. What, she wondered, would May's daughter have been like if she had lived? Would she have taken after her father or her mother? Daniel patted her wet face. Ruby came loping with a stick in her mouth. Hannah threw it for the dog to fetch, and Daniel screeched in delight. His laughter echoed over the hollow, reverberating through the beech trees. Crows cawed and crisscrossed overhead.

Gabriel called her. "It is ready." Hannah put Daniel in his packsack. He cried and struggled, but she was firm. She could hardly let him wander around if there was an open pit into which he might fall.

"Hush-a-bye. Don't cry. Be my brave boy." Straightening her shoulders, she moved over the mossy ground to the hole Gabriel had dug. Deep down, the soil went from black to red as though steeped in old blood. Just behind Gabriel lay the corpse. She couldn't let Daniel see it. She leaned him, still in his packsack, against a tree trunk so he faced away from the grave. She called Ruby. "Stay with Danny. Stay." She wiped his tears with her fingers and kissed him. "My brave, brave boy."

Gabriel opened the coffin with his raw, blistered hands. Part of her wanted to rub them in bear grease. She wanted to take him in her arms and rock his hurt away. His pain might ease if she spoke the magic words, told him she forgave him, that she cared for him still. But her eyes kept slipping past him to her sister's remains.

The shroud she had sewn was useless. Only remnants of skin and rotted cloth held May's bones together. It was doubtful that they could lift her out in one piece. Hannah's knees gave way. She found herself on the ground beside Gabriel, whose eyes were red and whose hands trembled, as hers did. Yards away, Daniel cried feebly.

"Hush-a-bye," Hannah tried to call, but she choked on the words. Taking the shroud, she ripped loose her careful seams. She shook out the sheet, then spread it on the bottom of the coffin. She thought of the graveyard in her old village, its tabletop tombstones raised to the sky, her parents resting side by side in the shadow of yew trees. When she tried to lift May's feet, they came loose in her hands. Hannah crawled off to vomit.

"The child screams," Gabriel told her when the retching stopped. "Go to him. I will do this."

She lurched to the spring to wash her hands and rinse out her mouth before running to Daniel. She took him out of his packsack and rocked him against her chest. Ruby rested her head on Hannah's knee.

"The thing is done," Gabriel called.

Daniel in her arms, she approached the coffin. The linen

sheet safely veiled what had once been her sister. She glanced at the knife on Gabriel's belt.

"Take a lock of my hair," she said, turning so he could cut it from the back of her head, thus keeping the blade away from Daniel. When he handed her the bright red lock, she dropped it on the white sheet. A part of her would go down with May, be buried with her forever.

"May I close it?" he asked.

"Aye." She clung to Daniel as the wooden lid slapped down.

Gabriel tied ropes around each end of the coffin. She put Daniel in his packsack and helped Gabriel lower the coffin into the pit. She handed him the Book of Common Prayer. He opened it to the page she had marked and started to read.

"'I am the resurrection and the life, saith the Lord: he that believeth in me, though he were dead, yet shall he live . . .'" His voice shook. "I cannot," he whispered, passing the book back to her.

"'I know that my Redeemer liveth,'" Hannah read, "'and that he shalt stand at the latter day upon the earth. And though after my skin, worms destroy this body . . .'" She swallowed. "'Yet in my flesh shall I see God.'" She continued reading the Order of the Burial of the Dead until she came to the Last Rites. "'Forasmuch as it hath pleased Almighty God of his great mercy to take unto himself the soul of our dear sister here departed: we therefore commit her body to the ground; earth to earth, ashes to ashes, dust to dust . . .'"

She cast down a handful of earth on the coffin. Turning the pages, she went on reading the words of prayer and blessing. After she had uttered the last *amen* and closed the book, Gabriel shoveled dirt into the pit. When at last the grave was filled, Hannah planted the cross in the firm ground beside the loose soil. Gabriel hammered it into the earth with a stone.

Her vision blurred, pinpricks of light dancing before her eyes. A pounding filled her head as she swayed. Had the fog come to seize her again, drag her down into a fit? She wished she could fall into Gabriel's arms, let him comfort and protect her as he had done in the old days. Instead she remained standing on her own two feet, with nothing but her will and her pain to keep her upright.

—✦—

That night, while Gabriel slept on his pile of furs, she tossed alone in bed to nightmares of May's bones snapping in the trap's steel maw.

"Would I win your pardon," he asked the next morning, "if I went to the Assembly Court in Anne Arundel Town and offered my confession?"

Hannah looked up from the tub of soiled clouts she was washing. "It is the deed that honor demands." The soapy water cut into her cracked hands. "I know not if they would find you guilty of murder. All I know is the punishment they would mete out on me."

"What punishment?" he asked, but she imagined he must already know. A shadow moved across his face.

"If you tell them your story, I must tell them mine. They would question me, the same as you." She kept scrubbing the clouts. "They would charge me with fornication and bastardy. And seeing that you owe four years' rent to the Lord Baltimore, they would confiscate all your furs in the name of your debts. I would have nothing to pay the fines." She spoke with weary certainty. "They would tie me to the post and flog me." In truth, she did not really care how people treated her, but she couldn't bear the thought of passing the legacy of shame on to Daniel.

"Hannah." His voice was stricken, but she did not look up from the laundry tub. "If we marry," he said fervently, "we will only be guilty of fornication. I will find a way to pay the fines. I promise you there will be no whipping."

"Mayhap if we sell the ring you gave to me." She wrung out the clouts, then plunged them into the tub again, scrubbing until her skin was raw.

"We must leave this place," he said. "We shall go away to-

321

gether where they will never find us. We shall change our names and begin anew. God willing, Hannah, we might still be happy."

It seemed a marvel to her that he could still feel love after all this. Everything inside her was dead. Her heart had become an empty chamber.

"Come spring," she said, "we shall quit this place." There was no use setting off now, with winter only a month or so away. "But not together."

His mouth went slack. "You wish to part ways?"

"I do." Her eyes followed the patterns in the soap scum as though she might read her future there. She had no idea where she would go. She wondered if Elizabeth Sharpe, from the ship, would welcome her. If everything else failed, she would be a servant to the Banhams. Her own happiness and pride didn't matter anymore—they were of the past. As long as the Banhams were kind to Daniel, she would scrub their chamber pots if they asked her.

"Then it will be as you say." Gabriel walked out the door.

—+—

Though they went on living in the same room, he was already beginning to fade. She saw him through a haze, which grew thicker and thicker until he appeared to be little more than a wraith. He spent nearly every waking hour out of sight and earshot—a thing for which she was grateful. It was easier to bear her burden alone, without his eyes on her, his sorrow filling the house. Each evening he brought home the animals he had trapped or shot with his musket. He seemed eager to make up for the time he had lain ill in bed. Perhaps bringing home the dead animals was the only way to banish his memory of May's body. Hannah did not pretend to understand the secrets of his heart. He tanned the hides and nailed up the furs in the old tobacco shed. She had never seen him bring in so many beaver pelts. It seemed he was trapping them up and down the river. Before, the beavers had been his allies, their dams and obstructions keeping the outer world at bay, but this year he killed as many as he could. Beaver pelts sold for a handsome price.

Part of her still wanted to tell him to spare himself the effort—all the beavers in the river couldn't redeem their debts. But she said nothing.

Sometimes she took the rolled-up maps from the chest of drawers and spread them out on the trestle table. How far would she have to go to escape her reputation as Gabriel Washbrook's whore, the woman who had fornicated with her own sister's widower? If she traveled south to Virginia or the Carolinas, or north to Pennsylvania, could she finally live in peace? Change her name, pass as a widow, meet another man? She would have given anything to have Joan read the cards for her, lay out her future on the table beside the map. What a comfort it would be to know for certain, even if the cards said her fortune would be full of woe. Anything would be better than the awful blank she saw before her.

—+—

Gabriel loaded the furs in his canoe and left to do his trading. Watching from the dock, she didn't wave goodbye. She knew that on his journey he would be furtive, not telling anyone his real name. A man could escape between the cracks so much easier than a woman, especially a woman with a child. It passed her mind that he might not return. The dogs seemed to sense this, too. Rufus kept mournful watch, always looking downriver. He hardly touched the food Hannah gave him.

In Gabriel's absence, she expected Richard Banham to pay a visit. She had avoided the graves by the river since the day she had pried the lid off the empty coffin. The box still lay open to the sun and wind. She had left May's ruined wedding dress on the grass, just couldn't bear to go back and dispose of it. If Banham came riding, that spectacle would greet him. She was too deadened to care what he thought; let him make what he would of the opened grave. But he did not come.

Days slipped by in silence. Hannah counted them on her fingers, and when she ran out of fingers, she cut notches on the doorframe. If Gabriel did not return in a fortnight, she would put

Daniel in his packsack, fill a basket with provisions, and set off for the Banhams'.

She picked a gourd from her garden and shook it so Daniel would hear the dry seeds rattling inside. "Look," she told him, "you have a new toy." Waving the gourd, he toddled through the long grass. Laughing, he trotted into her arms and let her sweep him in a circle. If only she could be as easily pleased as Daniel, who took delight in the simplest things. They threw a stick for Ruby to fetch until the dog flopped down exhausted at their feet. Sometimes when she fed him his supper, her son looked around and inquired, "Da-da?" But it didn't take long to distract him again.

⁘

The grass was brittle and dry underfoot on the thirteenth day of Gabriel's absence. It hadn't rained in weeks. The soil in her garden was cakey and dry. If there had to be a drought, at least it had come late in the year, when the harvest was already in. Edging close to the creek, she looked at the huge trees on the other side with their dead leaves lying in a thick carpet over their roots. The forest resembled a giant tinderbox. If the drought went on, one bolt of lightning or one careless cooking fire could set the whole woodland ablaze.

She hadn't dared set foot in that forest since May's burial. The place was haunted and cursed, the trees arrayed like an enemy army. She remembered the sense of futility when she had arrived here—the homestead was so fragile compared to the living wilderness, which waited for its chance to strike out and take back everything they had wrested from it.

⁘

Her heart raced at the noise of barking. Banham had come after all.

Why did the dogs sound so ecstatic? Their excitement proved contagious. Daniel, who had been sleeping in his packsack, awoke and kicked his legs back and forth. His weight slowed her down. When she reached the dock, tears pricked at her eyes. Gabriel stood surrounded by the leaping, joyous dogs. Rufus, paws on Gabriel's chest, licked his master slavishly. After stroking each of the dogs in turn, Gabriel took parcels out of the canoe. He didn't seem to notice her until Daniel cried, "Da-da."

She took the boy out of the packsack, passed him into his father's arms. Daniel shyly patted his beard. As Gabriel kissed the top of the child's head, his eyes locked with hers. Gabriel's deep blue eyes still had the power to undo her.

Clutching herself, she turned away. "You must be hungry." She picked up one of the parcels and carried it to the house, along with the empty packsack. Then she went to the hen house to butcher a chicken.

—+—

While she fried the chicken, he unpacked the parcels and laid out their contents on the table. Two cones of sugar, a box of gunpowder for his musket, a bolt of sober, dark blue linsey-woolsey, and a bolt of plain white linen.

"You chose well," she said. If she intended to pass as a widow, she couldn't have picked out better fabric herself. There was nothing fancy like last year's lover's gifts—the ruby ring and beautifully printed cotton. The ring was hidden in the Bible box for safekeeping, and the lovely dress was faded and worn. She bent her head over the skillet so he wouldn't see her tears.

"Was Banham here?" he asked in a weary voice.

"Not a sign of him." It occurred to her that she might ask him why he had been away so long this time, but the words eluded her.

He slumped on the bench with Daniel in his lap. The boy kept gazing at him as though afraid he might vanish again. Watching Gabriel ruffle their son's hair, Hannah saw how blistered his hands were from the oars. Leaving the skillet for a moment, she took the jar of bear grease from the pantry. After setting Daniel on the floor, she knelt at Gabriel's feet and gently rubbed the grease into his broken hands.

"Hannah." His eyes moved over her face. She flushed and

concentrated on his blisters. His lips moved, as if he were about to say something more. But then, at the smell of burning chicken, Hannah scrambled to her feet and snatched the skillet from the fire.

She split the chicken breast with a knife. Though the skin was blackened on one side, the flesh still looked white, juicy, and tender. Taking one drumstick for herself, she put the rest on Gabriel's trencher, then brought out the cornbread she had made that morning. While Gabriel ate, she prepared Daniel's mush. She stole glances at Gabriel, who devoured his meat in silence, leaving a pile of clean bones on the trencher. He was thinner and hungrier than ever before. If possible, he looked more ghost-ridden.

Could it be salvaged? He was not beyond comforting. A small voice inside her said that she still had the power to break the spell, banish the estrangement. She only had to kiss him. Let him hold her. Call him to her bed this night. She only had to tell him he was forgiven. But she just kept spooning mush into Daniel's mouth. The words she might have said clogged in her throat. After finishing his meal, Gabriel lay down on his bed of furs and fell asleep at once.

＊

Days slid by like slippery necklace beads falling from her hands. Then one day, no different from the ones that had preceded it, Hannah came back from gathering walnuts to find a map spread out on the trestle table. Her writing quill, inkpot, and blotter lay beside it. An X had been made to mark their house, then a line had been drawn, following the river down to the Bay and across it, to a place called Cleeve Hill on the Eastern Shore. The words *Quaker Village* were written in an unfamiliar hand. Hannah traced the sloping letters. At last she got to see Gabriel's handwriting.

Beaver pelts were piled high on his father's carved chair. She could not resist stroking the soft dark fur. But why were they still here? She thought he had traded all the furs for provisions. Then she noticed the message in the top right corner of the map.

Get you to the Quaker Village. They will give you Shelter and
Protection. I have spokken to them already and said you are a
good and honourable Widdow in need of Refuge. Take the Canu
downstream. I have cleared the Waterway. When you reach
Gardiners Point, await the Ferry to bring you to Cleeve Hill.
When you arrive, ask for Mrs. Martha Nuttall. She is the
Daughter of Father's old Housekeepper when we lived in Anne
Arundel Town. She will look after you and Daniel. God go with
you Hannah Powers.

"Gabriel?" She stepped out on the porch and called his name
until she was hoarse. It was nearly sunset. He should be coming in
for supper.

The day before, he had butchered a pig. The pork loin
roasted in its pan over the fire, with carrots, turnips, and potatoes,
and the rosemary and thyme she had added. Surely the smell must
be enough to draw him back to the house. She fried corncakes on
the griddle. Still he did not appear. When she went out with scrap
meat to feed the dogs, only Ruby came to eat. Though she whistled three times, the other dogs did not come. Back in the house,
she made Daniel his porridge. It grew dark. Leaping flames cast
shadows over the walls. When she couldn't bear to wait any longer, she ate the overcooked pork and griddle cakes alone.

The map, the message, the pile of beaver pelts. He had left
her. He was well and truly gone. He had grown fainter and fainter
until he had vanished altogether. Even his dogs had disappeared.
God go with you Hannah Powers. He hadn't signed his name.

That night, she left the door unbolted in case he returned.
Lying in bed, she started at every noise—the wind whistling
down the chimney, the straw rustling beneath Daniel as he moved
in his sleep. In the morning, she got up and combed every corner
of the house, every outbuilding, looking for signs. As indicated in
his message, he had left the canoe in the boathouse. He had taken
only his musket, his hunting knife, his traps, and his dogs. He
hadn't taken a blanket or a change of clothing. When she opened
the chest of drawers, she saw his second pair of buckskins, his old

wool breeches, his linen shirts, and the waistcoat she had never seen him wear. She kept hoping he would return for his clothes. She knelt down and prayed, *Dear God, bring him back.*

He had left her the canoe, beaver pelts, and provisions. He had cleared the waterway for her. There was still time to make her way to the Quaker village before winter set in. With the beaver pelts she could pay for her passage on the ferry and have more than enough left over to purchase a small cottage with a plot around it for growing vegetables. She could keep a pig and chickens. She could take the salt pork and cornmeal along, the cones of sugar, the barrel of raspberry wine. Gabriel wouldn't have wanted her and Daniel to winter here alone. It was time to return to society. But she couldn't leave this place if there was any chance he might come back. Gathering her courage, she crossed the creek into the forest where he had carved his name on the trees. One day faded into the next until the first snow came.

Cutting patterns in the linsey-woolsey, she made new gowns for Daniel. She sewed them with generous seams, to let out as he grew. Instead of sewing a new dress for herself, she stitched a new pair of breeches and a jacket for Gabriel. Sewing was a prayer to call him back. She wondered if he expected her to wait for him in the Quaker village. If she went there in spring, would he come looking for her?

As the days slid toward midwinter, each day darker than the one before, she forced herself to accept the truth. He had melted away into the forest, as he said he would all along. He was that fey, like one of the faeries, the vanishing people. *Once they lived amongst us like ordinary folk*, Joan had told her when she was little. *Long ago, before the reign of King Henry VIII, but then, one by one, they faded away, and now they can only be glimpsed at twilight and in dreams.*

If she had allowed it, he would have taken her with him. They would have been together forever, and no one—not the Banhams, not the debt collectors, not the judges from the Assembly—could have touched them. Now it was her lot to remain in this world while he passed into the next—that magic world deep in the forest. He would melt westward, toward those mountains he had once described for her, fleeing so far that no white man would ever lay eyes on him again. Maybe he would take an Indian name and an Indian wife. His children would be children of the forest.

As winter dragged on, a transformation befell her, too. An enchantment of sorts. To pass the lonely hours, she read her father's books of anatomy. She opened the case of surgical instruments, polished them with a clean cloth. *In faith*, Gabriel had once told her, *I always suspected there was something uncommon about you. You have powers few possess.* Come spring, she would leave this house, but not to pass as a widow in the Quaker village. And she would be no man's servant.

The dead end of the year reached its darkest point before slowly turning back to light. As the days grew longer, Hannah took in the seams of Gabriel's clothes. She shortened his buckskin breeches and cut out a new pair of boots to match her feet. She took an inventory of the physick herbs in the pantry, then wrapped them in scraps of linen and tucked them in a leather pouch. The raspberry wine was now ready for drinking. It helped steady her nerves for what she would do next.

She took one of the deerskins off the bed and cut out the pattern for a great roomy satchel, with a strap that she could wear across her shoulder and breast. Working with scissors, needle, and thread, she altered the packsack so it would accommodate Daniel's growth.

"You have to be my brave boy," she told him. "Your father has gone far away. I think we shall not see him again."

Ruby was growing up, too, in her loneliness away from the other dogs. She slept at the foot of Hannah's bed.

The winter, though cold, was dry with little snow. When spring came, she was grateful that the drought made the ground firm for walking. She sharpened her scissors. Daniel and Ruby watched while she cut her hair, the long red locks falling in a pile on the floor. She left them there. It hardly seemed worth the effort to keep the cabin tidy.

She had salt pork wrapped in cloth, a week's supply of cornbread, a bag of walnuts. She had a tin bottle for carrying water, a sharp knife to carry in her belt. She had a cloak and a blanket to sleep in. She had the map, her pouch of herbs, her father's books and instruments, and she had two changes of clothing. She flattened her breasts with a winding cloth before stepping into Gabriel's buckskin breeches and shirt. Her shorn head made her neck feel bare. Daniel kept looking at her in amazement. She stroked his face and kissed him. May's voice echoed in her head. *If I were a boy, I would run away to sea. I wouldn't come home until I'd seen the wide world.*

33 Ash

1695

DURING THE LONG DRY SUMMER, the Banham slaves spent hours dragging water from the river to the tobacco fields. In places, the creek ran dry, the bare rocks in its bed exposed to the sun like a crop of bones. The water smelled stagnant and foul. Mrs. Banham's little son fell ill with a raging fever and runny bowels. Within days, he was dead.

Weeks later, the black midday sky erupted. A jagged snake of lightning snapped down to strike a dead oak near the Washbrook Plantation. The parched forest burned, smoke billowing high as the wind blew the fire west. Orange flames licked the rotting timber of the manservants' shack, the tobacco barn, and finally the main house. The fire consumed the three crosses and the empty coffin on the riverbank.

When the wind changed direction, the fire spread east, heading toward the Banhams'. Every man, woman, and child was occupied digging fire ditches and passing buckets of water. Young Richard blindfolded the panicked horses. Smoke blackened the ivory faces of the Banham daughters as they watched their dowries go up in flames along with their home. The English spinet, the cherrywood tea table, and their gowns trimmed with Flemish lace all turned to ash.

34 *The Lost Sister*

May

OCTOBER 1690

THAT AUTUMN DAY, the sky was blinding blue, trees shimmering with color, the leaves as red as her sister's hair. The bitter wind chilled her to the marrow, even though her forehead burned. She clutched her bundle of clothes against her breasts, hot and swollen with useless milk, as she staggered away from the house, his raised voice. She laughed under her breath so she wouldn't cry. Adele took her elbow, urging her on. The girl's spine drooped under the weight of her satchel stuffed with blankets, cooking gear, and provisions.

"I am now a thief," May confided. "I have stolen his father's sovereigns." She had snatched the pouch of heavy coins from their hiding place under the floorboard, then concealed them beneath her skirts. With each step, their cold weight slapped her belly, still distended from childbirth.

Adele just looked at her, no doubt wondering whether she spoke the truth. May had been raving, she knew she had, ever since the baby turned cold and blue in her arms and Gabriel took it away.

"Come." Adele tried to hurry her along. "We must find a boat for to go downriver."

May dug her heels into the ground and burst into tears. "Not the river, Adele. No."

He had ordered her to be gone or he would have her punished for adultery, have her dragged behind his father's boat like the woman she had seen when she first stepped ashore in Anne Arundel Town. His eyes so full of hate, he had looked as though he could kill her with his own hands. Hold her head underwater until she drowned. The manservants said he had gone mad. After she had exploded at him, and he at her, the men had scattered and fled.

May tottered on her feet, but Adele caught her around the waist. Eyes wide with terror, the girl seemed determined to put as much distance as possible between them and Gabriel. They followed the path behind the servants' shacks.

"We will go to the creek," Adele said. "Walk along the creek until we come to the neighbors'."

"No. I will not go there and endure their pity. Never." For an awful moment, May imagined Paul Banham sending her back to her husband. "I have heard there is a track through the forest. We must flee north. Far away from here. To Philadelphia, if we can." She clung to Adele's arm. "If I perish along the way, you must go on without me. I will give you the sovereigns."

"You must not say such things."

The girl looked so frightened that May tried desperately to hold her torn body together and keep walking. Somehow they managed to cross the creek. *Escape evil by crossing water.* That was one of Joan's old superstitions. *Flowing water stops the devil in his tracks.*

Adele helped her clamber up the steep bank on the other side and into the forest of massive trees on which Gabriel had carved his name. By the letter of the law, May knew that she was his property, just as the trees were. He had every legal right to punish her as he saw fit. *I was sold to him, just as you were sold to his father,* she wanted to tell Adele. *Parceled off to a stranger for a heap of tobacco.*

"Watch yourself," Adele said as May stumbled blindly along. "We know not where his traps are."

Out of breath, May had to sit down. Adele gave her a piece of cornbread.

"You must eat to keep your strength."

"Why are you so good to me?" May asked. Only this girl had stayed with her through everything, after seeing her at her worst.

"Come. We must go on." Adele cast an anxious look back in the direction of the house.

They had covered another quarter-mile when Adele came to a halt, then pushed her body in front of May's.

"*Mon Dieu!*"

Adele tried to block her view, but it was already too late. The sight of the body in Gabriel's bear trap braced May like a dose of powerful physick. Her fever cooled and her vision cleared. She let her bundle of clothes drop to the ground, then crouched beside the dead girl and gingerly turned her over. Her gray face was frozen in a grotesque smile. Her fist clenched a knife. May reckoned that the girl had used the knife to try to free herself from the trap, but had lacked the strength to force the jaws apart. When had this happened? While she and Gabriel had been cursing each other? If it had been quiet at the house, might someone have heard the girl's screams and been able to save her? The smell was too much. May drew the edge of her cloak over her nose.

Adele sank down beside her. "Who is she?"

"Peter's girl." May let out her breath. "From the Banhams'. It looks like she did run away." She had seen the girl once, the previous autumn, when they had gone down to Banham's Landing with their tobacco barrels. Peter had confided about his sweetheart to Finn, then Finn had told May.

A shallow knife wound marked the girl's breast. Before she had fled, someone had stabbed her. Had she been ravaged by one of the men at the Banham Plantation? Or had Mrs. Banham, in a fit of jealousy, attacked the girl for catching her husband's eye? May had heard that Mrs. Banham was touched by madness. Perhaps the girl had stolen through the forest to beg asylum from the Washbrooks.

The decent thing would be to return and tell the news. But Peter had vanished along with the others. When May envisioned facing Gabriel, her strength ebbed with the blood that still leaked from her womb. If she wanted to keep herself alive, she couldn't afford to expend an ounce of effort or sentiment on this dead girl.

"May the Lord preserve us," she said. "Turn her over, Adele." She could no longer bear the sight of that ghastly face.

When the body was lying face-down, May could breathe again, pretend the girl wasn't dead but only sleeping. Her thick chestnut hair shone in the sunlight.

"Her hair." Adele shivered. "It is like yours."

An ugly laugh erupted from May's throat as the awful inspiration visited her. It was the devil moving through her, her wicked need to punish him. And her fear of him. He could still come after her, bring her to justice. The law was on his side. She reminded herself that she had stolen from him, too.

"Let us make her more like me."

Wrenching off her wedding band, she tried to force it on the corpse's swollen finger. She had to use her spittle before she could ease the ring over the knuckle. Shutting her ears to Adele's protests, she took the knife and carved on the smooth beech trunk near the dead girl's head. *Murderer.* Then she returned the knife to the dead fist.

Adele grabbed her shoulders. "How can you do this?"

A noise came out of May, halfway between a laugh and a moan. "He wanted me dead. Well, I've given him his wish." Drained from the effort of carving the letters, she collapsed against the beech trunk. "Do you not understand, Adele? I am that boy's wife." She breathed fast, praying that she wouldn't faint. "I own nothing, not even my clothes."

Reaching for the bundle of dresses, she untied the sacking and dumped them beside the body. The sun glanced off her embroidered green wedding gown. "Let him have it all," she panted. "You know I am not able to walk very fast or very far. If he comes after me, I am finished. But this way, he never will." She burst out laughing, but that hurt her and she had to clutch her belly. She thought of the tiny wrinkled infant, whom she had named after the sister she would never see again. Unbaptized, the baby would wander forever in limbo, as doomed and hopeless as her mother. Like the weakest of women, she began to weep. "There is nothing left of me, Adele."

"We must keep walking." Adele wrapped May's arm around her shoulder and hoisted her to her feet. The forest, the sunlight, the dead girl, the pile of discarded clothes, and the pain blurred together as Adele led her away. High in the trees, birds sang. May's soul floated out ahead of her broken body.

—┼—

Adele said an angel guided them through the forest. They were blessed with mild days and nights. Huddled together in Adele's blankets, they slept on piles of dead leaves. After their food ran out and snow began to fall, an Indian woman found them and took them to her village. May's memory of that time was a haze of the weight of deerskins over her fevered body and the bitter willow-bark brew the woman gave her. She dreamt of comets tracing brilliant paths across the heavens. Her lifelong dream had finally come true. Fatherless, husbandless, utterly masterless, she was her own woman. She was as free as the tinker she had kissed at the village dance all those years ago. She could wander the wilderness like an explorer, blazing her own trail. When she tried to raise herself from the deerskin, Adele and the Indian woman held her down and gave her more of the brew. Adele never seemed to leave her side. Sometimes she thought it was only that girl's devotion that rooted her to this world.

Something was rising in Adele. The Indian woman, whose language May could not speak, saw it, too—May could read the knowledge on her face. Adele wasn't a girl anymore. A light shone in her eyes. Her skin gave off a dark radiance. It was her mother's magic, May thought. Adele was coming into her powers.

When May could sit up without fainting, she made herself useful stitching buckskin with a bone needle and thread made from bear gut. The lifeblood flowed inside her once more. She helped the Indian woman make corncakes, which they cooked on hot stones. In spring, before she and Adele continued on their way, May gave the woman her tortoiseshell hair clasp and a gold sovereign. Adele gave her the white cockerel feather from the pouch she wore around her neck. A white feather for blessing and protection. Then they set off through the forest, following the way Adele insisted was north, until they reached Philadelphia.

To Mrs. Hannah Powers
Hare Wood Green
Gloucestershire
England

June 1691

My dearest Hannah,

I pray to God that this Letter reach your Hands before you set sail to America. Sister, I must tell you the Impossible, namely that my Marriage to Gabriel Washbrook was the worst Match anyone could have made. In Faith, I own that I am to blame for my own Fate. My Wantonness did earn my Husband's Scorn and I have escaped his House like a Fugitive, allowing him to believe that I had perish'd in the Woods. My deepest Grief is that my Daughter, named Hannah after you, lived only Seven Days. I shall never cease mourning her.

Despite my many Wicked Acts, God has seen fitt to bless me with a true Friend, Adele, whom I have to thank for my verry Life. We share a little House in Philadelphia, where we do earn our Bread as Seamstresses. Our Workroom below has a big glassed Windoe that we may make use of the Light for our Sewing. We sleep in the Garret above. In the Back we have a small Garden where we do grow Vegetables and keep Chickens and Rabbitts. I live under the Name of May Powers, for after what I have done, I will not have myself be call'd by my Husband's Name. Mine is a Simple Life, but one I cherish, for I am my own Mistress.

Dear Sister, please write to me with all Speed. If you should join us in Philadelphia, it would be my greatest Joy. If you

*choose to stay in England, you have my Love and Blessing, too.
But know, dearest, that there is Nothing for you at Washbrook
Landing.*

Yr loving Sister May

*To Mistress Hannah Powers
Washbrook Plantation
Sequose River
Maryland
Western Shore*

October 1694

*My dearest Hannah,
    I did write to you at our old Home in Hare Wood Green
only to have my Letter return'd to me with the News that you
had allready sailed for the Chesapeak. My dearest, will you ever
forgive me for not warning you in Time? I have fled the Washbrook Plantation, my Husband having cast me out. Now he
believes me to be dead. He has probably told you as much himself. I do write to you now under the name of Mistress Thorn to
conceal my Identity.
    Darling, please write to me with Speed. Seek Refuge on
the Banham Plantation and from there do make your way to
Philadelphia where I await you most anxiously. On no account
remain on the Washbrook Plantation. If you do so, you live
in peril. Ere I last saw Gabriel Washbrook, he was out of his
Mind. Hannah, I pray for you every Day. God willing, Adele
and I shall soon wellcome you to our Home.*

Yr loving Sister May

In January 1695, the letter came back in the mail, its wax seal
still unbroken. Hannah's name was smudged, the paper creased by
too many fingers. By the light of a guttering candle, May read the
message that accompanied the letter.

*Dear Mistress Thorn,
    It is with deepest Grief that I impart this News. The Wash-*

brook Plantation burned to the Ground this Summer last.
No Trace could be found of Mr. Washbrook, Mistress Hannah
Powers, or her Child. May God have Mercy on the Souls of the
Departed.

Yours truly, Richard Banham, Esquire

The letter slipped from May's grasp and fell to the floor. "She had a child." May pressed her fingers to her mouth. "She's dead. Had I but warned her."

"You did," Adele replied. "You did *try*," she amended. "The first letter . . ."

"Too late." May could almost see the flames enveloping Hannah. If it weren't for Adele's hands gripping hers, she thought she would blow away like a dry husk in the draft sweeping down from the eaves. "What must have happened?" May closed her eyes. "Coming to that place and finding *him* there. She would have had no money left. Nowhere else to go." She wept as she had when her baby died. "She bore his child, Adele."

Head bowed, Adele did not speak, only squeezed her hands.

"What must she have thought? He would have told her I was dead." Had her sister succumbed to him because she was helpless and bereft, adrift in the wilderness? A chill crept into her. Hannah had borne his child even though May had made it look as if she had perished at his hands. The specter of her sister's betrayal nearly overpowered her shame at the fiendish trick she had played. To think that her tenderhearted sister would bed the man who had driven her from her home with the threat of near drowning.

"Mayhap her child was not his," she blurted, in one last attempt to salvage Hannah's memory. "On her journey, someone might have taken advantage."

Adele regarded her sadly. "His child or no, she lived with him in his house."

"I wonder if she found the letter I hid in the Bible." The thought of her sister with Gabriel's baby made her loss even keener, the memory of the cold blue infant buried beneath that flimsy cross. *This is my punishment.* This was the plate of bitter herbs she must swallow to atone for her own treachery.

"I forgive her," she told Adele. "How can I not? She's dead. They're all dead. Burned alive." May could not get over the horror of the fire. How unspeakable Hannah's death must have been, flames scorching her flesh, devouring both her and the child she tried to shield.

Adele pulled May's hands from her eyes. "Listen to me. You know not if she is truly dead. You know nothing of what happened."

"Will you gaze into your glass for me? Look for Hannah in the glass?"

Adele opened the wooden box at the foot of their bed and pulled out a bundle wrapped in cloth. "Bring the candle."

May took the single taper from the wall sconce and set it on the closed box. Pulling the cloth away, Adele unveiled a sea float made of green glass that they had found while walking on the shore. Once it had been used to buoy up fishing nets.

"Take my hands." She spoke with the authority of an obeah woman's daughter. She and May sat on opposite ends of the box, hands joined on either side of the glass ball. Their breath fogged its surface. "Think of your sister."

My lost sister. Hannah on the Bristol pier. The wind whipped her hair loose from its linen cap. The wind braided their hair together, chestnut to the blinding red. Her sister begged her not to leave, tears flooding her green eyes. Sweet Hannah. May remembered her as a baby, tiny pink face and squeezing hands.

Candle flame cast its sheen over Adele's face. As she stared into the glass, seeing things invisible to May, her features seemed to shift, eyes widening, mouth curving. Even her voice sounded different.

"I see a girl. She is much smaller than you. Her hair it is like fire."

May nodded, tears streaming down her face.

"She carries a boychild on her back."

A son. Would he have looked like his father? May pushed her enmity away. Hannah had nothing left, no family, no one to protect her. Maybe Gabriel had been gentle to her, stitched her a pair of slippers. How could he help but fall in love with that girl whose innocence set her so far apart from May? Father had favored her, then Gabriel did, too. Hadn't she herself told Hannah to forgive and then forget her? *I was born under Cursed Stars and only bring Pain and Misfortune.*

"Do you see him anywhere?" May couldn't bring herself to utter his name.

"I see only her and the child. The forest it is on fire, but the flames they do not touch her. She is long gone, far away. She walks the forest. She shines bright like flame itself."

35
At the Sign of the Mortar and Unicorn

BEING THE TRUE STORY OF MY WANDERINGS
AND CAREER AS AN ITINERANT PHYSICIAN AND
APOTHECARER, BY MRS. HANNAH POWERS WARD,
LATELY OF PHILADELPHIA

1740

MY DEAR LOST Sister, though we are never to be reunited in this World, it is to you that I address my True History. In many Ways, you are the Author of my Journey, for it was on your Account that I renounced my true Love Gabriel Washbrook and became a Physician (despite my Sex) like our Father before us.

While I live, I carry the Secrets with me. I confess I told a Lie or two to safeguard my Son's Reputation—I let him believe that I was married to his Father, who died of Ague, leaving me no Choice but to don his Buckskins and earn my own Bread. After I depart from this World, Daniel and his Children may read these Words and make what they will from the plain Facts.

Daniel's Memory of the early Years of our Wandering is dim. He cannot recall how long we journeyed through Forests and over Hills, from Farm to Village and Town. Nor can he remember how many Times we slept in Haymows or some Farmer's Shed. In the beginning, I traveled on Foot, sometimes covering as many as twenty Miles a Day, with the Child and all my Gear strapped to my Body. Later, as I began to prosper, I purchased a Cart and a Mare that I named Fortuna.

In Faith, I cannot say how many were fooled by my male Disguise, for I am small and carried a Child, but I never lacked

Employment. It was to my Advantage that there were precious few Doctors in the Hinterlands through which I traveled. Most who called themselves Doctors were Quacks who demanded as much as a Sovereign for some Elixir made of nothing more than Horse Piss diluted with Water. Many could not read, much less understand the Latin Books of Medicine and Anatomy. Some of the Irregular Physicians prescribed so-called Heroick Measures, wherein the Medicine had to be as noxious as the Disease. They had their Patients swallow ground Cattle-Hooves, then plastered their Bodies with Poultices of Dung, then bled them till they fainted away. Nearly as bad were the Preacher-Physicians who reasoned that their Book-Learning gave them the Authority to practice Medicine, though they knew little of Physick or Anatomy. These Preachers blamed all Sickness on the Patient's Sins; the only succor they offered were Prayer and Bible Verses. When the Disease took its Course, killing the Patient, the Preacher-Physician proclaimed it the Will of God.

But as you well remember, when I was yet a Girl in Old England, our Father instructed me on the Handiwork of a Loving God—for every Ailment and Disease, the Creator gave us an Herb to cure it. Such is the Doctrine of Plant Signatures. Indeed, God provided Clues in the Shape and Nature of Wild Plants so that we Physicians could divine the Plant's Healing Properties. Iris, being Purple in Colour, was intended for Use as a Poultice for Bruises. The Leaves of the Quaking Aspen Tree are efficacious in the Treatment of Palsy.

Most of my Patients were too poor to afford costly Remedies such as imported Laudanum or Mercury, so I endeavoured as much as possible to work with the common Plants growing in our American Forests and Fields. Through Study of Indian Lore and then through my own Experiments, I learned the curative Properties of such divers Native Plants as Snakeroot (good for treating Snakebite); Wild Indigo; Seven Barks; American Senna (which unclogs even the most Stubborn Bowels); Sassafras; Gravelwort (its Name reveals its Use); Rattlesnake Plantain; and the

Cherokee Herb called Five-Fingers, which Botanists do liken to Asiatick Ginseng. I used each Plant on myself before dispensing it to my Patients.

I also practised the Art of Surgery. If they could tell I was indeed a Woman, none of my Patients objected when given the Choice between my clean and well-kept Instruments and the local Blacksmith's Saw and Pliers. Most Procedures I performed were of a simple Nature, such as pulling abscessed Teeth. Sometimes I cut for Kidney- and Bladder-stones. Once I removed a Bullet from a Man's Stomack.

No doubt you are wondering who looked after young Daniel when I was occupied with my Patients. I did my best to shield him from Contagion, paying a healthy Housewife in the Vicinity to watch him for me. When I took ill in a Smallpox Epidemick, I sent Daniel to the next Village until it passed. The Scars still mark my Cheaks, but my Son remained untouched. I confess our Life was never easy. Though he was a tolerant and good-natured Boy, I think he envied the Children belonging to regular Families.

We never lacked for Adventure. As we traveled ever northward, we encountered all Manner of People, from fiery Scotsmen who fired their Muskets with little Provocation, to the Quakers of Pennsylvania, and the Dutch of New York who pinched Daniel's Cheaks and called him "Mannekin." We met free Africans, Indians, and ascetick Puritans.

Though Daniel and I would have been welcome to linger in any Number of Hamlets, my Profession of Physick kept me pressing ever on. I still hoped to find some Clue of where Adele had gone that I might at last learn from her the Truth of your Last Days, May. However, I discovered that escaped Slaves were wont to change their Names and do all in their Power to elude Detection. Putting out Advertisements in Gazettes and Broadsides for Adele Desvarieux would have brought me Naught. I might as well have tried searching for a Coin lying at the Bottom of the Ocean. I kept reminding myself that you my Sister were well and truly Dead. Not even my deepest Longing could bring you back.

When I finally reached Boston, I was weary from the Years of Travel. By then Daniel was seven and needed proper Schooling and a settled Life. To this End, I adopted feminine Dress once more and set myself up as Midwife and Herb Woman, but the Rumours of my male Disguise and Surgery-practice never left me. To escape my Notoriety, I would have been obliged to board a Ship back to Old England.

Yet my Reputation attracted Admirers as well as Detractors. In this Manner, I happened to make the Acquaintance of Mr. Simon Ward, Proprietor of the Sign of the Mortar and Unicorn Apothecary. May, you would laugh to hear the Tale, for I was never a Beauty, even in the Bloom of my Youth when I first met Gabriel. By the time I met Mr. Ward, I was twenty-seven, scarred by the Smallpox, and grown very thin from my long Journey. Yet I did take his Fancy, and he paid Court. He loved me on Account of my Spirit and Wit; indeed he said we were Kindred Souls. A Widower with no surviving Children, he showed much Affection to Daniel and promised to bring him up as his own Son. In August 1702 we were married. Daniel and I both took Mr. Ward's Name.

It is true that a Late Love cannot quite match a First Love in terms of Passion, but at least this time, the Flames did not consume me. I never lost my Head. No Shadows hung over Mr. Ward and me. I must confess, however, that it was a bit frightening to marry after having lived such an independent Life, being my own Mistress and having no Master. But God blessed us. Mr. Ward and I were happy, except for one thing—I could give him no Children. The Smallpox had left me barren. Mr. Ward's dearest Wish was to sire not a Son but a Daughter, he said, with my Red Curls, so that he might see how I look'd when I was a Girl. Such was the Fondness of his Gaze when he teazed me so, I quite forgot the Smallpox Scars on my Face and felt myself a Maid again, full of Giddy Happiness and free of Care.

Once married, I gave up Midwifery and worked with my Husband in the Apothecary. We were as much Partners in Commerce as in Love, working side by side as we weighed the Ingredients and ground them with Mortar and Pestle. We sold our own Elixirs, Lozenges, and Pills. Once when Mr. Ward sailed to England, he entrusted to me the Role of Deputy Husband. I ran the Shop and handled all Business Dealings in his Absence.

Let me tell you that Mr. Ward, like our own Father, was a scholarly Man, possessing a modest Library of Books on such divers Subjects as Alchemy, Astrology, Chymistry, and the Wonders of the Natural World. Mr. Ward belonged to a Salon of Sorts, with other Learned Men and their Wives. Though I never quite escaped my Reputation, I made Friends with those who respected me for my Experience. They never tired in begging me to tell Tales of my Travels.

Daniel being an only Child, we could afford to send him to the best Grammar Schools. At fourteen, he completed his Apothecarer's Apprenticeship. Sister, he was a bonny Boy, blessed with Father's Mind and your Beauty poured into a male Form. He was also ambitious, and Mr. Ward and myself were ambitious for him.

"The Lad is so full of Promise," Mr. Ward said. "He could do better than run an Apothecary." Then I did confess to my Husband my Secret Wish that Daniel could study Medicine like his Grandfather after whom I had named him. There being no School of Medicine in the Colonies, we enlisted the help of a Wealthy Patron to send Daniel to Oxford. Daniel did stay there eight Years. In his Letters, he seemed happy in his Studies and pleased with his Life. He might have stayed on in Old England and led a comfortable Existence far from Home had not Mr. Ward died of an Apoplexy.

Having written this, May, I must lay down my Quill and collect my Thoughts. My doting Granddaughter has poured China Tea for me. I watch the Leaves settle at the Bottom of the Cup. Once I might have tried reading my Future therein, but at my Age, my Future lies not in this World but the Next. To make any Sense of my Life, I must keep looking to the Past.

I cannot describe in simple Words my Grief to have lost my

Husband. Daniel then returned from his long Sojourn and tried to comfort me as best he could. He had left me as a Boy and returned as a handsome Stranger. May, you would have been so proud to see him step off the Ship in his embroidered Waistcoat. He is tall like you and proud, also. Something of your Roving Spirit lives on in him. Though affectionate enough, he is of an independent Nature and did not linger long in Boston. He went to Philadelphia, where his Patron had taken up Residence. Being the only University-trained Physician in the City, my Son soon attracted Patients from the best Families. Although I was sad to have him living at such Distance from me, his Fame in Physick was a Source of deep Pride.

As for myself, I carried on with the Sign of the Mortar and Unicorn Apothecary. Daniel had little Interest in the Business, and I was grateful to have the Dignity of an Occupation to lighten the Loneliness of my Widowhood. Indeed, I had little Desire to be a Dowager reduced to living off my Son's Income. My Life in Boston was not unhappy, for I had my Friends, Mr. Ward's Collection of Books, and it might shock you to hear that I was known in the Tavern for my Skill at the Cards (tho' I never played for Money). As an old woman, I become more and more like our Joan.

Thus my Son and I did live Worlds apart, though he wrote regularly. Then in 1717, I received an Invitation to come down to Philadelphia, the Occasion being none other than Daniel's Wedding. His Bride was a wealthy Merchant's Daughter named Rebecca Barnett. If you saw her, May, you would be reminded of Paul Banham's Daughters. She had their Air of Refinement and Breeding, but, to my Son's Good Fortune, she was also possessed of a kindly Nature. After the Wedding, they moved to a Commodious House on Society Hill. Though Rebecca was kind enough to say there was Room for me should I tire of my lonely Existence in faraway Boston, I returned Home.

I might have lived in the Rooms above the Apothecary to my Death had the Letter not arrived from Daniel describing how his Wife had been stricken by Miscarriage more than once. Needless to say, poor Rebecca was at Wit's End. Her own Mother being dead, I took it on myself to offer her Solace and perhaps a Remedy to both lift her Spirits and act as a Tonick for her troubled Womb. I sold the Apothecary and sailed down to Philadelphia. At the Bottom of my Son's large Garden was a Cottage where the former Groundskeeper once lived. This became my new Domicile. I did not wish to live in my Son's own House, for young married People need their Privacy and I had no wish to interfere in the Affairs of their Household. But I took my Daughter-in-Law in Hand and it was then that I truly began to love her, for she was like the Girlchild I never had.

I nursed her with all manner of Herbs to strengthen the Womb and encourage Conception: among them were Red Clover Blossom, Peppermint, Nettle Leaves, Raspberry Leaves, Blue and Black Cohosh, False Unicorn Root, Life Root, Partridge Berry, Cramp Bark, and Motherwort. I bade her to walk outdoors with me every Day, taking in the Air in all Weathers. Within a Year, she conceived. I tended her through her Confinement, forbidding the Cook to add Parsley to the Soup. Then she did give birth to a lovely Girl named Arabella, the first of my seven Grandchildren.

It was a happy Time. I lived in my Cottage at the Boundary of the Yard, planted a Garden of Physick Herbs, and doted over each new Baby in turn. In some of the Children, I saw Glimpses of you, May. Benjamin, the firstborn Son, was small, dark, and secretive, so much like Gabriel that I felt my old Loss all over again. I prayed that none of the Children would inherit my own shrill Hair.

The Years passed and even Rebecca's Youth began to fade, her lovely Curls threaded with Silver as her Children grew older. Yet the Years would not rob my Locks of their violent Colour. My own Son teazed me for being a Witch, only half in Jest, I think. Since I lived with them, his Wife never suffered another Miscarriage.

God had blessed us for so many Years, but what is given is also taken away. Six weeks ago, Tragedy visited our House. Many in the Neighbourhood were infected with the Croup, but my youngest Grandson Henry died of it. He was only six, his Mother's Darling.

So distraught was she, I feared she would weep herself dry. Daniel was in a sorry State himself, having used all his Medical Arts to save the Boy, but to no Avail. With both of them paralyzed by Grief, I took it on myself to arrange the Funeral, hiring a French Stonemason to carve the Marker for little Henry's Grave — the first Tombstone in the Ward Lot of the Cemetery. I ordered black Stuff for Mourning Garb and Black Veils for Rebecca, myself, and the Girls. Then I sweated beside the Sempstresses to have it all prepared in time for the Funeral. I ordered the Coffin and hired the Hearse with six black Horses to draw Henry to his final Resting Place.

During the Funeral, Rebecca was so wan, I thought she might faint. I took her one Arm while Arabella held the other. Together we kept her on her Feet. A short while after the Burial, Rebecca recovered. Then I wandered off to find a Moment's Solitude as I often do these Days. Brushing the Veil back from my Face, I threaded a crooked Path between the Headstones in hope that Exercise might ease the Ache in my Head. Soon I arrived at the poorer Section of the Cemetery where I made a Discovery which made me quake with Near-Hysteria. I almost wondered if I suffered an Hallucination.

Though most of the Graves in this Section were simple wooden Crosses, someone had managed to procure a Headstone and on it was carved *Here lyeth May Powers, Spinster and Needlewoman, born in Glouchestershire, England, 1667, died in Philadelphia 1711.* At the Foot of the Grave was a simple clay Vessel filled with White Lilacs, for it was May, *her* Month. My Son found me on my Knees, weeping inconsolably. It took him and his two Sons to lift me off the Ground.

How could this come to pass, May? I found your Body, your Leg in Gabriel's Trap. Or was it another May Powers buried in the Philadelphia Cemetery? How many May Powerses can there be, born in Gloucestershire in 1667? What if it was really you that lay there? What if I had put Gabriel through that Torment only to find that you had escaped him and lived on, far away from him, passing as a Spinster, bearing your own proud Name?

"May Powers," I kept saying. "That's my May."

My secondborn Granddaughter took my Hands. "Don't you know *I'm* your May?" For that was the Name her Parents had given her—May Lucinda Ward.

They took me Home and put me in my Bed. Daniel gave me Wine and then Laudanum, which made me see Visions of you, my Sister, laughing in your embroidered Wedding Gown. And Visions of Gabriel, the Boy I had once sworn I would love forever. I loved him still. Even after Mr. Ward and the Decades of Separation. I do not think a Woman ever recovers from her First Love. Gabriel was branded on me, his Name burning on my Skin. I wondered if he still lived. Part of me, a ghostly Self, still walked at his Side and shared his Blanket.

"Why do you carry on so, Mother?" asked my Son, who was ever ruled by Reason. He looked at me with his Father's Scrutiny. "Surely this is mere Coincidence. What point is there weeping your Eyes out on Account of some dead Stranger?"

36
The Vanishing Point

1740

HANNAH MOVED WITH a shadow's stealth, dogskin slippers making no noise as she trod the cropped cemetery grass. Daniel and Rebecca did not know of her mission. They would disapprove, would think that, at the age of sixty-six, her good sense had deserted her.

Dressed for mourning, she wore a dove-gray cotton gown with a black neckcloth and a black straw hat. She carried a small bouquet of honesty, which she had cut from her garden before slipping out the back gate. Walking up the aisle of headstones, she felt strangely like a bride—a thought that made her laugh under her breath. May, she remembered, always laughed when confronted with anything too troubling or absurd.

When she reached the grave carved with her lost sister's name, she caught her breath. The white lilacs she had seen there previously were gone, replaced by a posy of heartsease. Her eyes filled when she remembered May's wilderness garden, planted from the seeds she had given May before she left their father's house. Hannah regarded her own bunch of honesty, pale purple flowers tied with black ribbon. She hadn't thought to bring a vase. Untying the ribbon, she arranged the honesty among the heartsease.

The dates carved on the grave informed her that this May Powers had passed away in 1711, twenty-nine years ago. The one who kept bringing flowers must have loved her well. Folding her hands, Hannah tried to pray, but her mind was too unquiet. She wished she had the powers of divination, like Joan. Every morning when she awoke, Hannah had to marvel that she was older by far than Joan had been when she last saw her, older than Father had been when he died. Once she had believed that age would deliver wisdom, but she felt as confounded as ever. If only she could read tea leaves or consult a crystal ball to ascertain the true identity of the woman beneath this grave. If only she possessed the powers of necromancy so she could raise the dead woman's ghost and hear her story.

She yearned for knowledge of Gabriel, too. Did he still wander the forest, as she once had? As much as she tried to imagine him as a man grown old, she could picture him only as the boy to whom she had offered up her heart and soul. Like May, he would never age. While she grew ever older, Gabriel and May would remain eternal as the spring leaves that budded out each year, fresh and new. How she wished she could read the cards, read the patterns in the stars, to learn what had become of them both.

If Daniel knew the shape of her thoughts, he would shake his head and patiently explain that there was no magic, no secret power to be harnessed. He would tell her that she was simply an old woman haunted by her past. Everything outside the circle of Science was a sham, mere superstition, consolation for the ignorant and weak. He would tell her that she should be above such things. Let the feeble-minded mutter over tea leaves and pretend to divine the future. The truth lay elsewhere. Daniel discounted the doctrine of plant signatures and his stepfather's books of astrology and alchemy, even dismissed Galen's teaching of the humors. There were no mystical secrets, he believed; Nature itself could be ordered, neatly labeled in Latin, and explained by rational laws.

She could not prove by logic or rational deduction that this May Powers was her sister. By all rights she should banish the grave from her mind and focus her thoughts on Arabella's wedding the following spring. They were already preparing her trousseau. But before Hannah could retrace her steps home, her vision clouded. When she closed her eyes, she saw a heart pierced by three arrows.

Her granddaughter May kept a pet ferret that was forever getting lost, only to reappear in the garden or cellar, its coat dirty from burrowing. Rebecca didn't like the beast, but May would not be parted from it. She swore that the ferret was better at hunting mice and rats than her sister's lazy cat.

I am like a ferret, Hannah told herself as she stole off to the cemetery for the second time that week. A dogged creature running down dark tunnels, searching out buried, hidden things. She concealed her bouquet of harebells in the folds of her skirt. Lest the neighbors see her and gossip, she took a roundabout way, heading down back streets and alleys before arriving at the cemetery.

When she reached the grave, she saw that the heartsease and honesty had been removed to make way for a glorious bunch of foxglove. Hannah hesitated before arranging the delicate sprays of harebell around the edge of the clay vessel. Her hands trembled. The foxglove bells shook in the wind.

Hannah kept her cemetery vigil. She waited as the foxglove and harebells started to droop. Standing in the shade of a cedar tree, she watched a woman with a bouquet of dark red roses approach the grave. Hannah wondered if this stranger knew that their mother's maiden name had been Thorn. The woman was her own age, even her size — short and small-boned. Watching her take the old flowers from the vase, Hannah noted how delicate her wrists were. Her skin was tawny brown, and the bit of hair peeping from her linen cap was gray. She wore a necklace of glass beads around her throat. Despite her age, there was something girlish in the way she moved. Hannah was willing to bet that if she raised her fawn skirts, her ankles would be as graceful as her wrists.

Upending the clay vessel, the woman poured the spent water on the grass. Leaving the flowers beside the grave, she strode off toward the well at the edge of the cemetery. Hannah closed her eyes and felt almost faint as the roses' fragrance reached her hiding place. In her basket was a bunch of sweetpeas, stems wrapped in damp cloth to keep them fresh. Sweatpeas would look lovely among the dark roses.

The stranger returned with freshly drawn water. Limber as a person half her age, she sat on her heels and arranged the roses in the clay vase. She sang softly. Hannah could not catch the words, but the melody made her ache. It sounded like a tune her sister used to hum while spinning. May had died at forty-four—a stalwart age. Had she grown stout with the years? Had her beautiful hair turned gray? Hannah could only see a laughing girl on the Bristol pier.

Hannah started. The woman had noticed her. Springing to her feet, the stranger stared. Hannah picked up her bunch of sweetpeas and walked toward her, held out the flowers as an offering. Certainty flooded her—there was no question anymore. She didn't falter but spoke loud and clear.

"So you are May's Adele."

The woman lowered her face as she took the flowers.

"She wrote of you in her letters," Hannah said. Hastily she added, "I am her sister."

When the woman lifted her face again, Hannah saw that she was crying.

"You are Hannah," she said. "I kept praying that one day you would come." Her speech had a foreign ring to it, a soft melody beneath the words.

The pounding in Hannah's head became a roar. She burst into tears like an eighteen-year-old girl who had just been told that her sister was dead. "But *how?* I did find her body in the woods." She quivered like wind-tossed foxglove, remembering the boy she would never see again. The boy she had falsely accused, over and over. Adele caught her as she collapsed. Her last thought before

357

she went under was that this would be the final attack. She would fall into the bottomless green well and never come up again.

—✦—

She opened her eyes to see the tranquil sky, Adele's face.

"You will be fine now." Adele spoke as though she willed it to be so. She wiped the spittle from Hannah's face and helped her sit up. "May never did forget you," she said after a moment had passed. "She did have dreams of you. She did wake up weeping for you."

Hannah tried to speak but could not.

"I have a story to tell you," said Adele.

—✦—

When Hannah felt well enough to walk, Adele led her down a back lane to a narrow house squeezed between a wig shop and a cobbler's. The sign over the door read *Madame Desvarieux, Dressmaker.* A young black girl sat stitching at a scrubbed pine table in the center of the shop. When they entered, she stood up.

"Mistress, I am nearly finished." She held up the silk petticoat she had been hemming.

"This is Esther, my apprentice," Adele told Hannah. "Esther, you may have the rest of the day free."

With a smile, the girl folded the petticoat, took her shawl, curtsied to Adele and Hannah, then let herself out the door.

"This was where your sister and I did ply our trade," Adele said. "May could stitch like an angel."

Hannah stepped up to the hearth. In the evenings, she reckoned that Adele would pull the curtains over the front window, set her stool by the fire, and cook a simple meal to share with her apprentice. Centered on the mantelpiece was a box covered in faded wool tapestry, a pattern of roses and doves. Before she could stop herself, she stroked it.

"This is May's handiwork, is it not?" Hannah's heart beat so loudly, she thought Adele must hear it.

"Aye. Her workbox."

Hannah tried to smile. Her sister loved beautiful things—even her workbox had to be pretty. Wandering along the shelves, she fingered a bolt of watered silk and imagined her nieces coming in to order new gowns. Ah, but Rebecca wouldn't think this quarter of the city respectable; it was too close to the harbor where sailors and whores congregated.

Opening the back door, Adele revealed a small garden crammed with a riot of vegetables and flowers. Creamy white roses climbed the walls of the earth closet. A rabbit hutch occupied one corner. The big hive beside the rear gate looked to be an excellent defense against thieves. The hum of bees nearly drowned out the hammering of the cobbler next door.

"At our childhood home," Hannah said, "we also kept bees at the bottom of the garden."

"We led a simple life, but we never went hungry. Below is a cellar where we kept our conserves." Lifting the edge of a rag rug with her toe, Adele revealed a trapdoor.

Before Hannah could think what to say, Adele led her up a narrow staircase. "Above is the bedchamber."

Hannah followed her to a garret with a slanting ceiling. On either end were tiny gable windows. She surveyed the sparse furnishings: a bed with a box at its foot, a few baskets of scrap cloth and empty thread spools, a washstand, a chest of drawers, and a stool. There were no decorations on the whitewashed walls, only a candle sconce. The floor was bare wood, everything so plain that it reminded her of the wilderness house she had shared with Gabriel. The bed curtains were tied back, allowing her to view the room's one extravagance—a quilt stitched from scraps of cotton, wool, linen, silk, and velvet. How long, she wondered, had it taken to gather all those tiny squares and triangles, all those different colors that glowed as rich as jewels?

"That is May's work," Adele told her. "It did take six years to finish."

Hannah caressed a patch of brocade as blue as May's eyes had been. "How did my sister die?" Having this conversation twice in one lifetime was a cruel fate. Sometimes she thought that, even taking into account her many sins, God had dealt too harshly with her. She and Adele had lived in the same city for more than twenty years. Why did this meeting have to take place now, when she was too old to endure the tragedy? Twenty years ago, at least, she would have been able to wrestle more bravely with her grief. Not crumple on the edge of Adele's bed.

"It was the pneumonia." Adele sat beside her. "We were both ill from it. I lived and she died." She went to rummage through the wooden box and pulled out two yellowing letters. "I think you would like a remembrance of her. She did write these to you. But they were returned."

The faded words running across the paper ripped open the old wound. So May had tried—and failed—to find her again. She read Richard Banham's note about the fire, saying that she, Gabriel, and the child had most likely perished.

"She knew about our child. Did she hate me for it?"

Adele shook her head. "May loved you. She prayed for your happiness. Here, take this, too." She passed a square of folded silk. "There is something inside."

Hannah unfolded the silk to find a slender plait of chestnut hair bound in a circle. Father's voice sounded in her head. *A circle has no beginning and no end.* She closed her fingers around her sister's hair, untouched by gray.

"I wish I had something more to give you," Adele said. "We did live a very plain life." She drew in her breath. "We came through the forest with nothing but the clothes on our backs and some money May did steal from Gabriel Washbrook. We used the money to buy this house and start our business."

Hannah flushed at the sound of her lover's name, which had remained unspoken since he had disappeared.

"This is treasure to me." She opened her hand to see her sister's hair. "I just wish—" She broke off. Her heart was so full of loss and regret, she didn't know where to start. *A circle has no beginning.*

"I think I know what you suffer," Adele said. "You loved him. You love him still."

"How would you know such things?" There was a ringing in Hannah's head. Father had told her that the place where a ship was lost over the horizon was called the vanishing point. Gabriel was as lost to her as May.

"You are so pale." Adele spoke with solicitude, reminding her of how Gabriel had spoken to her forty-eight years ago when he first took her in. When he fried the fish for her, taking care that she ate and didn't just shrivel up in grief.

"What he did to her was cruel." Adele's voice was grim. "What she did to him was crueler, letting him think she had died in his trap. I could not stop her. Hannah, I wish I had, but I was so afraid. I knew not if we would survive the journey."

To think her sister had been capable of such a hateful jest. To think she had gone so far to punish him. A long green tunnel yawned before Hannah. She willed herself down that passage that would take her back to the past, back to her youth. She would have believed him, would have embraced him with all her love. She would have never let him go.

"Later she did sorely regret it," Adele said. "She was most sorry on account of what happened to you."

Hannah saw her sister's face. *Darling, forgive me. I was so lost.* May had lost her baby, then Gabriel had driven her out of the only home she had left. The salt tears burned. This was more than she could bear. Really, she should leave at once. Back home, they would worry and wonder why she had been gone so long. Her granddaughters would alert Rebecca, who would then send Benjamin out to look for her. Young Benjamin, who had Gabriel's black hair and melting eyes. When Hannah tried to stand, she found she was dizzy. She sat back down on the edge of the bed.

"We were dressmakers." Adele resumed the conversation, steering it into calmer waters. "For two spinsters, we did better than most."

Hannah had to concede that the room was soothing in its simplicity, far more peaceful than Rebecca's drawing room with its walls covered in patterned French silk and pictures in gilt frames. This had been the home of two masterless women, forging their way through life without husband, father, or children. She could almost see her sister on the stool by the window, brushing out her long hair. *Hannah, can't you see that this is an adventure?*

"You were very devoted to my sister. I am happy to know she had such a loyal friend."

"I loved her, but sometimes she tried me sorely. She never stopped chasing the men. I had to cure her of the French pox more than once."

With a lurch, Hannah imagined May leading sailors up to the garret, letting them unlace her dress, then lying with them beneath the dazzling quilt.

"In the end, she settled on one." Adele thumbed a patch of red velvet on the quilt. "A sea captain with a wife in England. He and May only saw each other once or twice in a year. I think this is why they never tired of each other. Their love . . . it was always brand-new. He wrote long letters to her. But May was never his whore. She refused to take anything from him, not a trinket, even when we had hard times. Her pride made him love her more. He could not buy her anything until she did die. Her sea captain paid for her headstone." Adele turned her head away and wiped her eyes. "I could never afford such a thing."

Hannah touched her arm. "Did you have many hard times?"

"The business of dressmaking is fickle. Either we did have more work than we could take on or no work at all. When business was poor, we did other things to earn our bread."

Digging in the box again, Adele unwrapped a ball of sea-green glass. "I tell fortunes. From my mother I did inherit the powers. The older I get, the stronger they grow."

"I envy you," Hannah said. "I do wish that I could see into the future."

"The future, the past, the present," said Adele. "All the things that are hidden. I taught your sister to gaze into the glass when she was lonely for you."

Hannah brushed back tears. "Will you teach me, Adele?"

—+—

She saw him in the glass. He walked the snowy forest, dogs gathered around him, different dogs from the ones she remembered. Rufus was long gone. Gabriel wore buckskin and the fur of wolf and lynx. Snow crystals caught on the fur and glittered like tiny stars. Age had marked his face, yet she could still clearly see the boy he had been. He glided through the forest on Indian snowshoes, leaving behind strange tracks that did not look as though they had been made by a human. Except to whistle to his dogs, he was as silent as when she had first met him. Unused to speech. He was slim as ever, spine unbowed.

"He thinks of you every day," Adele told her. "He remembers you with love."

━┼━

In a shack on a faraway mountainside, Gabriel awoke with a start and sat up panting on his bed of skins. Though it was summer, he had dreamt of deep winter, of a girl with snowflakes in her flame-red hair. Even as he pinched himself and gazed at the moon through the glassless window, the dream lingered. Snowflakes touched his face. The girl's warmth overpowered him as she wrapped her arms around him and laid her head against his pounding heart. *You have an angel's name. They named you after an angel.*

He struggled to push the vision away, but she wouldn't be banished. Her fingers fanned out on his cheek. *Gabriel, I think I am in love with you.* A ghostly fire blazed in his empty hearth. He saw her young body, golden in its light, as she spread out on the furs, as she gave herself to him in perfect trust.

He couldn't sleep any more that night. At dawn, he opened his leather pouch. Inside, knotted in a scrap of old cloth, was a lock of her hair.

━┼━

Father taught her that the place at which two receding parallel lines met on the horizon was known as the vanishing point. Beyond that point they disappeared from sight.

The day the *Cornucopia* set sail from Bristol, May cupped her face in both hands and kissed her. "Courage, Hannah. This is no time for tears."

But Hannah wouldn't let her go. Finally May took her arm and led her up the gangplank. This time they set sail together, Hannah taking her place with May at the ship's prow. The wind whipped her sister's hair as she turned to her, eyes and cheeks glowing. She had never seen May so happy.

"A wilderness, they say the New World is. Have you never wondered, Hannah, what a wilderness is like?"

They both turned toward the western horizon over which they would vanish on their voyage. They were young, their lives still before them, their future an apple waiting to be tasted.

Afterword

THE FIRST SEED of this book was planted in 1986 at the University of Minnesota when I took part in Dr. Annette Kuhn's seminar "The Making of the Female Character (1450–1650)," which explored the lives of women in a rapidly changing world marked by the decline of the feudal agrarian system and the rise of mercantile capitalism. For me, one of the most intriguing periods of social transformation was the English Civil War and the English Revolution, which underlay it. For several decades in the seventeenth century, the world was turned upside down. Groups like the Ranters, Seekers, Diggers, and Levelers demanded an end to the rule of feudal lords. The newly founded Quaker religion offered a vision of gender and racial equality, a world without slavery or war, in which people bowed to God alone and not to their lords or kings. Of these groups, only the Quakers endured, but not without persecution. Many fled to the American colonies.

What tugged on my curiosity was the possibility that the idealism of the English Revolution somehow survived into the Restoration in the minds of ordinary people who were not willing to forsake their dreams and bow down to the new order. What would happen to a late-seventeenth-century woman who was determined to carve out her own destiny and who demanded the same liberties, both social and sexual, as a man? This was how May's character was conceived.

However, this proved to be my most daunting book to write. I was living in Germany in what, for me at least, was the pre-

Internet age, and finding good research material was a perpetual challenge. Years later, when I showed an early draft of *The Vanishing Point* to my agent at that time, she advised me to scrap it; books set in this era didn't sell unless they were genre romance novels. Moreover, in her opinion the English setting of the opening chapters would be of no interest to American readers.

I will always regard *The Vanishing Point* as the book that no one wanted me to write and that perversely became my strongest book thus far, because I was forced to fight so hard to make it happen. This manuscript stretched me to my utmost through a period of considerable upheaval, as life circumstances took me from Germany to California and then to the north of England. In the Lancashire countryside the novel finally took root and gained a life force of its own. My characters' surnames were lifted from seventeenth-century grave markers in village churchyards. My present home is situated at the foot of Pendle Hill, on top of which George Fox received the ecstatic vision that moved him to found the Quakers. Commonword, the nonprofit organization I work with, is housed in the basement of a Friends meetinghouse in Manchester. The yew trees and hawthorn hedges that May longs for in her American exile grow outside my door. Every week I go horseback riding in the village of Grindleton, which, in the seventeenth century, gave its name to a short-lived utopian religious sect: the Grindletonians.

The writing and research for this book stretched over a decade, during which I consulted many books. Standout texts included Antonia Fraser's *The Weaker Vessel*, David Hackett Fischer's monumental *Albion's Seed: Four British Folkways in America*, and *Frauen in der Geschichte*, volumes 2 and 3, edited by Annette Kuhn and Jörn Rüsen. Much of the herb lore comes from Nicholas Culpepper's *Complete Herbal*. The recipes Hannah discovers in her mother's receipt book are taken from Eliza Smith's *The Compleat Housewife*—an admitted anachronism, since that book wasn't published until 1742. Perhaps the most valuable information was imparted by the good people at Colonial Williamsburg and Jamestown Settlement, who answered in detail my many questions about life in the colonial Chesapeake. The Sequose River, which appears in this book, exists only in my imagination. At a storytelling retreat at Ty Newydd in Wales, Hugh Lupton's inspired telling of the tale "Glamoury Eye" had a powerful impact on my story.

My thanks go out to all who read this manuscript in draft form, especially to Susan Ito and everyone at Readerville, Cathy Bolton and everyone at Womenswrite, Jane Stubbs, Margaret Batteson, and Susan Stern. My friend Cath Staincliffe, the acclaimed crime writer, taught me much about advanced plotting and how to weave multiple narrative threads together to achieve maximum impact and suspense.

I wish to express my profound gratitude to my agent, Wendy Sherman. This book would have taken much longer to see the light of day without her belief and commitment. My foreign rights agent, Jenny Meyer, worked hard to bring this book to an international audience. I am deeply indebted to my editor, Jane Rosenman. *The Vanishing Point* would be a much poorer book without her insights and critique.